BRUISED SPIRITS

BRUISED SPIRITS

DAISY GUMM MAJESTY MYSTERY, BOOK 11

ALICE DUNCAN

Book and cover design by eBook Prep
www.ebookprep.com

April, 2019
Paperback ISBN: 978-1-64457-067-8
Hardcover ISBN: 978-1-64457-068-5

ePublishing Works!
644 Shrewsbury Commons Ave
Ste 249
Shrewsbury PA 17361
United States of America

www.epublishingworks.com
Phone: 866-846-5123

For Nicky in Australia. She knows why, and I hope no other women ever have to learn the way she did. And, as ever, thanks to Lynne Welch and Sue Krekeler, my wonderful beta readers, who always tell me what I've done wrong and where to go. Wait. That didn't sound right. Oh, well...

ONE

What's that feeling you get when you think you've been somewhere and experienced an incident before? It doesn't last long, but it's jarring. I think the alienists call it déjà vu or something like that.

Whatever it's called, I had a distinct case of it when I opened the door to my family's tidy bungalow on South Marengo Avenue in the fair city of Pasadena, California, and beheld on my front porch Flossie Buckingham. Flossie, after a very difficult start in life as a poor girl in a dreadful slum in New York City, had moved to Pasadena with her then-lover, a gangster named Jinx Jenkins. She had once shown up at my door battered almost beyond recognition.

That morning Flossie was fine. Her companion, however, looked very much as Flossie had looked that other morning a few years prior. I think she was in even worse shape than Flossie had been, because Flossie seemed to have to hold her up to keep her from collapsing onto the hard concrete of the porch.

"Flossie!" I cried, bewildered, and slapping a hand to my chest, where I felt both the Voodoo juju given to me by a Voodoo mambo a year or so ago, and the gorgeous emerald engagement ring given to me by Detective Sam Rotondo the prior Christmas. More about that later.

"Daisy, please let us come in," said Flossie in a soft voice, as if she didn't want others to overhear her. "This is Lily Bannister, and she desperately needs your help."

My help? *My* help? The woman looked like she needed to be in the hospital, or at least under a doctor's care. I searched the curb next to our front lawn, where I espied Flossie and Johnny's Ford Model-T. "Where's Johnny?" I asked, sounding as befuddled as I felt.

"Taking care of Billy," snapped Flossie, which was most unlike her. "Let us in, Daisy. Now."

Billy, if you care, is the name of Flossie and Johnny's baby boy. They named him after my late, beloved husband, Billy Majesty. What was going on here?

However, I trusted Flossie as I trusted few other people, so I stood back, making sure my family's black-and-tan dachshund, Spike, didn't jump on either Flossie or Mrs.—Miss?—Bannister.

"Come in," I said, grateful the rest of my family was out. Ma and Aunt Vi were at their daily employment, and Pa had gone out to meet some friends and chat. My father is one of those folks for whom the expression "he never met a stranger" was invented. Great guy, my father.

"Can you help me, Daisy?" Flossie asked, cocking her head for me to take Lily Bannister's other arm. So I did.

Flossie and I carefully maneuvered the poor woman into the living room and over to the sofa, where we tried but failed to lower her gently. She sort of plopped onto the sofa with no other sound than a muffled groan and then a sob or two. I looked a question at Flossie, who appeared quite flustered, not a usual state for the gentle and loving Flossie Buckingham I'd come to know since she'd met and married my old childhood chum, Johnny Buckingham, a captain in the Salvation Army.

"May we speak in private, Daisy?"

My gaze was riveted on poor Lily Bannister, who sagged on the sofa. Both of her eyes were black and swollen, her lip was split, and she had bruises all over her face. I expected the rest of her body had been similarly bashed up. Then I transferred my gaze to Flossie. "Yes. I guess so. Come into the dining room."

So she did and, with a worried backward glance at Flossie's battered companion, I joined her.

"What the heck is going on, Flossie? Who is that woman, and why did you bring her here? I thought Johnny was the one who helped folks in distress. That's his business, for Pete's sake. I'm just a phony spiritualist."

I guess I should enlarge upon that last remark, too, but I'll save an explanation until later.

"That's just it, Daisy. Johnny *can't* help her. He wants to, but he can't."

Huh? Last I heard, the Salvation Army took in all the strays and orphans and drunkards and drug fiends and poor folk and immigrants and so forth that no one else would touch with a barge pole. "But Flossie, Lily Bannister has clearly suffered a...a...Well, I don't know what happened to her, but she needs medical help. I'm not a doctor."

"Daisy, just listen to me, please. Unless you know a doctor who is absolutely true to his oath of privacy, we may even have to forego medical help."

"But why? She obviously needs it badly."

"Her husband beat her to a pulp and then kicked her down the basement steps—concrete basement steps, Daisy—and she barely managed to escape with her life. Fortunately for her, Billy and I were out walking, and I spotted her nearly crawling down Fair Oaks Avenue, trying to get to Johnny's church."

For the record, I don't believe Billy Buckingham could walk a whole lot yet. I suspect Flossie meant she'd been pushing him in his baby carriage.

"Her husband did *what?*"

"You heard me," Flossie said in a harder tone of voice than I'd ever heard issue from her gentle lips.

"But...But isn't that a crime? Can't he be prosecuted for nearly killing her?"

"He can be prosecuted for murdering her, which he probably will do eventually, if she's forced to go back to him," said Flossie. "Until then, he's her husband in the eyes of the law and her church. *And* her parents." Her mouth pinched up. "She's a Roman Catholic, and she once made the

3

mistake of asking her priest if he could intercede and help her get away from her husband. The priest said it was her duty to abide by her solemn marital oath, although he did speak to her husband and ask him to treat her more gently. Naturally, that infuriated the horrible man, and he beat her senseless for daring to expose 'family matters' to anyone outside the family."

Flossie jumped up from the dining room chair in which she'd been sitting and commenced pacing. "Oh, it just makes me *furious*! I've been in that woman's position, you know. Well, of course you know." She whirled around and looked fiercely at me. "But I didn't face the obstacles Lily faces. I wasn't married to that awful Jenkins man. I wasn't married to anybody! If I'd gone to the law after he'd beaten me up, they'd probably have arrested Jinx. But the law won't arrest Mr. Bannister. He's her husband, and therefore, the law considers her his property. They'll send her *back* to him. So will her church! So will her *parents*, who believe she must have done something wrong to deserve being beaten. As if anyone deserves *that*. You *have* to help me help her, Daisy! You *have* to!"

Boy, I'm glad my parents weren't like Mrs. Bannister's. Not that my darling Billy would ever have beaten me, but if he had, they'd have been on my side. I think. Oh, dear.

"Can't Johnny do anything at all?" I asked in a small voice, wishing I knew what to do.

"Johnny has to abide by the law, Daisy. If he hides her somewhere, he's liable to be arrested and prosecuted himself! Oh, it's all just *so* unfair!"

"Yes. Yes, it is." However, that didn't negate the fact that I didn't have a clue what to do for poor Mrs. Bannister. "But...Oh, but Flossie, I can't keep her here. There's no room. And besides that, I don't think my parents would like it. They don't like breaking the law any more than Johnny does."

Flossie glared at me and I held up a hand. "Honestly, Flossie, *I* don't mind breaking the law for a good cause, and Mrs. Bannister is definitely a good cause, but—"

The telephone rang. I do believe it was the first time in years I'd been glad to hear it, primarily because anyone calling the house wanted to speak to me, usually to engage my services as a spurious spiritualist-medium. Not that my clients didn't think I was for real. But never mind that. I'd just been saved by the bell! At least for a moment or two.

I walked into the kitchen followed by Spike, who loved the kitchen because it contained food. I lifted the receiver from the cradle of the wall-mounted 'phone, and spoke my typical greeting, "Gumm-Majesty residence, Mrs. Maj—"

"Daisy!" cried a voice I recognized.

Joy and hope bloomed in my heart. "*Harold!*"

"Cripes, Daisy, don't yell at me. I think you just busted my eardrum."

"I'm sorry, Harold, but I'm *so* glad you called."

"I should hope so, because I'm going to take you out to lunch today and—"

"Harold, come to my house right this minute. It's urgent. It might even be a matter of life and death."

A pause on the other end of the wire preceded Harold's puzzled, "I beg your—"

"Oh, *please* don't argue with me, Harold! I need you now."

And Harold, bless his heart, said, "Be right there," and he hung up.

Turning to Flossie, I actually managed a smile. "If anyone can help Mrs. Bannister and us, it's Harold Kincaid. I'll bet Harold even knows a discreet doctor he can call upon to tend to the poor woman."

"I've met him, but I don't really know him," said Flossie doubtfully.

"Harold is the most kindhearted, useful, dependable man in the universe, Flossie. He's one of my very best friends. I tell you, if he can't help Mrs. Bannister, nobody can." I thought about the wilted woman on the living room sofa and said, "We'd probably better go see how she's doing."

"Yes. Yes. I'm sorry, Daisy. But when I heard what Lily told me, you were the only one I could think of who might be able to help her."

Lucky me. "I hope your faith wasn't misplaced." I meant it.

Mrs. Bannister had either succumbed to her injuries and passed out, or had fallen asleep. Or died, although I hoped not. I wasn't quite sure if it would be wise to wake her, but Flossie had no such compunction. She gently shook the woman's shoulder. "Lily, wake up. You probably have a concussion, and you shouldn't go to sleep yet."

Mrs. Bannister uttered a pitiful groan. I still didn't know what to do, but I made an effort.

"Um...does she have any open wounds or anything? I can get iodine and bandages from the bathroom."

"I think some of her ribs might be cracked or broken. If we can't get a reliable doctor to treat her, one of them might puncture a lung or something."

I grimaced, although I didn't mean to.

"Her ribs should probably be bound, at the very least." Flossie chewed on her lower lip. "But I hate to bind her ribs when I don't know precisely what's wrong."

Made sense to me. "Under the circumstances, and I know this sounds idiotic, but would some aspirin tablets help, do you think?" Clearly, the woman needed more than aspirin, but aspirin was great for easing one's aches and pains.

"Good idea. Can't hurt. Thank you, Daisy."

Little did Flossie know. I was so glad to get out of that room holding the brutalized woman, I practically ran to the bathroom. There I regret to say I dawdled, not because I didn't want to help Mrs. Bannister, but because I didn't want to have to see her awful injuries again. You'd think that, after nursing my husband through his last years—he was shot and gassed by the cursed Germans in the Great War—I'd have become accustomed to tending to sick people. But Billy hadn't been battered, as had Mrs. Bannister. At least, by the time he got home to me, his flesh wounds had been tended to and only scars remained. His lungs were ruined, he couldn't walk, and he was in constant pain, but he had no open wounds.

Oh, Lord. I didn't want to think about Billy.

I carried the package of aspirin tablets into the kitchen, thinking the next time I bought aspirin tablets, I'd get a bottle of them instead of packets. It's easier to shake tablets out of a bottle than to rip open a packet or three to get at the pills. In the kitchen I poured a glass of water, and carried both the water and the aspirin to the living room.

Flossie had tried to make Mrs. Bannister more comfortable with sofa cushions, but her efforts went for naught. The poor woman needed more help than sofa cushions could provide.

"Here," I said, holding out the aspirin packets and the glass of water to Flossie.

"Can you please give me...I don't know...three aspirin tablets, Daisy? I don't want to let go of Mrs. Bannister's shoulder in order to open the packet, because she might fall over."

See what I mean? From then on, it would be bottles for the Gumms and the one remaining Majesty in our household.

Oh, God. I hoped to heaven Harold had called from nearby, because I *really* needed him.

"Certainly. Here you go." I ripped open the packets and gave Flossie three aspirin tablets and the glass of water, stuffing the empty paper packets into my apron pocket as I did so. Before Flossie arrived with her burden, I'd been dusting; hence, the apron.

"Can you prop her up so she doesn't fall over, Daisy? I'm so afraid that if she has any broken ribs, one of them might puncture her lung if she moves around too much, so it's best if we can keep her as still as possible."

"Right. Will do." And I did. Hating every second of it. I don't believe I'm a natural-born care-giver, if you know what I mean. I'd had to nurse my husband, but I'd loved him all my life. Even then, I hadn't enjoyed the experience. I'd never even heard of Lily Bannister until a few minutes earlier. I suppose that doesn't speak highly of my character, but it's the truth.

Mrs. Bannister groaned miserably as Flossie told her to open her mouth. I winced when the woman obeyed. Her mouth was a mess: swollen, bloody, both of her lips were split, and when she finally got her mouth open wide enough to accept the aspirin tablets—one at a time—I saw that her ghastly husband had broken a couple of her teeth. Probably the insides of her cheeks were minced meat. But she gamely accepted the tablets and swallowed some water, her eyes tearing up with the effort.

Where, oh where, was Harold?

"There. Maybe that will help you feel better, Lily," said Flossie in a soothing voice. Flossie, unlike yours truly, was definitely a natural care-

7

giver. That was why she and Johnny made such a perfect couple. Heck, they'd even tended to someone with leprosy once.

After Mrs. Bannister had swallowed the aspirin tablets, Flossie sat next to her on the sofa, put an arm around her shoulders, and held her upright. I stood before them, wringing my hands. Big help I was, huh?

"Is there anything else I can do before Harold gets here, Flossie?" I asked because I thought I should.

"I don't think so." Flossie gazed up at me, her big blue eyes appearing almost tragic. "I just hope your friend can help."

"Me, too," said I. "Um...I'll go make some tea." I have no idea why, but folks seemed to like sweet, milky tea after catastrophes.

"That sounds good."

I think Flossie was humoring me. Nevertheless, I practically ran to the kitchen, where I took my time boiling water in the kettle, warming the teapot—my Aunt Vi, who is the best cook in the known universe, had taught me always to warm the pot—dumped some tea leaves into the warm pot, and filled said pot up with water. Aunt Vi claims tea isn't fit to drink until it's strong enough to walk out of the pot by itself, so I took a few more minutes, watching the tea brew and praying Harold would arrive. Now.

He wasn't at the house by the time the tea was almost black. I figured it was strong enough. Darn. However, I thought of another way to waste a few seconds, so I went into the living room again and asked Flossie if she and Mrs. Bannister would like tea.

Mrs. Bannister only groaned a little. Flossie said, "Thank you, Daisy. I would like a cup."

"Um...It's kind of strong. Do you want milk and sugar?"

"A little of each, please. And perhaps you should prepare a cup for Lily, only with more sugar and milk."

Flossie grinned at me. I'm sure she was remembering the time, a couple of years prior, when I'd been coerced into teaching a cooking class at the Salvation Army for poor women, most of them immigrants who'd fled their native lands after the Great War. To understand her grin fully, you probably ought to know that cooking and I are mortal enemies. I'm a crackerjack spiritualist-medium, and I can sew like a Paris couturier, but I can burn...well, pretty much anything.

"All right. Be right back," said I, and trotted back to the kitchen. There I retrieved two cups, two saucers, a tray, put milk into a milk pitcher, and sugar in the matching sugar bowl. Then I put the full teapot on the tray along with a slotted spoon for catching loose tea leaves, remembered to add a couple of spoons, one for each saucer, and staggered out to the living room with my heavy tray.

I'd just set the tray on the table in front of the sofa when our doorbell buzzed. We had one of those doorbells that you twist from the outside, and it makes a buzzing sound in the house.

Harold! Oh, please, thought I, let it be Harold!

Spike, naturally, went crazy, racing to the door and barking up a storm. I noticed Mrs. Bannister wince in pain, and told my dog to hush. Spike, who had gone to obedience training school and come in first in his class, hushed. I wish people obeyed me so well.

It was indeed Harold who stood on the front porch with a puzzled frown on his face. I saw he'd parked his shiny red Stutz Bearcat on the street in front of the house behind the Buckinghams' battered Model-T. They made an incongruous pair, the Bearcat and the Model-T, but that doesn't matter.

"Harold! I'm so glad to see you! You'll never know *how* glad." And I reached out, grabbed his arm, and yanked him inside the house.

TWO

I made quick introductions. I don't think Mrs. Bannister comprehended what was going on, but Flossie smiled at Harold, who smiled back, still clearly puzzled.

"Come here, Harold," I said, and tugged him into the dining room. "Nuts. I left the tea things in the living room, but I can get you a cup of tea if—"

"Just tell me what's going on, Daisy. Who is that poor woman, and what happened to her? You know I'm apt to faint at the sight of blood. I'm not really the best person to call on if you need a damsel in distress rescued."

"Oh, but you are, Harold. Let me tell you Mrs. Bannister's story." In truth, Harold had assisted me in the rescue of a damsel in distress once before, but that's another story entirely, and Harold only had to provide clothing that time. This time, I feared, would be a whole different kettle of problematic fish.

So I told Harold Mrs. Bannister's tale of woe. Harold's lip curled when I told him the poor woman was a Roman Catholic. His lover, Del Farrington, also went to the Catholic Church. Hmm. I guess I sort of spilled the beans about Harold there, didn't I? To expand on the subject a trifle, let me just say here and now that I don't want to hear about how sinful men like Harold and Del are, or how unnatural. There's not a thing unnatural about either one of them, and they didn't choose to be what they were. Don't argue with me about it, because I'm right.

That's not the point anyway.

"Does she go to Saint Andrews, like Del?" Harold asked.

"I don't know."

"If she lives close enough to the Salvation Army that Flossie and her kid found her, I'll bet she does. Poor woman. I'll never understand how people can stand that place. You know I call it Our Lady of Perpetual Malice."

"I know, Harold, but that's not important right now. What I need to know is if you can help Mrs. Bannister. Do you know a doctor who can tend her and not give her away to her husband or that stupid priest or her family? They all want to send her back to her husband."

"Even her *family*?"

"Evidently so."

"That's brutal of them."

"Yes, it is."

"Hmm," said Harold. "Let me think for a minute."

So I did, fingering my juju on its woven string and my engagement ring on its lovely golden chain through my faded blue housedress. Although I wanted to, I didn't even bite my nails while Harold thought. I had to protect my nails. In fact, I had to protect my entire self. I made my living dishing up fake spirituality to the wealthy denizens of Pasadena, California, and I needed to look the part. Therefore, I always wore gloves when I worked in the garden and protected my face with a wide-brimmed hat. I cultivated the pale and interesting look, and had my act down to perfection. Why, I could waft better than your average ghost. Not that there are such things.

Heck, I made my living pretending to conjure dead relations for people who'd lost loved ones. If I could actually do that, I'd be talking to my Billy all the time. Unfortunately, I couldn't.

When I could no longer stand the silence created by Harold's mulling, I said, "I can't keep her here, Harold, because the authorities, the church, and her parents want to send her back to her husband, and my parents wouldn't want to break the law or anything. And then there's Sam." Sam Rotondo, my fiancé—although nobody knew that but Sam and me—was a detective for the Pasadena Police Department.

"And you think I do?"

"No. But I know you. Your entire life is lived in the breaking of laws. Surely you know a doctor or someone who could treat Mrs. Bannister and not turn her in."

"Yes, I know a doctor or two of Del's and my persuasion," said Harold in something of a grumble. "But where the hell am I supposed to keep her?"

In a very small voice, I said, "At your place?"

"At *my* place?"

"Well...Yes?"

Harold heaved a sigh at least as big as he was. Harold wasn't awfully tall, but he was kind of plump. "Your family's out now, right?"

"Right. Aunt Vi and Ma are at their jobs. I don't know where Pa is, and I don't know when he's coming home, but..." My voice trailed off, because I couldn't think of anything else to say.

"I can call Dr. Fred Greenlaw right now, and he can come here to doctor the poor soul. Then we'll probably have to discuss what to do with her. What's her name again?"

"Mrs. Bannister. Lily Bannister."

"Hmm. Is she married to Leo Bannister?"

"I don't know what her husband's first name is. All I know is that he's a beast."

"Agreed. If it's Leo, he's also a pervert."

My mouth fell open. I started to ask, but Harold held up a hand. "I'll tell you later. The 'phone's in the kitchen, right?"

"Right."

Harold walked through the kitchen to the telephone. I debated whether to wait with him or return to the living room. Recalling what lay in the living room, I followed Harold into the kitchen, praying the whole time that his Dr. Greenlaw would agree to treat Mrs. Bannister and keep her whereabouts—wherever those whereabouts ended up being—a secret.

Because we Gumms and this Majesty weren't rich enough to afford a single telephone line to ourselves, I scooted all our party-line neighbors off the wire before Harold used the telephone. It was always most difficult to get rid of Mrs. Barrow, who loved to listen in to other people's conversations, but I managed to shoo her off the wire eventually, and then I handed the 'phone to Harold, who dialed a number he'd evidently memorized.

Dr. Greenlaw's nurse or receptionist answered the wire, and Harold said, "Dr. Greenlaw, please. This is Harold Kincaid, and it's an emergency." Pause. "No, I can't tell you the nature of the emergency. I need to speak with Dr. Greenlaw instantly."

I don't recall ever hearing Harold sound so authoritative. Good for him. He rolled his eyes and glanced at me. "Officious nurse," said he.

"I'm sorry," said I, although I don't know why.

I guess the officious nurse got hold of the doctor, because Harold sort of sagged a bit and said, "Fred? I need you to come here and treat a woman who's been badly beaten by her husband. And you have to promise me you won't tell anyone about her or where you saw her or anything."

Another pause. Longer this time.

"I don't care. Don't you take some sort of oath to keep your patients' cases a secret?" Pause. "Dammit, Fred, it's the Hippocratic Oath, not the hypocritical oath, right?" Pause. "Well, then, honor your oath and get the hell over here. The woman looks as if she's knocking on death's door." Pause. "No, I'm not kidding." Pause. "Thanks." And Harold gave Dr. Fred Greenlaw my address.

Lordy, I hoped Pa wouldn't come home any time soon.

Harold hung the receiver on the cradle and heaved another huge sigh. Turning to me, he said, "There. I hope you're happy now."

"No, I'm not happy, and I'm sorry I dragged you into this, but Flossie brought Mrs. Bannister to me, and I couldn't think of a thing to do for her until you called."

"Lucky me."

"Precisely what I thought."

The stupid telephone rang. "Oh, for Pete's sake," I muttered.

"It's probably Mother, so you should brace yourself."

13

Harold's mother, Madeline Pinkerton, who used to be married to Harold's father, Eustace Kincaid, was pretty much always hysterical for one reason or another. I suspected this time her hysteria would be related to her idiot daughter's latest love interest. "God save me," I whispered as I lifted the receiver. "Gumm-Majesty residence, Mrs. Maj—"

"*Daisy!*" shrieked the voice of Harold's mother. I shut my eyes, prayed for patience, and glanced at Harold, who had the nerve to grin at me.

"Good morning, Mrs. Pinkerton," said I, knowing I lied as I spoke the words. For the record, I always speak softly and soothingly to my clients. I did so now to Mrs. Pinkerton in the vain hope my gentle voice would encourage her to shriek less. This ploy had never worked before, and it didn't this time either. I wasn't surprised.

"Oh, *Daisy!* I need you. *Now!*"

Great. Just great. "I'm so very sorry, Mrs. Pinkerton, but I am unable to visit you right now. I have a...family emergency."

"Oh, *nooooo!* But when can you come over. I need you to communicate with Rolly for me!"

Rolly is the name of my spirit control. I know he has a silly name, but I conjured him out of thin air and my imagination when I was ten, so his name isn't really the adult Daisy's fault. Anyhow, most of my clients believe his name is spelled R-A-L-E-I-G-H, so it doesn't really matter.

"What is the trouble, Mrs. Pinkerton?" I asked in a calming tone.

That didn't work, either. "It's *Stacy!*"

No surprise there. Stacy, whose given name is Anastasia, is Mrs. Pinkerton's idiot daughter.

"Is it related to her engagement to Mr. Percival Petrie?" I asked even more softly.

"Yes!" The woman began to sob at me.

I cast my gaze to the kitchen ceiling and wished for all sorts of things that couldn't be. Harold remained seated and grinning. I stuck my tongue out at him. Childish, I know, but we've already established that I'm not among the world's most mature adults.

"I'm very sorry, Mrs. Pinkerton. I honestly don't know when I'll be able to visit you, but I think I can come over this afternoon." I lifted my eyebrows at Harold, who shrugged at me. Made sense. He didn't know how long the Bannister crisis would last any more than I did. "And if it can't be this afternoon, it can be first thing tomorrow. That is to say, about ten forty-five tomorrow." I knew better than to stick to the "first thing" promise. If I did, she'd expect me at some ungodly hour. Six a.m. or something equally ghastly.

"Oooooh," she whimpered. "Please try to come today, Daisy. *Please!*" She sobbed some more.

"I shall. I'll give you a ring if I'm able to come to see you this afternoon." Bother the woman!

"Th-thank you," she said with what I deemed to be a snivel.

"You're more than welcome."

"But what is your family emergency?" she asked. She would.

"I'll have to explain later. I'm needed at once. Good morning, Mrs. Pinkerton."

And, by gum, I hung up on her. I don't believe I'd ever done that before, although I'd wanted to several million times.

I turned, heaved a huge sigh, and saw Harold still grinning at me. "It's not funny," I said.

"Is too," he said. He heaved himself to his feet. "Honestly, I don't know how you can tolerate the woman, even if she is my mother."

"It's because of Stacy," I told him. "She's engaged—"

"I know. I know. Percival Petrie. He's probably a filthy fortune-hunter. Who else would want Stacy?"

Good question and one I couldn't answer. I braced myself mentally and told Harold I supposed we'd better go to the living room and see if Mrs. Bannister was still alive.

"I'm no nurse," said Harold, shuddering slightly.

"I'm not one, either. But the poor woman needs help."

"Yes, I understand that. What I don't understand is why I should take her in. I'm not a field hospital in Belgium or anything."

"I know it, but you're the only person I know who has the room to house an invalid in secret for a while. I've been to your home, so don't pretend you don't have room for her."

"Oh, I suppose I have room for her, but I don't have a single idea what Del will think of taking in a woman who's running away from her husband. He's a Catholic, too, you know."

"I know it. I also know the two of you living together is a violation of Catholic law. And probably the law of the U.S.A., too. Not that I personally care, as you well know, but you can't use Mrs. Bannister's being Catholic as a reason to keep her out of your home."

"You've got me there," said Harold in something of a grumble. "But maybe I don't *want* an invalid cluttering up the house. Did you ever think of that?"

"Yes, I did think of that." But I suddenly had a brilliant idea. Or maybe it wasn't. It sometimes takes a while to know for sure if an idea is brilliant or not. "But if I hire a home nurse for her, will you take her in? That way, you won't have to deal with her at all. Just provide room and board. If she can ever eat again. Her husband broke some of her teeth, and her face is so bruised and swollen, I doubt she'll be able to do much except sip clear broth for a while."

"You can't afford a home nurse! Anyhow, do you know any home nurses who won't rat out the woman?"

Oh, dear. "No," I admitted.

"Well, don't despair yet. When Fred gets here, maybe he'll be able to think of something."

"Thank you, Harold," I said, sounding as humble as I felt.

So I left the kitchen, walked through the dining room and, sucking in a deep breath for courage, walked quietly into the living room.

Mrs. Bannister was still there. I guess she was still alive, too, because Flossie was speaking gently to her and sort of stroking the poor woman's head. She stopped at one point, drew her hand away, glanced at her fingers to find them bloody, and gave a deep sigh. She must have heard me enter the living room, because she showed me her hand.

I shook my head. "I'm so very sorry. But a Dr. Fred Greenlaw—well, I guess his name is Frederick—will be here soon. He can see to Mrs. Bannister's ribs and...and head...and everything. I'll get you a wet rag."

"Thank you, Daisy. I'm not sure how I'll pay for—"

I held up a hand. "Don't even say it, Flossie. I'll take care of the medical bills." Oh, boy, I only hoped they wouldn't bankrupt me. I'd definitely try to see Mrs. Pinkerton that afternoon. If I could tell her some sob story about my so-called family emergency, she'd probably give me a big lump of money. She was good about stuff like that, and the good Lord knew she had enough money to hand out to needy people. I hurried to the kitchen, got a clean rag from the drawer and wetted it under the faucet. Holding the rag, I returned to the scene of the crime. So to speak.

"Here. You can clean your hand with that." I thought about telling her she could wipe the blood from Mrs. Bannister's head but didn't. For all I knew, she had a gaping hole in her head. I stood back and tried not to show how inadequate I felt.

Behind me, Harold spoke, making me jump slightly. "Don't worry about the cost, Mrs. Buckingham. Fred's a good man, and he probably won't charge anyone anything. If he does, I'll cover the cost. Lord knows, I have enough money for three dozen people."

That was true, and I knew Harold wasn't boasting. He was quite matter-of-fact about his inherited wealth, in fact. Not only that, but he also worked for a living as a costumier at a Los Angeles movie studio. Great guy, Harold.

"Th-thank you, Mr. Kincaid." Flossie started sniffling.

"For God's sake, don't start crying. The money doesn't mean anything to me, but your poor friend's health clearly needs some work."

Flossie tried to stop her tears, but couldn't quite manage to do so. She used the other side of the wet rag to blot her tears. Fortunately for Harold, the doorbell sounded. He, Spike and I all turned and rushed to the door.

"Fred!" cried Harold. "Thank God you're here. There's a poor woman in her who needs all the help you can give her. Or sell her. I'll take care of her bill."

"Harold Kincaid," said the nice-looking man standing at the front door, "you're a kick in the pants, you know that?"

"One of my more endearing characteristics." Harold turned to me. "Daisy, please allow me to introduce you to Dr. Fred Greenlaw. Fred's a very discreet gentleman, mainly because he has to be, but he's also a good doctor. Fred, Daisy Majesty, spiritualist-medium extraordinaire."

Dr. Greenlaw, who was tall and trim, had dark hair and eyes, and was clad in a stunningly tailored dark gray suit with a white shirt and an attached collar, bowed slightly, and said in a beautiful baritone voice, "Happy to meet you, Mrs. Majesty."

If I didn't already know Dr. Greenlaw was of Harold's persuasion, I might have swooned. "Thank you so much for coming, Dr. Greenlaw." I held out my hand for him to shake, he shook it, then I stepped back, and he walked into the house. I locked the door as a precaution. If Pa came home and discovered the front door locked, he'd be surprised, but better he be surprised by a locked door than a surreptitious medical procedure being carried out in the living room.

I don't know why these things always seemed to happen to me.

But I'm being selfish. Something awful had happened to Mrs. Bannister. Flossie only foisted her on me because she didn't know what else to do with the poor woman.

It sounds awful, but I still wish Flossie had taken Mrs. Bannister to someone else's house.

I'm not really an evil person. At least I don't think I am.

Oh, never mind.

THREE

"Oh, my," said Dr. Greenlaw when he took in the full glory that was Lily Bannister. "Who did that to you?"

"I don't think she can speak, Dr. Greenlaw. Her mouth is all torn up. Her husband beat her to a pulp and then pushed her down the cement basement steps."

"Threw her down the stairs," Flossie said, correcting me.

"Good Lord." Dr. Greenlaw removed his coat and rolled up his sleeves. He set his medical bag on the floor next to the sofa and turned to me. "Do you have a sheet we can lay over the sofa so it doesn't get bloody while I'm treating the woman? Or, if you have a spare bed somewhere, that might give me better access to her various wounds."

"You may use my bed," I said, wincing inside. "I'll go pull back the covers. I expect you or Harold will have to carry Mrs. Bannister."

"Thank you, Mrs. Majesty."

"Oh, call me Daisy. Thank *you* for coming here and helping. I didn't know what to do for the poor woman."

"No more did I," said Harold.

"I know all about you, Harold," said Dr. Greenlaw with a smile.

Because I didn't much like the inference that seemed to be contained in the doctor's comment, I said, "Harold saved my life in Turkey." That was the truth.

"Doesn't surprise me in the least," said the doctor. "He likes people to think he's useless, but he's not."

"I do not," said Harold, plainly irked.

"Let me get my bedroom ready," said I in an attempt to forestall further argument.

"Thank you, Mrs.—Daisy," said Dr. Greenlaw. "Please call me Fred."

"Will do." I scurried to my bedroom, pulled the quilt and blankets off the bed and draped them over a chair. Then I rushed to the linen closet and got a clean sheet, which I put over the sheets already there. Spike was so interested in what I was doing, I darned near tripped over him. He leapt aside so a collision was avoided. Wishing I had an oilskin or something to put under the clean sheet so my own sheets wouldn't get bloody, I said, "All ready in here."

"Thank you," said Flossie. "I think we can assist Mrs. Bannister to walk to your room."

"It's kind of a long walk for an injured person," I said doubtfully.

But Harold, Fred, and Flossie managed it. Poor Mrs. Bannister was weeping by the time she got to my room, but Dr. Greenlaw proved his worth by gently settling her on top of my newly sheeted bed. He turned to me. "Do you have a clean apron, Daisy? And if you could boil up a couple of pots of water, I'd appreciate it. I'll need a large bowl and some clean rags if you have them, too."

"Right away," I said, and scrammed out of my room as if I were on fire. I hoped Dr. Greenlaw wasn't going to ask me to assist him with his medical attentions to Mrs. Bannister, because I *really* wasn't cut out for nursing.

Flossie trotted behind me. "You boil the water, Daisy. I'll help Dr. Greenlaw. I've had a good deal of nursing experience since I married Johnny."

Better you than me, I thought unkindly.

"Where are the clean rags?"

"In that drawer there." I pointed to the proper drawer as I put a huge pot in the sink and began filling it with water. "Would you mind sending Harold in here? I'm not sure I can carry this pot once it's full of water."

"Sure thing," said Flossie, grabbing all the rags in the drawer and heading back to my bedroom, which was right off the kitchen and handy for midnight snacks, emergency medical procedures, and stuff like that.

Harold entered the kitchen almost instantly. "Thank God. I was afraid they'd ask me to help out in there. Want me to get some bowls or something?"

"Thanks, Harold. Yes. If you'll look at that cupboard there, you should find a couple of large mixing bowls. Those will have to do. I'm going to fill another pot and put it on the stove. You'll probably have to help me carry them into the operating room. I mean my bedroom."

"Sorry, Daisy, but you started it."

"Did not. Flossie started it."

"Leo Bannister *started* it, if you want to get technical."

"True." I heaved a sigh as I lugged the pot to the stove, spilling a little water as I did so. I grabbed the mop out of the broom closet and cleaned up the puddle. Grabbing another pot, I set it in the sink and filled it with water. "I don't know how men get away with doing things like that."

"That's not all he gets away with," said Harold, a dark tone to his voice.

"Yes, you've hinted as much before, but I still don't know what you mean."

"Tell you later," said Harold as he trotted to the bedroom carrying three large mixing bowls.

It was a darned good thing Aunt Vi was such a great cook. If supplying the kitchen with implements had been left up to me, we'd probably only have bread, peanut butter, and a couple of knives to spread things with.

Harold came back into the kitchen almost as soon as he left. "Fred needs two clean aprons, one for himself and one for Mrs. Buckingham."

"Oh, Lord," I said, pressing a hand to my forehead. "I forgot about the aprons. They're in that drawer there." I pointed to the apron drawer, and Harold withdrew two aprons decorated with lovely embroidery. I'd sewed them up and stitched the embroidery, although I had a feeling Dr.

21

Greenlaw wouldn't care what they looked like or appreciate my handi-work if he even noticed.

"Good God. Fred's going to love these."

"I made them," I said with something of a snap.

"And they're lovely. Not sure they're precisely the thing for medical operations."

Harold took the aprons into the bedroom before I could compound my many sins with that of pride. Well, I guess I'd already committed that one. Fiddle. Emergencies and I don't get on all that well together.

"Is the water hot yet?" asked Harold as he again walked into the kitchen *sans* flower-bordered aprons.

I lugged the second pot of water to the stove and clanked it down. I gazed into the one that had been heating for a few minutes and said, "I don't know how hot he wants it. It's not boiling. If he wants boiling water, he'll have to wait another minute or so."

"And I'm supposed to carry a pot of boiling water into your bedroom?"

"Harold! Yes. I mean, grab some pot holders. They'll protect your sensitive hands." I shouldn't have been sarcastic with the fellow, who was being awfully helpful. I allowed my head to droop for only a second. "I'm sorry, Harold. The pot holders are in that drawer there." I pointed to yet another drawer, in which rested a whole slew of potholders sewn together by my own skillful hands. Most of them were layers and layers thick, and really did prevent burned hands.

"It's all right, Mrs. Majesty. I understand your trepidation in this matter," said Harold with mock severity. "Mine's at least as large as yours. If I'd wanted to go into the medical profession, I would have."

"Yeah. Me, too. The notion of doctoring wounds makes me want to run out of the house screaming."

"If you decide to do that, I'll join you." He left to ask the good doctor how hot he wanted the water, and returned a moment later. "He'll take the first pot. When the second pot boils, I can take that in to him."

"Thank you, Harold. You really are a good friend."

"I know." He snatched four pot holders out of the drawer, made sure his hands were well protected, and tried to lift the pot. "Holy Moses, are all your pots this heavy?"

"I guess they are when they're filled with water. I'm sorry."

"Never mind." With an audible "Umph," Harold lifted the pot and toddled to my bedroom.

It occurred to me to check to see where Spike was in the overall order of things. I *really* didn't want Harold to stumble over Spike whilst holding a gigantic pot filled with hot water. Fortunately for all, Spike was supervising conditions in the bedroom and stayed out of Harold's way.

Harold came back into the kitchen after having delivered the water and said, "I'm to wait until the next pot boils. While it does, Mrs. Buckingham and Fred are preparing the woman for surgery."

"*Surgery?*"

"If not precisely surgery, then something I don't want to watch. And Mrs. Buckingham doesn't want me in there, either, because it would be immodest to disrobe Mrs. Bannister while a non-medical man is in the room with her."

I squinted at Harold, but I believed he was telling the truth. "Well," said I after a pause, "I wouldn't want to see what's going on, either. I didn't even like looking at the poor woman when she had all her clothes on."

"Precisely."

So Harold and I sat at the kitchen table and chatted softly. We heard muted sounds coming from my bedroom. Spike joined us and sat at our feet, disappointed, I know, that we weren't eating, even though we were sitting on the kitchen chairs. I reached down to pet him.

"Since neither of us has had lunch, I don't suppose you have a sandwich or something available, do you?" Harold asked me doubtfully. He knew about my cooking failures, too, because my family had told on me.

I felt extremely inadequate in that moment. I couldn't cook, I couldn't nurse, and my few real skills didn't seem to be of much importance under the current circumstances. Nevertheless, I rose from the table and said, "Let me look." I went to our lovely almost-new Frigidaire and opened the door. The pickings weren't vast.

Harold came up behind me and peered over my shoulder. "Hmm," said he. "You have a largish block of yellow cheese, I see."

"Yes. My father is particularly fond of a good sharp cheddar, he says. He says it's because of his English ancestors, who liked cheddar and stilton, whatever stilton is. He likes that, too, although I'm not sure we can get it here."

"Daisy, Daisy, Daisy, your education is sorely lacking."

"It is when it comes to food and cooking," I admitted.

"Stilton is sort of like Roquefort, only British. We ate stilton when we were in England, if you recall."

"No. I wasn't eating much when we were in England," I reminded him.

"How could I ever forget? Well, if you've had Roquefort cheese, and you have, because we had it when we were in France, stilton tastes something like that."

"Oh. I think I had Roquefort cheese once here. I don't remember eating it in France. I think Vi sprinkled some on a salad. It was good."

"It's delicious. Oh, I see you have a couple of tomatoes, too."

"Yes. Those are left over from last night's salad."

"What kind of bread do you have?"

"Um...I don't know. I'll see." I moved over a tick and lifted the lid of the bread keeper. "Oh! It looks like Aunt Vi made some more pumpernickel! I love that. Especially with roast beef and mustard."

"Good Lord, child. Your vistas have expanded greatly since we last discussed food."

"Well, Sam had a roast beef and pumpernickel sandwich at Webster's soda counter a year or so ago, and Vi was kind enough to make pumpernickel for me since I asked about it. It's really good with ham, too."

"Yes. Ham and cheese on pumpernickel can't be beat."

"I don't think we have any ham," I said, feeling more like a failure than ever.

"No matter. Cut four slices of bread, and I'll fix us some spectacular sandwiches. Provided you have a skillet I can use. And some butter."

"Of course, we have a skillet and butter. You mean you're going to cook the bread and cheese and tomatoes and butter?" I'd never heard of such a thing. Which was probably just as well, given my ability to ruin anything I tried to fix in the kitchen. I mean, Aunt Vi fixed the occasional toasted cheese sandwich for us to have at lunch some weekends, but cheese and tomatoes? And pumpernickel? Well, Harold knew more about these things than I did. He could scarcely know less.

"Lord, Daisy." Harold peered at me, doubt writ large on his features. "You can't even cut a straight slice of bread, can you?"

I set the brand-new loaf of pumpernickel bread on the cutting board and clasped my hands behind my back in shame. "No."

"Fear not. It's as well I'm here."

Before Harold could perform any miracles, however, Flossie appeared in the doorway of my bedroom. "Is the water boiling yet? Dr. Greenlaw can use it if you don't mind bringing it in, Mr. Kincaid."

"Call me Harold, please. Yes, I'll bring in the pot of water. Would you and Fred like a sandwich? Neither Daisy nor I have had lunch yet."

Flossie looked at the two of us oddly for a moment then said, "We don't really have time right now. Maybe later."

"Right. Well, you tell me when you're ready to eat, and I'll fix you a sandwich. I'll bring in the water now."

So he did. When he came out of my bedroom, he looked a trifle green.

"Are you sick, Harold? Want me to put the cheese and bread away?" I was disappointed, being rather hungry myself.

"Oh, no." Harold shook himself like Spike after he gets a bath. "I'm all right. I just don't like the sight of blood."

"There's lots of blood?" I asked, thinking of my bedclothes. Petty, I know.

"Not a lot. I don't like any blood at all, as you should know by now. But never mind that. Where's that bread?"

I pointed to the lovely loaf of pumpernickel.

"Bread knife," said Harold, holding out a hand and eyeing the bread I'd set on the cutting board.

I handed him the bread knife.

"Scalpel," said he.

"I beg your pardon?"

"Just a little medical humor." He cut the bread into four perfectly perfect slices. I was impressed. "You can wrap this up and put it back in the keeper," he said, handing me the rest of the loaf.

So I wrapped the cut loaf in waxed paper and put it back in the keeper.

Harold said, "Cheese, and a sharp knife."

I handed him the cheese and a sharp knife.

He cut the cheese into as many pieces as would fit on a slice of pumpernickel. He was most dexterous with that knife and precise in his measurements. I remained impressed.

"Tomato," he said, handing me the remains of the cheese.

I put the cheese back in its wrapper and handed him a tomato, washing it first under the kitchen faucet and drying it on a clean kitchen towel.

He cut it into rings, cut the rings in half, and placed precise half-rings of tomato on top of the cheese on top of the pumpernickel.

"Butter," he said, holding out his hand.

I got the butter dish from the kitchen table, removed its lid, and handed it to Harold.

"Butter knife," he said.

I handed him a butter knife.

"Skillet," he said.

I handed him a cast-iron skillet, which he settled onto a stove burner. He grabbed a match out of the match-holder on the counter, lit a burner under the skillet, and put a couple of pats of butter into the skillet. He then adjusted the flame and watched the skillet as if he expected it to get up and fly out the window. I'd seldom seen such concentration of my friend's face. I guess he took food as seriously as did Aunt Vi.

Since I didn't want Harold to feel left out, I watched the butter melt in the skillet, too. When the butter was melted to his satisfaction, Harold said, "Spatula."

I grabbed the spatula out of the jar in which Vi kept things like that and handed it to him.

Harold stirred the butter in the skillet until it fairly uniformly covered the skillet's bottom. Then he carefully lifted one slice of loaded pumpernickel and set into the skillet, which sizzled. He did the same to the second slice, then covered both of the bread-cheese-and-tomato concoctions with the third and fourth slices of pumpernickel. Using the butter knife, he spread butter on the latest slices of pumpernickel to hit the skillet. Then he stood back and smiled with satisfaction.

"There. You just wait and see if I haven't created a masterpiece."

After watching the bread in the skillet for a moment, I said, "I guess I'll have to wait, won't I?"

"Hmph," said Harold. "Not for long, you won't."

FOUR

H e was right. After lifting the edges of the sizzling bread a couple of times, he deftly flipped both sandwiches so that their other sides would toast. My state of impressedness remained intact.

"If I tried to do that, the sandwich would fall apart and there would be a big mess on the stove. And probably on the floor. Spike wouldn't mind, but I would."

"You just need to concentrate on what you're doing when you cook, my dear," said Harold.

"That's what Vi always tells me."

"She's right."

"I guess so. But I don't like to cook."

"Tut, tut. Cooking is an art to be cultivated. But you may haul out a couple of plates now, because my masterpieces are about ready." He gingerly lifted each sandwich's edge once more and peered at each one's bottom.

I got the plates and put them on the cool side of the stove. Harold gently placed one sandwich on each plate, picked up the knife he's used for the cheese, and cut each sandwich in half. "Got any dill pickles?"

"I think so. Let me look." I did, we did, and I got the bottle down from the cupboard where Vi had stored them when she'd preserved them last summer when our cucumber crop was at its vine-busting best. Those things grow fast.

Harold fished out a pickle, let it drip into the jar for a moment or two, and plopped it onto a plate. He did the same with another pickle, then sliced the pickles in half. "There," he said with a satisfied sigh. "Lunch is ready."

"Thanks, Harold." I quickly set two places at the kitchen table. Harold brought over the plates and set one at each place.

"Dig in," said he, demonstrating.

So I did. "Oh, my, this is delicious. I don't know why I never even thought about toasting cheese-and-tomato sandwiches before. Why hasn't Vi done this for our lunches? Well, she's not usually home for our lunches, come to think of it."

"Your aunt has enough to do dealing with my mother and stepfather, Daisy Majesty. *You* should learn to be more useful in the kitchen."

Stung, I said, "You're right."

Harold and I had finished our sandwiches and pickle halves, and I'd just finished washing the few dishes we'd dirtied, when Flossie appeared in the bedroom door, looking slightly frazzled.

"How's Mrs. Bannister?" I asked her hastily.

"Dr. Greenlaw says she should go to the hospital, but she refused to go. She's sure her husband will find her there, and I think he will, too."

"You're both probably right," I said, wishing I had a million dollars and could take care of Mrs. Bannister's medical costs. "She probably didn't have any money with her when she escaped from that basement, did she?"

"No. And she has no way of getting funds. Her parents won't help her. The church won't help her. The police won't help her. *Nobody* will help her. It's so unfair!" Flossie said, wiping angry tears from her eyes.

I walked over and hugged her. "We're trying to help her," I said in an effort to cheer her up.

"Don't get blood on your clothes, Daisy. Do you have any idea where we can take Mrs. Bannister now, since we can't take her to the hospital?"

I looked at Harold, who looked back at me. Then he heaved a huge sigh and said, "Oh, for the good Lord's sake, take her to my house. I'll hire a hospital nurse to take care of her. I'm sure Fred can suggest someone who won't blab, especially if I pay her enough."

I ran to Harold and hugged him hard. "Oh, Harold. You're the *best*."

"Thank you *so* much!" said Flossie, crying harder.

Dr. Bannister appeared at Flossie's back. His once-clean apron was stained with blood and other goop I didn't want to know about. "Did I hear you volunteer a room in your house, Harold?"

"Yes," said Harold, plainly exasperated. "It looks like I'm being drawn into this melodrama whether I want to be or not. And I don't. Say, Fred, do you know a nurse I can hire who won't tell the world we're hiding Leo Bannister's mutilated wife?"

Dr. Greenlaw's nose wrinkled. "Leo Bannister? *He* did that to her?"

"Yes," said Flossie.

I glanced at her for confirmation, and she shrugged. I got the feeling she didn't know the evil Mr. Bannister's first name either, but figured Leo would do if it would assist Mrs. Bannister.

"In that case, yes. My sister Hazel can nurse her. She won't tell a soul."

"You're sure?" asked Harold.

"I'm sure," said the doctor grimly. He gave Harold what I considered to be a significant glance, and I wondered exactly what kinds of perversions Mrs. Bannister's husband perpetrated.

"Right," said Harold. "So now all we have to do is get the woman to my house." He turned to me. "Daisy, I can't drive her in my Bearcat. Can you and Mrs. Buckingham take her in your Chevrolet?"

"I'd better go with you," said Fred Greenlaw. "It will take two people to keep her from re-injuring herself. I had to give her a dose of opium so I could tend to her various injuries, and she's too woozy to sit upright without help."

"Good heavens," I whispered, appalled.

"There's nothing good about her condition," said Dr. Greenlaw. "And I wish to God her case didn't have to be kept secret. I think men who do that to women, husbands or not, should be prosecuted."

"I think they should be beaten to a pulp and then shot," I said, truly angry, both on Mrs. Bannister's behalf, and on behalf of all the other women who were forced by the law, their churches, or their parents to remain with brutish men. "They make me sick."

"I should be forgiving," said Flossie, her tears finally dry. "But I'll have to pray about that one, because I can't find an ounce of forgiveness in my heart for Mr. Bannister."

"Wise woman," said Harold.

"But first we have to do something about these aprons and that bloody sheet," said Dr. Greenlaw.

"Oh. Shoot. I guess I'll have to hide them somewhere until I can launder them in private."

"You might try hydrogen peroxide first and then bleach mixed with your washing water," suggested Dr. Greenlaw. "Both are good for getting out tough stains."

He sounded kind of like my aunt Vi or an advertisement in the *Saturday Evening Post*, but I appreciated his suggestions. "Thanks. In the meantime, pile the dirty stuff in my bedroom." I bit my lip for a second. "Let me fetch a basket from the basement. We can shove everything in there, and I'll stick the basket in my closet."

"Sounds like a good idea." I don't know who said that, because I was already headed to the basement, which was off the kitchen, sort of on the way to the hall. Well, I can't explain it very well, but it doesn't matter. I pulled the light chain, charged down the stairs, thinking they were hard and concrete and would hurt a whole lot if one were to fall or be thrown down them, grabbed a laundry basket, and carried it back upstairs.

By the time I got to the kitchen with my basket, the doctor and Flossie had more or less carried Mrs. Bannister out of my room and deposited her in a kitchen chair, where Harold held her steady.

Flossie, the doctor, and I traipsed into my bedroom, where I couldn't quite avoid looking at my bed. Oddly enough, the sheet covering the mattress pad didn't look too horrifying. Nevertheless, I ripped it off the bed, thought for a second, and then took the rest of my bedclothes off too, dumped them all in the basket, and told Flossie and Dr. Greenlaw to deposit their aprons and other rags and so forth in the same basket, which I then shoved into my closet and closed the door. I pulled up the quilt to cover my bed so that it appeared to be made up just as it normally would be. Spike jumped on the bed and sniffed interestedly. I patted him and said, "You can stay there if you want to, but don't chew on the quilt." Turning to my companions, I said, "I'll put on fresh sheets and bedding later. First we need to get Mrs. Bannister to Harold's house."

"Right. I'll follow in the Bearcat," said Harold.

"Actually, you'd better lead," said the doctor. "You'll have to unlock the door for us."

"Good point," said Harold, and he headed for the front door.

"But first help us get Mrs. Bannister into the Chevrolet," I told Harold.

Fortunately, my family's bungalow had a side entrance off the dining room. It led to a porch and stairs, and our automobile was parked handily right beside the bottom step. I raced down the steps and opened the car's back door, since I presumed Dr. Greenlaw and Flossie would be attending to Mrs. Bannister there.

Harold and the doctor carried the wounded and bewildered Lily Bannister down to our auto, where Dr. Greenlaw got in first, and carefully helped Harold arrange Mrs. Bannister beside him. Flossie got in next to her and assisted in keeping her upright.

Only then did I realize I still wore my frowzy day dress. Oh, well. Emergencies happened. I raced back into the house, unlocked the front door in case my father came home before I did. Then I noticed the lovely red automobile parked behind Flossie's Model-T and Harold's Stutz Bearcat. "Oh, my, what kind of car is that? The doctor's, I mean."

"Marmon Wasp," said Harold walking toward his car. He turned and said, "See you soon."

"Right." Again, I gazed down at my dumpy dress, sighed, and told myself not to be silly. None of my clients would see me this way. I hoped. Couldn't be helped anyway. So I returned to the Chevrolet.

I carefully backed out of our driveway and headed south on Marengo Avenue. When I got to Del Mar Boulevard, I turned left and drove east toward Allen Avenue. At Allen, I turned right and headed down into the lush and lovely San Marino, where Harold and Del lived. So did Miss Emmaline Castleton, whose railroad-robber-baron father had built a monumental estate there. Emmaline had shown me around the place once. It was spectacular.

Harold's house wasn't too shabby either. Situated on Lombardy Road, it was, according to Harold, built in the Spanish style. I'm not quite sure what that means, but the house itself was two stories, and enclosed a *spectacular* patio laid with bricks in a lovely pattern, and with a tiled fountain at one end. Harold had invited me to parties there, I'd conducted séances there, and I wish I could afford to live in a house just like it with my family. Silly me.

But Harold had built the thing with his own money, and I didn't begrudge him anything he owned. He and Del both worked hard for their livings, even though neither man actually *had* to work, unlike like those of us born into the middle and lower classes.

Do I sound the least bit envious? That's because I was. But that's merely me being human, I think. I hope.

Harold had arrived before us and already gone into his house, I presume to give instructions to whatever servants he employed. As we pulled up in front of his house, he hurried to the curb to assist with Mrs. Bannister's transport. "There's a room upstairs she can use. Roy—he's my houseboy—is making it up as we speak. There's a full bathroom off the room, and I can have a cot or something set up for Hazel." He eyed Dr. Greenlaw doubtfully. "Will Hazel mind sleeping on a cot?"

"Hazel's a nurse, Harold, and she'll do pretty much anything for another victim of Leo Bannister's evil."

Another victim. This Leo Bannister character was beginning to sound not unlike Satan himself. But Harold had said he'd tell me about the evil man later, so I'd just have to wait.

"Thanks, Harold," I said, getting out of the car. I walked to the back door. "Is there anything I can do to help?"

"I think Harold and will be able to lift her from the machine," said Fred Greenlaw. "Mrs. Buckingham, will you come with us? You, too, Daisy."

"Very well."

I winced as the two men carefully maneuvered Mrs. Bannister out of the car. Then the doctor gently lifted her into his arms. She was sort of skinny—her beast of a husband probably wouldn't allow her to eat more than bread and water—so she wasn't much of a burden for the tall, well-built man.

Flossie and I followed the men and Mrs. Bannister to the front door, which stood open. I heard Flossie gasp when she first viewed the wonders of Harold's home.

"Amazing, isn't it?" I whispered.

"Mercy, yes," she whispered back.

The entryway of the home was tiled, and a staircase rose on the left. The entryway itself had a spectacular Oriental rug on the floor. A couple of decorative chairs perched against the walls. I knew from experience that the hallway leading from the entryway led to a beautiful front room, which Harold called the "family room," a dining room, and a kitchen that was even larger than Harold's mother's kitchen. I guess Harold got a lot of practice cooking up various delectable nibbles in there. What's more, according to him, he enjoyed it. There's no accounting for taste.

"Be careful carrying her up the stairs," said Harold. "They're red brick and tile. They're not slippery but they're hard as hell, and there's no carpeting."

"I've been here before don't forget, Harold," said the doctor drily. He didn't even seem out of breath. This time I was impressed with him and his stamina. And his goodness of heart, if that's what it was.

"It's the last room on the west wing," said Harold. He hurried ahead of the doctor up the stairs, and turned right when he reached the top. The upstairs hallway, which bent in the middle sort of like the staircase, had a lovely Oriental carpet laid, but we could still hear Harold's footsteps as he dashed to the room being prepared to receive Mrs. Bannister. We also heard him call, "Roy! Is the bed ready?"

"Yes, sir," a voice answered him.

Flossie and I followed the doctor slowly, taking in the beauty all around us.

"Oh, my," whispered Flossie, "I don't believe I've ever seen anything so grand."

"I know. Harold has really good taste." At least I suppose that was what he had. An artistic eye, for sure. I don't see how his and Del's home could have been made to look any better, whoever had been responsible for its furnishings.

I knew from having been in the house before that the two wings of the house sheltered the patio and that all the rooms on the second floor had doors leading onto a balcony that circled—squared?—the patio from above.

Dr. Greenlaw seemed to have no trouble carrying Mrs. Bannister up the stairs and down the hallway to the last bedroom on the west wing of Harold's gigantic home. Flossie and I sped up a bit in order to help him settle her if he needed help.

He didn't. Roy waited at the head of the bed and rushed to assist the doctor. I'd met Roy before. He was a young Negro man, slender and not awfully tall, but extremely polite. He'd always seemed to me to be a gentle and kindly lad, which made me suspect he belonged to the same segment of society to which Harold and Del belonged. I don't know that for sure, but it wouldn't have surprised me.

"Good Lord, Mr. Harold, what happened to the lady?" asked Roy as he took in the full glory of Mrs. Bannister once Dr. Greenlaw had settled her onto the bed.

"Her husband happened to her," said Harold grimly. "And no one is *ever* to know she's here. Right, Roy?"

Harold gave Roy a meaningful glance, which was returned along with Roy's, "Yes, sir."

"Cut it out with the 'sir' and 'Mr. Harold' nonsense, all right? Just pull the covers up over Mrs. Bannister—"

Roy jumped an inch or so and blurted out, "Bannister? You mean that's Leo Bannister's wife? And he did *that* to her?" Roy had a soft voice with some kind of lilting, musical accent. I wanted to know where he came from, but I didn't think this would be an appropriate time to ask.

"Yes."

"I won't tell a single soul on this green earth," Roy promised.

Golly, Leo Bannister was surely a monster if even this young boy had heard of him. I wonder why no one in my circle of acquaintances had told me about him before now. Odd, that.

FIVE

D
r. Greenlaw called his sister, Hazel the nurse, on the telephone extension in the upstairs hallway, and then he, Harold, Flossie and I descended the staircase.

"I'd like to remain here until Hazel arrives," the doctor said when we were downstairs. "My machine's in front of Daisy's house, however. Harold, would you mind riding up there with Daisy and Mrs. Buckingham and driving it down here?"

"Happy to," said Harold.

Fred Greenlaw turned to Flossie and held out his hand. "Mrs. Buckingham, I can't tell you how much I appreciate your help with that poor woman. You were brave, able, and useful, and I'm sure your efforts will be rewarded." He glanced at Harold, who started slightly, then nodded.

"There's no need for a reward for me," said Flossie. "I only hope her old man won't find her and drag her back. If he does, he'll probably kill her one of these days."

I hadn't heard Flossie sound so much like she used to sound in the bad old days for a couple of years.

"Well, thank you," said the doctor. "I need to get back upstairs and monitor the patient until Hazel arrives."

"Thank you so much, Dr. Greenlaw," said I, holding out my hand to him. "You might have saved her life. In fact, you probably did."

"She didn't have any broken ribs, which was the main concern, barring concussion. She has a concussion, which might or might not get better with time. Sometimes concussion can cause long-term problems with a patient. I bound her ribs, which might be cracked, although none were broken."

"I can't imagine a husband doing that to his wife," I muttered.

"Happens all the time," said Flossie, who knew.

My life had been terribly sheltered, I suppose, and I'm really glad of it.

So Flossie, Harold and I left the doctor and Roy to tend Mrs. Bannister and headed to my Chevrolet. As we walked the brick pathway leading through Harold's beautifully tended lawn, I said, "When we get to my house, I think I'll call your mother, Harold. She was in a dither when she 'phoned me this morning, and maybe I can sneak some information from her about the Bannisters."

"I can tell you everything you'll ever need to know about Leo Bannister," Harold told me.

"I don't even *want* to know about him," said Flossie. "I know all I need to know right now."

"Actually, you probably don't," said Harold. "But I'll talk to Daisy, and then, if she deems it appropriate, she may tell you, although I don't think the word should be spread far and wide. Leo Bannister should burn in hell, and the sooner the better, but his wife doesn't need any more grief in her life. If word of his antics spreads, she'll certainly be the one who suffers."

"Oh, dear," I said. "That bad, is he?"

"Probably worse," said Harold.

Flossie said not another word, and neither Harold nor I spoke as I drove the Chevrolet back up to my family's bungalow on South Marengo Avenue. We did talk after they both exited the car.

"Thank you so much, Daisy," Flossie said. "And Harold, I don't know how I'll ever be able to repay your kindness and that of Dr. Greenlaw."

"No need," said Harold, blushing slightly.

"There's every need." Flossie pulled out her hankie and sniffled as she walked to the Model-T. I hoped she wouldn't get scolded by Johnny. She could just tell him that she came over to my place and we gabbed for slightly longer than usual, I guessed.

"Criminy," muttered Harold. "If she only knew. It's Fred she needs to thank."

"And you, too, Harold. You let poor Mrs. Bannister stay in your house."

"Only because you forced me to," he grumbled. "You deserve to deal with my mother today for embroiling me in that drama."

"And thanks for lunch!" I called as he stomped to Dr. Greenlaw's beautiful red automobile. He didn't turn around, but did acknowledge my thanks with a wave. Oh, dear. I hoped he wasn't too mad at me for involving him in this day's work.

Pa had come home while I was carting invalids and caretakers around town. He met me with a questioning glance. I preferred Spike's greeting, which was as happy and exuberant as ever.

"Where have you been, Daisy?" he asked, eyeing my charming frock. I'm joking.

"Just out for a bit. Flossie came over, and then Harold came over, and then a friend of his came over."

"You don't generally leave the house without looking like a picture from a fashion magazine."

I heaved a sigh. "I know."

"And who belongs to that Marmon Wasp out there? Harold hasn't traded in his Bearcat for the Marmon, has he?"

Inventing at the speed of lightning, I said, "No. That belongs to Dr. Fred Greenlaw, Harold's friend. I took us all for a little spin, but when we got to Harold's house, the doctor got a 'phone call from his nurse and had to deal with an emergency—"

"How'd his nurse know where to get hold of him?" asked Pa. It was a reasonable question, drat it.

"He called his office, and that's when his nurse told him about the emergency. Harold said he—the doctor—could use his Bearcat, and I drove Harold and Flossie back up here. Harold's going to take the doctor's car to his house, where Dr. Greenlaw will pick it up after he's dealt with his emergency."

Pa peered at me for several seconds before he said, "Oh."

"I didn't mean to be away for so long," I said feebly.

After heaving a large-sized sigh, Pa said, "I'm sure you had your reasons, and I'm sure they were good ones." He held up a hand as I took a breath to respond. "I won't ask. But I hope you aren't getting into another pickle."

Darn it! This wasn't the first time my otherwise-wonderful father had accused me of poking into things that were none of my business and getting into trouble for it. And perhaps I had experienced one or two little problems in the past due to my tendency to snoop, but today's catastrophe wasn't my fault in any way whatsoever. However, I couldn't tell Pa that.

"It's not another pickle," I lied.

Then, for the second time in the history of me, salvation came unto me with the ringing of the telephone in the kitchen rang. I hurried to the 'phone.

As I scuttled to the kitchen, Pa called after me, "Mrs. Pinkerton called. She's upset."

"Thanks, Pa," I called back, pretty sure the 'phone call was for me and that the party on the other end of the wire was going to be Mrs. Pinkerton. Again.

I was right. "Gumm-Majesty—" was as far as I got before she interrupted me.

"Daisy! Oh, please tell me you can come over this afternoon. It's after noon now, and I so hope you can visit. I desperately need your help with the Ouija board and the tarot cards." As an afterthought, she added, "I hope your family emergency worked out all right."

"It did, thank you. And yes, I can come over in..." I looked at the clock on the wall. Shoot. It was already two o'clock. "I can be there in forty-five minutes. Will that be all right?"

"Oh, yes! Thank you so much, dear! I can't tell you how much I appreciate this!"

I'm sure she would figure out a way. She'd also undoubtedly hand me boocoo bucks, which I aimed to give to Mrs. Bannister. I might make the gift conditional. If she stayed away from her brutish husband, she could keep the dough.

But that wouldn't make it much of a gift, would it? And the poor woman needed help more than anyone else I knew at the moment.

"I'll be there soon," I promised Mrs. Pinkerton.

"Thank you, dear." She hung up.

I hung up. When I turned to go to my bedroom—only then recalling the bundle of laundry tucked away in my closet—my father stood at the kitchen table, watching me. So did Spike, but he was hoping for food. My father seemed puzzled and somewhat irritated. I hated to make my family unhappy.

But I still couldn't tell anyone about Mrs. Bannister.

Lordy, how do I get into these messes?

It would probably be better if you didn't answer that.

"Gotta go see Mrs. Pinkerton. You're right. She's upset. I think it's about Stacy and her fiancé. Mrs. P doesn't approve."

"She probably has good reason."

"I'm sure she does. In fact, I know she does, because Miss Petrie at the library told me a whole lot about him. Stacy's fiancé and she are distantly related."

"Good Lord. Isn't she the one who was related to those Ku Klux Klan idiots?"

"Yes, but that's not her fault. There's a good side to the Petrie clan and a bad side. Miss Petrie belongs to the good side. The bad ones belong to...well, the bad side."

"I see," said Pa, and this time I could tell he was the liar.

I didn't call him on his fib, being in rather deep and dubious waters myself right then. "Anyhow, I can't imagine that anyone but a miserable, conniving fortune-hunter would want to marry Stacy."

"That's not very nice, Daisy," said my always-nice father.

"I know it. But it's the truth." I felt rather beleaguered as I went back to my bedroom with Spike, who pretty much followed me everywhere, and opened the door to my overstuffed closet. I loved to sew, and I had a wardrobe fit for a queen. Pa was correct when he said I seldom left the house looking less than spiffy.

Still, I didn't have much time, so I grabbed a mid-calf length tan-colored dress with a brown collar and low-waisted belt. It was comfy, and I didn't have to do any wriggling to get into the thing. I just slipped it over my head and it settled, like the good dress it was, to fit precisely. I hadn't paid much attention to the weather when I'd been out earlier, but I'd worn a short-sleeved day dress and hadn't been cold, so I didn't bother with a coat, but slipped on some flesh-colored stockings, my brown shoes, and then tackled my hair.

I have dark red hair, but it's not difficult to manage since I had it bobbed a couple of years ago at the local barbershop. I combed it into submission, made sure my juju and Sam's engagement ring didn't show at my neck, and put some rice powder on my cheeks. No rouge or lip color for me, since I aimed to look as spiritualistic as possible. Fortunately, I buffed my fingernails almost every single evening, so my nails, even though I'd been doing housework before Flossie'd ruined my day, looked all right. Peering into my mirror, I decided I'd pass muster. To be on the safe side, I squirted a little bit of lavender water on my armpits. Nobody wants a stinky spiritualist. Then I made a dash for the bathroom where I took care of essentials, went back to the bedroom, picked up my brown handbag, settled my cream-colored cloche hat on my hair, and headed for the side door.

"That was quick," said my father. "You look swell, sweetie."

"Thanks, Pa." I gave him a quick kiss on the cheek, bent to pet Spike, apologized to both of them for having to dash rather than take a walk with them, and scooted out to the Chevrolet.

Mrs. Pinkerton has the most wonderful butler in the world. His name is Featherstone, I've never seen him the least little bit rattled—which is kind of a miracle, given for whom he worked—he was always neat as a pin, and he even had an elegant English accent. As soon as I'd picked up the brass lion's brass knocker and clumped it against the brass knocking plate, Featherstone opened the door.

"I'm here to see Mrs. Pinkerton, Featherstone." I only said that because it was a tradition. He knew why I was there.

"Please follow me," said he, as he always did.

So I followed him, and he led me to Mrs. Pinkerton's vast drawing room. In anybody else's house—well in anybody else who didn't have a fortune's house—it would have been called a living room or a parlor.

As soon as I wafted gently into the drawing room, Mrs. Pinkerton, who had been standing at a window looking out, swirled around and screeched, "Daisy!" I didn't even flinch. "I'm so glad you could come!"

And, also as usual, she charged at me. It was a darned good thing Mrs. P favored heavy wooden furniture, because I braced myself against a mahogany chest so that when she hit I wouldn't fall over backwards. She was a good deal larger than I.

"Oh, Daisy," she sobbed onto my shoulder. "I'm so very worried about Stacy! That man she wants to marry is a bad lot. I just know it."

"Let's consult with Rolly," said I soothingly. "Shall we?"

Thank the good Lord, she let go of me. One of these days, she's going to knock me down, and smother me. Or maybe not. I can be dramatic myself sometimes.

"Oh, yes. Thank you so much, dear!" She hurried over to a beautiful sofa, and I pulled up a lovely medallion-backed chair. I think her furnishings were Louis the Somethingth, but I'm not sure which one. Fourteenth or Fifteenth, I suppose. I should ask Harold.

A shining mahogany table sat in front of the sofa, so I took my Ouija board from the lovely embroidered bag I'd made for it, set it on the table, set the planchette on top of the board, and said sweetly, "What would you like to ask Rolly first?"

"Oh, dear." She pulled out a hankie and sniffled into it. "I don't know what to ask!"

Great. Perfect. She'd pestered me all day to bring my Ouija board to her house, and now she didn't know what she wanted to ask? Rather than show my state of peevedness (I don't think that's really a word), I said, still sweetly, "You know Rolly can't answer questions for anyone other than the person using the planchette with me." She needed this reminder almost every time I visited her.

"Yes, yes. I know that, dear." She wrinkled her powdered brow and thought. Thinking didn't come easily to her. I know it for a rock-solid fact. That may not be a nice thing to say, but it's true.

"Perhaps you should ask Rolly if there's anything *you* can do to unearth any unsavory details about Mr. Petrie's life." Mind you, if Percival Petrie turned out to be a mass murderer, Stacy would probably want to marry him anyway, but oh well.

"What a wonderful idea!" Mrs. P cried.

"Not at all," said I, reflecting that anyone with a rational thinking brain could have come up with the same suggestion.

So we settled our fingers lightly on the planchette, and Mrs. Pinkerton repeated my question to Rolly, who recommended she either hire a private investigator or ask around for information pertaining to Percival Petrie.

Mrs. Pinkerton said, "A private detective?"

Rolly said yes, in that special way he has which, in this case, means I sent the planchette up the board to land on the big YES on the upper left-hand corner of the Ouija board.

And so it went. Last of all, I dealt out a tarot pattern, which told Mrs. P pretty much what Rolly had told her. Well, that's not precisely true. With the cards, you can deal out various patterns and depending on what cards show up, you can sort of tell a person what to expect. In Mrs. Pinkerton's case, that day the cards, which consisted mainly of swords—not the most encouraging cards in the deck—told her to expect trouble before peace came down upon her. I swear, my job sounds idiotic sometimes.

But our session finally ended. Mrs. Pinkerton, as I'd expected she would, handed me a big gob of money, I thanked her graciously, and then I headed for the door, aiming to walk to the kitchen and see if Vi was ready to come home.

As I exited the drawing room, Mrs. P called after me. I turned and smiled graciously at her.

"You know, dear, I've been thinking about marriage lately."

"Yes, I know."

"But I've not merely been thinking about Stacy. You know she's always been just a little bit wild."

A *little* bit. Stacy was a hellhound of the first order. Well, she'd calmed down a trifle since she'd joined the Salvation Army, but I didn't trust this phase of hers to last. "Indeed," said I sweetly.

"But I've also been thinking about Harold," said Mrs. Pinkerton.

Uh-oh. "Do you think Harold wants to get married?"

"I don't know, but I *do* think that you and he would be the perfect couple!" She clasped her hands to her large bosom and beamed at me.

Uh-oh again. And again and again and again.

SIX

I can't even remember how I responded to Mrs. Pinkerton's suggestion that Harold and I should get hitched. He and Delray Farrington had been living together in their mansion in San Marino for as long as I'd known Harold, and I knew darned well he didn't aim to marry a woman any time soon. Or ever. Harold wasn't attracted to women.

Besides that, he was one of my all-time best friends. I knew from experience that marriage and friendship, unless you're extremely lucky, don't always go together.

It was a rattled Daisy Gumm Majesty who pushed open the swing door to the Pinkertons' kitchen that miserable day. Not that the weather was bad or anything, but my day so far had not been blissful. I didn't mean to, but I startled my wonderful aunt, who jumped an inch or so and looked over her shoulder at me.

"Daisy!"

"I'm sorry, Vi. I didn't mean to scare you."

"It's all right, sweetheart. I'm just getting ready to pack up and go home, so your arrival is timely."

"Oh, good." I sank into a kitchen chair and sniffed. "Boy, it smells good in here. What are you fixing?"

"Lamb stew. There's enough for us at home, too, but I wasn't sure

45

how to get it there. Now that you've come, you can drive me home, so we can have lamb stew for dinner."

"Yum. You're the best, Aunt Vi. And you know you can always telephone me, and I'll be happy to pick you up and drive you home."

"I know, sweetie, but I don't like to burden you with even more telephone calls."

"I wouldn't mind getting a call from you, Vi. It's the other calls I don't like so much." I buried my head in my hands with my elbows on the table. I didn't mean to; it just sort of happened.

She turned and studied what she could see of my face while wiping her hands on her apron. "What's the matter, Daisy? You look a little upset. I know Mrs. Pinkerton has been in a tizzy lately over Stacy, but you should be used to her tizzies by this time."

"It's not just that, although you're right. She's upset about Stacy, but that only makes sense. Anyone with half an ounce of common sense would be upset about Stacy."

My darling aunt chuckled. "I guess that's not very nice, but it's true. So what's wrong?"

I couldn't tell her about Lily Bannister, so I decided to tell her about Ms. P's plan for my future. "Mrs. Pinkerton wants Harold and me to get married."

"She *what?*"

"You heard me," I said with a massive sigh. "Now that she has this bee in her bonnet, she'll probably pester me about it forever."

Vi shook her head. "It's your own fault. You ought to marry Sam and get it over with."

Lifting my head from my hands, I stared at my aunt. I think my mouth fell open. In fact, I know it did, because I shut it with an audible clack of teeth before I stuttered, "But...but...What do you mean, 'marry Sam and get it over with?' How can I marry Sam? For heaven's sake, Vi, Billy died not two years ago. I haven't recovered from losing him yet!"

"Yes, yes, I know," said Vi, turning again to fill a large container with lamb stew, I presume for our family dinner. "But you know Sam adores you. You could do a whole lot worse."

Actually, I already had done a whole lot worse, although that was neither Billy's nor my fault, and I would *never* tell Vi so. But when Billy and I were a starry-eyed young couple marrying right out of high school, we didn't anticipate a war ruining our lives.

"I'm not ready to marry again. Not anyone." I fingered Sam's engagement ring at my bosom, thinking I probably ought to give in and tell everyone we were engaged. Every time I thought about that, though, my heart twanged. Bother.

"It's all right, Daisy. I know how grief can hurt. I lost my husband and my only child, you know."

"I know. I'm sorry, Vi. I don't mean to wallow, but...Well, I'm not ready to remarry. Anyone. And especially not Harold." The thought suddenly made me giggle.

Vi eyed me as she stuck her container full of lamb stew in a cardboard box and added a bunch of dinner rolls wrapped in waxed paper. Oh, boy, were we going to stuff ourselves that night! I could hardly wait.

"You know, sweetie, Harold is a very nice man. I can't quite seem him as the marrying kind, though."

"You're absolutely correct on that count, Aunt Vi."

"Um...Well, I know this is a shocking thing to say, and I do dearly love the boy, but...Well, do you think he might be one of those fellows who...Oh, dear." She stopped speaking.

I had a feeling I knew what Vi was thinking, but I wasn't about to spill Harold's deep secret. I just blinked innocently at my aunt.

"He is, isn't he?" said Vi, squinting at me with speculation writ large on her features.

"He is what? I do know he's not the marrying kind."

After a moment or two, Vi said, "Right," and put the lid on the cardboard box. "Let me get my apron off and my coat on, and I'll carry this out to the car. Thanks for driving me home, sweetie."

"Happy to do it, Vi." Which was the absolute truth.

As luck—or something—would have it, Sam came over to dine with us that evening. This was nothing unusual. Sam usually dined with us in the evenings unless he was wrapped up in a case or something. But everyone in the family liked him. Heck, I loved him. I think. But he wasn't the liveliest of companions sometimes, perhaps because his job as a detective with the Pasadena Police Department could be grim. However, I aimed to grill him like a fish after dinner, and find out why the police couldn't do anything about husbands beating their wives nearly to death. That seemed totally unfair to me.

"Delicious meal, Mrs. Gumm," said Sam. This was a customary comment from him. It was also well deserved, my aunt being the greatest cook of her generation. Maybe others as well.

"I love lamb," said I. "And this is special, Vi. Thank you for being so good to us."

"Oh, get along with you, Daisy. You know I love to cook as much as you love to sew."

"Yes, but your skill is more useful than mine."

"Not necessarily," said my wonderful mother. I adored my family, including Spike, who sat beside the table, hoping for someone to drop something. "You helped Lucy alter her wedding gown and made all those bridesmaids dresses, don't forget."

My friend and fellow choir member, Lucille Spinks, had married an older gentleman named Albert Zollinger approximately a month prior, and Ma was right. "Hmm. I guess sewing comes in handy sometimes, but cooking can save a person's life. I mean, if he's starving or something. Sewing can't do that." How do I get myself mired in these verbal mud puddles, anyhow?

"No chance of anyone starving with Vi around," said my father, winking at me. "And no one will go unclad with you around. I think you both use your special talents to good effect."

"Absolutely," said my mother.

"All Daisy need to do in the kitchen is concentrate on what she's doing," said Vi.

I doubted that. I'd honestly tried to cook. Heck, I'd even taught that stupid cooking class at the Salvation Army and hadn't ruined anything during class time. When I tried to re-create my one and only masterpiece at home, however, things didn't turn out so well.

"I think there's more to it than that, Vi," said I.

Sam said, "Huh," which was also a customary comment from him.

I wanted to ask him if he'd do the cooking if we ever got married, but couldn't. Not in front of my family.

"Well, I don't know which skill is the more useful, but this stew is delectable," said Pa. "By the way, Daisy, how'd it go with Mrs. Pinkerton today. She must have telephoned a dozen times while you were out."

"You were out?" said Ma, interested. "Where did you go, dear?"

Nerts. I didn't want to tell anyone anything about my morning's travels. Or travails. Whatever you want to call them. "Flossie and Harold came over, and we went for a drive in the good old Chevrolet."

"Oh?" Ma appeared puzzled, probably because if anyone went for a drive with Harold, it would be natural to take his Bearcat, which was a most excellent automobile and ever so cunning.

"Yup. It was fun." Oh, boy, I hoped God didn't fling a lightning bolt at me for that enormous stretcher.

"Oh," said Ma, who promptly lost interest. My mother, who was a wonderful person, didn't have much imagination. And I thanked my stars for it a whole lot.

"How's Flossie?" asked Sam. "Haven't seen her for a while."

"She and Johnny and Billy are doing fine. They're a darling family."

"Must be nice," said Sam.

I eyed him suspiciously. Was he implying that he'd like to marry and start a family of his own? Sam's late wife, Margaret, had died of tuberculosis, and they had produced no offshoots. In a way, that was a good thing. Sam had told me that if he and Margaret had children, they would probably be in the care of his own family, and they lived in New York City where Sam originally hailed from. You could still hear it in his voice, although he didn't have a hideous accent like that of our peskiest party-line neighbor, Mrs. Barrow.

"It's very nice for them," I said noncommittally.

"You and Billy wanted children, didn't you, dear?" said Ma.

After heaving a largish sigh, I said, "Yes. Three kids. Two boys and a girl, although you can't predict those things, I guess."

"True," said Ma. "I was happy with a boy and two girls."

"And I was happy with my Paul," said Aunt Vi, looking a trifle misty-eyed.

"I liked Paul a lot," I said, getting a little misty myself. "Rotten Kaiser took both him and Billy, although Billy lasted a little longer."

"I don't even want to think about that dreadful war," said Ma.

"Sounds good to me. Let's talk about something else," I said. Turning to Sam, I said, "Anything interesting going on with the PPD, barring death and dismemberment?"

"Daisy!" said Ma, who didn't appreciate my sense of humor sometimes, mainly because she didn't possess such a thing.

Sam actually grinned, something he seldom did. Don't get me wrong. I loved the guy, but he was big and solid, and he had to be gruff and policemanly for his job. However, he definitely had a softer side. He also possessed a superb bass voice and had even sung a role in *The Mikado* the year earlier. After the fellow who was originally set to play Go-To, a noble lord of Titipu, got locked up for murder, Sam played the part and was fabulous in it. It was one of the first times I'd seen him be other than rock-like. He actually *acted*, and was funny as heck. I got to play Katisha, a role I loved because I got to be mean and nasty, which I'm never allowed to be in real life.

Hmm. Somehow I see I've strayed from the point.

Ah yes, I remember. Sam grinned. Then he said, "Not much. No dastardly murders or anything."

"I'm glad to hear it," said I, foregoing the mention of a near-murder because it would cause a whole lot of trouble, and not merely for Lily Bannister.

"Yeah?" said he. "And just why is that?"

I tried to look bewildered. "What do you mean, 'why is that?' I'm glad there haven't been any murders or anything awful that you have to solve. That's all."

"Ah," said Sam. "I see."

Doggone it! He didn't trust me. Well, nerts to Sam Rotondo! "Darn you, Sam Rotondo. I do have a question for you, since you're being so nosy. Flossie came over today and she was really upset by something that happened at the church."

"The Salvation Army?" asked Sam.

Taking a page from his book, I rolled my eyes. "Whatever other church would Flossie be interested in?"

"Just asking."

"I'll bet. But anyway, Flossie said a woman came to her and Johnny. Her husband had beaten her up, and she was hoping for a place to stay, but Johnny couldn't help her."

"What? I've never heard of such a thing!" said my mother, who might not have a sense of humor, but definitely had a well-developed sense of what's right and what's wrong in this nasty old world.

"My thought exactly, Ma. But Johnny said it would be against the law for him to hide the woman from her horrible husband."

"That doesn't sound right," said Pa, who was likewise endowed with a sense of how things should be.

"That's awful," said Vi.

See why I love my family?

"Well, Sam, what about it?"

"Since I don't know the particulars, I can't answer that question," said Sam, hedging for all he was worth.

"Flossie said Johnny said he couldn't help the woman escape from her husband, because it would be against the law for him to do so. Evidently, the police don't care if men beat their wives to smithereens unless they end up murdering them, and then the police can arrest them for murder. Seems to me they ought to be able to do something before things get that dire."

"I don't know what to tell you," Sam said as if he didn't want to admit it. "We can't interfere between a husband and wife."

"Even if the husband beats the wife to a bloody pulp?"

Sam heaved a large-sized sigh. "Even then. I'm sorry, but that's the way it is. What about the woman's family? Can't they take her in?"

"Evidently, according to Flossie, they *won't* take her in. And she's a Catholic, so her church won't help her, either."

Sam stared at me, squinty-eyed, for a moment. "Just who is this woman, anyhow?"

"How should I know?" I asked, trying for all I was worth to sound indignant. "Flossie was upset, and I don't blame her. She's a wonderful woman, and she was in tears about the mess. Flossie, I mean. And it hurt her that she couldn't help the poor beaten woman."

"Huh. Did Mrs. Buckingham at least take her to a hospital?"

"*I* don't know! Flossie came over here because she was so rattled, and I tried to comfort her. Then Harold popped by."

"He popped by, did he?" said Sam. Suspiciously, I'm sure I need not add.

"Yes. He popped by. So I decided we all needed a ride to help calm Flossie's nerves."

"And you took your Chevrolet," said Sam, still suspicious.

"Yes! Flossie didn't want to ride in Harold's Stutz Bearcat. Said she was afraid to ride in sporty cars." Boy, I could improvise with the best of them sometimes, couldn't I?

"Huh," said Sam. Unremarkable comment.

"And then," said Pa, darn it, "a friend of Harold's *popped* by. You forgot that part, sweetie."

"I didn't forget it," I said, sounding almost as resentful as I felt. "It was irrelevant. But we couldn't all fit in Harold's Bearcat, even if Flossie wasn't afraid to ride in it."

Sam said, "Hmmm."

I didn't like the sound of that *hmmm*.

SEVEN

As you can probably tell from the dinner-table conversation, it wasn't Sam but I who was grilled like a fish after I'd cleaned up the dinner dishes. Dagnabbit!

"If you know something about a woman beaten half to death by her husband, Daisy, you need to tell me about it."

By this time, we were seated on the front porch steps. The front porch steps were where Sam and I had most of our meaningful conversations, mainly because it was the only place we could get away from my family. Not that my family was nosy. It's just that we didn't live in a fabulous mansion with sixty or seventy superfluous rooms in which Sam and I could chat if we felt like it.

"Why? It's not as if you'd do anything about it even if I knew the woman's name," I said. Resentfully, I'm sure I need not add. But I see I did anyway. Oh, never mind.

"We could at least talk to the woman and see if she wanted to press charges."

I eyed my beloved in the evening gloom. The weather that day had been pleasant, even if the activities therein had stunk, but there was a nip in the air that night. Therefore, I'd bundled up in a sweater before going outside with Sam. "That would do a lot of good, wouldn't it?"

He shrugged. "Couldn't hurt."

Little did he know. And I didn't quite dare tell him. I'm pretty sure Sam wouldn't care for a man who beat up women for sport, but I also knew that he couldn't—or perhaps wouldn't—interfere between a husband and wife. Doing so seemed to be off-limits for the police. Or the Catholic Church. Or poor Lily Bannister's parents. The poor in that sentence belongs to Mrs. Bannister. Her parents were nitwits. Worse than nitwits. Not that I knew them personally, but any mother or father who could fail to help a woman in Mrs. Bannister's situation had to be a nitwit, if not downright evil.

Speaking of evil, I really wanted to know more about Leo Bannister. I opened my mouth to ask Sam if he'd ever heard of the man, but shut it again instantly. There was no way in the world I'd even *hint* that Lily Bannister was currently being hidden away from her evil husband by Harold Kincaid, Dr. Fred Greenlaw, Fred's nurse sister Hazel, Flossie Buckingham, and me.

Since I wanted to leave the subject of beaten women behind me for fear I might reveal more than would be good for Lily Bannister, I told Sam, "Mrs. Pinkerton thinks it would be a swell idea if Harold and I were to marry."

I felt Sam's startled reaction because we were snuggled up together.

"She *what?*"

"You heard me. She thinks Harold and I ought to get married. Because we're such good friends and all."

"You mean she doesn't know her son's a fairy?"

"A fairy?" Harold was a lot of things—a good man in a crisis, to name only one—but I couldn't form a mental image of him flitting about with little translucent wings. "Is that another term you big, bad men have created for people like Harold? He saved your life once, if you'll recall."

"I recall," said Sam. "But his mother must be blind if she doesn't know what he is by this time in her life."

"Mrs. Pinkerton isn't blind. She refuses to see what she doesn't want to see."

"You know your buddy Harold could be arrested for his proclivities, don't you?"

"That's so unfair," I said. I was not merely resentful this time, but downright crabby. "Harold can't help being what he is any more than you can help being what you are."

"Huh."

"It's the truth!"

"Whatever you say."

There was a perceptible pause in the conversation at that point. I got the feeling Sam realized he was already in hot water with me for a couple of reasons and didn't want the pot to boil over and scald him to death.

At last he said, "I don't suppose you'd condescend to wear my ring in order to dispel Mrs. Pinkerton's fantasies, would you?" He sounded a little sad.

Fingering my gorgeous engagement ring through my dull gray day dress—it used to be blue in its youth, which was several years ago—I thought about Sam's suggestion. It actually wasn't a bad one. It would shut Mrs. P up in a trice. Whatever a trice was. But was I ready to take off Billy's ring and wear Sam's instead? My heart instantly gave a gigantic lurch, and I knew the answer to that question.

"I'm sorry, Sam," I said, resentment having fled for the nonce. Whatever a nonce is. "Every time I think about taking off Billy's ring, my heart squishes."

Sam heaved a sigh approximately as large as Mount Wilson and said, "Very well. I understand."

"Do you?" I asked, mainly because I really wanted to know.

"Yes, I do, believe it or not. It took me three years before I could even imagine being married to anyone other than Margaret. So from that perspective, you've got another year or two to go."

"I don't like to think of it that way," I muttered, still fingering the ring through my dress. It was a gorgeous ring and would look quite elegant on my finger. It was, in fact, considerably more beautiful than the plain gold band I'd been wearing since my wedding to Billy in 1917, seven years prior to that front-porch conversation. The ensuing years had been rough, but losing Billy had darned near killed me, and I just flat wasn't ready to announce to the world that I was ready to move on to another man, even a man I loved as much as I loved Sam.

And I didn't even want to *think* about how long it had taken me to admit to loving Sam.

"I don't know how else to think about it," said Sam. "I lost the love of my life, too, don't forget."

"I'm not forgetting anything." After a second, I added because I'd just thought about it, "I wish I'd met Margaret. She sounds like a wonderful woman."

"She was," said Sam. "Billy was a wonderful man, too."

"Yes," said I. "He was."

We sat there in silence for another few minutes until Sam heaved another large sigh, put his big hands on his big knees and said, "Well, I'd better get going. Have to get up early for a court case in which I have to testify tomorrow."

"Oh, really? How often do you have to testify in court?"

I felt him shrug. "As often as it takes. This is a preliminary hearing, actually. For Mr. Gerald Kingston. I'm sure you remember him."

"How could I ever forget him? He tried to murder me. He killed his own brother, for heaven's sake. *And* Mr. Underhill. Granted he was no great loss, but still."

"Yeah. I know. You'll probably have to testify at the trial itself unless he pleads guilty, and I doubt he'll do that."

"I wonder if Miss Betsy Powell will have to testify." Miss Powell had been sweet on Mr. Kingston, although she wasn't lily-pure herself. Then again, how many of us are?

"Lord, I hope not. The woman screeches like a banshee every time anyone even looks at her funny."

"True, true."

"All right. I'm off."

I refrained from making any smart comments, but I rose too, and called for Spike to come back from his search for the next-door neighbors' cat, Samson. Spike had held a grudge against Samson for years now. Then again, according to Mrs. Bissel, from whom I'd received Spike in payment for an exorcism—which is a whole 'nother story entirely—dachshunds were bred to be mighty hunters. Spike took his role in life seriously. Fortunately for me, he also took his obedience training seriously and came running at my call.

"Have a good night, Sam," I said.

"Thanks." He bent and drew me into his arms and kissed me.

I kind of melted for a moment or two. Then Spike spoiled—or perhaps he saved—the moment and jumped on us. We broke apart with a couple of sighs.

Sam bent and patted Spike. "Spoilsport," he said, but he grinned as he did so.

"Spike, you know better than to jump on people."

"Go easy on him," said Sam. "He was jealous."

"I bet." But I smiled.

So Sam got into his Hudson and drove south on Marengo. I knew he lived in a small court of darling little cottages on South Los Robles Avenue. I wondered if I'd one day live there with him, or if he'd come live with us. If he valued his digestion, he'd better opt for the latter scenario.

I moped back into the house, feeling as if I'd let Sam down, and not merely for not being able to wear his ring yet. I hadn't told him about a serious crime having been committed in the City of Pasadena. But how could I? He couldn't do anything about it if he did know. Poor Lily Bannister. I decided to visit her the next day. I also wanted to know more about her husband, so I hoped Harold would be there.

The next morning dawned gloomy and overcast. This wasn't normal weather for May in sunny Pasadena, California, but I figured you couldn't depend on much of anything when it came to weather.

Aunt Vi had made one of her spectacular breakfast casseroles for the family, and there was a bowl full of oranges in the middle of the kitchen table, so I dined well that morning. I did not, however, dine peacefully.

I'd just forked up a bite of my egg-and-potato casserole when the 'phone rang. I glanced up at Pa, who wrinkled the morning newspaper and peered at me over it.

"Mrs. Pinkerton?" he asked as if he felt sorry for me.

"Probably." I glanced at the kitchen clock. "Shoot, it's only seven-thirty. The woman's not even supposed to be alive this early in the morning. Edie told me once she sleeps until nine most mornings." Edie Applewood, a high-school friend of mine, worked as Mrs. P's lady's maid.

"Must be nice," said Pa.

"I guess. I pretty much wake up at seven every day unless I've been up late the night before." Sighing, I replaced the forkful of food on my plate and rose to answer the telephone.

I'd just begun my routine, "Gumm-Majesty residence, Mrs. Majesty speaking," when Mrs. Pinkerton's shrill voice attacked my eardrums, interrupting me before I was half finished with my greeting.

"Daisy! Oh, *Daisy*!"

Oh, Lord. "Yes, Mrs. Pinkerton?" I said. I said it sweetly, too, darn it.

"Oh, Daisy, it's *Stacy*!"

I wondered what the brat had done now, but didn't ask the question so crudely. "What about Stacy, Mrs. Pinkerton? Are you still concerned about her young man?"

"Oh, Daisy, they *eloped*!"

They what? But..."Um, didn't Stacy want Captain Buckingham to perform the marriage ceremony for them?"

"*No*! Oh, Daisy, they both left the Salvation Army! I don't know what to *do*!"

I didn't know what she should do, either. I didn't think suggesting she pray they both leave town and never come back would be appreciated. Rather I said, still sweetly, "I'm not sure you can do anything, Mrs. Pinkerton, providing they had a valid marriage license and were married by a minister or a judge or something."

"Oh, but *Daisy*!" she bellowed. Needless to say, I'd removed the earpiece from my ear and was at the time of the bellow holding it about four inches from my poor, beleaguered ear.

Pa heard the shriek and turned in his chair to stare at me. I shrugged back at him.

Then, after heaving an internal sigh that didn't leave my lips, I said, "Would you like me to visit you with the Ouija board and my tarot cards, Mrs. Pinkerton?" Not that either of those nonsensical devices would do any good, but at least I'd make some money plying my phony trade.

I don't mean to sound cynical.

Or maybe I do.

"Oh, yes." Mrs. Pinkerton had begun sobbing. "Thank you so much, dear. When can you be here?"

Huh. I glanced again at the clock. It was seven thirty-two. And I wanted to 'phone Harold and take Spike for a walk with Pa before I tackled Mrs. P's problems, about which I could do absolutely nothing. "I can be there at ten forty-five, Mrs. Pinkerton."

"Ooooooh! You can't come any sooner?" Now she was wailing. I was used to it.

"I'm very sorry, but no. Ten forty-five is the earliest I can get there."

After sobbing another couple of times, Mrs. P said, "Thank you, Daisy. I'll try to maintain my sanity until you arrive."

Maintain it? She might, possibly—although chances were slim—gain a modicum of sanity before I got there, but I doubted it.

"Try to calm down, Mrs. Pinkerton. You know, there's not really much you can do to alter the fact."

However, there might be something I could do. I could visit the library and chat with Miss Petrie and make sure I understood precisely how much of a rotten apple her cousin Percival really was. She'd given me an earful a month or so earlier, but I wanted to get my facts straight.

"I know," she said pathetically. "I know it. Oh, I don't know what to *do*!"

Here we went again. I didn't say so. "I'll be there soon," I promised. "Good morning, Mrs. Pinkerton." And I hung up on the ridiculous woman.

"Stacy?" asked Pa as I headed back to my breakfast, hoping it was still warm.

"Yes. She eloped with Percival Petrie, and Mrs. Pinkerton is hysterical."

"She's always been hysterical when I've spoken to her," said Pa. "Sounds like it's her usual state."

"It is."

I'd no more than sat down again when the blasted telephone rang *again*. Thinking the day was off to a really bad start, I rose once more and stomped to the instrument of torture. Again, I wasn't able to complete my normal spiel, only this time I was interrupted by a more welcome voice. Harold's.

"Daisy, can you come over to my house today? I think I'd better tell you something about you-know-who's you-know-what."

I glanced at my father. I didn't want to say anything that might give away Harold's and my secret. "Sure. I can do that. I have to see your mother first, though."

"Oh, Lord. Did she weep on your shoulder about Stacy marrying that yahoo?"

"She wept in my ear, and yes. She even shrieked once or twice. But I think he's worse than a mere yahoo, Harold. His cousin works at the library, and she told me some pretty awful things about him." Oh, nuts. I'd forgotten to shoo our party-line neighbors off the wire. Oh, well. At least I was glad Harold didn't mention Mrs. Bannister by name. "But we'd better talk later. We aren't rich, so we don't have a private line, you know."

"I know, I know," said Harold. I couldn't tell if he was amused or annoyed.

"I'll visit about noon. Will that be all right?"

"Fine. My place. I'll feed you. Thanks," said Harold, and he hung up.

Sighing heavily, I went back to my rapidly chilling breakfast.

"Harold?" asked Pa.

"Harold," I agreed.

"Nice guy, Harold."

"Very nice," said I.

Pa went back to reading the newspaper, and the telephone rang yet again. This wasn't fair. Nevertheless, I got up, gazing wistfully at my breakfast, and answered the stupid thing.

Sam. At least he let me get my greeting out.

"Daisy, if you know something about a woman being beaten by her husband, you need to tell me about it."

"Why? You already said you can't do anything. But wait a minute." I cleared my throat. "Will everyone who isn't a Gumm, a Majesty, or a Rotondo kindly hang up your telephones." I used my gritty voice; the one few people ever heard. Two clicks sounded along the wire. I waited another second and said, "Mrs. Barrow. Hang up your telephone. This call is for me." Another click, this one sounding grumpy, floated across the wire. "There. I think we're alone. I don't know a single thing about the woman, Sam Rotondo, and even if I did and I told you, you already said you couldn't help her."

"I might be able to think of something."

"Right. Listen, it's early, and my breakfast is getting cold."

"Sorry. You heard that Stacy Kincaid married that bozo, right?"

"Of course. Mrs. Pinkerton called me first thing this morning."

"I think he's crooked," said Sam, not mincing words.

He didn't usually discuss his cases with me. I had to pry and snoop and turn over rocks to get information about them. I said, "I know he's crooked. His cousin told me as much."

"Your librarian friend?"

"That's the one, all right."

"She has a hell of a family."

"That she does. I'm going to visit with her today, and if she says anything about him that might prove him to be something other than a mere fortune-hunter, I'll let you know."

"Thanks. We've got something going on in the city he might be involved in, if anything you find out about him points that way."

"Something going on in Pasadena? Something bad."

"Very bad."

"What is it?"

"Can't go into it now."

"Sam Rotondo, you're the most mean-spirited, cruel...I don't know what you are, but you're awful to tell me something to pique my curiosity and then not satisfy it."

"Sorry. Nature of the job."

"Phooey."

"Well, go eat your breakfast. But I want to talk to you about what this particular Petrie's deficiencies are."

"Come to dinner tonight."

"How about lunch?"

"Can't. I'm meeting Harold at noon."

"Criminy." And he hung up on me.

I'd no more than returned the receiver to the cradle than the blasted telephone rang *again*! Yanking the receiver off its cradle, I'd started to speak when Flossie's voice interrupted me. I could tell she'd been crying. "Flossie! Whatever is the matter?"

"Oh, Daisy, I need to see you!"

"What's the matter, Flossie? I hope it's nothing to do with...you know." Lordy, how did I get myself in these messes?

"It is, but I don't want to talk about it on the 'phone."

"Good idea. Meet Harold and me at his place at noon. Can you do that?"

"Yes. Thanks, Daisy. You're such a special friend."

And, of course, that made me feel guilty, because at that moment I didn't want to be anybody's friend, especially if the person had problems —or came to me with people who had problems.

So once more I trod to the kitchen table, sat, and glumly ate the rest of my portion of Vi's now-cold breakfast casserole, thinking I was going to have a hard time wiggling out of all my current tribulations. Phooey.

EIGHT

Fortunately for me, Pa didn't ask any questions about my many telephone calls during breakfast. I think he wanted to, but couldn't quite figure out how to ask them without incurring either wrath or lies from yours truly. Pitiful situation.

Because I felt so guilty about deceiving my family, I said, "Poor Flossie is really upset. I have a feeling it's because Stacy Kincaid married that Salvation Army private, and according to Mrs. Pinkerton, they've both left the church."

"That doesn't sound good."

"It's not. I know the guy she married is a bad apple, because he's related to Miss Petrie, the librarian, and she's told me some stuff about him."

"Oh, boy. Another Petrie in the woodpile, eh?"

"Yes, and one of the bad ones."

"Well, don't get involved in anything that'll make trouble for you. You always seem to get into danger when you nose into other people's business."

"I'm not nosing into anything!" I cried, furious with my formerly practically perfect father. "People are dumping me into their problems head-first. I don't want anything to do with them, but I'm too nice to say no."

Pa eyed me for a couple of seconds and then said, "I see. I'm sorry I accused you of prying."

I swallowed my last bite of what had started out being a delicious egg-and-potato casserole, but had ended up being a congealed lump of cold glop before I said, "That's all right. But you weren't being fair, Pa."

"If you say so, sweetie."

Oh, for Pete's sake, he didn't believe me. Not that he should, but for once in my life, it wasn't my fault. I didn't take him to task for his disbelief. He did have reason to doubt me, I guess, although I swear, except for a tiny bit of snoopery the month before, most of the situations I'd been involved with truly hadn't been my fault.

Instead, I tried to sound pleasant when I said, "I'm going to clean up the breakfast dishes and get dressed. Then do you want to go for a walk with Spike and me?"

Spike instantly became alert at the mention of a walk. Smart dog, Spike. I'd even taught him to add, subtract, divide and multiply. Sort of. But he was so alert that I could barely wiggle my little finger and he'd stop barking when he'd hit the appropriate number after I'd presented him with a math problem. "Spike," I'd say. "What's two plus two?" He'd start barking, I'd wiggle my little finger when he barked four times, and he'd shut up. Brilliant dog.

He'd been alert as Pa and I ate breakfast, too, but that was because he was hoping we'd drop something he could eat. I tried to avoid giving him too many treats because, according to Mrs. Bissel and Mrs. Hanratty, two of my dog-loving friends, dachshunds' backs were too long to accommodate extra weight. Dachshunds also tend to be slightly piggish, so it was a battle to keep his weight down.

But back to the breakfast table.

"Sure. It's cold out there, so bundle up," said Pa.

"Will do."

So I washed the few dishes left from everyone's breakfast—Ma and Vi had already left for work by the time I'd sat down to my own breakfast—and then Spike and I went to my room. And, of course, I instantly remembered the pile of bloody bedclothes and rags, etc., in the basket in my closet. Bother. I had no idea when I'd be able to launder them. It had to be sometime when Pa was out of the house, or he'd wonder about the hydrogen peroxide and the bleach, etc., I'd have to use to get the stains out.

Deciding I'd think about bloody things later, I opened the door to my closet and instantly decided I'd have to think about them sooner than that. The stupid basket stank. I hadn't noticed the smell last night when I was getting ready for bed, but I guess bloody fabric gets foul, kind of like dead bodies do when they sit around for a while. Spike was so fascinated by the terrible smell, he began rooting around in the basket.

"Spike, no!" I commanded softly. I wasn't about to holler at my dog for fear Pa would wonder what was going on and visit my room to find out. Spike, who was terribly disappointed, backed away from the basket and looked at me reproachfully.

Great. Even my dog was against me. Well, I couldn't help that.

I peeked out of my bedroom to find my father had left the kitchen. I didn't know where he was, but I sped through the kitchen to the laundry room, grabbed the bottle of hydrogen peroxide and the bottle of bleach, and hurried back to my room. There I carefully laid out the various bloody objects and poured hydrogen peroxide on them. Boy, did they fizz! Hoping like mad that nobody would snoop in my room while I was away that day, I left them on the floor to let the peroxide do its work and went back to peer into my closet.

Because I didn't have to dress up to walk the dog, I grabbed a formerly pink day dress—I didn't wear much pink because it didn't go well with my hair—threw it on, and grabbed a warm woolen coat I'd sewn for myself a couple of years prior. Since wool makes me itch, I'd lined the coat with flannel. Then I grabbed a scarf, a hat, some cotton stockings and my walking shoes, put everything on, and headed out of the bedroom again.

And there was Pa, holding Spike's leash, waiting for the both of us. When Spike saw the leash, he stopped moping about not being able to snuffle through a pile of bloody sheets and rags and bounced around like the happy dog he almost always was.

"Spike's ready for his walk," Pa said.

"He always is," I said.

And so we took a nice long walk around the neighborhood. Spike marked territory all along the way, barked at a stray cat or two, and had a grand old time. Pa seemed pensive and didn't talk much. That was all right by me. I had too many unpleasant troubles on my mind to deal with pointless conversation.

When we got home again, Pa and Spike retired to the living room to read and I returned to my bedroom, where I was greeted by a bunch of wet cloth on the floor. Bother. I didn't have time to deal with the mess before I went to Mrs. Pinkerton's place, so I gathered everything up again, replaced it in the basket, and returned the basket to my closet. Maybe I could take it all to Harold's house and launder it there. In fact, I decided that was a brilliant idea. Have I mentioned that it sometimes takes a while to determine if an idea is truly brilliant or not? Well, it's true.

However, that day, I managed to get dressed in a dark green wool flannel suit with a three-quarter-length unfitted jacket. It had a wide collar banded with dark brown braid and a set-in shoulder cape over wrist-length sleeves. The skirt matched the jacket and was mid-calf length. Under the jacket I wore a white blouse and a brown tie. It was a charming outfit and went well with my hair. It was also sober and sophisticated enough for a serious-minded spiritualist-medium to be seen in without being thought fast or flapper-ish. I wore flesh-toned stockings and my brown shoes with a short Louis heel. My engagement ring from Sam would have gone smashingly well with my costume, but I still wore it on its gold chain around my neck beside my Voodoo juju. One of these days....

When I peeked into the kitchen from my room, I saw my father was still not there, so I quickly grabbed the basket out of my closet and walked as quietly as possible to the side door off the dining room. My luck held when I managed to get the basket out the door, down the porch steps to the Chevrolet, and stuff it onto the car's back seat. I heaved a sigh of relief when I returned to the house to fetch my hat and gloves. There I bade my father and Spike a fond farewell.

By the time I left the house, it was only around nine-thirty, so I decided to take a detour to the Pasadena Public Library before I visited Mrs. Pinkerton. I wanted to gather some more information about Stacy Kincaid's—I mean Stacy Petrie's—husband before I tackled Mrs. Pinkerton. I knew the woman would be in a frenzy so I intended to be well-armed before I had to deal with her.

Fortunately for me, Miss Petrie sat behind her desk in a little cubicle. She smiled hugely when she saw me. We were pals, Miss Petrie and me.

"Mrs. Majesty," she whispered—she always called me Mrs. Majesty even though I'd told her more than once to use my first name, "it's lovely to see you. You don't generally visit me so early in the morning."

I whispered back, "I have some news and need to ask you some questions, if you don't mind."

"Not at all. Is this about my rascally cousin Percival?"

Rascally. I guess that was one word for a gold-digging snake in the grass. "Yes, it is. He and Mrs. Pinkerton's daughter got married. I guess they eloped, because Mrs. Pinkerton was in a great fuss when she telephoned this morning."

"No!" cried Miss Petrie in a whisper. If you can whisper a cry.

"Yes. Evidently they both left the Salvation Army, where your cousin was a private—"

Miss Petrie snorted, an undignified sound coming from the youngish, staid librarian who looked more like a librarian than she might have if she'd taken a little trouble with her hair and makeup. But I make my living via my looks, more or less, so perhaps I'm not the best judge of these things.

"I'm not sure where they are now, but according to Mrs. Pinkerton they weren't married by Captain Buckingham, who's a friend of mine."

"Percival Petrie doesn't have a devout bone in his body. He was a bad boy, and he's a bad man."

"You told me some pretty awful things about him a month or so ago."

"Yes, but I didn't tell you the worst of his many sins. If I had, perhaps you could have warned the young woman's mother, and she wouldn't have become ensnared in his trap."

"I wouldn't bet on that," said I, perhaps more frankly than was proper. "Stacy Kincaid is the most obstinate, least sensible person I've ever met. Before she joined the Salvation Army, she used to get picked up in raids on speakeasies all the time. Why, she even punched a policeman once, and got sent to jail for three months. Didn't cure her of her nastiness, as far as I can tell."

"My goodness. Perhaps the two of them deserve each other."

"I'm sure they do. However, as much as Mrs. Pinkerton drives me crazy, and as much as she's an ineffectual parent, she doesn't deserve a total rotter in the family. Another total rotter, if you count her daughter. Well, and her ex-husband, I guess, which would make a lump sum of three total rotters."

"I see. Well, you'd better pull up a chair, because this will take a while in the telling. And please, Mrs. Majesty, don't judge me by Percival's side of the family. My side is perfectly respectable."

"Of course it is, and I'd never judge you by the bad side of the Petrie clan. I'm sure none of your close relatives have any connection at all with the Ku Klux Klan or any other awful things the bad side are involved with."

"Hmph. Yes. I'd just as soon cut the ties to that side of the family completely, but they keep popping up here in Pasadena. Sometimes I think they come here out of spite, because my parents, siblings and I won't have anything to do with them."

"A wise choice on the part of your parents and siblings and you."

"Indeed."

I pulled up a chair. They were heavy, those big, wooden library chairs, but I didn't even scrape it as I carried it across the floor. My muscles weren't as strong as they'd been when I'd assisted Billy in and out of his wheelchair and supported him as he walked, but I wasn't total mush yet. I decided to think about starting a regimen of Swedish exercises later. Maybe.

When I was settled in the chair and leaning over Miss Petrie's desk, she said, "Very well. Perhaps I should begin with Percival's tainted youth."

Interesting. I'd heard of flaming youth, mainly because there was a flicker by that title starring Colleen Moore (which I didn't bother seeing, not being interested in flaming youths), but never tainted youth. "Yes, please do," I said.

"Percival used to torment animals," said Miss Petrie in a sepulchral whisper. "He went on to torment children in his school classes."

"What do you mean by 'torment?'"

"He'd tease them unmercifully and hit them with sticks."

"The animals?"

"Yes. And the children. He was sent home from school more than once for hitting other children with sticks and rocks. I do believe one of his victims landed in the hospital with a bad concussion."

"Good heavens. Didn't his parents ever try to correct him?"

"His father is just as bad as he is. *And* he drinks. His mother only makes excuses for him. Ghastly people. It was embarrassing to live in the same town with Percival and his family."

"I can imagine." The thought nearly sickened me, in fact. I was *so* fortunate in my family.

"He was sent to reform school when he was thirteen years old."

"Oh, my goodness." I'd heard of reform schools, too, but never knew anyone who actually knew anyone who'd been in one. If that makes any sense.

"It gets worse. While he was in reform school, he killed another boy. Worse, he got away with it, claiming the other boy had been trying to kill *him*. But the other boy was two years younger than Percival. I have a feeling his father and older brothers might have threatened the gentleman who ran the reform school."

"Good heavens."

"Percival," said Miss Petrie firmly, "has *never* had anything to do with heaven." She sniffed. "I'm surprised your friend at the Salvation Army allowed him in."

"I guess Mr. Buckingham, who has had a troubled past, tries to see the good in people." Very well, it wasn't a ringing endorsement. At that point, even I was beginning to question Johnny's judgment in allowing the evidently wicked Percival Petrie into his ranks. On the other hand, he'd allowed Stacy in, so maybe he had his blind spots.

69

"I trust Mr. Buckingham's past isn't riddled with murder and...Please move a little closer. I don't want anyone else to hear this."

So I leaned even closer to Miss Petrie. "Yes?"

"Percival ran a *brothel* in Tulsa," Miss Petrie said in a thrilling whisper.

It makes absolutely no sense, but I was more shocked about the brothel than I was about the murder. We humans have inexplicable capacities for emotional responses.

"That's *awful*," I said. "Do you think he might be doing something of the sort here in Pasadena?"

"It wouldn't surprise me. And it also wouldn't surprise me if he turned out to be part of a bootlegging gang, either."

"Is he a leader or a follower?" I asked. Then I decided that had been a stupid question. "I mean, does he organize and run these illegal gangs and brothels, or does he have partners?"

"Percival has never been able to get along well with others. If anyone gets in his way or tries to alter his course, he tends to eliminate whoever it is. My family—and others, including police officers—believe he had something to do with the disappearance of two or three young women in Tulsa."

"Good heavens! They just disappeared? And were never found?"

"That's correct. I think Percival kidnapped them and...did awful things to them. Then he probably killed them and tossed their bodies into his father's pig pen."

"The *pig pen*?" I repeated, appalled.

"Pigs will eat anything," said Miss Petrie, as if a pig eating a human child was a normal, every-day thing. Maybe it was in Tulsa, Oklahoma, but it sure wasn't in Pasadena, California, where we were extremely civilized. For the most part. I could think of a few exceptions, but none quite as rotten as Percival Petrie.

"It's difficult for me to believe you and he belong to the same family."

"Hmph. It's difficult for me to believe it, too. I wish it weren't so. He's a blight on the family tree. Well, so are his parents and siblings."

"Oh, dear. How awful for you. Thank you, Miss Petrie. I'm sorry to learn this, but I guess I have some ammunition for Mrs. Pinkerton to use.

Although her idiot daughter will probably say everyone has merely misunderstood poor Percival."

"Ha. That's what his mother says about all of her children. The rest of them are all nearly as evil as Percival."

"I feel sorry for her."

"Don't. She's too stupid to see what's in front of her face. And she allows her bully of a husband to...well, to bully her."

There seemed to be a lot of that sort of thing going on in those days. I didn't approve. Which made as much of a difference then as it ever did, which is none at all.

Before I left the library, Miss Petrie loaded me down with books, bless her. She'd saved Mr. G.K. Chesterton's *The Man Who Knew too Much*; Miss Edna Ferber's *So Big*; Baroness Orczy's *The Triumph of the Scarlet Pimpernel*; and Mr. E. Phillips Oppenheim's *The Great Prince Shan*. Boy, I'd much rather have gone home and read for the rest of the day than perform the duties that morning's telephone calls dictated.

Too bad for me, huh?

NINE

However, being the slave to duty I was—I think that's a line from Gilbert and Sullivan's *Pirates of Penzance*—as soon as I left the library with my loot, I drove the Chevrolet up to Mrs. Pinkerton's grand home on Orange Grove Boulevard.

Featherstone, Mr. and Mrs. Pinkerton's perfectly splendid butler—I think I mentioned that before—met me at the door and, as always, said, "Please follow me." Never mind that I could have found my way to the drawing room blindfolded by that time. He always said it, and I always did it.

Bracing myself for an assault, I sucked in a big breath for courage, and entered the room. To my surprise, rather than leaping up and running at me, Mrs. Pinkerton sat more or less crumpled on a sofa across the room. I paused for a moment, then dared to waft gently up to her.

"Mrs. Pinkerton? Whatever is the matter?" Stupid question. I knew what the matter was.

She glanced up at me with tear-streaked cheeks and red, puffy eyes. The poor thing was truly in a state. "Oh, Daisy, I don't know what to *do*. I don't even know where they *are*! How could Stacy do such a thing?"

Given her past record, I figured Stacy could and would do anything hateful just because she wanted to. Naturally, I didn't say so to Mrs.

Pinkerton, who was already more distressed than I'd ever before seen her. I sat next to her on the sofa and placed a gloved hand lightly on her arm.

"I'm very sorry Stacy has done such a...despicable thing," I said, being more candid than I normally was to the sensitive mother of Stacy-the-brat. "I can't believe she didn't even invite you to her wedding."

"She...She..." Mrs. P paused to sniffle and wipe her eyes and cheeks with an already-soggy handkerchief. "She knew we didn't approve of Mr. Petrie. *Private* Petrie, as he called himself, although according to Stacy they weren't married in the church, and she wouldn't tell me where they are now."

"I'm so sorry, Mrs. Pinkerton. I'm not sure how I can help you, but I'll be happy to summon Rolly for you." I briefly contemplated regaling Mrs. P with Percival Petrie's ghastly criminal history and decided not to heap coals of sorrow on her head. Or whatever that saying is. "I chatted with Miss Petrie at the library, and evidently Mr. Petrie had a reputation as being a bad egg back in his home town, which is Tulsa, Oklahoma. Miss Petrie and he are distantly related, but evidently Miss Petrie's side of the family has nothing to do with his side of the family."

After sniffling and swallowing and wiping away more tears, Mrs. Pinkerton gazed at me dolefully. While I often didn't have much sympathy for her tizzies and fits, this time I was quite sorry for her. Granted, she'd been a lax parent, but still and all. She had two children and one of them had turned out to be a total peach. I'm talking about Harold, of course. Stacy had turned out to be a rotten apple. But I didn't mean to mix my fruits.

"I knew he was a wrong one," said Mrs. P. "Can you tell me what your librarian friend had to say about him? If I knew where they were, I might be able to tell Stacy about some of his more awful traits."

"Well...I'm not sure that would be wise, Mrs. Pinkerton. You know Stacy. She seems strangely drawn to dreadful men. If you regale her with Percival Petrie's shortcomings, she might stick up for him all the more."

"But if he's a *really* bad man, don't you think she'd see reason?"

No, I didn't. "I honestly don't know. But do I suspect he is a really bad man. However, if you don't even know where they are, I don't think it

73

matters at this point. And I'm not sure how you're going to be able to find them."

"Can't your detective friend help? Detective Rotondo?"

Glory be! She remembered Sam's last name! I guess Stacy was important enough for her to go to the trouble of actually recalling his name. This was a first. The fact that it was prompted by more hideous behavior on her daughter's part didn't precisely endear her to me, but there you go. Never happy, some of us.

"They're both over twenty-one, aren't they?"

"Well, I know Stacy is. I suspect that awful man is, too."

"Then I don't think the police can help you. They can search for children who are missing, but I think adults are on their own, especially if they've married and run away. Or whatever they've done." Curious, I asked, "How do you know they got married?"

"Stacy telephoned and told me." Many sniffles and tears followed this admission. "She said she knew I didn't like her precious Percival, but she knew him to be a good man, and they were being married by a judge, and they were no longer associated with the Salvation Army."

"Hmm. Perhaps Captain Buckingham might know something about where they went."

"Oh, would you ask him for me, dear? I'd appreciate it *so* much!"

"Of course, I'll ask him." I'd at least ask Flossie, whom I intended to see soon. I didn't even bother asking why Mrs. P hadn't called the Salvation Army and spoken to Johnny herself. She didn't do things like that.

"Thank you *so* much, Daisy. You're such a comfort to me."

Right. A fake spiritualist was the comfort of her life. You figure it out; it's beyond my understanding.

"Would you like me to consult Rolly for you?" To be on the safe side, I said for approximately the three millionth time, "Don't forget that Rolly can't tell you anything about Stacy or where she and her new husband have gone, but only answer questions pertaining to you."

She heaved a sigh about as big as her mansion. "I understand. Yes, please. I'd like you to talk to Rolly and then deal the tarot, if you wouldn't mind."

"I don't mind at all," I fibbed.

So I talked to Rolly, who said she might achieve comfort if she spoke to Father Frederick, a very nice Episcopal priest she knew, and pray. Gee, I didn't usually have Rolly advise people to pray, but I figured it couldn't hurt. Might even help. Then again, we were dealing with Mrs. Pinkerton here, and helping her was nigh on to impossible.

"Of course. I should have spoken to Father Frederick before this," said Mrs. Pinkerton, brightening fractionally, so I guess Rolly's suggestion had been a good one.

Chalk up a point for Desdemona Majesty!

Then I dealt out a tarot pattern and was disappointed to see the devil and several swords appear. Swords were the iffiest cards in the tarot arcana, and these particular cards predicted trouble ahead for Mrs. P. I tried to put as bright an interpretation as I could on the hand I'd dealt, but a cheery future, at least in the short term, didn't look good for the poor woman. Well, the rich woman. Oh, bother. You know what I mean.

"Those cards aren't good, are they?" she said, surprising me as she pointed to the ten of swords. I'd been dealing out tarot hands for her for more than half my life, and until this minute I'd have sworn she'd never learned anything at all about the cards. Guess I was wrong.

"They're not the most favorable cards, the swords," I said, trying not to sound glum.

"I thought not."

We sat in silence for several seconds. Silence and Mrs. Pinkerton didn't generally go together, so this was another unusual happenstance.

Finally, she heaved another huge sigh and said, "Well, thank you very much, dear. I feared neither Rolly nor the cards would be able to help me much, although Rolly's suggestion about Father Frederick was very good. And prayer, of course. I suspect the cards are just telling me the truth. I don't like the truth sometimes."

I do believe those were the most introspective words I'd ever heard from this source. "I think there are times in all our lives that are difficult to get through, Mrs. Pinkerton. Be sure to use the assets you have to see you through this period of trouble. Harold is a superb son, and Mr. Pinkerton is a dear. Definitely speak to Father Frederick. And you always have me." Darn. I wished I hadn't said that as soon as it popped out of my mouth. Too late not to say it, though.

"Thank you, dear. I suppose one should always count one's blessings. Stacy has been...well, you know better than anyone that she can be a sore trial sometimes."

Sometimes? All the time was more like it in my admittedly biased opinion. "True. I do know that." And I didn't add anything nasty to those words. Sometimes I can hold my tongue.

"But you and Harold are always sweet to me. I do wish you and he would consider marriage to each other, dear. You and he would be a perfect couple." A few new tears trickled from her swollen eyes. "Unlike Stacy and that unspeakable fellow she's gone and married. But you haven't told me what your librarian friend said about him. I'd like to know, even if it won't do much good at this point."

So I related a sanitized version of Mr. Percival Petrie's primary sins to the mother of his new wife. Unless Stacy had lied about that. I wouldn't put much of anything past her. I didn't mention the missing girls he'd supposedly violated and fed to the pigs. That was too appalling even to think about, much less relate.

"Oh, dear. He's even worse than I feared. I thought he was just a fortune-hunter."

"I suspect that's his main object in marrying Stacy," I said, keeping my tone and manner spiritualistically subdued. A spiritualist-medium who gloats over another's misfortune wouldn't have much of a career. And really, I wasn't gloating. I didn't care what happened to Stacy, but I liked Mrs. Pinkerton a lot, even if she was dithery. After all, she'd been the mainstay of my family's income for lo, these many years.

We spoke softly for another few minutes, and then I wafted out of there as kindly as I could, my heart feeling heavy for Mrs. Pinkerton. I'd have loved to visit with Aunt Vi in the kitchen, but I had to hie myself to Harold's house where, with luck, I could talk with Harold and Flossie. I had lots of things to tell, and lots of things to learn. Wasn't sure I wanted to do either one of those things. Oh, well. Too late by then.

Harold and Dr. Greenlaw were both at Harold's house when I pulled up in front of the magnificent mansion on Lombardy Road. I didn't see Flossie and Johnny's decrepit Model-T, but it rolled up before I got out of the Chevrolet. So I waited on the sidewalk until Flossie joined me. She'd been crying; I could tell.

Therefore, because I honestly liked her a lot even though she had dumped me in the soup the day before, I walked over and gave her a hug. "What's the matter, Flossie? Are you still worried about Mrs. Bannister?"

"Yes, but it's even worse than that," she said, a tone of tragedy in her voice.

"How could it be worse?"

"Johnny knows I'm hiding her somewhere."

"How could he know that?"

"He just knows. I know he knows. He hasn't tried to coerce me into telling him where she is, and I hate lying to him. Well, not lying exactly. I just hate keeping secrets from him, especially when he...*knows*. You know?"

"I know. But in this case, don't you think I it's a necessary lie? Or...not a lie, but a...what would you call it? A deception? A necessary deception?"

"Is there such a thing?" Flossie grabbed a hankie and held it to her usually pretty eyes. She no longer wore piles of makeup, so nothing got smeared, but her face had a slightly ravaged look about it.

For just an instant, I wanted to rush to the Salvation Army and give Johnny a piece of my mind. I didn't tell Flossie so. "Yes, I firmly believe one sometimes has to prevaricate or keep secrets in order to help other people. You told me Johnny couldn't help the woman. And if you told him where she was being hidden, don't you think he'd feel honor-bound to tell her husband or the police or her parents or someone? Mrs. Bannister doesn't need her wicked husband to find her. *Or* her ghastly family. She needs to recover from Mr. Bannister's cruelty to her. If she can. Dr. Greenlaw didn't sound awfully positive about her recovery yesterday."

Flossie didn't respond for a moment. Then she straightened her shoulders and said, "Thank you, Daisy. You're right. Johnny is a truly saintly man, but in this case, I believe I did the right thing."

"I know you did."

Flossie and I started up Harold's beautifully bricked walkway. "Say, Flossie, don't you have a private in the Salvation Army named Petrie? Percival Petrie?"

She stopped dead in her tracks, grabbed my arm, and said in a shocked whisper, "Oh, Daisy, that man is a devil! He stole the children's charity fund and ran off with that awful Stacy Kincaid!"

I gasped. "I knew they'd eloped and left the church, because I just came from Mrs. Pinkerton's house. She's in a rare state about what her revolting daughter has done this time, and she doesn't even know about the children's charity fund." Although I would have thought it impossible until it happened, Stacy sank another degree or two in my estimation. And she'd been below the line for a decade or more even before she met Percival Petrie.

"Johnny hadn't been happy with his performance for some time. I knew he was a cheater even before Johnny suspected him, because I've had lots of experience with cheats and liars in my life."

"I know, Flossie. Some people's lives are a whole lot harder than other people's lives. You didn't deserve to go through your miserable childhood, although it worked out all right eventually."

"That's true. I love Johnny with all my heart." She swallowed. "I didn't mean to complain to you, of all people. You, who lost your beloved husband before you even got started in life together."

"Maybe. But I didn't have a dreadful childhood. My parents are great folks, and my aunt can cook like a master chef. Hmm. Is there a word for a woman chef? A cheffess or a cheffette or something?"

I was glad when Flossie gave a short laugh. "Probably not. Women don't get much respect in this old world, do they?"

"No. It's a crying shame, too."

"But at least neither of us has had to endure what Mrs. Bannister has gone through," she said.

I gaped at her. "You did, too! That beastly Jenkins man beat you nearly as badly as Mr. Bannister beat his wife."

"I guess so. It didn't seem so bad at the time."

I would have gaped some more, but we'd reached Harold's beautiful front door. I pressed the doorbell and heard chimes. The chimes were pretty. Our doorbell kind of scratched. But we weren't rich enough for chimes, I reckon.

Oh, pay no attention to me. I was getting downright depressed on that stupid day, and it was only noonish.

Roy, Harold's houseboy, opened the door to Flossie and me. "Please come in, Mrs. Majesty and Mrs. Buckingham. Mr. Harold and Dr. Greenlaw are in the family room."

"Thank you, Roy," Flossie and I said in a musical duet. Flossie, by the way, had a lovely soprano voice, which she'd used to good effect in *The Mikado* the year before, when she'd been roped in to sing a part after the original singer of the role got arrested for murder.

Maybe my father is right. Maybe I do get into trouble all the time.

I still maintain it's not my fault.

TEN

Harold and Dr. Greenlaw were in a conversational huddle when Flossie and I entered the room. I smelled delicious aromas coming from somewhere, so I presumed Harold aimed to make good on his promise to feed us lunch. That was all right by me. My stomach felt empty, and it had already been a trying day. Harold spotted us first.

"Daisy! Mrs. Buckingham! I'm so glad you could come over. I have some information you might eventually be able to use against Mr. Leo Bannister, although not until Mrs. Bannister is out of the woods. Medically speaking."

"How is she today?" I asked to both men.

"Not well," said Dr. Greenlaw. "She's not regained full consciousness, and I don't believe she could talk even if her wounds were to allow her to do so. Concussion is a difficult problem with which to deal. Sometimes its effects are permanent, and sometimes they don't show up until long after the initial event."

"Oh, dear," Flossie whispered.

"I'm sorry to hear it," said I.

"Indeed," said the doctor. "After examining her, I suspect this isn't the first time Mr. Bannister has used her as a punching bag."

"The beast," I growled.

"The fiend," Flossie growled.

"He's both of those things, for sure," said Harold. "And probably worse. Well, Roy's fixed us some luncheon, so let's partake of our meal and then get into the grisly details of Leo Bannister's sinister career."

"Grisly details of a sinister career, eh? That doesn't sound good." I wasn't joking.

"It isn't good. He's a genuinely evil man."

"Oh, dear," I said upon a sigh. "Not another one."

"What do you mean, 'not another one?'" demanded Harold as he led the way down his gorgeously tiled hallway to the dining room, where a table sat, set and ready—and, of course, beautifully presented with a floral centerpiece—for us.

"I'm afraid your sister's new husband is another genuinely evil man. Wait until you hear what Miss Petrie told me about him. In fact, maybe he's in cahoots with Mr. Bannister. Wouldn't surprise me much."

"Good heavens," said Dr. Greenlaw. "There's another person like Bannister out there?" He turned to Harold. "And he married your *sister*? Oh, my word. That doesn't sound good."

"Sounds like precisely what Stacy deserves," muttered Stacy's not-very-fond brother.

"According to his distant cousin, he's even worse than she is," I said.

"And he stole the children's charity fund from the Salvation Army," added Flossie.

"The Salvation Army?" Dr. Greenlaw appeared confused.

I clarified the matter. "Flossie's husband Johnny is head of the local Salvation Army Church and charity."

"Ah," said Dr. Greenlaw.

"But let's talk about all this after lunch," said Harold.

I knew several leaves had been taken from the table, because it was small enough to seat us without our having to holler at each other. I'd been to dinners at Harold's home during which all the leaves had been put in the table, and it could seat twenty people with ease. Big table. Big house. Expensive, all of it.

"Thanks, Harold," I said. "I'm hungry. I felt so sorry for your mother when I was over there. She's devastated about Stacy and Mr. Petrie."

"Well, at least she's got something to worry about this time and isn't just wasting your time," said Harold, sounding not exactly like a dutiful son. Not that I blamed him. If I'd had to grow up with a mother like Mrs. Pinkerton and a sister like Stacy, I'd probably feel the same way.

After we were seated, Roy came in with soup and set a plate before each of us. It was a delicious soup made primarily with onions, and it had a piece of bread with some kind of cheese melted on it on top of the soup.

"This is delicious, Harold," said I after taking my first bite.

"French onion soup. We had it in France, remember?"

"No. But I wasn't eating much at that time if you'll recall."

"How could I ever forget? By the time we got to Egypt, I could practically see through you." Harold gave an eloquent shudder.

"I hadn't lost *that* much weight," I protested.

Harold and Flossie both stared at me for a moment, and I decided not to argue anymore. I suppose I had lost a little too much weight during that dreadful time in my life.

"Anyhow, French onion soup is one of my favorites," said Harold after giving his head a swift, short shake.

"I can see why. I wonder if Aunt Vi can make this for the family."

"Don't know why not. She feeds it to my mother and stepfather all the time."

"Hmm. Don't know why she hasn't given it to us. It's really good. In fact, this could be an entire meal. Oh, wait! She used to feed us French onion soup. I remember now." I frowned into my soup plate. "Wonder why she hasn't made it for so long."

"Maybe she doesn't like peeling and slicing onions," said Harold.

"That makes sense," said I.

"I don't like peeling and slicing onions, either," said Flossie. "They make me cry."

"Precisely," said Harold.

"Although," said I, "this might be worth it. Maybe she'd fix this if I peeled and sliced the onions for her."

I got another pointed look from Flossie and Harold.

Irked, I said, "It's not like I'd cut my finger off or anything. I've sliced onions before."

"Just be careful," said Flossie, giving me one of her sweet smiles.

"I will be," I said, grumbling slightly.

Appearing slightly confused, Dr. Greenlaw—I should probably call him Fred from now on, since he told me to—said, "Have you hurt yourself cooking, Mrs. Majesty? I mean Daisy?"

Bother. I hated admitting to being a failure in the kitchen.

"I don't think she's hurt herself," said Harold. "But evidently she poisoned her family once." He snickered.

"I did not! I just...well, I used baking soda instead of flour in a dish, and it tasted...Very well, it tasted awful."

Harold snickered again.

Flossie said, "But you taught that cooking class for our poor ladies without a single accident, and they all loved you."

"Oh, hell, everybody loves Daisy," said Harold. "That doesn't mean she should be set loose in a kitchen any time soon."

"Ah," said Fred.

Silence, except for discreet sipping sounds, prevailed at the luncheon table for several minutes. I, for one, was glad of it.

After we'd finished our French onion soup, which was possibly the very best soup I'd ever eaten in my entire life, Roy brought in a platter of lamb chops, roasted potatoes, and green beans. Boy, I could see why Harold was chunky if he ate like this every day. And this was *lunch*. All this stuff would have made a special dinner for us middle-class Gumms and Majestys.

A peach cobbler with cream finished the meal, and I was pretty sure I wouldn't be able to waddle away from the table, I was so stuffed.

Fred, however, showed no such compunction. On the other hand, I don't think he ate as much as I did. Restraint is probably a quality I should cultivate.

At any rate, Fred stood and said, "Let's go into the family room and discuss what we know about Leo Bannister and how we can help his wife, shall we?"

"I'm too full," said Harold.

Troubled, Flossie said, "Oh, please, Mr. Kincaid, we truly need to do something about poor Lily Bannister."

Rising from his chair with a laugh, Harold said, "Only joking, my dear. And will you please call me Harold? When you call me 'Mr. Kincaid', I am reminded of my father, and he's one of the world's biggest louses."

"Oh, dear," said Flossie, clearly regretting she'd brought up a touchy subject.

"Think nothing of it," said Harold. "My father is a bad man, and I prefer not to think about him."

"Oh," said Flossie.

"Don't mind Harold," I said, taking her arm. "He's right about his father. But he's stuffed away in San Quentin now, and it doesn't look as though he'll be able to escape again."

"Interesting people you know, Harold," muttered Fred. I think he was amused.

"My father's not my fault. Daisy and Flossie are both top notch. But we're not here to chat about my criminal father. We're here to talk about the ghastly Mr. Bannister and come to some conclusion about what can be done for his poor wife."

We'd walked to the family room, and I plopped down in an over-stuffed chair, thinking it and I had a lot in common just then. "So far, it doesn't look as if anything can be done to help her," I said, feeling disgruntled. "The police won't help, her church won't help, her family won't help, and Johnny *can't* help."

"He'd like to," said Flossie softly, as if in defense of her husband.

"Nobody's blaming him," I assured her. "It's just the truth."

She sighed. "Yes."

"You don't suppose your awful sister's new husband is in cahoots with this Bannister creep, do you? You haven't yet told me about his evil ways, but like tends to find like, and if they're both involved in the same perverted practices, perhaps they've found each other."

Three pairs of eyes focused on me, and I felt my face heat. "Well, it's possible," I muttered.

"Tell us about Stacy's beau, and I'll tell you if I think they might have found each other. It might be a match made in hell." Harold grimaced. "Awful thought."

So I told my audience what Miss Petrie had said about her cousin. As I spoke, I sensed Harold and Fred's interest becoming keener. Flossie appeared suitably appalled. Made sense to me. No one interrupted me as I spoke, although I did hear a gasp or two from Flossie, and she uttered a horrified, "*Pigs?*" once. Understandable.

After I finished talking, Fred and Harold locked gazes for a moment. Then Fred gestured to Harold as if asking him to take the floor.

"It's too soon to know for sure, of course," Harold began. "But this Petrie guy sounds like he might be right up Leo Bannister's alley."

"Why is that? You still haven't told me about Mr. Bannister," I reminded Harold.

"Right. Well..." Harold glanced at Fred.

Fred said, "Let's go up and see how Mrs. Bannister is doing. You had Roy take Hazel some lunch, didn't you?"

"Of course," said Harold.

"Wait! I want to know about Leo Bannister!" I cried, miffed.

"Hold your horses a little while longer, Daisy," Harold told me. "It's not a pretty story, and you might want to give Mrs. Bannister a look-see, since you and Flossie are the heroines of the piece."

"Heroines, my foot," said I. "But I do have some money for her."

"Money? You're giving her money?" Harold squinted at me.

"How sweet," said Flossie, bless her.

"I told myself yesterday that if your mother gave me a gob of money, I'd give it to Lily Bannister. She did, and I aim to do what I said I'd do. I'm sure Mrs. Bannister had no money with her after her old man beat her nearly to death."

"You're right about that," said Flossie with an eloquent shudder. "She barely had a dress on, and it was torn to ribbons."

"Good heavens." I wrinkled my nose.

"There's absolutely nothing heavenly about what that man did to her," Flossie told me in a hard, flat voice.

"Can't argue with you," said I.

"Come on, everyone. With luck, maybe she's gained some degree of consciousness, although even if she has, she might not be able to tell us anything about any of Bannister's friends or current occupations."

Doggone it! I wanted to know about Leo Bannister *now*, not after seeing Mrs. Bannister. I'd seen too much of her the day before, and what I'd seen then had sickened me.

"It's all right, Daisy," whispered Flossie, taking my arm. "Perhaps it's better to find out from Lily if she knows anything before we begin speculating about devilish conspiracies."

"Devilish?" I stared at Flossie. I mean, I knew she was a good Christian woman, but *devilish*?

She grinned. "Just a figure of speech."

"Oh. Good. For a minute there, I was afraid you'd gone 'round the bend."

"You don't believe in the devil?" she asked me as we started up Harold's elegant staircase.

I hesitated before answering her question, which was, admittedly, a fair one. "I...I honestly don't know, Flossie. If I believe in God, I suppose I should believe in Satan, but Satan's a little more difficult for me to get a grip on than God is."

"I'm glad of that, anyway," she said, laughing.

Harold and Fred turned to look at us. They'd started up the stairs ahead of us.

"You two all right?" asked Harold, frowning. I guess he didn't think the present situation called for levity.

"We're fine, thanks," I said. He was right, of course. There was nothing the least bit funny about the Lily Bannister problem. I suppressed a heavy sigh.

We were quiet as we all walked the carpeted hallway to the last bedroom in the west wing. Fred knocked quietly on the door, and I heard a slight rustling sound of someone walking across the carpeted floor. When the door opened, I instantly saw the resemblance between brother and sister. Hazel Greenlaw also had dark hair and eyes, and she was statuesque. I think that's what you're supposed to call tall woman, of which I'm not one, although I've always wished I were. Being short is a distinct handicap sometimes. She smiled a lovely smile at her brother and stepped back a pace or two.

"Come on in, Fred, and the rest of you." She held her hand out to me. "I'm Hazel Greenlaw."

"Daisy Majesty," I said, shaking her hand. "And this is Flossie Buckingham. She's the one who first saved Lily Bannister's life."

Hazel turned to Flossie with what looked like intense satisfaction. "How wonderful of you, Flossie! I wish the law would do something to Leo Bannister to prevent the abuse he heaps upon women, but it prefers to look the other way."

Slightly flustered, Flossie said, "Oh, well, I really didn't do much. I only drove her to Daisy's house. Daisy is the one who got hold of Harold—"

"Huh," said Harold, reminding me of Sam.

"—and Harold telephoned your brother, and he went to Daisy's. Then Dr. Greenlaw treated her as well as he could at Daisy's house, and Daisy drove her here, and...Well, I do so appreciate you for helping the poor woman." She sniffled and had to grab a hankie from her pocket.

"I will do almost anything to assist the victims of Leo Bannister's evil proclivities," proclaimed Hazel.

Darn it, now I was practically jumping up and down, I wanted so much to know more about the evil Leo Bannister. I told myself to possess my soul in patience, and all would be revealed, but myself told me it couldn't happen soon enough to satisfy me. Patience is another one of those virtues I haven't cultivated a whole lot.

"Well, come over and check her out," said Hazel to her brother. "She's still not awake. Her eyelids have fluttered a time or two, but she doesn't respond when I whisper to her." She turned to Harold. "Thanks for the delicious lunch, Harold. Roy just picked up my tray a minute ago and carted it downstairs."

"You're welcome," mumbled Harold, who didn't look as though he wanted to see Lily Bannister again.

I took hold of his arm and yanked him along behind me though, so, when Lily Bannister's eyes fluttered open a second or two later, her bed was surrounded by four people who were probably strangers to her. Unless she remembered Flossie, which I doubted.

ELEVEN

When I say Lily Bannister's eyes fluttered open, I'm not being technically accurate. Her eyes were two swollen purple blobs, and I could scarcely see a shiny strip of eye between the slits in each blob. The shiny strips were more red than white, probably due to broken capillaries and so forth. Ugh. She blinked once, groaned, and closed the blobs once more.

"Mrs. Bannister?" Fred said softly. He had a most comforting voice.

No answer.

"Mrs. Bannister, I'm Dr. Greenlaw. I'm here to help you. My sister is Hazel Greenlaw. She's a registered nurse, and she's been assisting you, too."

Her battered mouth moved a bit, but she couldn't seem to open it.

Hazel, who seemed to think of everything, picked up a glass of water holding a straw that sat waiting on the side table, lifted Lily's head slightly, and held the straw to Lily's mouth. It seemed to take Lily a great, exhausting effort, but she sipped a bit of water. Then she lay back down on her pillow and groaned again while tears slid from her slitted blobby eyes. Hazel gently wiped them from her black-and-blue cheeks with a soft cloth.

We all stood there in a state of profound anticipation. Well, that was my condition anyway. I can't really speak for anyone else.

Finally, after resting for long enough that Harold began fidgeting, Lily said mushily, "L-leo?"

"Leo doesn't know where you are, Lily," Hazel assured her.

Lily sighed and might have said, "Thank God," but I'm not sure since her mouth, tongue and lips were so badly swollen and brutalized.

"And he never will know where you are," said Fred. "We'll make sure of it."

Harold, Flossie and I nodded, but poor Lily couldn't see us. Oh, well.

"Do you think you can answer a question or two, Mrs. Bannister?" Fred asked then.

Lily lay on the bed, unmoving, for what seemed like three hours, but at last I think she said, "Yesh."

"Do you know what provoked Leo's attack on you yesterday?"

Silence.

More silence.

Then a muffled, "Yesh."

Fred turned and whispered to the group, "I can't see us getting very far questioning her today. She's in wretched shape. But I'll just ask her one question she may be able to answer with a nod or something." He turned back to Lily. "Did it have something to do with children?"

Yet more silence.

Then, "Yesh."

"I see. Thank you, Mrs. Bannister. You rest up now. Hazel will remain with you, and she'll see that you're well taken care of. I'll be back in a bit to make sure you don't need more medication or anything of that nature."

I think the poor woman tried to say "Thank you," but it didn't come out quite right. I felt like crying. When I turned to Flossie, I saw she *was* crying. Gently, I took her arm.

"Let's go down to the family room, Flossie. Harold is going to tell us all about it." I glared at Harold. "Aren't you, Harold?"

Harold said, "Yes."

The four of us trooped down the hallway and then down the staircase and headed for the family room. When we got there, I took one of two comfy-looking chairs sitting one on either side of a lovely table decorated with a vase filled with what looked like freshly cut roses. The vase was a new addition from when we'd been in the room before.

Gesturing to the roses, I asked Harold, "From your garden?"

"Not bad for early May, eh?" said Harold with some satisfaction in his tone.

"Not bad at all."

Don't ask me why, but it was at that precise moment I remembered the basket of wet laundry in my Chevrolet's back seat. I must have gasped, because Harold looked at me oddly and said, "It's not *that* strange to have roses blooming in May, Daisy Majesty."

"I know. I know. But I just thought of...Oh, dear." I rose from my chair, flustered.

Flossie, who'd just taken a seat in the chair across the table from mine, stood and held out a hand to me. "Daisy! Whatever is the matter? Do you need help?"

"No, no. Yes. No. I just remembered...Oh, Harold, I put all the bloody sheets in a basket in my closet, and this morning they stank horribly, so I poured peroxide on them, bundled them into the basket again, and now they're sitting in the back seat of the Chevrolet!"

Harold and Fred stared at me for approximately three seconds each, and then both men burst out laughing.

I scowled at Harold, not knowing Fred well enough yet to scowl at him. "It's not funny, Harold Kincaid! I don't want my family to know what went on at our house yesterday. I have to get those sheets and rags and aprons washed and dried and put away before anyone realizes they're gone!"

"I'm not l-laughing at you, Daisy," Harold said, lying through his teeth.

"You are too!" I more or less bellowed.

"Take it easy," Harold told me, sobering slightly, but still grinning like a monster. Then he reached for a button set into the wall beside the sofa upon which he then resided and pressed it. The button, I mean. "I'll just have Roy launder your bloody rags, and you'll be all set."

Startled, I said, "Oh. But..."

"Don't be silly, Daisy. It's the least I can do after you gave up your rags and aprons and sheets for such a good cause yesterday."

Smiling at me, Fred said, "I'll even buy you some new sheets."

Embarrassed, I sat again and said, "There's no need for that. If Roy would be kind enough to launder everything, I'm sure I can pick it all up tomorrow and everything will be just fine."

"Fiddlesticks. You at least deserve new sheets," said Fred.

"But it's May," I said softly, feeling not merely embarrassed, but also a trifle befuddled.

"What's May got to do with anything?" Harold asked.

"All the white sales are held in January. Sometimes in July, but mostly in January," I told him, wondering why he even had to ask. Then I remembered. "Oh, that's right. You're rich. You can buy sheets any old time you want to, can't you?"

"Not personally," said Harold in what I considered a faintly snide tone of voice. "But yes. I can have sheets purchased any old time of the year. And so can Fred."

Roy entered the room at that point, and Harold said, "Roy, will you please fetch a basket of laundry out of Mrs. Majesty's Chevrolet and wash the load for her? She deserves it, believe me."

"Use lots of bleach," added Fred. "There's blood on them."

"Happy to, Mr. Harold and Dr. Greenlaw," said Roy, who turned and smiled at me.

By that time, I'm sure my face was as crimson as several of the roses in the bouquet I'd admired earlier. "Thank you, Roy."

"Is your car locked?" asked he.

"No."

"Then I'll begin right away."

"Thanks, Roy," said Harold.

"Thank you," I said.

"Happy to help," said Roy, who seemed a genuinely cheerful individual. He left the room and, I presume, did what Harold had asked him to do. I loved his accent and told myself to remember to ask where he'd originated.

It must be nice to have a servant or two to do chores for you. I didn't say so, having by that time humiliated myself beyond redemption.

"I'll bring some sheets to Harold's tomorrow," said Fred. "White is, I believe, the color you prefer."

That's because I'd mentioned the white sales held annually at Nash's Dry Goods and Department Store and several other places in the city. But, darn it, they *did* hold those sales in January! And, while I made a decent income for my family and me, that didn't mean I could rush out and buy expensive sheets any old time I wanted to. In fact, I actually felt a trifle guilty about not sewing the family's bed linens, etc., on the White side-pedal sewing machine on which I made so much of the family's clothing. But sewing bed sheets wasn't fun. Sewing dresses, shirts, suits and so forth, was.

"Really, there's no need for you to buy sheets," I muttered to Fred.

"Nonsense. You and Mrs. Buckingham saved a woman's life yesterday. That's worth at least a sheet or two."

Deciding it would be best to drop the subject I wished by that time I'd never mentioned, I said merely, "Thank you," and shut up.

Harold rubbed his hands together. "Very well then. Leo Bannister."

Fred sort of growled. "Yes. Leo Bannister."

"You two both seem to know him and dislike him. Does he beat up women all the time or something?" I asked. "If he beats up women who aren't married to him, can't they complain to the police? I mean, does he go around the city, looking for women to pick up and torture? Why don't they report him? And why did you ask Mrs. Bannister if her beating was precipitated by children?"

Fred and Harold exchanged what looked to me like a speaking glance or two.

Then Harold heaved a sigh. "They don't dare. He imports them. He brings in men and women—often mere children—and holds them in various places. Then he allows fellow perverts to pay for the privilege of...of...Oh, dear. What's a polite way of saying this?"

"Do you mean to say he brings young girls and boys into the country to work in *brothels*?" Flossie demanded, sitting up straight in her chair, her blue eyes blazing. Mercy sakes. I'd never seen her so incensed.

After blinking at her, I presume in confusion, Harold said, "Well, yes. That's precisely what I mean."

Flossie gave the right arm of her chair a good, solid whack with her fist. "*Damn* the man! He deserves to be horsewhipped! He deserves to have his heart ripped out of his chest! He deserves to have his balls cut off with dull, rusty scissors!"

Fred's mouth fell open. Harold's didn't, but he looked a trifle surprised. Then he probably remembered the Flossie from the old days, and I could swear his lips curled up slightly.

"You're right," said Harold.

"Yes, you are," said I, shocked beyond measure, although I'm not sure why. I'd already figured the guy was a horrible person. I just hadn't quite imagined how repugnant a specimen of humanhood he was. "He imports little *girls?*"

"Girls and boys," said Harold and Fred in a baritonal duet. Well, Harold sang tenor, but you probably know what I mean.

"That's...that's...that's...I can't think of anything vile enough to call a man who does that sort of thing."

"I can," said Flossie. At that moment, if you'd looked up the word "grim" in the dictionary, you'd probably have found a picture of Flossie Mosser Buckingham. "Although it's difficult to stick to just one," she continued. "He's evil. He's a rotten, lousy bastard. He's a disgusting pervert. He's the devil incarnate. He's a son of a bitch. He's a—"

"I get the picture!" said I, my voice rising a trifle, primarily from shock. I had never, since the day I'd met her, heard Flossie pronounce so much as a "damn" in my presence. Given the company she'd kept until Johnny came into her life, I didn't doubt she knew the words. I'd just never heard her say them.

"He's a depraved monster," said Flossie as if she hadn't heard me. "He's a corruption of a human being. He's a repulsive viper. He's the worst kind of ogre to walk the earth."

"Well, there was the Kaiser—" I said, attempting to stop the flow of vitriol. Although, I must say, I was impressed by Flossie vocabulary.

"*Damn* the Kaiser!" shouted Flossie. "Damn Leo Bannister! They're both wicked, degraded villains who don't deserve to live!"

And with that, Flossie sank back into her comfy chair, whipped her hankie out of her pocket, and commenced to sob uncontrollably.

"Flossie!" I cried, hurrying around the table between our chairs and kneeling before her, laying my hands on her trembling arms. "Oh, Flossie. Is that what happened to you?"

She'd evidently run out of words, because she only nodded as she wept. Then she threw her arms around me and sobbed some more.

"Good God," said Harold.

"I'm so sorry," said Fred. "Here, Mrs. Buckingham, will you allow me to get you something for a composer?"

Flossie's head, still buried on my shoulder, shook back and forth. I heard a rustling sound that might have been Fred rising and then sitting again.

I don't know how many minutes that went on. Poor Flossie. I was so horrified and sorry she'd been through anything as awful as what Harold had described, I didn't even care when my knees began to ache. And when she was a little *girl*! My mind boggled and didn't seem to want to stop.

At long last, Flossie withdrew from me, mopping her face with her hankie as she did so. After she blew her nose, she said in a shaky voice, "I-I'm sorry. I...I just can't *believe* anything like that goes on in Pasadena."

"Me neither," said I, because it was the truth. I creaked to my feet and brushed down my skirt.

Flossie reached out a hand. "Oh, Daisy, I've got your shoulder all wet."

"Don't even think about it, Flossie. I don't care. But I must say I'm glad you have Johnny and Billy now instead of...that." I made a vague gesture meant to indicate Lily Bannister's room.

"Me, too," said Flossie and sniffled some more. Then she snorted, sounding not unlike a horse I'd seen in the park once. "Once upon a time, I thought Jinx was my salvation."

"Good Lord," I whispered, wondering how anyone, even a young, beleaguered girl, could regard the disgusting Jinx Jenkins as a savior. Her circumstances must have been even worse than I'd guessed.

"The good Lord sent me you," Flossie said thickly. "And you gave me Johnny."

I wouldn't have put it in those precise words, especially since I'd more or less flung Flossie at Johnny in order to get her out of my hair. Ignoble, I know.

No one spoke for a while. Not sure how long.

Then someone, I think it was Harold, heaved a large-sized sigh and said, "How do you think I got Roy?"

Flossie and I both snapped to attention. Flossie's eyes widened substantially, considering they were puffy from crying.

So did mine. My mouth also fell open, but words spilled out. "Harold Kincaid, do you mean to tell me you frequent dens of iniquity like that—"

"For God's sake, Daisy! You know me better than that! If you don't, you damned well should!"

Merciful heavens. I'd never seen Harold look so peeved. "I'm sorry. I mean...Well, how did you get Roy then?"

"I'll let Fred tell you," said Harold, grumbling slightly, probably irked that I could even think he'd frequent such a disgusting place. Speaking of which, where did Leo Bannister perpetrate his vile trade? I'd have to ask later.

It was Fred's turn to sigh. "One of Leo Bannister's customers got a little rough one night. I don't know who did it, but poor Roy was dropped off at the Castleton Hospital. He and a few other children, who were likewise tormented. Poor Roy was in rough condition, worse than any of the others. He'd been...Um, he'd been violated and beaten."

"Oh. How horrible," I whispered.

"It was horrible, all right," said Harold. "Some bastard had used a beer bottle to—"

Fred coughed loudly. "There's probably no need to go into details."

"The hell there's not!" Flossie said, erupting from her slump. "Some jerk raped him with a beer bottle. Is that it? And the poor kid was all torn up inside and bleeding? I swear, if I could find every man in the universe who did things like that to little girls and boys, I'd hang them all!"

"But...But...But what do you mean? I don't understand. How can—"

"You're not as innocent as most young women your age," said Harold

95

in a voice I can only describe as kind of crunchy. "But your experiences are limited to what sane people do to each other. There are people who get their thrills tormenting other people. Sexually, I mean."

"With...With beer bottles?" My mouth pursed up with distaste.

"I'll explain it to you later," said Flossie. "It's not pretty, and I expect these men would prefer we not discuss it right this minute."

"Precisely," said Harold, and I could tell he was relieved beyond measure that the subject of beer bottles and rape had been dropped.

TWELVE

Wentifield e talked in a desultory manner for a little while, and I managed to ask my question about where Leo Bannister's...well, brothel, I guess, was situated in my formerly sainted city. It was difficult for me to imagine such wickedness being carried out in my home town. I didn't like it, either. Naturally, my not liking it made as much difference as it ever did, which, as I've already mentioned, is none.

Life can be downright depressing sometimes.

Anyway, back to the conversation.

"If we knew that, we might be able to stop him, although it will be difficult, since most of his victims are foreign, are here illegally, and are too afraid to talk to the police," said Harold. "And his customers come from a high echelon of society."

Ew.

"What about his wife? Do you think she knows?" I asked.

"We can't know that unless she tells us. And that depends on whether she ever recovers from this latest beating," said Fred. "She's badly concussed, and I wouldn't be at all surprised if this wasn't her first concussion at her husband's hands. Repeated concussions can cause brain damage."

"Oh, my goodness," I said. "That's truly...awful."

"Yes, it is," said Fred. "But it's going to take some time before we know if she'll even be able to talk to us once she regains full consciousness. If she does. And, of course, if she remembers details of what happened to her."

"Do they have any children?" asked Flossie. "I mean, if they have children, and the children are old enough, they might be able to help."

After exchanging a glance with Fred, Harold said, "I don't know. I don't recall hearing about any children."

"I hope they don't," said I. "I can't imagine having a monster like that for a father."

"Me, neither," said Fred.

"I can," said Harold. "I must say, though, that while my old man wasn't exactly a saint, he didn't beat my mother. Or Stacy or me."

"Might have been better if he had beaten Stacy," I said, thinking about Stacy's latest indiscretion.

"Speaking of Stacy, if this fellow she married is as bad as your librarian friend thinks he is, he's the exact sort of man who might be in league with Leo Bannister." Harold peered at me. "You'll probably be visiting my mother again tomorrow, won't you?"

"Oh, yes. I have a feeling I'm going to be spending a lot of time with your mother until the Stacy-and-Percival situation is resolved. One way or another."

"Maybe they'll die in a fiery accident," said Harold with some relish.

"Or drive off a cliff," I said, smiling.

"Daisy!" said Flossie, shocked, although I'm not sure why. She knew Stacy, too.

I only shrugged. "Only a thought," said I.

"Well," said Harold, "since nobody seems to know where Stacy and her beloved are at the moment, we'd probably better concentrate on what to do about Leo Bannister."

"If we can," said Fred. "Folks have tried to do it before."

"Have they?" I asked.

Fred opened his mouth to speak, but no words emerged. He shut it again and glanced at Harold. Harold shrugged.

"Actually," he said, "perhaps they haven't. All I've ever really heard are rumors. Except for Roy, and he can't tell anyone where his assault happened. He'd just come here from somewhere in the Caribbean, and he didn't know the geography of Pasadena at all."

"Oh. I wondered where he was from. He has a delightful accent."

"He's a good kid, Roy," said Harold.

"Very useful, too," I said, nodding. "But doesn't he miss his family back home? Wherever home is?"

"See?" said Fred. "That's where this whole thing gets tricky. The kids who end up with Bannister are generally orphans. In fact, it wouldn't surprise me if he passed himself off as some sort of humanitarian or something, and the places where these children come from think he's doing them a great favor out of the goodness of his heart."

"What heart?" muttered Flossie.

"True," said Fred. "But until someone figures out where he's keeping these children and finds proof of what he's done to them, I don't know what we can do."

"I can certainly do some snooping," I said, picturing my father's face in my mind's eye as I did so.

"So can I," said Flossie.

"I suppose I can, too," said Harold with a shrug. "Don't have any work at the studio for a week or so. What the heck."

"How do you propose to go about this snooping of yours?" asked Fred.

Flossie, Harold and I looked at each other. I'm sure we also blinked.

"Um...I'm not sure. Do you suppose you could ride around with Roy and see if he recognizes anything familiar?" I asked Harold doubtfully.

"I guess. He might spot something." He didn't sound awfully enthusiastic.

"I can ask Johnny," said Flossie. "He doesn't talk much about stuff like this, but he's wise to every vice carried on in the city. He prays about it all the time."

"Don't mention Mrs. Bannister," I warned her.

"Of course I won't. He already thinks I'm doing something on the sly. But I can mention that I ran in to you or Harold and one of you mentioned something about one of his friends taking in a child who'd been injured by a beastly pervert or something like that."

"I guess. Probably better not use any names except mine," I said. "Not that I want Johnny to distrust me, but I *really* don't want to get Harold or Fred into any trouble. Or Roy, for that matter."

"I second that sentiment," said Harold.

Fred nodded.

"Very well. I'll just mention I bumped into someone who told me a terrible story about what happened to a child here in Pasadena. I guess I don't need to name names at all."

"Good idea," said I. Then I got to my feet. "This has been an... enlightening afternoon, and I do appreciate the lunch—and the laundry—Harold, but I'd better be getting home. Sam's coming to dinner tonight, and I aim to tell him about your sister's beloved. He asked me to, in fact. I think, although of course he won't tell me, that he already suspects Stacy's precious Percival of being some kind of hoodlum."

"No surprise there," said Harold. "Sam might not be the most genial of fellows, but he's not stupid."

"True," said Flossie. "And he's been very helpful to Johnny and me a few times. He's a good man, Daisy."

It seemed to me as if everyone in the room were staring at me with some kind of suggestion in his or her eyes. Nerts. "I know he's a good man," I said somewhat snappishly. "By the way, your mother again today told me I should marry you, Harold. You've got to get that notion out of her head."

Harold lifted his arms as if in despair. "If you can tell me how to get my mother to do anything, you're a better man than I am, Daisy Din."

I shook my head at him in pretended horror at his adaptation of one of Kipling's more heroic poetic fictions. "Harold, that's bad, even from you."

He got up, too, smiling. "Yeah, well I'm having your sheets laundered for you. That should buy me some slack."

"I guess so."

"I should go, too. Thank you very much, Harold." Flossie turned from

Harold to Fred. "And, Dr. Greenlaw, I don't even know *how* to thank you. And your sister."

"Don't even think about it," murmured Fred, clearly embarrassed.

"I'll be praying for you and Hazel and Lily Bannister," said Flossie a little thickly. She'd been crying a whole lot that day.

"Thanks," said Fred doubtfully.

"Thanks," said Harold, and I could tell he was biting his tongue to hold back a sarcastic comment about prayer.

"Come on, Flossie. Let's get out of this paradise and head for the grubbier side of town."

With a sniffle and a strained chuckle, Flossie said, "Daisy, you're a caution."

Whatever that meant.

I hate to admit it, but when I got home, I took off my spiritualist's garb and lay on the bed, feeling tired and sad and wishing such things as wife-beating husbands, child-peddling perverts, and people who fed children's bodies to pigs didn't exist on this earth. Spike snuggled with me and told me not to despair. *He* was there for me, no matter what the rest of the world got up to behind our backs. I appreciated my dachshund a whole lot that afternoon.

Anyhow, the short nap I took perked me up some, so I dusted the house, ran the carpet-sweeper over the carpets, and dust-mopped the wood floors, so I didn't waste the entire afternoon.

Pa came home when I was wielding the dust mop.

"Busy girl," he said as he hung his cap on a hook in the kitchen.

"That's me, all right."

"I hope this morning's telephone calls didn't ruin your day for you," he said.

"No. The calls didn't. They only ruined breakfast. Other things ruined the rest of the day."

"Mrs. Pinkerton having fits again?"

I took the dust mop out the front door and shook it out over the hydrangea bushes, which didn't deserve such treatment. But they were handy. "Oh, my, yes. She deserves them this time, though. I have to admit that for once she has a reason for her hysteria."

"Her daughter?"

"Yes. Stacy's run off with a very bad man this time."

"How do you know she ran off with him? Because she didn't tell her mother? And how do you know he's a bad man?"

"Before they skipped out of sight, Stacy and her beloved stole all the money in the Salvation Army's children's charity fund. That's according to Flossie."

"Good heavens. That is pretty bad."

"It gets worse. But Sam's coming over for dinner tonight, and I don't want to have to tell this story more than once, so can you wait until he gets here?"

"Sure. I don't know why you don't just marry that man, Daisy. You'll never find a better one."

I touched Sam's engagement ring, which was warm against my chest as my father spoke those words, and felt like a world-class crumb.

"I know you're probably right, but...Well, I just don't think I'm ready yet."

Pa came over and deposited a kiss to my head. "That's all right, sweetie. Didn't mean to put any pressure on you. I just feel sorry for Sam, is all."

Sorry for *Sam*? What about *me*? I didn't ask. I just sighed and finished my housework. Then I set the table and hoped that Vi had something scrumptious for us to eat that night.

Of course, she did. I heard a motor rumble up to the curb along about five o'clock that afternoon, and when I went to the front door to see who'd come to call, hoping for Sam oddly enough, I saw Harold's Stutz Bearcat. There was Harold. And there was Aunt Vi! Harold held a cardboard box that appeared to be quite heavy, unless Harold was exaggerating slightly. Or more than slightly.

"Vi!" I cried, running down the porch steps. "Here, let me help you!"

"I'm the one who needs help," Harold grumbled. "This box weighs three hundred pounds."

"Harold Kincaid, you naughty boy." Vi giggled. Harold has that effect on middle-aged ladies.

"May I help with anything?" I asked.

"Just don't let Spike trip me up," said Harold.

Sound advice. And appropriately given, since Spike was at that very moment racing toward Vi and Harold. I preempted his assault and scooped him up. He wriggled in my arms, but he didn't mind being held.

"Boy, whatever that is, it smells tasty," I said.

"It is tasty," said Harold, grunting slightly as he carried the box up the porch steps, across the porch and into the house. "I've sampled it."

"Well, I hope you've left enough for us," I said, trying to sound playful, but not succeeding very well.

"Daisy! That was unkind!" said Vi.

See what I mean?

"It was supposed to be a joke, Aunt Vi."

"Never mind, Mrs. Gumm," said Harold. "I'm used to being bullyragged by your niece."

"Oh, piddle," said I, following Harold and the heavenly smells as he deposited the box on the kitchen table.

"Can you take that platter out of the box and put it in the warming oven, Daisy? I want to keep the tournedos of beef warm until dinnertime. Put those hominy and horseradish croquettes in a separate platter and stick them in the warming oven, too, please. Then you can help me string these beans." Vi held up a paper sack that looked as if it were stuffed to the brim with green beans. When Harold and I ate green beans in Turkey (which has the best food in the world, no matter what France says) they were called *haricots verts*, which is French for skinny green beans.

"Sure, Vi. Thanks. Oh, my, this whole dinner smells wonderful. What's the meat called again?"

"Tournedos of beef. They're just cuts of tender beef cooked in a certain way and covered with a savory sauce."

"And the croquettes? Hominy, did you say?" My father liked hominy grits for breakfast sometimes, but I'd never considered them *haute cuisine*. Learn something every day, I reckon.

"Yes, hominy and horseradish. The horseradish goes well with the beef."

"Good. Sounds good." Sounded weird to me, but I've already acknowledged I'm no cook, much less a chef. Or a cheffette.

"Must be off," said Harold, kissing me on the cheek and then doing the same to Vi. "Mother needs me." He heaved a large-sized sigh, for which I had every sympathy, said goodbye to my father and Spike, and vanished out the front door again.

I stringed—strung?—and snipped the green beans, and Vi made magic with them.

By the time Sam showed up for dinner, the table was set, the house was full of enticing food scents, and my mouth was watering.

THIRTEEN

Spike and I met Sam at the door when he knocked at precisely six p.m. Sam was punctual unless he was unable to keep an appointment at all because of his job, but he always managed to 'phone when that happened.

His eyes widened after he greeted Spike and me, Spike with a pat and me with a kiss. "Wow, something sure smells good."

I recited the menu as if I knew what I was talking about. "Tournedos of beef with hominy and horseradish croquettes, and green beans amandine. Or *haricots verts* with whatever the French words for toasted almonds is."

"I'm a lucky guy," said Sam, removing his overcoat and hat and hanging them on the coat rack beside the front door.

"We're all lucky to have Vi cook for us."

"We certainly are," said my mother, smiling up a storm and coming at Sam and me with her hands extended. I wasn't sure what to do with them, but Sam took them both and then kissed Ma on the cheek.

Huh. Maybe he'd been taking lessons on gracious behavior from Harold. As if.

"It's good to see you, Sam," said Ma.

"Thank you. It's good to see you, too, and the rest of Daisy's family."

"Especially Vi," I muttered.

Ma said, "Daisy."

Sam only laughed. He was doing that a lot more lately, and it made me happy.

When we were about halfway through with dinner, Sam said, "Delicious meal, Mrs. Gumm." He always said that, and it was always true.

"Thank you," said Vi, beaming. She loved feeding people.

"It's wonderful," said I, wanting to close my eyes to more fully savor the beef with the horseradish and hominy croquette. Vi had been correct when she said horseradish and beef make good companions. "And I love the almonds in the beans."

"Thank you."

"I'm so glad you can cook for us, Vi," said my mother. "Neither Daisy nor I can cook a lick."

"Well, now..." I began, but then realized I'd be lying if I disagreed with her. So instead, I sighed and said, "Ma's right. I'm glad we have you, Vi."

"You just don't keep your mind on your job when you're in the kitchen, Daisy," said Vi. She'd said as much before, but I know she's wrong. I just can't cook. Period.

Anyway, the meal was grand, and we all enjoyed it. Even Spike once, when I sneaked him a bite of beef. I really shouldn't do that, since dachshunds have long backs and being heavy isn't good for them.

After we'd finished dining (the meal was too good to call it mere eating), I cleaned up the dishes, and the rest of the family retired to the living room to gab. Probably Sam and Pa would haul out the card table and play gin rummy at some point, but I wanted to talk to Sam before that point came, so I sat next to him on the sofa (to the not-so-hidden delight of my family; I generally sat on a piece of furniture separate from Sam) and said, "What are you guys talking about?"

Sam shrugged. "Not much. I was telling your family about Stacy Kincaid running off with that fellow from the Salvation Army."

"Did Pa tell you Petrie stole the money from the Army's children's charity fund before he and Stacy did a flit?"

"What's a flit?" asked Ma.

"They eloped after stealing the children's charity money."

"Goodness!" cried Ma. "That's terrible."

"Awful," said Vi.

"That's the least of his sins," said I, relishing the story I was about to tell my family.

"And how do you know all of this?" asked Ma as if she suspected me of being about to tell tall tales to my family.

"Because Percival Petrie's cousin, Miss Petrie at the library, told me all about him. He's really evil, Ma."

"Well...I don't know that you should be spreading stories, Daisy. That's not how I raised you."

Peeved, I said, "You didn't raise me. You reared me. And Sam needs to know this stuff."

"Oh. Well, then," said my mother. Then she smiled and sat back, ready to hear the juicy details.

Because she'd irked me, I said, "But you're probably right. I should take Sam out to the front porch and spare the rest of you these squalid, ugly details."

"Oh, no," said Ma, rushing her words slightly. "That's all right. I'm sure we won't go telling anyone else."

"That's good, Mrs. Gumm," said Sam, and he was being deadly serious. "Please don't relate any of this to anyone else. If I'd known Daisy was going to spill it to the whole family, I'd have taken *her* out on the front porch. But the Pasadena Police Department has an investigation going on, and it's one in which Petrie might possibly be involved. So please don't spread this anywhere else."

Blast. That took the wind out of my sails. "I didn't know you had an active investigation of the booboisie, or I'd have talked to you alone," I said, feeling silly.

"What," said my mother in a sternish voice, "is a booboisie?"

"A dimwit. A punk. A—"

"*Will* you speak English, Daisy Majesty!" my mother said, and loudly too.

"Sorry, Ma. I meant he's a petty criminal. Only maybe not so petty."

Sam huffed slightly, and when I jerked my head to look at him, I saw he was trying to smother laughter. Blast them all.

Nevertheless, I told my story as Miss Petrie had told it to me. Naturally when I got to the pigs part, I heard two or three horrified gasps. When I'd finished regaling my audience, I turned to Sam. "So what do you think he's involved in, Pasadena-wise, Sam?"

"I don't know. And if I did know, I couldn't tell you. You know that, Daisy."

"That's so unfair! I just spilled my guts—"

"Daisy!" Ma. Naturally.

"Sorry, Ma. But it's so frustrating that Sam can never tell us about his cases."

"Not until they're solved," said Sam.

"Makes sense, Daisy," said Pa in a consoling tone of voice. "You can't expect the police to tell everyone their business. If they did that, everybody would know, and the crooks would find out, and then Petrie would probably abscond with more than the Salvation Army's children's charity fund."

"I guess," I said, sounding sullen even to my own ears.

Aaaaand, the telephone rang.

"What's going on with that stupid telephone today?" I asked nobody in particular when I went to answer it.

Apparently no one knew, because no one spoke.

So I trudged to the kitchen and picked up the receiver. "Gumm-Majesty residence, Mrs. Majesty speaking," said I in my best, most restful voice, expecting an eruption of hysterics from Mrs. Pinkerton to interrupt me before I got my message out. But no. There were no hysterics. Only a polite, male voice that said, "May I please speak to Detective Rotondo?"

"Sam?" I said, surprised. "Sure. One moment, please."

I'd started to lower the receiver gently so it wouldn't bang against the wall and break the caller's eardrums when it occurred to me that Sam might not like an audience for this particular call, which, I figured, could only be from the Pasadena Police Department.

Therefore, I held the receiver to my ear again and said, "Will our party-line neighbors please hang up your 'phones? This is a private call."

I heard three clicks, and heaved a sigh of relief. Sometimes it was difficult to get Mrs. Barrow to hang up her telephone. Guess she was reading a good book or the "Detective Rotondo" part scared her or something, because she didn't linger this time.

So I gently let the receiver dangle and went to get Sam.

"Me?" He pointed to his chest when I summoned him.

"You. How come your office knows where you are, anyway?"

"I have to tell them where I am at any given time. My job requires me to work odd hours, you know."

"I know."

"And they like to know where they can get in touch with me."

"Oh."

So Sam walked off to the kitchen, and I didn't even follow him to hear his half of the conversation. I wanted to, but I knew Sam. He wouldn't even begin to speak to a colleague—if the caller was, indeed, a colleague—until I left the room.

I flopped on the sofa and looked at my family. They looked back at me.

"Who was that?" asked Ma.

"I don't know," I said with a shrug. "Probably the police department. Who else would telephone our house and ask for Sam?"

With a little frown, Pa said, "There are sure a lot of mysterious goings-on going on around here lately."

"What do you mean, Joe?" asked Ma.

"Daisy got about six thousand telephone calls this morning, and now Sam gets a call at our house this evening. Something's going on." Pa gave me a pointed look.

"Don't ask me," I said in some frustration. "Sam *never* tells anything about his cases."

"What about all those calls?" asked Ma.

"One was from Harold, who asked me to lunch." Not a lie. Maybe a tiny bit of a stretcher. "Another was from Sam, who asked me to find out about Percival Petrie. Another one was from Mrs. Pinkerton, who was in a tizzy because Stacy had run off with Percival Petrie. And the other one was from Flossie, who was distraught because Percival Petrie and Stacy had gone on the lam after stealing the children's charity fund." There. I got through them all without telling a single real lie. I was proud of myself.

"I presume 'on the lam' means running away," said Ma.

"Right," said I.

"I do wish young people today would speak proper English," Ma muttered.

I heaved a sigh.

Pa chuckled.

"According to Daisy," said Vi, "we had our own slang in our generation, too."

"We did?" Ma sounded as if she didn't quite believe it.

"Perhaps young people today are more apt to speak their slang whilst among company than we were," said Vi.

"You aren't company!" I cried. "You're *family*! If I can't speak plainly among my family, whom can I speak it among? Or to. If that makes any sense."

"It makes sense, sweetheart," said Pa with a grin. "I guess we were more afraid of our parents than young folks today are. If I'd used slang around my father, I'd have had to cut a switch for him to whack me with."

"Oh." I felt sorry for my poor father. "I'm glad you didn't do that to Daphne, Walter and me." Daphne and Walter were my two older siblings.

"Maybe he should have," grumbled Ma.

"Tut, tut, Peggy," said Vi. "I think it's fine for young people to have their own vocabulary. Or whatever you'd call it."

We didn't get to discuss the term of usage, however, because Sam returned to the living room just then. I stood up. "What was it?"

"Just got called out to check out a matter," he said, his Great Stone Face firmly back in place.

"A police matter?"

"Yes." He sighed, then turned to my relations. "Thank you very much for the fine dinner, Mrs. Gumm. And I hope we can play cards the next time I'm able to visit, Mr. Gumm." He nodded at my mother. "Good night, Mrs. Gumm." It might seem confusing to have two Mrs. Gumms in the family, but it wasn't, really. We knew who we were.

"I'll walk you out to your car," I told Sam.

He frowned a bit, but not as if he didn't want my company. Spike instantly jumped off the sofa, where he'd been peacefully ignoring the family chatter, and raced to the front door. He sat before the door patiently while Sam put on his overcoat and hat.

"I'm sorry you can't stay and play cards, Sam," I said as he opened the door and Spike dashed out. Sam gestured for me to precede him, being a trifle more polite than my dog.

"Yeah. Me, too," said he as we began the short march to his Hudson.

"Can you at least tell me what kind of case you were called out for?" I asked, not expecting much.

Sam surprised me. "Murder."

"Goodness gracious! We don't get too many of those in Pasadena."

"I dunno about that," said he. "People seem to drop dead around you quite frequently."

He was joking, but I didn't appreciate the joke. "Thanks a lot, Sam."

"You're welcome." He bent and kissed my cheek. I turned my head so that we ended up kissing with our lips.

As he stood straight again, he sighed. "Well, off to the races."

"Can you at least tell me who got bumped off?"

"Guess so. I expect it will be in the papers tomorrow anyway. Fellow named Leo Bannister. Shot to death in his own home."

"Good heavens!" I cried, forgetting I wasn't supposed to know anything about anyone named Bannister.

Sam squinted down at me. "Why so shocked? You know the guy?"

Quickly getting my scrambled wits together, I said, "No. No, I've never heard of him. I...well, it's shocking when someone in Pasadena, of all civilized places, gets shot. I mean, people in New York and Chicago shoot each other all the time, but Pasadena?"

"Yeah." Sam continued to stare at me for a second or two. "Daisy, if you know anything at all—"

I held up my hands. "I've never heard of Leo Bannister in my entire life."

Very well, so I finally told a lie.

I called Spike as Sam tootled off, aiming, I expect, for the home of Leo and Lillian Bannister.

Leo Bannister. Who'd just been shot to death.

Unless it was a day-or-two-old crime that had only just been discovered.

Good Lord in heaven, could Lily Bannister be a murderer as well as a victim?

It was a perplexed Daisy Gumm Majesty who walked her dog back up the porch steps and into the family home.

FOURTEEN

I had a hard time getting to sleep that night because I kept shuffling through possible scenarios that might have left Lily Bannister beaten to a pulp and Leo Bannister dead. I wanted to telephone Harold, who was probably awake, but I didn't because I didn't want my family to know I knew anything about the Bannisters, either one of them. Life gets so complicated sometimes.

The following morning, however, after one hysterical telephone call from Mrs. Pinkerton, and after Pa and I had taken Spike for a walk around the neighborhood, Pa went off to gab with some of his friends. Then I picked up the telephone, shooed our party-line neighbors off the wire, and dialed Harold's telephone number.

I'd looked in the *Pasadena Star News* and found no article about a bloody murder, so I didn't know what was going on.

At any rate, Roy answered the telephone. "Mr. Kincaid's residence." I guess he didn't dare say, "Mr. Kincaid and Mr. Farrington's residence," because people would get the wrong idea. Or the right idea. Well, you know what I mean.

"Roy, is Harold around? This is Daisy Majesty, and I need to speak with him if he's available."

"Yes, ma'am, Mrs. Majesty. I'll just go fetch him."

"Thank you, Roy."

"You're welcome, ma'am."

It occurred to me that people spend a whole lot of time on the social amenities. I'm not complaining. The world is a hard enough place, even when lived in with manners.

"What's up, Daisy?" came Harold's rather light voice.

"Sam came to dinner last night, but afterwards he was called to the scene of a murder. Somebody shot Leo Bannister to death."

A shocked pause emanated from the other end of the wire. "*Leo* got shot? Did Lily do it?"

"I don't know. Sam won't talk to me about his cases. I don't even know when the man was killed. He was shot to death in his home. Maybe she shot him after he beat her up. I wouldn't blame her, but I don't suppose it will look good if she did, especially not now that she's disappeared. Well, not disappeared to us, but to everyone else it will look as though she ran off after shooting him. I guess."

"Cripes," said Harold.

"Couldn't have put it any better myself."

"Well, come here for lunch again today. Bring Flossie with you if you want. Fred will be here. Maybe we can get something from Mrs. Bannister, although I doubt it. She's still practically unconscious. Hazel is quite concerned about her."

"That poor woman."

"Yeah. I suppose you have to visit my nutty mother this morning?"

"Yes. I'll come over after that. Thanks, Harold."

"You're welcome. Roy has all your sheets and rags laundered. I do believe he managed to get all the stains out."

"He's a miracle-maker."

"Yeah, he's pretty talented, all right."

We ended on that note, and I went to my bedroom with Spike, where we took a gander at my wardrobe. Because I'd already been outside, I knew the day to be a pleasant one. Therefore, I selected an ivory-colored linen dress with an unfitted bodice. The dress had long sleeves. It wasn't perhaps my most successful effort at dressmaking, but that's because the dress and I were practically the same color. But I wore a brown cloche hat and brown shoes with it and, therefore, didn't totally disappear when I viewed myself in the mirror.

"I don't know, Spike," I muttered to my intelligent hound. "I should have chosen another color of fabric, I suppose, but this was so cheap. A bolt end at Maxime's." Cheapness mattered a whole lot to yours truly, mainly because I felt like a selfish pig for having so many clothes. But I made 'em myself using the least expensive fabrics, thereby justifying my greed. If greed it was.

It was a fairly ghostly Daisy Gumm Majesty who bade her hound a fond farewell and drove up Marengo to Orange Grove Boulevard, turned left, and wound my way to Mrs. Pinkerton's splendid home.

Featherstone evidently didn't find my uniform coloring off-putting. He merely opened the door and said, "Please come this way," as usual.

Mentally bracing myself, I went that way, to the drawing room, where Mrs. Pinkerton sat wilted on the sofa. She didn't hop up and charge at me, but gestured for me to join her. So I did.

We called upon Rolly via the Ouija board, and I dealt a tarot hand that was as full of swords as the last one I'd laid out for the dear woman, and she cried some more. Rolly did suggest she might perhaps take a restful trip up the coast or somewhere, just to get her mind off her problems. I hoped she'd take his suggestion because if she did, I'd be free of her hysterics for a day or two.

"Have you heard anything from Stacy?" I asked during our session.

"Nooooo!" she wept. I guess you can't really weep a word, but she sort of did.

"I'm really sorry, Mrs. Pinkerton. I wish there was something I could do to help you, but—"

"I know. I know. Stacy is *such* an ungrateful child."

Mercy sakes, I'd never heard her say anything the least bit critical of Stacy before this latest episode of hers.

"Yes. She's a very ungrateful child. And she and her new husband stole money from the Salvation Army, too. They took the money from the children's charity fund."

Mrs. Pinkerton gasped and nearly choked to death. When she finally stopped coughing, she whispered, "They did?"

115

I nodded. "They did."

Shaking her head, Mrs. P said, "I don't know what will become of that girl. But wait a moment." She got up from the sofa, walked to the cord hanging from the wall and pulled it. "I'm going to have Featherstone give you some money to take to the Salvation Army."

"I'm sure that's not necessary, Mrs. Pinkerton. You weren't the one who stole the money."

"No, but my child did, and I'm ashamed of her. And me, if you want to know the truth."

Good heavens. "I'm sure you did your best under extremely trying circumstances," said I, thinking that might even be the truth. Mrs. P didn't have much in the way of a backbone, but she did have one great child, in Harold. If the other was a stinker, it might or might not be partially her fault, but I figured Stacy got most of her bad qualities from her bad father.

Featherstone appeared, almost as apparition-like as I, and said, "Yes, ma'am?" Very dignified and correct was Featherstone. I loved the guy.

"Featherstone, please get Edie to fetch my handbag."

"Yes, ma'am." He turned and walked through the doorway to the hall.

In other words, it took two servants to get Mrs. Pinkerton's handbag to her. If I weren't in my spiritualist pose, I'd have shaken my head in wonder. In my world, one fetched one's own handbag if one wanted to get something from it. Even after working for them for so many years, wealthy people still amazed me.

A few minutes later, Edie Applewood, a pal of mine from our school days and now Mrs. Pinkerton's lady's maid, entered the room, dressed in a nice black dress with a crisp white apron. She smiled at me as she carried Mrs. Pinkerton's handbag to her.

"Good morning, Edie."

"Good morning, Daisy."

She gave a tiny curtsey and handed Mrs. P her bag. Mrs. P smiled at her and said, "Thank you, dear."

At least she was nice to her employees. Her awful ex-husband used to pinch Edie's bottom and try to corner her with his wheelchair. Horrid man.

Anyhow, Edie and I stood quietly while Mrs. P dug around in her handbag. When she pulled out a handful of bills, Edie's eyes went round as saucers. I was more accustomed to seeing gobs of money than she, but even I was surprised when Mrs. Pinkerton handed me an inch-thick wad of money.

"Please give this to Captain and Mrs. Buckingham, Daisy. And please tell them how sorry I am that my daughter caused them grief." She sniffled and wiped tears away. If Stacy had been in that room at that moment, I do believe I'd have stabbed her with one of my hatpins.

"I'm sure this is much more than they stole...er, took from the children's charity fund, Mrs. Pinkerton," I told her.

"Nevertheless," said she. "Stacy is my daughter, and what she did is not only criminal but vicious. After all the Salvation Army has done to help her, too." She shook her head. "I can't believe my daughter is so wicked. That Petrie fellow has a lot to answer for."

Ah. I understood it then. She was blaming Petrie for Stacy's stinky behavior. Never mind that he was a recent addition to Stacy's life and she'd always been a rotter. It figured, though. Mrs. Pinkerton had always found excuses for her ghastly daughter, even though this time she had to stretch to achieve one. And she'd said she was ashamed of Stacy, so that was a step in the right direction.

Or not. It was difficult to tell about these things, life being the muddled mess it is.

Edie executed another graceful curtsey, retrieved Mrs. Pinkerton's handbag from her and retreated to the upper reaches of the Pinkerton mansion. I gave her a finger wave, and she grinned back at me.

Mrs. Pinkerton sighed. "Edie is such a treasure, Daisy. Of course, you're my mainstay through all my travails."

Her travails. Hmm. Well, why not? I sat back down in my chair and asked, "Mrs. Pinkerton, do you know a couple named Bannister?"

"Leo and Lily? Yes, I do, although not at all well. I have to admit I don't much care for Leo." She lowered her voice, even though we were the only two people in the room. "I think he bullies Lily sometimes. He's a hard man and quite rude."

"I understand he was murdered. Shot to death."

117

"Good heavens!" Mrs. P was as shocked as I'd ever seen her. "When did it happen? Who did it? Why? Oh, my goodness, Lily didn't finally snap and shoot the beastly fellow, did she?"

"I don't know. I only know he was killed because Detective Rotondo dined with us last night, and the police station called him to the scene of the crime. I barely got the name of the dead man out of him, he's so closed-mouthed about police investigations."

Mrs. P sat forward on the sofa, her expression avid. "Was he killed at home? Was he doing something he oughtn't? Oh, poor Lily! I know what it's like to be married to a bully. I've always thought she deserved better than Leo, but did she kill him? He probably deserved it, but still, I just don't know if murder is the answer."

"No, I don't, either. As far as I know, the police don't have any suspects yet."

"My goodness."

"Did they have any children?"

"I don't believe so. Oh, poor Lily. I wish I knew her better. I should probably visit her or something. Or telephone, at least. "

She could do either or both of those things, but she wouldn't get to talk to Lily Bannister. I began to feel the least little bit of niggling panic as I considered Lily Bannister. I hope she hadn't killed her awful husband, but if she had and Harold, Flossie, Fred, Hazel and I were hiding her, would we be in trouble with the police? I had a sinking sensation the answer to that question was yes. Oh, dear.

"Well, Mrs. Pinkerton, I'd better be on my way. I'm sure you'll telephone me if you hear from Stacy, won't you? I believe the police will want to talk to Mr. Petrie about the money he stole from the Salvation Army."

"Of course, I'll telephone you, dear. Stealing from a church! How low can a person sink? Even if it was the Salvation Army, theft is a crime and a sin."

Even if it was the Salvation Army? I sighed. "Indeed, theft is definitely a crime and a sin. I suspect Captain Buckingham has called the police about the theft."

"I hope the police find him."

"And Stacy," I said for the heck of it.

Tears began to leak from Mrs. P's eyes. "Yes. And Stacy. Oh, Daisy, I do hope she didn't know about the theft of that money. I know she's been in trouble before, but I never thought she'd sink so low as to steal from the people who were trying to help her."

"I fear that sort of thing happens more than we like to think about," I said, wondering if that were true.

"I suppose it might," said Mrs. P on a sigh. She gave a last swipe of her leaky eyes with her damp handkerchief, rose from the sofa, and embraced me. Fortunately, she released me before I smothered. She was *much* larger than I. After she let me go, she sat back on the sofa. "Thank you again, Daisy. I don't know what I'd do without you."

I shook her hand. It was a trifle moist but oh, well. "You're too kind, Mrs. Pinkerton," I said, thinking she'd be totally lost without me. And I'm not bragging. Mrs. P, for all her wealth and connections with the finest elements in our fair city, was innocent as a lamb when it came to the so-called "real" world. "I think I'll just pop down to say good day to Aunt Vi before I leave."

"Your whole family is heaven-sent, dear. Your aunt is the best cook in the entire city of Pasadena. We're so fortunate to have her."

"Yes, she is, and we're fortunate to have her, too," I said.

Mrs. P actually gave a short laugh at that. "You must eat well at your house, dear."

"Thanks to Aunt Vi, we do."

She gave another wistful sigh. "I suppose that when you and Harold marry, you'll give up your career and live in his house. It's beautiful, but I wish the two of you would choose to live here."

What? "Um...Harold hasn't asked me to marry him, Mrs. Pinkerton. We're very good friends, but..." My voice trailed off, since I didn't know what else to say.

"Oh, but you're so perfect for each other," she said, clasping her hands to her ample bosom.

"I'm very fond of Harold," I said as noncommittally as I could. "But I really must go now."

And with that, I stuffed the wad of bills into my own handbag, picked up my other prettily embroidered bag that held my Ouija board and the tarot cards, left the drawing room and headed to the kitchen.

When I pushed open the swing doors to the kitchen, Aunt Vi had on one of the lovely aprons I'd made for her, and she was punching the heck out of some dough in a bowl. "I bet you have strong arms from doing that," I said to her back.

She didn't seem surprised at my entry into her domain. She turned, smiled, and said, "I do, so you'd better watch yourself, young lady." Sobering, she said, "I hope you were able to offer Mrs. Pinkerton some solace. She's been in a state ever since that ghastly daughter of hers ran off with that ghastly man."

"I did my best," said I with a sigh. "Just thought I'd pop in for a minute. Mrs. P gave me money to take to Flossie and Johnny, to make up for the money Stacy and her husband—"

"If that's what he is," said Aunt Vi with a stringent sniff. "For all we know they just ran away together like a couple of naughty children and are living together in sin. Only neither one of them is a child."

"That's true. Anyway, I hope your day is going well. I'm heading to the Salvation Army now to drop off all the dough Mrs. P gave me before I suffer a brain wave and spend it all on frivolities."

"Get along with you, Daisy!" said Aunt Vi, giving me one of her pat phrases. I'm still not quite sure what it means. "You'd never do anything underhanded, and you know it."

I thought about Lily Bannister hidden away in the west wing of Harold's second story and wondered about my aunt's good opinion of me.

"Say, Aunt Vi, have you ever heard of someone named Leo Bannister?"

She stopped punishing her dough, patted it into a ball, left it in the bowl, and covered the bowl with a damp towel, pondering my question as she did so. "Bannister. Bannister. I do believe I've heard the name. Why do you ask?"

"He was the subject of the call Sam got at our house last night. Somebody named Leo Bannister got shot to death. Just wondered if you knew anything about him."

"Mercy sakes! What an awful thing to happen."

Once more I pictured Lily Bannister, but I said, "Yes, indeed," anyway. "Do you know them or anyone who works for them, Vi?"

"Them? Was the man married?"

"I believe so. I think his wife's name is Lillian or Lily or something like that."

Heading to the sink to wash the dough and flour off her hands, Vi muttered, "Bannister. Lillian. Pretty name. I don't...Wait! I know their cook! Evelyn McCracken has cooked for them for some time." Vi turned to stare at me. "Goodness gracious, Evelyn said that man used to abuse his wife regularly. I believe he even hit her a time or two. A virtual tiger, that man was. I hope his wife didn't shoot him, but I wouldn't blame her if she did. If he hit her, I mean. That's just cruel."

"My goodness. He beat her, eh? Terrible. I'm so glad our family isn't like that."

"I am, too. Your uncle Ernest used to drink some, but he was a good man, and he never hit me."

"I know, Vi. I loved Uncle Ernie. And Paul." Ernest and Paul were Vi's late husband and her late son, who was another victim of the Kaiser's insanity. Only Paul died on the field. He didn't linger like my Billy did. Not that it matters, I suppose; they're both still dead.

"Yes." Vi heaved a huge sigh and dried her hands on another towel hanging on a rack beside the sink. "Well, I don't know any more than that. I hope his wife didn't kill him, but I'm glad for her sake he's dead. Men like that...I just don't know."

"I don't, either."

Vi was still shaking her head sadly as I left the kitchen via the service entrance and walked around to the front to retrieve our Chevrolet.

FIFTEEN

It didn't take long to get to the Salvation Army, which sat on the corner of Walnut Street and Fair Oaks Avenue. I was glad I had a genuine reason to visit, because, while I was happy Mrs. Pinkerton was assuaging the damage her daughter had done to the church's coffers, I was even happier to know I'd get to see Flossie and tell her the dire news about Leo Bannister.

Flossie and Johnny lived in a little house in back of the church itself, so I walked to their front door and knocked. Flossie, her cheeks pink with heat, came to the door wearing a pretty apron she'd made herself. I wasn't the only seamstress in town.

"Daisy! How nice to see you." Flossie grabbed my arm and yanked me into the house. In a whisper, she asked, "Have you heard anything about Mrs. Bannister's condition?"

"Not much. Harold told me she's not doing very well, and he asked the both of us to come to lunch today."

"Oh, dear. I can't make it today. I'm busy baking cookies for fellowship after this coming Sunday's service. But you're going to see her, aren't you? I do hope the poor woman survives."

"I do, too. But Flossie, I need to tell you something else." I remembered the money in my purse and said, "Two things, actually."

"Oh? Come to the kitchen with me. You can help me form the dough into balls."

"You trust me in your kitchen? You're a brave woman, Flossie Buckingham."

She only laughed, even though she knew all about my kitchen catastrophes.

"Before I touch your dough, I have some dough Mrs. Pinkerton gave me to make up for what her daughter and Mr. Petrie stole from the children's charity fund."

Flossie swirled around, her hands to her cheeks. "She did *what?*"

"You heard me. Here." I reached into my purse, which I'd set on the kitchen table and pulled out the thick wad of money.

Flossie's eyes went as round as pie plates. "Good Lord, how much is in that bundle?"

"I don't know. But I'll count it now."

And I did. After I finished counting the mazuma, it turned out Mrs. Pinkerton had donated the lofty sum of five hundred dollars to the Salvation Army's children's charity fund. Even my mind boggled as I looked up at Flossie, still holding the last bill in my hand.

As for Flossie, she sort of sank into a kitchen chair, as if not quite believing what she was seeing and hearing. She whispered, "Five hundred dollars? But that's...that's...that's far too much. I think the children's charity fund contained about forty-seven dollars when those two ran off with it."

"Don't be silly, Flossie. I know you and Johnny can use the money. Refill the children's charity fund, and use the rest for whatever good purposes you want to. I have a feeling Johnny can use all the money he can collect."

"Yes," said Flossie, still dazed. "Yes, he can. He's such a good man, Daisy. I don't deserve him at all."

"Stop that!" I told her firmly. "You're a wonderful wife and mother, and you're precisely the right woman for Johnny. You and he have both been to hell and survived. This money is a mere drop in the bucket."

"No. No, it isn't. There's nothing mere about it." She hopped up from her chair. "Oh, but I must fetch Johnny. He'll be so thrilled!"

"Wait a second, Flossie," I said, catching her flying apron as she sped to the door. "There's something else I need to tell you."

She turned. "Oh?"

"Yes. Um, you'd better sit down for this one, too."

Looking nervous, Flossie sat in the chair she'd just vacated. "What is it?"

"Leo Bannister is dead. Murdered. Shot to death."

Flossie's mouth dropped open. Then she covered it with one of her hands. Then she said, "Oh, my Lord."

"Something like that."

"Did...did Mrs. Bannister do it?"

"As far as I can tell, nobody knows," I said, shaking my head. "Sam came to dinner last night, and he got a 'phone call from the police department. He wasn't going to tell me what it was about, but he finally did. He said Leo Bannister had been shot to death. I'm afraid it's going to look bad for Mrs. Bannister, since, except for a few of us, nobody knows where she is."

"Whatever should we do?"

"I wish I knew. I'm going to Harold's today, as I told you. Maybe he and Fred and I can figure out something. I hope she didn't do it."

"If she did, it was in self-defense, I'm sure," said Flossie. "That man would have ended up murdering her if somebody hadn't knocked him off before he had the chance."

"I agree. I'm not sure the police department will see it our way, though."

She heaved a deep and heartfelt sigh just as Johnny walked through the kitchen door, holding the Buckinghams' son, Billy, in his arms.

"Daisy! How nice to see you." His gaze, after paying a loving visit to his wife, got stuck on the pile of money on the table. "Good heavens, where did that come from?"

"Daisy brought it," said Flossie. "She said Mrs. Pinkerton gave it to her to give to us, to make up for the money Stacy and Mr. Petrie stole."

"Good Lord," said Johnny, a little more faintly.

"Yes, indeed," said I, rising. "But I can't linger. I need to visit..." My mind stalled for a moment. To hide my confusion, I chucked little Billy under the chin. He giggled and trapped my finger against his cheek and chest. By the time we'd all stopped laughing, I'd made up a new lie. "I have to visit another client. I just came from Mrs. Pinkerton's. She still hasn't heard from Stacy."

"I don't care if anyone ever hears from Stacy again," said Flossie, her voice flinty.

"Now, now, Floss. She is what she is. I had hopes for her once, but I'm not so sure anymore."

"You're a better person than I am, Johnny Buckingham," said I. "I've loathed the woman for as long as I've known her. It's a good thing I'm a fake spiritualist instead of a minister, because I'd be a total flop at forgiveness."

"You're a gem, Daisy," said Johnny, giving me a quick peck on the cheek.

"You truly are," said Flossie, rising from her chair and giving me a hug. Because Flossie and I were relatively the same size, her hug didn't threaten to suffocate me. As she hugged me, she whispered, "Please tell me whatever you find out, will you?"

"Absolutely," I whispered back. Then I tickled Billy's tummy, which made all of us giggle, and I took my leave.

The drive to Harold's house took me from the west side of Pasadena to the east side, and then down Allen Avenue into San Marino. Orange Grove Boulevard might have been Millionaire's Row, but it couldn't stick up its nose at San Marino, which was full of wealthy people and huge, glorious mansions. Flowers bloomed everywhere, the day was lovely, and I enjoyed the ride.

Then I got to Harold's place and things went downhill from there.

Roy admitted me to the house. "Good morning, Mrs. Majesty."

"Good morning, Roy."

"Mr. Harold and Dr. Greenlaw are in the family room. Just follow me, please."

I wondered if Roy had been taking lessons from Featherstone. But no. Featherstone never offered grins when he opened the great doors at the Pinkerton Palace. Very stiff and proper was Featherstone. I had a feeling Roy liked a good time when he could have one.

Sure enough, Harold and Fred were huddled on two fancy chairs in the family room, discussing, unless I missed my guess, the Bannisters. Harold saw me first, leapt to his feet and charged me, not unlike what his mother did most of the time. Fortunately for me, Harold stopped before he could run me down.

"My dear Mrs. Majesty," said Harold, eyeing me critically. "How perfectly...bland you look today."

"I'm supposed to look spiritualistic, Harold Kincaid. I know, I should have chosen another color, but this was so cheap. Bolt end at Maxime's."

"I see. Well, even though you're nearly invisible, your frock is perfectly tailored."

"Thanks, Harold."

"But Daisy, what the hell are we supposed to do now? Sit anywhere." Harold gestured at the room.

I took a seat next to the ones Harold and Fred occupied. Fred had stood upon my arrival, and we shook hands politely. "How should I know?" I said, answering Harold's question with my own. "Is Mrs. Bannister conscious yet?"

"Not fully," said Fred. "I honestly don't know if she's going to be able to survive this latest attack without significant brain damage. Even if she does, she most likely won't remember the incident. And now the police will probably believe she killed her husband and ran away after committing the crime."

"That's what I'm worried about, too."

"Can you find out from Sam when the man was killed?" said Harold. "If his death occurred after you brought Mrs. Bannister here, that would let her off the hook."

"I don't know," I said upon a sigh. "Sam doesn't like discussing his cases with me."

"Too bad," said Fred. "I might be able to find out the time of his death through medical channels, but I don't want people to think I know anything about either one of the Bannisters."

"It's a problem, all right. I feel like a low-down sneak for keeping Lily's whereabouts from my family and Sam. But until we know more about Mr. Bannister's murder, I'm not sure what to do. If he was murdered after she ran away from him, there won't be any reason to keep her hidden. She'll be a widow, and can live safely from him from now on."

"I hope she didn't kill him," said Harold. "Even though he needed killing."

"You sound like a character out of a dime novel, Harold Kincaid," I said.

"I only spoke the truth."

"You're right." I agreed.

We all sat there, looking at each other, and I suspect we all felt helpless. I know I did. After a moment or two of that, Harold sighed and said, "Well, Daisy, I think it would be good for you to see Mrs. Bannister before we dine. She might be more comfortable with a strange woman than with strange men."

"Are you calling me strange, Harold Kincaid?"

It was a dumb joke, but we all laughed. Truth to tell, I didn't much want to see Mrs. Bannister. Even to look at her hurt. I can't even imagine what she continued to go through, pain-wise.

But I wasn't a total coward, so I walked upstairs with Harold and Fred, and when Hazel opened the sickroom door, we all walked silently (because of the thick carpet) to Lily Bannister's bed. I took one look at her face and shut my eyes. It didn't look any better today than it had the day before. If anything, the bruises were turning even more virulent colors. How could a man do that to someone he was supposed to love? Never mind. I don't expect an answer.

Leaning over the bed, Fred said, "Mrs. Bannister?"

The lump on the bed moaned a little, and one of her eyes blobs opened slightly. She said, "Uhhh."

Trying again, valiantly, I thought, Fred said, "When you left your house, was your husband still there?"

Another, "Uhhh," answered that question.

After a small sigh, Fred stood and asked his sister in a quiet voice, "Has she said anything, Hazel?"

"No. She's opened her eyes a couple of times, but I don't think she even knows where she is."

"That makes sense. She was unconscious when Daisy brought her here," said Harold.

"Yes," said Hazel. "But what I meant was, I don't think she even knows she's anywhere. If you know what I mean."

I did. That poor woman.

"Let me know if she looks to be in pain or if she says anything, please," Fred said to his sister.

"Oh, for pity's sake, of course I'll do that, Fred. I'm a trained nurse, you know." Hazel grinned as she said it, so I guess this was some kind of long-running conversation between the siblings.

"I know. I know," said Fred, grinning back at her.

Thank the good Lord, we left the room then. I'd make a terrible nurse. I can't even stand to *look* at injuries like those Mrs. Bannister had sustained, much less touch and tend to them. I guess we all have our gifts. Mine wasn't nursing. Or cooking. Or lots of other things, too, actually. In fact, I felt pretty useless as Harold led us to his breakfast room for luncheon.

That day's spread was as good as the one the day before. Roy regaled us each with a green salad, a chopped beef patty smothered in sautéed onions (I'm using the word sautéed rather than fried, because Harold is so much classier than I), roasted potatoes, and a tapioca pudding for dessert. For Daisy Gumm Majesty, whose daily luncheon generally consisted of an orange and a peanut-butter sandwich, this was gourmet dining at its best.

The only lighthearted moment during the meal came when I told Harold, "By the way, when we get married, your mother wants us to live with her."

Poor Harold almost choked to death, but we all laughed after he finally caught his breath.

By the time the meal was over and we'd retired to the family room to discuss Mrs. Bannister's problems and whether or not she might have killed her husband, I left, none the wiser about anything at all. Fiddlesticks. If the police department ever hired women, I might just apply so I could be on the inside of these bothersome investigations.

Or perhaps not. I wouldn't make as much money as a police woman as I would as a spiritualist-medium. Probably. I don't really know, but since women make about half as much as men make, even when they do the same jobs, I expect that would be the case.

More fiddlesticks. And applesauce, too.

On the other hand, I did receive a nicely laundered piles of sheets, aprons, rags, and so forth from Roy, whom I thanked, and another package of sheets from Dr. Greenlaw. I thanked him, too. Life isn't all bad. Usually.

SIXTEEN

Sam didn't come to dinner at our home that night, probably because he was knee-deep in the Bannister case, so I left the house for choir practice with no more information than I'd had when the day began. Such a state was quite frustrating to a person who likes to be in the know about what was going on around her.

Nevertheless, my knowing-nothingness couldn't be helped, so I tried to be pleasant when I opened the door to the choir room at seven o'clock. Lucille Zollinger, a soprano who had been Lucille Spinks until a little earlier in the year, must have been on the lookout for me, because as soon as I stepped into the room, she was on me like a fly on a dead rat. That sounds awful. Sorry.

"Hey, Lucy, what's up?" I asked her, not suppressing my surprise at her avidity.

She grabbed my shoulder. "Oh, Daisy! Have you heard? There's been a *murder* in town!"

As there had been a murder and a half in our very own church a couple of months earlier, I didn't know why Lucy was so excited about one that had nothing to do with the church. Unless...

"Mercy sakes! Who was killed?"

"A man named Leo Bannister."

Great. Just great. "Where did it happen?" I asked, wondering if someone was going around my fair city, bumping off its citizens.

Lucy wrinkled her brow. "What do you mean 'where did it happen?'"

"Well, I mean, was the murderee run over or knifed in the back as he left his club or—?"

"Oh, I see. It happened in the very home of Mr. and Mrs. Bannister, and Mr. Bannister was shot! With a *gun*!"

What else could he have been shot with? I suppose someone might have shot him using a bow and arrow, but...Oh, dear. I started toward the closet where our choir robes were stored and where we hung our coats and sweaters on Thursday evenings. "My goodness. I don't believe I know either one of them, but I'm sorry about the murder."

Lucy sniffed. "You wouldn't be if you'd ever met Mr. Bannister. I don't know how his wife managed to stay with him for so long. If I'd been she, I'd have shot him years ago. Well, I wouldn't have, because I don't have a gun and I would never marry such a horrible man, but...Oh, you know what I mean."

"He was a stinker, was he? How so?" As Lucy began to tell me, I pulled my coat over my head, so I said a muffled, "Wait a minute. I can't hear you." When I finally got the coat on the hanger, my dress had risen slightly. With a tug, it fell back into place and I started smoothing it down. "Very well, why was Mr. Bannister so awful?"

Lucy spoke in a titillated whisper. "Oh, Daisy, they say he used to beat poor Lillian! And there was some sort of scandal having to do with him and Dr. Greenlaw's daughter."

"Dr. Greenlaw has a daughter?" I asked, confused.

"Yes."

"But I thought Dr. Greenlaw was a youngish man. He couldn't have a daughter—" I stopped speaking suddenly, realizing that if I used Hazel's name, Lucy might guess I knew more than I wanted her to think I knew.

"Oh, *that* Dr. Greenlaw." Lucy laughed. "No. Not him. Dr. Greenlaw's a doctor, and his son is a doctor, too."

Her explanation wasn't broad, but I got the picture. "Ah. I see. So the

Dr. Greenlaw I met is following family tradition by going into medicine or something like that."

"Yes, and Hazel, the one in the scandal, is his sister, and she's a nurse."

"I see. That makes sense, although I'm sorry about the scandal."

"But you've met the younger Dr. Greenlaw?" asked Lucy, sticking to me like glue as we picked up our music books and headed for the chancel where our choir sat in a place set off for it. Lucy and I always sat together in the front row mainly because, while Lucy is a soprano and I'm an alto, we were often asked to sing duets. Which, I might add, we did very well. "I hear he's awfully handsome. I almost wish our family doctor wasn't Dr. Benjamin, or I might go to the younger Dr. Greenlaw." She blushed crimson and said, "I don't mean that. I adore Mr. Zollinger. I only meant—"

Giving Lucy a sympathetic smile—I personally all but swooned over Rudolph Valentino—I said, "I understand what you meant, and yes, he's very handsome. But tell me about this scandal. What kind of scandal?"

"Umm...I'm not altogether sure. It was several years ago, and my parents wouldn't talk about it in front of me. I gather Mr. Bannister tried to do something...indelicate to Miss Greenlaw."

Indelicate, eh? I'd just bet it was indelicate. I pretended dismay. Actually, it wasn't much of a pretense. As the hours passed, I was more and more pleased that Leo Bannister was no longer alive to plague the earth and its occupants. I still hoped his wife didn't kill him, though.

Lucy and I sat in our places, and I leaned over and whispered, "So who killed him?"

"Nobody knows, precisely, but everyone thinks his wife did it."

Wonderful. "Ah. So has his wife...I mean his widow, been arrested? Was it in self-defense?"

"Nobody knows," said Lucy, clearly enjoying telling this tale. "They can't *find* her! Oh, Daisy, I hope someone didn't kill him and kidnap her."

I blinked. "Um, yes, that would be awful. But how do you know all this, Lucy? I didn't see anything about a murder in the paper this morning."

"It's in the evening *Herald*," said she. "I read all about it before I came to choir practice tonight."

Nuts. I could have picked up the Gumm-Majesty copy of the *Pasadena Evening Herald* before I'd come to choir practice, too. But had I? No. Stupid Daisy Gumm Majesty. Oh, well, I could read about it after I got home.

Our choir director, Mr. Floy Hostetter, called us to attention at that moment, so Lucy and I could no longer gossip. Piffle.

However, our Sunday anthem, now that Easter was over and we could be joyful again, was "O Happy Day that Fixed My Choice," which was lively and pretty and even rather bouncy. During the Lenten season, hymns could get downright dismal, but after Easter Sunday, we got happy again. Makes sense.

We sang the hymn once through, and Mr. Hostetter frowned. I wondered what we'd done wrong, since I thought we'd sounded pretty good.

"You sang that very well, ladies and gentlemen," said Mr. Hostetter, relieving me somewhat. "However, the tune is simple, and even though we sing verse two as a round, it gets a trifle boring. Perhaps we could break up the monotony if you, Mrs. Fleming," he said, squinting at the organist, "could improvise a little melody between verses two and three?"

Mrs. Fleming, a lovely middle-aged woman with gorgeously marcelled gray hair, said, "There's no need for me to improvise. I have the music at home, and the version I have has a charming little interval that I can play between verses two and three."

"Excellent. And then," said Mr. Hostetter, fixing his gaze upon his choir members once more, "perhaps Mrs. Majesty and Mrs. Zollinger will sing the fourth verse as a duet."

Lucy and I looked at each other and grinned. "Happy to," I said.

"Excellent," Mr. Hostetter said again. "Then let's sing it again, with those two little changes."

So we did, and we sounded great. Lucy and I might not be opera-quality singers when we each sang alone, but together our voices blended beautifully. After that, we went over the upcoming Sunday's hymns —"Lead, Kindly Light," "Come, Ye Faithful, Raise the Strain," and

"Fairest Lord Jesus." Then we attempted the next Sunday's anthem, "Love Divine, All Loves Excelling," which is one of my favorites. I regret to say that I select as my favorites the hymns that have the prettiest tunes. I think that's not awfully pious of me, but there you go.

As we prepared to leave the church at nine p.m., Lucy again sidled up to me. "Oh, Daisy, do you think Detective Rotondo will be investigating the Bannister case?"

Indeed, I did. Rather than saying so, I said, "I'm not sure. I can ask him the next time I see him, but he doesn't like talking to me about his cases."

"Oh." Lucy looked disappointed. "That's too bad."

"I think so too." Which was the absolute truth.

I was happy to see Sam's big old Hudson parked on the street in front of our house when I drove home from church that Thursday. I rushed up the steps, opened the side door, and instantly had to kneel down to address my hound. Spike was pretty much the joy of my life, so I always paid attention to him because he deserved it. When Billy died, I think I might have faded away entirely if it weren't for Spike and Harold. And Sam, I guess.

"How was choir practice?" Pa asked.

He and Sam sat at the dining-room table. Pa smiled at me. Sam, as was his custom, frowned. Lest you get the wrong impression of Sam, he really wasn't a big old grump, although he was big. I think his job had hardened him some, and he saved his smiles and laughs for special occasions. As he and I were secretly engaged, I considered any evening when we were together a special occasion, so I frowned back at him.

"Choir practice was nice," I said to my father. "Lucy and I are singing a duet in the fourth verse of 'O Happy Day that Fixed My Choice.'"

Sam's frown deepened. "I've never even heard of that one."

"If you come to church with us on Sunday, you'll get to hear it. It's kind of old, I think. Sounds...I don't know...folksy, if you know what I mean," I said, rising to my feet with a little grunt. I kept telling myself that I needed to exercise more, but so far I hadn't responded to the demand with action.

"Folksy, eh? I hope I'll be able to go to church with you," said Sam, grumbling slightly. "What with this murder investigation on...Well, we'll have to wait and see."

"Have you told Pa about Mr. Bannister?" I asked my beloved (I'm talking about Sam here), taking a chair beside him at the table.

"Yes. Evidently your family didn't know the Bannisters."

"I told you that. Never heard of 'em," I said, which had been true until a couple of days prior.

"I've never heard of them, either," said Pa.

Sam said, "Hmm," which was typical.

"Mrs. Pinkerton knows them slightly, though, and she said Mr. Bannister was cruel to his wife."

Sam said, "Huh."

"That's not very nice," said Pa.

"I agree," said I. "Do they know who killed him yet?" I asked, and instantly held my breath.

"His wife," said Sam.

"Oh." Darn. "Have you guys arrested her?"

"Can't."

"Why not?"

"She's disappeared."

"Then how do you know she killed him?"

I thought it was a good question, but Sam said, "When a husband or wife is murdered, it's usually the mate who turns out to be the murderer. True love, and all that."

"You're cynical, Sam. What if somebody murdered him and kidnapped her?" I silently thanked Lucy Zollinger for this plot point.

With a shrug, he said, "Unlikely. She's gone, and there's no evidence of a struggle."

No evidence of a *struggle*? Was he telling me there was no evidence that Leo Bannister had battered his wife nearly to death two days ago? There had to have been blood everywhere. "Would you expect a struggle?" I asked, feeling unable to ask what I wanted, which was, did they find blood from poor Mrs. Bannister anywhere.

"Yes, if someone is kidnapped, there's usually a struggle."

"So..." I didn't know what to ask next. Then I recalled the *Pasadena*

Herald. "Lucy Zollinger said she read that Mr. Bannister had been shot to death. Did you find a gun? Maybe he committed suicide."

"No gun," said Sam succinctly.

"Did his wife own a gun? I mean, does anyone know if she did?"

"Nope."

Darn the man! "I wish you'd use more than one or two syllables, Sam Rotondo! When was he killed? Does anyone know that yet?"

"Won't know that until after the autopsy. There, that was several syllables." He smiled at me.

"You drive me nuts, Sam Rotondo."

Pa laughed.

"Sorry. Can't talk about my cases," said Sam, still smiling.

"Lucy and Mrs. Pinkerton both said there are rumors that Mr. Bannister used to beat up Mrs. Bannister, and that Mr. Bannister did awful things to little girls."

"Yeah?" Sam appeared interested.

"That's what Lucy said. She said Mr. Bannister interfered with Dr. Greenlaw's daughter."

"Is that the Dr. Greenlaw who came here the other day?" asked Pa in all innocence.

Blast! "No, my Dr. Greenlaw is that Dr. Greenlaw's son."

"Oh?" said Sam, his smile gone. "You know the younger Dr. Greenlaw, do you? He's *your* Dr. Greenlaw, is he?"

"Well, not to say *know*," said I, wishing I were somewhere else. Preferably Turkey. I'd enjoyed Turkey except when I was sick, which was most of the time I was there.

"But he came here?" Sam persisted.

"Yes, but only for a minute. Then we all—that's Flossie, Harold, Dr. Greenlaw and I—went for a little spin."

"In our Chevrolet," Pa added, unnecessarily in my considered opinion.

"I see," said Sam as though he'd already put the worst interpretation possible on my meeting with Dr. Greenlaw. If he only knew. If they'd ever find out when Mr. Bannister died, maybe I could tell him.

I decided to change the subject a little bit. "So, when will you know when Mr. Bannister died?" I asked. "And do you think Percival Petrie might have anything to do with his demise? I mean, he's a certified crook, and according to Miss Petrie, he's killed people before. He'd probably be more likely to kill someone than poor Mrs. Bannister."

"Poor Mrs. Bannister?" said Sam, raising one of his bushy eyebrows.

I don't know how he managed to lift one brow like that, but I wish he couldn't, because when he did it I became nervous. "Well, I mean if her husband beat her and interfered with little girls, I do feel sorry for her."

"Tell me where she is, and maybe I'll feel sorry for her, too," said Sam in an insinuating tone of voice.

Frustrated and peeved, I said, "I don't even *know* the woman! How should I know where she is?"

"Huh."

"Well? What about Petrie? Are you looking for him? He stole money from a church, for pity's sake!"

"We took a report from Captain Buckingham. The children's charity fund had in it a little less than fifty dollars. That's considered petty theft, and the department doesn't have enough officers to hunt down every petty thief in Pasadena."

"There are that many of them?" In my fair city? I didn't approve.

"I'm afraid so."

"But aren't you considering Petrie for something else? Isn't that what you told me a few days ago?"

"I can't talk about my cases, Daisy."

"You are the most frustrating man in the entire universe, Sam Rotondo!"

He grinned again, the fiend. "It's the nature of my job. Sorry."

"Nerts."

Pa laughed. "I'm going to bed. Don't you two come to blows now, you hear?"

"I'll make sure we don't," said Sam, and he laughed, too.

What the heck, I laughed along with them, and Spike and I walked out to Sam's car with him.

SEVENTEEN

"So," said Sam as we stood beside his Hudson. "Precisely who is this Dr. Greenlaw who visited you the other day?"

"He didn't visit me. He visited Harold, because Harold called him and asked him to come over."

The way Sam cocked his head and peered down at me didn't fill me with optimism. "Perhaps you could explain that a little more clearly?"

How did I get myself into these pickles? I decided maybe sticking kind of close to the truth might work. "Flossie came to my house, worried and terribly upset. A woman had come to the Salvation Army, begging them to help her because she'd been nearly beaten to death by her husband—that's why I wondered about Mr. Bannister beating Mrs. Bannister—and she was afraid to go to the hospital for fear her husband would find her. So, since I couldn't think of anything else to do, I called Harold."

"Why Harold?" asked Sam. Reasonably, blast it. "Why not a doctor? Shoot, the Buckinghams could have called a doctor for her."

"I know that, but Flossie said the woman was afraid if she went to a regular doctor or to the hospital, her husband would track her down, and Johnny said he couldn't keep the woman from her husband, because that would be against the law."

"Smart fellow, Buckingham."

"Yes, he is. And he's nice. It hurt him that he couldn't hide the woman."

"And how does Dr. Greenlaw fit into this scenario?"

"Harold 'phoned him, and he came over to discuss the beaten woman with Flossie."

"Huh."

"Oh, stop saying 'huh' all the time!" I said, tired and cranky.

"Even you have to admit the story's a little thin, Daisy."

"I can't help it. It's the truth."

He eyed me for a moment, then said, "If you say so." Then he bent and kissed me. I kissed him back, but without much enthusiasm. I was extremely tired by that time. The day had been stressful, and I suddenly realized I hadn't opened the package Dr. Greenlaw had handed me as I left Harold's house.

Before he shut the door to his machine, I decided what the heck and said, "I love you, Sam, even if you do keep everything from me."

"I love you, too," he said in a not-very-lover-like voice. "And one of these days we'll have to discuss who keeps what from whom."

And with that he tootled on down the road. It bothered me to admit it, but he was right. I was at present keeping a whole lot of things from Sam Rotondo.

When I opened the packet of new sheets given to me by Dr. Green-law, I wasn't sure what to do with them. They were much too fancy for the Gumms and the one Majesty residing at our little bungalow on South Marengo Avenue.

Ultimately I decided to save them until July and then pretend I'd bought them for the family as something "special." I swear, I was getting better and better at lying as the days passed. That probably wasn't a good thing.

Friday morning dawned clear and fresh and quite lovely. Pasadena is a beautiful city. Heck, even our street, Marengo Avenue, is gorgeous. Lined on both sides by pepper trees, the branches of which nearly formed a canopy spanning the street, Marengo was a happy place to live. Until your life was interrupted by brutality.

Darn Leo Bannister to perdition. And he could take Stacy Kincaid and Percival Petrie with him.

But never mind that. Spike and I rose at about seven a.m., as usual. I stuffed my feet into my old slippers, opened the back door so that Spike could do his duty as a dog, paid a visit to the bathroom, and meandered into the kitchen. I was surprised to see Vi there, as she generally had already started her trek to Colorado Boulevard to catch the bus to the Pinkertons' place. I was overjoyed to see her. Anywhere Vi was, food was, and it was invariably delicious.

"Good morning, Vi!" I said, walking over to the stove and giving her a little kiss on her cheek. "Why are you here so late?"

"Good morning, Daisy. I'm not going to work today." She preened a little.

"*What*? Did Mrs. Pinkerton finally faint to death or something?"

"Daisy!" But she giggled. "No. She paid me a visit late in the afternoon yesterday."

"She came into your *kitchen*?" I asked, astonished.

"She visits me quite often to discuss menus and whatever."

"I'm surprised she doesn't order you to see her."

"She doesn't order anyone to do anything. You should know that by this time, Daisy. She claims she likes our little chats. I'll make a pot of tea, and we'll plan out the next day's menu. Or the next dinner party, or whatever she wants."

"Interesting."

"I don't know what's so interesting about it. Anyway, she paid me a visit yesterday afternoon and said she was going to take Rolly's advice that she get away for a few days, so I won't have to go to work there again until Monday."

"Mercy sakes. I don't think she's ever taken Rolly's advice before." I thought about that. "Well, maybe once or twice." I took an orange out of the bowl filled with same that always resided on the kitchen table. We had both a navel and a Valencia orange tree in our yard, and this was the season for the Valencias. They weren't as easy to peel as the navels, and they had seeds, but they sure tasted good. I commenced peeling it as Spike gazed at me longingly from the floor. "You don't like oranges," I told him.

His sad brown eyes told me he didn't believe me.

"Anyhow, she said she wanted to pay a visit to Father Fredrick. Then she said she's going to have Jackson take her and Mr. Pinkerton up the coast, just to contemplate things and get away from the stress and strain of her life." Vi's gaze paid a visit to the ceiling, a gesture I'd never seen before from her.

"Well, she's got a stressful daughter," I said in mitigation of Mrs. Pinkerton's nervous problems. Even if she did have all the money in the world. I'd heard all my life that money couldn't buy happiness. I'm sure that's true, but I'd a heck of a lot rather be melancholy and depressed in, say, Tahiti, or somewhere else exotic than in my little rut in Pasadena. Not that I didn't love my city, my home, my family and my rut, but I'm sure you understand. "I'm glad you get a day off. Although you're not taking very good advantage of it. You're standing over our stove instead of hers."

"Indeed, but I can go lie down and read a book afterwards if I want to."

"Sounds like heaven to me. Whatever you're fixing sure smells good, Vi."

"I'm experimenting this morning. I aim to make something no one in this house has ever eaten before."

"Oh?"

"Yes. You know I told you I know Evelyn McCracken, who cooks—or cooked—for the Bannisters?"

"Yes, I recall you telling me that." I sat at the table, munching a piece of orange and hoping Vi might spill something useful to our investigation. By "our," of course, I mean Harold's, Flossie's, Hazel's, Dr. Greenlaw's and mine. If it turned out to be pertinent, I might even tell Sam.

"Well, she told me that Leo Bannister loved something called chorizo with his eggs in the morning."

I frowned slightly. "What the heck is chorizo?"

"It's a Mexican sausage. Quite spicy, Evelyn told me."

"How did he learn about chorizo?" I wanted to know, sticking another bite of orange into my mouth. Valencias are very sweet oranges, bless them.

"Evelyn told me he visited Mexico quite often for business."

"Ah. I see." Huh. Some business. Finding little kids to satisfy the depraved whims of evil men. I didn't say that out loud.

Vi continued, "So, when I visited Jorgenson's last week, I asked Mr. Larkin"—For the record, Mr. Larkin was the butcher at Jorgenson's Grocery Store, which was where the staff of all the rich folks in Pasadena bought their foodstuffs—"if he carried chorizo. He said only two people have ever asked him for it, and one was Mrs. McCracken and the other was Olive Peterson, who cooks for Mr. and Mrs. Gaulding."

Aha. Perhaps we might be getting somewhere with this information.

"I don't think I know the Gauldings."

Vi sniffed. "You probably wouldn't want to. I understand they're very high and mighty. And also, there's something slightly...what would you call it? Sniffy about them."

"Sniffy? And here you decry my use of slang. What do you mean by sniffy?"

"Oh, you know. Like that expression, smelling a rat. Something like that. Not quite upstanding. Rather like Leo Bannister, in fact, I suppose. Of course, they're as rich as the Pinkertons, so I guess nobody minds if they dip into the seamy side of life from time to time."

Aha again. "I see."

"But here. Try this." Vi set a plate before me. It contained eggs scrambled with what I presumed was chorizo sausage. She'd buttered a piece of toast and cut it, so that it sort of made an artistic presentation alongside the eggs and chorizo. She stepped back to observe my reaction to this new creation of hers.

I took a bite. "Oh, my, this is delicious, Vi!"

"I'm so glad! Mr. Larkin ordered some chorizo for me when I asked about it, and he had it in the last time I went to Jorgenson's."

"I love it. I wonder if Mijare's uses chorizo in anything." Mijare's was a

Mexican restaurant that had opened four years earlier in Pasadena. My family and Sam and I had eaten there a few times, and the food was really good. Our horizons were expanding in the Gumm-Majesty household. I'd brought my wonderful aunt a cooking book from Turkey, and now she was cooking food that had originated in Turkey *and* Mexico. Well, and India, too, if you want to count the curries Mr. Pinkerton favored, and which Aunt Vi prepared for us, too. We were becoming, in fact, quite the international family, culinarily speaking. I don't think culinarily is a word, but who cares?

I began gobbling up the rest of my fine breakfast when—you guessed it—the telephone rang. Vi and I exchanged a glance.

Vi said, "Let me get it for a change, Daisy. You finish your breakfast. If it's Mrs. Pinkerton, what should I tell her?"

"Um...Oh, what the heck. Tell her I'm here, and I'll speak to her."

Pa walked into the kitchen, rubbing his hands. "What's that delicious aroma?"

"Chorizo sausage and scrambled eggs."

"*What* and scrambled eggs?"

"Chorizo. It's a Mexican sausage."

"Daisy," said Vi, holding the receiver in her hand. "It's Harold. He'd like to speak to you."

"Harold? Good heavens!" I glanced at the kitchen clock. It was only seven-thirty in the morning. Whatever could Harold be calling me about this early?

I snabbled one more bite of breakfast and went to the telephone, took the receiver from Aunt Vi, and said, "What are you doing up this early? I thought all you rich people slept until noon."

"Very funny," said Harold in a not-at-all amused voice. "You need to come over here today. I think I may have an idea where my idiot sister and that fortune-hunter of hers are staying."

"And I want to know this why?"

"Because it might have something to do with..." Harold ran out of words and cleared his throat. "You know."

"Oh. Right. Very well, I'll be over there as soon as Pa and I walk Spike."

"I'm so glad you have your priorities in order," said Harold in perhaps the most sarcastic tone I'd ever heard issue from him.

"Darned right I do," I told him.

"God," said Harold, and he hung up.

So I hung up, too, and went back to Vi's spectacular breakfast. By that time she'd joined Pa and me at the kitchen table, and we all enjoyed our food. Spike looked up at us mournfully, as if he hadn't had a meal in decades. If one only looked at his eyes, one would be tempted to throw him some food. If one looked past the eyes to the plump belly, one would know those pitiful eyes fibbed. Nevertheless, I tossed him a little piece of buttered toast.

"Tsk, tsk," said Pa, his eyes twinkling at me.

"Don't tell Mrs. Hanratty or Mrs. Bissel," I told him.

"I won't, but if Spike gets too fat, you're going to hear from both ladies, you know."

I heaved a sigh. "I know."

So. No more buttered toast for Spike. Poor doggie.

After we'd all cleared our plates, we sat back and sighed in unison. "That was spectacular, Aunt Vi," I said, wishing I could eat more, even though I was stuffed to the gills.

"Thank you. I enjoyed it, too," said Vi, beaming.

"Me, too," said Pa.

Spike didn't speak, but if he could have, he'd probably have griped that he didn't know how it tasted, having been given only one tiny piece of buttered toast.

"I'd better get the dishes cleaned up. I guess Mrs. Pinkerton won't be pestering me today, but Harold wants me to pop by for a minute or two. He thinks he might know where his sister and Percival Petrie are."

"He should probably call the police," said Pa.

That's right. He probably should. Oh, dear. I paused, wondering how I was going to get out of this one. "Maybe. But he isn't sure. I think he wants us to do a little snooping before he calls the police."

"Ah, Daisy, that's how you always get into trouble," said Pa.

"I do not!"

"Yes, you do," said Vi.

144

I humphed, gathered the breakfast plates, and began washing and drying them, deciding that to fight this battle would serve no useful purpose. When I was finished, I asked, "Anybody want to use the bathroom? I want to take a short bath and brush my teeth."

"No, thanks," came a duet from Pa and Vi.

So I brushed my teeth, took a shorter bath than I wanted to, washed my hair, combed it out, and went to the bedroom, Spike following like the good dog he was. Since I'd had my hair bobbed and shingled at the local barbershop a couple of years ago (and continued to do so at regular intervals), it dried all by itself into a perfect "do" that I didn't have to mess with. At least something in my life worked right.

Oh, all right. I have a lot to be thankful for. I just hoped I wouldn't be locked up for harboring a fugitive.

EIGHTEEN

After Pa and Spike and I took a longer-than-usual walk around the neighborhood—I felt almost as free as Aunt Vi, since I didn't have to visit Mrs. Pinkerton that day—I changed into a nicer outfit. I always wore a faded day dress when Pa, Spike and I went for our walks, but when I visited Harold, I wanted to look prime.

Therefore, that day I selected a nice two-piece dress made of "Pamico" cloth (whatever that was) I'd found on sale at Nash's Dry Goods and Department Store. The dress had an embroidered top sewn onto a solid-colored (in this case, blue) skirt, and had a sleeveless blue jacket with embroidered pockets. Naturally, I'd done the embroidery myself with embroidery thread I'd found at Nelson's Five- and Ten-Cent Store. I thought it was one of my nicer outfits and hoped it would make up for yesterday's blandness. I was sure Harold would let me know.

And I was right. As soon as I rang Harold's doorbell and heard the chimes, Harold himself opened the door, frowning. His visage softened as he looked me up and down. "Well, I'll say this for you. You're only bland once in a while. That's a charming creation, Daisy."

"Thank you, Harold."

"But come in. I think I might know where Stacy and her beloved are holed up."

My nose wrinkled all by itself when Harold called Percival Petrie Stacy's beloved. It couldn't help itself.

"How's Mrs. Bannister?" I asked as we walked down the hallway to the family room.

"Terrible."

"Oh, dear. I'm so sorry."

"I wish somebody would tell you when Leo Bannister was killed. Life might become a whole lot easier. Or," he added glumly, "it might not."

"Yes," I said, and sighed.

Hazel Greenlaw sat in the family room, sipping a cup of tea, her nurse's cap sitting tidily beside her on the sofa. "Good morning, Mrs. Majesty."

"Good morning, Miss Greenlaw."

Harold squinted from Hazel to me and back again. "What is this Missus and Miss stuff. You're Daisy and Hazel. Get used to it."

Hazel and I both grinned at Harold, and I saluted. "Yes, sir."

"Oh, go sit down. I'll get Roy to bring you some tea. Lunch will be ready soon."

"I'm only taking a break while my brother visits with Mrs. Bannister," Hazel told me, still smiling. "I'll be back at work as soon as Fred comes down and fills us in." She shook her head. "The poor woman isn't doing very well, I fear."

"I hope she recovers," I said, meaning it sincerely. If the woman died in Harold's home, God alone knew what we could do about it. Of course, if she lived and it was determined she killed her husband, the police would probably want to lock her up and I, for one, didn't think she deserved so dire a fate. Well, I guess dying is more dire a fate, but after living with the brutish Leo for years and being beaten for her trouble, it seemed a shame that she might be imprisoned for standing up for herself.

Hmm. Maybe Harold knew a good lawyer. A good lawyer should be able to get Mrs. Bannister off on a self-defense charge. If she ever regained consciousness. If she did indeed shoot her husband. Bother.

I felt quite discouraged that morning.

Roy entered the room (Harold had pressed the bell) and Harold asked him to bring more tea for Hazel and me. "And bring me a sherry," he added.

"Harold!" I cried, shocked. Don't ask me why.

"Don't you *Harold* me, Daisy Gumm Majesty. You're the one who got me into this mess. If I want a sip of sherry before lunch, I'll *have* a sip of sherry before lunch."

"Yes, sir, Mr. Harold," said Roy, grinning up a storm.

"I didn't mean to get you into it," I said sincerely. I also didn't point out that it had been Flossie who'd started this whole thing. Looking at it from that light, I guess it was Leo Bannister himself who started it. But never mind.

I also didn't mention that it was officially Prohibition, and the drinking of alcoholic beverages, including sherry, was illegal. Rich folks have never had to worry much about laws, I reckon.

Harold shook his jacket sleeve down and peered at his wristwatch. "It's eleven-fifteen. We'll have lunch as soon as Fred can join us."

"Please have Roy bring my lunch up on a tray, Harold," said Hazel. "I don't want to leave Mrs. Bannister alone. She's too fragile at this point."

Harold shuddered. "I never want to see another person in her condition in my life."

"Me neither." I was sincere that time, too.

"Nor do I," said Hazel drily. "I wish we could show the police what that brute did to her, but I don't suppose they'd care."

Instantly I felt defensive of Sam and his cronies, even though I'd bemoaned the same thing to Sam's face. "I don't think it's that they don't care so much as that they can't do anything about it. Evidently it isn't a crime to beat your wife nearly to death. If you *do* beat her to death, that's another story."

Hazel stood, shaking her head. "It's a sad story then."

I couldn't disagree.

Fred joined us at that point.

Hazel asked, "Is it all right for me to be here while you fill us in on Mrs. Bannister's condition? I don't want to leave her alone for too long."

"I've given her a dose of morphia, so I don't think she'll be awfully lively any time soon."

The mere mention of morphine or morphia made my innards wrinkle up and ache. That's the stuff my Billy had used to kill himself. Not that I blamed him. He'd been in frightful agony. But that's neither here nor there.

Hazel sat again and Fred took the floor, pacing. "The bruises on her body are beginning to take a recognizable form. The man not merely punched her with his fists, but he kicked her while she was down. She was probably trying to get away from him. If we can discover when Bannister was shot, and if it was after Mrs. Majesty found Mrs. Bannister—"

"It was Flossie Buckingham who found her," I corrected, interrupting him. Rude, I know.

"Whoever found her, if we discover Bannister was killed after whoever found her found her, we might be able to transfer to the Castleton, where she could get X-rays and full-time care."

"I've been giving her full-time care," said Hazel mildly.

"I know, Haze, but you can't X-ray her ribs."

"True."

"I didn't know the Castleton could perform X-rays these days," I said, surprised. X-rays had been around for a while, but not all the hospitals in the United States were equipped to give them. "I hope we can get her to the hospital soon."

"Me, too. But we can't do much until we know when her husband died," said Fred.

"I know." I heaved another sigh.

"Anyway," Fred went on, "she continues to come in and out of consciousness, but she's never alert enough to speak. The most she can do is moan. That's partly because the swine battered her face so badly, but I think kicks to the head might have wrought more harm overall. I'm not sure she'll ever be fully conscious."

"Kicks!" I cried, appalled all over again.

Fred nodded grimly. "I fear brain damage."

"Yeah. You've said as much before," said Harold, sounding the least bit surly. I didn't really fault him for that. After all, he might be harboring a murderess.

Naw. If Mrs. B killed Mr. B, it was because he deserved it.

It might be difficult to convince the police of that, however.

"Anything else to report?" asked Hazel, preparing to take her leave.

"I don't think so," said her brother. "I'll be up again before I leave for the practice. You know to call if anything changes in her condition."

"Yes, sir. I know my job." Hazel saluted her brother and left to tend to Mrs. Bannister.

"I can't imagine living with someone who does things like that to his wife," I said, feeling not merely discouraged but downright melancholy by that point.

"Lots of men do it," said Harold.

He sounded terribly callous. "I hope not that badly, they don't," I said fairly snappishly.

"Face it, Daisy," said Harold. "You might not have been born rich, but you were born into a good family and married a good man. There are many women in the world who aren't that lucky. Look at Lily Bannister, for pity's sake. I understand her family was wealthy, and look at her now. And her family won't do a single thing to help her. Hell, look at my own mother, for that matter. My father might not have been a beater, but he was a lousy husband and father." He glanced at his wristwatch again. "Speaking of which, I'd better tell you what you came here to learn."

"That might be nice," I said.

"I don't know how to prove it unless we go over there, though."

"That's what I was thinking."

"What are you two talking about?" asked Fred reasonably.

"I think I know where my idiot sister and her criminal husband—if they bothered to get married—might be holed up," Harold informed him.

"Oh. I'm glad of that, but I'd better be off. I have work to do and patients to see."

"You aren't staying for lunch?" I asked him.

"No. I have too much work piling up. I hadn't anticipated having to visit Harold's house every day for days on end."

And now, besides discouraged and melancholy, I felt guilty. "I'm sorry," I said in a small voice.

"Not your fault," said Fred with a nice smile for me.

"The hell it isn't," growled Harold.

I sighed.

Anyhow, Fred left, and Roy entered to say luncheon was ready. That day we dined on a salad made with chicken, chopped apple pieces, celery, walnuts, little green onion bits, lettuce, and I don't know what all else. It was magnificent. I told Roy so.

"It's a recipe from my mother," said Roy proudly.

"It's wonderful. I'll have to tell Aunt Vi about it."

"You can make it with tuna fish, too," said Roy.

"Tuna fish? Where do you get tuna fish? I mean, isn't that an ocean fish? Do you have to go fishing to get it or something?"

"For the love of God, Daisy, where have you been all your life?"

"In Pasadena, California, Harold Kincaid!"

"Well, canned tuna fish has been available for two decades or more. It's good, too."

"Oh. I didn't know that."

"Clearly," said Harold. And he, clearly, was in a grouch.

Roy laughed when he left the dining room for the kitchen. It was nice to have one cheerful person in the house.

I sniffed. "This salad is delicious, whatever's in it. And Roy makes rolls almost as good as the ones my aunt makes."

"These are your aunt's rolls, so you'd better alter that opinion in a jiffy," snarled Harold.

"Why are you so grumpy today, Harold."

Harold put down his fork and glared at me.

Feeling guilty again (or still), I said, "It wasn't my fault."

"Right."

We finished our meal in silence. When we'd conquered our salads and rolls, Roy came back with some tapioca pudding for us. That was delicious, too.

Feeling it might be safe to offer another comment, I said, "Roy's a good cook."

"Yes, he is. He trained with the best."

"The best?" I asked, thinking my own very aunt was the best when one were talking about cooking.

With a wicked grin, Harold said, "Your own aunt, Vi."

My mouth fell open for a second until I shut it with a snap. "*Vi? Vi* taught Roy how to cook?"

"She did indeed."

"Golly, she never told us she had apprentices."

"I asked her a couple of years ago—after Roy had healed from his ordeal—if she would mind helping a poor orphaned child learn how to cook. He already had a head start, because he used to cook for his family in wherever the heck he's from."

"I thought he said this was his mother's recipe."

"I'm sure it was. He was kidnapped and brought to the good old U.S.A. when he was around fourteen, and he'd been helping his mother around the house for a few years before that."

"Huh."

"That's because he comes from a resort island, and he had the goal of becoming a chef in one of the grand hotels there."

"And you can't remember the name of the island?"

"Let me think." Harold proceeded to think. "Ah! Tortuga! That's it. Tortuga."

"I think I've heard of Tortuga."

"It's near Haiti."

"I've definitely heard of Haiti."

"Well, then, now you know more than you did when you came over today. Does that make you feel better?"

I gave him a good grimace. "Not perceptibly."

"Didn't think so. But you would press, wouldn't you?"

"I think where people come from is interesting."

"Yeah, yeah."

"But what about Roy's poor mother? Does she know what happened to her son? Is she still wondering what became of him? That must be awful."

"I know you don't think much of me, Daisy Gumm Majesty, but I'm *not* a monster. I brought his whole family over here after I learned Roy's story. They all have jobs in rich people's houses or in various restaurants."

"Oh, Harold, that was so nice of you."

"Yes, it was, wasn't it? But let's retire to the family room, and talk about my idiot sister."

"I hope you don't call her your idiot sister in front of your mother."

"I don't, although I'm not sure why. One of these days, Mother will figure it out for herself and probably call her the same thing."

"I doubt it," said I, folding my napkin and wishing I had the recipe for Roy's mother's salad. Then again, since Vi can fix almost anything on the face of the earth, I could probably just list the ingredients and she'd put it together. For all I knew, Roy had already taught her the secrets to this wonderful salad. I'd ask her when I got home.

NINETEEN

W e retired to Harold's family room. After learning about Harold's kindness to Roy and his family, I decided not to scold him about being an old grouser or drinking sherry during Prohibition. He had a big heart, did Harold Kincaid.

"Very well, so where do you think your sister and Mr. Petrie are hiding out? And what are they using for money? The Salvation Army's children's charity fund wouldn't take them too far."

"Stacy gets an allowance," said Harold with a telling grimace.

"Does it come to her...I don't know. Automatically? Or does she have to go home and pick it up?"

"Bank. She goes to the bank and they cut her a check every month."

"Wish I had an arrangement like that," I said, thinking I might not be worth much, but I deserved an allowance more than Stacy Kincaid did.

"You don't need it. You can fend for yourself. My sister would die in the street if she had to make her way in the world without someone handing her everything on a tray."

I couldn't help myself. I smiled. Evilly, I'm sure. "What a lovely idea."

"Don't get too attached to it. Mother would never allow that to happen to even so disgusting a specimen of humanity as my gawd-awful sister."

"A shame, that," I said upon a sigh.

"When Stacy and her love first ran off, I asked Mother if she couldn't stop payments on Stacy's allowance, but Mother wouldn't hear of it. She nearly had a spasm and said she'd never cut off one of her children without the means to live. My mother is an extremely silly woman. But you already know that."

I shrugged. "She loves her children. Even if one of them is Stacy."

"Gawd."

"All right. Tell me where you think Stacy and her man are hiding out?"

"Do you remember Adele Knowles?"

"Um...No."

"She was engaged to Eddie Hastings, who was murdered by a crony of my father's. Surely you can't have forgotten Eddie."

I shuddered. "How could I ever forget Eddie? His ghost actually showed up at one of my séances. Scared me to death."

"You weren't the only one."

"I hope no other ghosts of people ever show up at another one of my séances," I told Harold with fervor.

"You're not the only one there, either. I thought poor Mrs. Hastings was going to suffer an apoplectic fit or something."

"I darned near did."

"What kind of spiritualist-medium are you, if you cringe at the sight of ghosts?"

"A fake one."

Harold grinned.

"Anyway, so do you remember Adele Knowles now?"

"Yes, I do, poor thing. She was terribly cut up about her fiancé's death."

"Yes, she was. A lot of us were. Eddie was a good fellow. Unlike his father."

"Indeed."

"Well, Adele told me she thought she saw Stacy with a young fellow somewhere around the California Institute of Technology the other day. She stopped her motor and tried to speak to her, but Stacy—if it was she —scuttled off with her man friend."

"Did Adele see where they went?"

"She said she thinks they went up a driveway not far from Caltech. A little east of the university, she thinks."

"Why did she tell you? Did you ask her about Stacy?"

"Good heavens, no! As far as I'm concerned, Stacy is a blot on the family escutcheon."

"Not unlike your father."

"Right. Not unlike my father. Or my mother, for that matter."

"That's not fair, Harold. Your mother might be a silly woman, but she's not evil."

After thinking about it for a half-second or so, Harold said, "I suppose you're right."

"So why did Adele tell you where Stacy was hiding out?"

"For one thing, she didn't know Stacy was hiding out. We met at a party last night. Adele's engaged to be married again, this time to a fellow who will appreciate her properly." Eddie Hastings had been a fine man, but of Harold's persuasion and, therefore, not particularly attracted to the ladies. Harold had told me once that Eddie had planned to do his duty and sire children with Adele, but it might have been a burden on him. All things considered, I guess Adele becoming engaged to a fellow who liked females was a better bet for her. Although, I have to admit, sometimes I wonder.

But enough of that.

"I'm glad to hear it. I hope they have a long and happy marriage. Who's she marrying?"

"A lad named Delbert Franklin, who originated in New York City, not unlike your favorite detective."

"Right," said I, deciding to say nothing more.

"Only Delbert's the son of a rich man. He works for a living, though, unlike my idiot sister."

"What does he do?"

"He's a lawyer, like so many other rich men's sons."

"You're a rich man's son, and you're not a lawyer," I pointed out.

"My father married my mother's money, so I don't count."

"You do so count, Harold Kincaid!"

"Not as a rich man's son."

"I suppose not. So how did the subject of Stacy come up?"

"She actually cornered me, because she thought Stacy's behavior was odd."

"Stacy's behavior has always been odd."

"True, but she didn't used to scurry away when former friends stopped to talk to her on the streets of Pasadena."

"Interesting. Your sister is such a jive jane. But how can we find out if she saw Stacy or not?"

"Adele gave me the approximate address, so I guess we can drive around in that area and look."

"Sounds kind of hopeless, doesn't it?"

Harold sighed. "Yes. It does. But I'm not sure how else to go about it. Damnation, I wish you could find out when Bannister was killed. If we could find out that much, I wouldn't give a hang about finding Stacy. But I'm afraid her beloved might somehow be involved in Bannister's evildoings. Especially after you told us his history."

"I think so, too. But I don't know how to determine when Bannister died, unless Sam lets it slip at dinner tonight."

Harold's eyebrows lifted. "Dinner tonight? My, my, you two seem to be together a lot, don't you?"

Feeling defiant, I said for the first time ever to the first person ever (aside from Sam himself), "Yes! Yes, we're together a lot. We're engaged to be married, as a matter of fact!"

Harold's surprise was unfeigned. I could tell. "Good Lord. Where's your ring?"

I felt for the chain around my neck. The first thing I pulled out was the juju Mrs. Jackson had made for me. Harold gaped.

"For God's sake Daisy, that's not an engagement ring!"

"Darn it! No, this is the juju Mrs. Jackson made for me. It's supposed to bring good luck. So far, it hasn't worked too well." I managed to grope around until I found the right chain. "Here! This is my engagement ring. I hope you're satisfied now."

Harold reached out and fingered the lovely emerald ring set in gold Sam had given me. "That's beautiful, Daisy."

"Thank you. Sam's father designed and made it. He's a jeweler in New York City."

"Fancy that. Why in the world don't you wear it?"

I clutched my left hand with my right and looked down at them both as they gripped each other on my lap. "I...I can't quite make myself take Billy's ring off."

"Well," said Harold acidly, dropping my ring, chain and all, so that it thunked against my chest. "I suggest you get over *that* romantic notion soon, or my mother will have the two of us marrying each other and living under her roof."

Ghastly thought. Not marriage to Harold. Living with Mrs. Pinkerton. "You're right. I should bolster my courage."

"You should indeed. Poor Sam."

"You don't even like him. Why call him poor Sam?"

"Because I feel sorry for the fellow. And I do like him. He doesn't like me."

That was probably true.

"Imagine how he feels, you wearing his engagement ring on a chain around your neck and Billy's ring on your finger." Harold shook his head as if he worried for my sanity or something.

I decided to change the subject. "So how do you want to go about this sleuthing on California Street?"

"Drive, I guess."

"We'd probably better take my Chevrolet. If Stacy sees your Bearcat, she'll run for the hills. It's not an inconspicuous car, Harold."

"Darned right, it's not," said Harold with some pride. He did have a wonderful automobile. Bright red and low slung, it was a beaut.

"Say," said I, thinking, which can be a dangerous occupation occasionally, "do you know anyone who lives near there? I mean, a whole lot of wealthy Pasadena residents live around there, but do you know any of them?"

"And in San Marino, as do I," said Harold with justifiable pride. He had a pretty snazzy house.

"Yes. Oh, my goodness, she couldn't have been heading for your house, could she?"

"Not if she values her hide and liberty. I'd call the police in an instant if I saw either one of those pills near me or my home."

"Know anyone else who lives around here?"

"Let me think."

"Don't strain yourself," I joked. The joke was undoubtedly in poor taste, but sometimes I can't help myself.

"Thank heaps. Very well, let me see...There are the Jenkins. They live on California east of the university. And there are the Gauldings—"

Instantly my eyes lit up, and I interrupted Harold. "The Gauldings! They're the ones whose cook told Aunt Vi about chorizo sausage!"

Harold peered at me blankly. "I beg your pardon?"

"Oh, I'm sorry. But listen, Harold! Vi cooked us a delicious breakfast this morning. She scrambled eggs with chorizo sausage, which is Mexican. When she asked the butcher about it, he said only the Bannisters and the Gauldings had ever ordered it from him before. There might be a connection! Aunt Vi said there was something fishy about the couple. Well, she said 'sniffy', but when I asked her what she meant, she told me it was like when you smell a rat."

"Interesting. Not sure if it adds up to a conspiracy."

"It might not. But the Gauldings might be involved if that's where Stacy and What's His Name went. Especially if Mr. Bannister went on his hunting expeditions for children in Mexico. He couldn't get them all from Tortuga, could he?"

"I suppose not. Hmm. Interesting idea, Daisy."

"Thank you," said I with becoming modesty. "By the way, what's Roy's last name?"

"Why?"

"Just wondered."

"Castillo."

"Isn't that Spanish?"

"I suppose. I think Tortuga belonged to Spain for a while. Maybe it still does. I don't know much about geography."

"No. I don't, either." I considered it a serious flaw, too, but one that couldn't be cured that afternoon. "So, do you want to take a drive?"

"Sure. I'll drive, unless you want to."

"No, I'll be happy to let you drive. Even if Stacy recognizes our Chevrolet, which is doubtful, she won't expect to see a man driving it."

"Good." He rang the bell for Roy, and when he appeared, he said, "Roy, will you please bring me the telephone directory?"

"Yes, sir, Mr. Harold."

Harold rolled his eyes as Roy left the room. "He won't leave off calling me 'Mister Harold.'"

"He's a good servant, I guess."

"I guess."

Roy trotted in with the 'phone book, and Harold looked up addresses for the Gauldings and the Jenkinses.

"All right," said he when he was through. "Let's go." He plopped the telephone directory on the table beside his chair.

So we went. Harold's house wasn't far from the California Institute of Technology, so we didn't have to drive far. We peered and peeked and searched, but we didn't see Stacy or Percival Petrie.

Harold pointed out the Gauldings' house. It was big and beautiful. Just what you'd expect in that neighborhood. He pointed out the Jenkins' residence, which was likewise lavish.

But no Stacy or Percival.

"I think Percival is a stupid name," I said at one point, being completely irrelevant.

"I think so, too, but wasn't he a big hero at King Arthur's table or something?"

"I think so. Can't remember the story."

So much for conversation. Harold continued to drive, and we continued not seeing Stacy and Percival.

"Well," Harold said after we'd scoured the neighborhood for about forty-five minutes, "I vote we give up for the day."

"All right by me."

So, disappointed, but with at least a hint of where the evil pair might be lurking, we went back to Harold's house, and I drove home.

The time was around two-thirty or thereabouts, and after greeting an enthusiastic Spike and talking to my father for a few minutes—he asked where I'd been, and I'd said I'd been to Harold's, and he just looked at me —I decided to hie myself off to the sewing room and begin working on birthday presents for my nieces. Vi was nowhere to be seen, so I presumed she'd gone upstairs for a much-deserved nap or reading time or something.

Polly and Peggy were my sister Daphne and her husband Daniel's two girls, and both had birthdays in October. Polly would be ten on October fifth, and Peggy would be seven on October fifteenth. I planned to make them both lovely frocks to wear to church or special occasions. Naturally, since their birthdays came right before Thanksgiving, I aimed to make them suitable for the Thanksgiving and Christmas holidays.

And how, you might ask, did I know the sizes of my two nieces, since Daphne, Daniel, Polly and Peggy lived in Arcadia, which was more than a wee hop from Pasadena? I called Daphne and asked, is how. Then, after having done so, I motored myself up to Maxime's Fabrics on Colorado Boulevard and bought two patterns that would fit the girls. I also bought some gorgeous fabric, one in a splendid jade green and another in a deep, vivid blue. Because Polly had hair that was more auburn than brown, I'd make the green dress for her, and because Peggy had blond hair, I'd make the blue dress for her. I tell you, I might not be good for much, but I could sew like a champ.

Sewing always made me feel peaceful, which was a blessing that day, believe me. Aunt Vi said the same thing happened to her when she was cooking. Cooking always made me tense and nervous. I guess that just goes to show that different people have different tastes.

Naturally, as I cut and pinned, I thought. How, wondered I, could we find Stacy and Percival Petrie? Was it worth finding them? Could they be involved with Mr. Bannister's evil deeds? Could Percival be the villain who had rid the world of the evil Leo Bannister? If he had, it was prob-ably the only good deed he'd ever performed, but also probably, no one else would consider it as such. Well, except those of us who knew Lily Bannister's story.

And then there were the Gauldings. Did they have anything to do with Leo Bannister and his sinister goings-on? How the heck should I know? Just because someone liked chorizo sausage with his or her eggs, it didn't necessarily follow that he or she was involved in wicked dealings.

If Sam refused to tell me, how could I find out when Leo Bannister died? I considered asking our family doctor, Doc Benjamin, who might be able to find out for me, but he would probably want to know why. Could I tell him?

Not without risking Lily Bannister's freedom. And probably Harold's, Fred's, Hazel's and mine, too.

Bother. Life was so troublesome at times.

TWENTY

Merciful heavens, but Vi certainly did more than nap and read that day! She actually fixed us, her family (and Sam), beef Wellington for dinner! She'd made it once for my birthday, and she fixed it from time to time for the Pinkertons, but generally she didn't have enough time to bother with making it for the family.

Not that day. That day, Vi had managed to procure a sirloin of beef, some liver pate, some onions and mushrooms, chopped the latter two articles, spread the liver pate on the sirloin, pressed the chopped onions and mushrooms into the pate, and wrapped the whole thing in a pastry that was so light, it might have floated off the table without the beef to anchor it.

"I've never tasted anything this good in my life, Mrs. Gumm," said Sam as he savored his beef, thereby deviating from his usual "This is delicious, Mrs. Gumm." He was right, though. Vi served the encrusted beef with buttered carrots, potatoes mashed with something wonderful—I didn't ask what—and her usual flaky dinner rolls.

"Me neither," I said, trying not to gobble like a pig. "I'm surprised you went to this much work on your day off."

"You know I love to cook, Daisy. Sort of like you love to sew. It relaxes me, and it makes me happy when people enjoy what I've made for them."

See? Told you so.

"I can't imagine how cooking can be anything but a hideous chore," I admitted. I felt like apologizing to Sam after I said it, but didn't, knowing my family would want to know why I was doing so. Fiddlesticks.

Sam actually grinned at me. "Well, maybe you can learn someday."

"I doubt it," said I, recalling with chagrin the one time I tried to prepare a dish for my family. The same dish had been quite a success in the cooking class I taught at the Salvation Army, but when I tried to duplicate it at home, I managed to use baking soda instead of flour for a part of it, and it didn't work. At all.

"You have your own special gifts, dear," said Ma, who was almost as dismal a failure in the kitchen as was I.

"Thanks, Ma." I shoved more food into my mouth in order to keep it from making a noise. I kept fearing I'd let something slip about the Bannister case.

"So what did you and Harold do this afternoon?" asked Pa.

Nuts. "Not much. His house boy made lunch for us—Oh, Vi!" I cried, recalling that Roy Castillo had apprenticed under my very own aunt when he learned to cook. "Harold's house boy is Roy Castillo, and Harold said you taught him how to cook!"

"My goodness gracious," said Vi, her eyes widening. "I certainly did. Nice boy. I understand he had some problems with illness when he first came to this country. Harold was extremely kind and rescued him and his family from dire straits, from everything Roy told me."

"Yes. Harold didn't precisely announce his heroism, but that's what it was, all right. He brought Roy's entire family over here from Tortuga."

"Tortuga?" asked Sam, one of his bushy eyebrows lifting dramatically.

"Yes. Tortuga. I didn't even know where Tortuga was until Harold told me it's near Haiti. I mean, I still don't know precisely where it is, but at least I've heard of Haiti."

Sam's eyebrow dipped and he frowned slightly as he gazed at me. Uh-oh. What did this mean? I soon found out.

"Say, Daisy, you don't know what type of illness this guy suffered from when Harold rescued him, do you?"

Well...Yes, I did. But I'd never tell Sam so. "No. Harold didn't say."

"Hmm." Sam went back to his dinner as my curiosity soared.

"What do you mean 'hmm'? Sam? Do you know something about Roy Castillo that I don't?"

"Don't know. All I know is that we've found several young children who have been badly abused in recent years in Pasadena. I only wondered if this Roy character was one of them."

"Abused? What do you mean abused?" asked Ma, shocked. "What kind of abuse?"

Oh, Lord, I hope Sam wouldn't tell her.

"Nothing specific," said Sam, the sly dog. "But a couple of the kids were from Tortuga. Another several were from Mexico."

"*Mexico*?" I blurted out before I could think better of it. Aha! Another link! I refrained from showing my interest. Still, I wished I'd kept my mouth shut.

For good reason. Sam turned in his chair to frown at me. "Why the interest in Mexico, Daisy? I swear, if you know anything—"

"I don't know anything!" I fibbed. "It's only that Vi fixed us a delicious breakfast today, using a Mexican sausage called chorizo, and she said that she only learned about it because the lady who cooks for the Bannisters ordered it from Jorgenson's."

"Hmm," said Sam, unconvinced if I was any judge, and I was.

"Anyhow, so you found children from Tortuga and Mexico who were abused?" I said to change the subject. "Where did you find them?"

"Someone dumped five children off in front of the Castleton Hospital," said Sam. "A couple of them, and I think your pal Roy was one of them, were in pretty bad shape."

"He's not my pal," I muttered. "He's Harold's house boy. And he's a very good cook, too, thanks to Aunt Vi."

"Right," said Sam.

"Goodness. I'm sorry to learn he was abused," said Vi. "Roy was a good worker and a fine boy, for all he's colored."

"What do you mean by that? 'For all he's colored?' What does that mean, Vi?" I was nettled. The Ku Klux Klan had made severe inroads into Pasadena the prior year, and I didn't like to think a member of my family harbored prejudices against anyone because of the color of his or her skin.

"Don't get in a lather, Daisy," said Vi. "I only mean that he was a colored child who spoke very little English. I know there's nothing wrong with colored people. If I didn't know it before you met Mrs. Jackson, I certainly know it now. I've never made such splendid beignets as those from the recipe she gave you to give me."

I sniffed. "Good. I'm glad to know that."

"Didn't Mrs. Jackson also give you one of those Voodoo doll things?" asked Sam, grinning again.

"She certainly did. I wear it on a chain around my neck." Then I blushed. I know that because I could feel the heat creep up my neck and into my cheeks. Doggone it!

"Ah," said Sam. "I see." I knew he was thinking of his ring, which I also wore on a golden chain around my neck. I had to remedy that situation one of these days.

Oh, dear. "Say, Aunt Vi, Roy made us a really good salad for lunch. It had chopped up chicken, apples, walnuts, celery, little green onions, and I don't know what all else in it. I think it would make a splendid luncheon for us one of these weekends. Roy said he got the recipe from his mother."

"Oh, yes!" said Vi. "That's delicious. He prepared it for me once, only he used sweet green grapes. You know, the ones without seeds, in the salad. You're right. I need to fix that one of these days. It would make a splendid luncheon on a hot summer's day."

"Sounds rather strange, to me," said my mother, who wasn't an adventurous diner.

"It was delicious, Ma. So that makes two delicious meals in one day!" I beamed at my wonderful aunt.

"Get along with you, Daisy," said Vi, blushing.

"She's only telling the truth," said Sam, sticking up for me.

That was nice for a change.

Naturally, it didn't last long.

Sam had to depart shortly after our scrumptious meal had been consumed—Vi served us lemon meringue pie for dessert. If you haven't eaten Vi's lemon meringue pie—well, I know you haven't—you've missed a delight. I cleaned the table, told my folks I'd be back to wash up the dishes in a minute, and Spike and I walked him out to his Hudson.

"Do you have to work on the Bannister case?" I asked him, trying to sound disingenuous.

"Yes. And I'd like to know precisely what you know about the Bannisters, Daisy. Please stop keeping things from me. The man was murdered, and his wife is suspected of having done him in. If you know anything at all, please tell me."

Gee, he didn't usually say please. "All I know about Mr. Bannister is that, from all accounts, he was a terrible man. He was rumored to beat his wife, and Dr. Greenlaw's sister had a run-in with him. I guess he tried to take advantage of her or something. That's what Harold said," I hurried to add.

"Dr. Greenlaw?" Sam squinted at me.

"Well, there are two Doctors Greenlaw. Father and son. I met the son and his sister, Hazel, who's a nurse, and she said he tried to assault her."

"Assault her? What does that mean?"

"Sam Rotondo, you know as well as I do what that means!"

He sighed. "Yeah. I guess so. So why didn't they call the police?"

I gaped at him. "*Nobody* calls the police about things like that. I guess his wife never called the police when he beat her, either, because there's nothing they would—"

"Could," Sam interrupted. "We can't interfere between married people."

"Even if one of them beats the other one to a bloody pulp?"

Another sigh. "Well...I guess if she were to press charges, but that sort of thing is awfully hard to prove, especially if he has other people to vouch for him."

"Why would anyone lie about something like that?"

"I don't know. Say, Daisy, do you know anything about where Mrs. Bannister is? If she didn't kill her husband, she might be in some other kind of trouble."

I sniffed. "Maybe he killed her."

"We only found one body in the house."

"Did you search through the whole house?"

"Of course, we did."

Something occurred to me then. "Even the dumbwaiter shaft?"

"The *dumbwaiter* shaft?"

"Yes. I read in *The Window at the White Cat*, by Mary Roberts Rinehart, that a fellow fell down the dumbwaiter shaft when he was chasing a crook."

"You read too many detective novels."

"The man who fell down the dumbwaiter shaft wasn't a detective. *Did* you search in the dumbwaiter shaft?"

"We searched the house."

"Including—"

"Including the dumbwaiter shaft."

"Oh. Well, maybe he drove her corpse up into the foothills. She could be feeding coyotes and bears and vultures by this time."

"By what time?"

"By whatever this time is from the time he killed her! Darn you, Sam Rotondo!"

He held up his hands in a peace-keeping gesture. "I'm sorry we can't make our own laws, Daisy, but that's just the way it is."

"Violating little children is the way it is? I thought that was against the law."

"It is."

"Well, then?"

"There's nothing we can do if people won't tell us what's going on."

"Or even if they do," I said grumpily.

Sam heaved a sigh. "Sometimes. But if you know anything about the Bannister woman, I wish you'd tell me. For all we know, she killed him in self-defense."

"Was a gun found on the premises?"

"No."

"When did he die?" I held my breath, hoping I could sneak that one past him.

Didn't work. "We don't know yet. Even if we did...Well, you know I can't talk about my cases."

Nerts. "I know, Sam. I don't know either of the Bannisters, but if it's any help, there's another family in Pasadena that also orders chorizo sausage from Jorgenson's. The Gauldings."

"Why would that help?"

I threw my arms out. "*I* don't know! All I know is that I think it's suspicious that the only people in Pasadena who ever ordered chorizo sausage from Mr. Larkin were the Bannisters and the Gauldings. And now Aunt Vi. And I *know* she didn't shoot Mr. Bannister."

"Who's Mr. Larkin?"

Details, details. Fussy man. "He's the butcher at Jorgenson's. Vi knows him quite well."

"Hmm. I don't know if it's worth looking in to, but maybe I will."

"Probably wouldn't hurt."

"Maybe not."

He bent and kissed me. The kiss lasted a little too long according to Spike, who jumped up on the two of us and effectively broke us apart.

"Stupid dog," grumbled Sam.

"Yes, Spike. You really could improve your timing, you know."

Sam was silent for a moment or two, then said, "So could you."

"Me?" I said, pointing at my chest.

"Yes, you. You keep my ring on its chain around your neck right next to that stupid Voodoo doll Mrs. Jackson made for you. How do you think that makes me feel?"

Crumb. "I..." I didn't know what to say. Finally I said, "I told Harold today that we're engaged."

"Harold, eh? Well, I guess that's a start."

"And Harold said the ring you gave me is beautiful."

It was getting dark out there, but I'm pretty sure Sam rolled his eyes. "So glad it meets with Harold's approval."

And with that and one more deep sigh, Sam walked to the driver's side door of his Hudson and climbed into the car.

I waved at him as he rumbled away, but I doubt he even looked to see what I was doing.

"Spike, why is life so complicated sometimes?"

Spike didn't know any more than I did.

TWENTY-ONE

I went to bed after I cleaned up the dinner dishes, taking with me *The Great Prince Shan*. Sleep overcame me before I read half a page, and I awoke a bit later than usual on Saturday morning with the book still in the bed with me, alongside Spike.

Another day. I wasn't sure I wanted to face it.

However, as there didn't seem to be much choice in the matter, I rose, donned my robe, skedaddled to the bathroom, and then staggered into the kitchen, where Vi was humming a lively tune. "Tea for Two," I believe it was.

"Morning, Vi."

She turned a beaming smile upon me. "Good morning, Daisy. You look like you could sleep for another hundred years or so."

"That bad, is it?"

"You do look tired, dear. Have you been working too hard?"

Hardly working, was more like it, although there were so many other things going on around me, it felt as though I carried the burdens of the world on my shoulders. "Not really. Especially not yesterday and today, what with Mrs. Pinkerton gone."

"Yes. Life is more peaceful without her constant telephone calls, isn't it?"

"You bet." I slumped into a kitchen chair, plucked an orange from the bowl in the middle of the table, and started peeling it.

"Here's a cup of coffee, dear. Your father's already eaten and has gone down to the Hull Motor Works to chat with some friends there."

Pa had friends everywhere. "And Ma's already at work, I bet. I'm a lazybones this morning." Guilt attacked me like a vicious grizzly bear.

"Nonsense. You've been busy lately, what with people calling you every other second and worrying about Stacy and that awful man of hers and Harold calling you day and night." Her blue eyes sparkled at me. They would. "Why *is* Harold calling you so often, dear? Is there anything amiss with him?"

Fiddlesticks. "Not wrong, exactly. He's worried about his mother worrying about Stacy, mainly. I don't know if he wants to find her to bring her home or if he wants to find her and bribe her to stay away."

"Daisy!" But Vi giggled.

"Poor Mrs. Pinkerton would probably be better off without her."

"I'm sure that's true, but one can't just throw away one's children."

"I guess not."

"Here. I made you an omelet for breakfast."

And darned if Vi didn't set a plate in front of me loaded with a perfect cheese omelet, bacon, and toast.

"You're too good to us, Vi," I said, digging in. It was *so* good.

"Nonsense. I'm glad you finally got your appetite back."

"Yes. So am I."

Spike muttered something under his breath. I looked down at him. "I'll feed you in a minute, Spike," I told him.

He grumbled again. I should have fed him before I ate. More guilt. Bother.

"What do you plan to do today, Daisy? What with Mrs. Pinkerton gone, I don't suppose you have to do anything, really. You cleaned the house a couple of days ago. My goodness, maybe we should both just sit down and read all day long. Doesn't that sound splendid?"

"It sure does," I said wistfully, pretty sure my day was going to be interrupted by someone or something ugly that would interfere with Vi's delightful plan.

As if in answer to my unspoken thought, the telephone rang.

Vi and I looked at each other. I sighed and said, "I'll get it."

"I'm sorry, dear," said Vi, bless her.

"Thanks, Vi." I picked up the receiver. "Gumm-Majesty residence. Mrs.—"

"I know who you are," said Harold Kincaid, sounding crabby.

"Hey, Harold." I heaved a sigh.

"Hey yourself. Come to the Raymond Pharmacy around noon. Fred and I will meet you there. You know where it is?"

"On Fair Oaks, right? In South Pasadena?"

"Right."

"They serve food there? I thought they had a soda fountain."

"They do, but they also have decent sandwiches. Fred can get away from his hospital duties, but not for long. We have to discuss—" I guess he suddenly remembered our party line, because he stopped speaking abruptly, and then said, "Well, you know what."

"Yes. I do," I said, feeling beleaguered.

"Anyhow, Fred needs your help."

"He does? But..." My voice trailed off, mainly because I didn't know what to say.

"Don't worry. The news is...Well, it's not good exactly, but it's better than it was."

"I'm glad to hear it."

"See you then."

"Right. Bye, Harold."

But Harold had already hung up.

"Meeting Harold for lunch again?" asked Vi, curiosity writ plain upon her features.

"Yes. He wants to meet at the Raymond Pharmacy in South Pasadena today. I think he may know where Stacy and Mr. Petrie are staying. Or something like that."

"Oh. Well, I guess that's a good thing. At least for Mrs. Pinkerton."

"I guess."

My appetite had fled, but I tried to do justice to Vi's delicious breakfast. I hate to admit that Spike himself dined on most of a cheese omelet and some buttered toast for breakfast that morning. I ate the bacon.

After I washed the breakfast dishes, Spike and I went for a walk around the neighborhood. The weather was pleasant and Spike enjoyed himself. I tried to do likewise, but my mind was occupied with a dozen other things. What did not-exactly-good-news mean, anyway? I guess I'd find out at lunch that day.

Dining at a luncheon counter in a drug store didn't require me to dress up, although I always attempted to look fashionable and spiritualistic no matter where I went for the sake of my business. Therefore, that day I wore my trusty blue-and-white checked gingham frock with an unfitted waist and a low belt. Decoration Day (or Memorial Day; whichever you prefer) had not yet come so I couldn't wear white shoes or a white hat with it, but I compromised with my all-purpose straw hat, wrapped with a blue-and-white checked ribbon around it, tied with a bow in the back, with the ends dangling prettily. Bone-colored shoes, gloves and handbag completed the ensemble, and I was ready to drive into South Pasadena in plenty of time to reach the Raymond Pharmacy. By that time, after not eating breakfast, I was feeling a little peckish. And what a silly word *that* is.

After saying a fond farewell to my loyal hound, who didn't know why he couldn't come with me, I walked past Vi, who was sitting at the dining room table with a book propped in front of her, eating a sandwich. She looked up as I opened the side door.

"You look charming, dear. I've always liked that frock on you."

"Thanks, Vi." I glanced down at my checks. "Do you think I've worn it too much? I mean, is it getting to be old-hat or anything?" Such things bothered me a bit, since I had an image to uphold.

"Don't be ridiculous, Daisy. That's a perfectly lovely dress, and you can wear it for years to come without being unfashionable. I know you have to protect your image as a sober-sided spiritualist-medium, but you needn't go to extremes."

"You're probably right," I told her. But I still wondered as I opened the side door and crossed the porch, walked down the steps, and went to the driver's side of the Chevrolet. It looked to me as if Pa had washed the machine that morning, because it gleamed in the bright May sunshine. Pa loved cars almost as much as my darling Billy had. A twang tugged at my heart at that memory. I ruthlessly shoved it aside, and drove down Marengo, took a right on Glenarm, a left on Fair Oaks, and headed into South Pasadena.

The Raymond Pharmacy's soda fountain was relatively empty on that Saturday, which kind of surprised me. But Harold and Fred were there, and I didn't worry about why more folks hadn't come to dine at the pharmacy's soda fountain.

Harold met me with a little peck on the cheek. Fred and I shook hands. Harold said, "I've always liked that dress, Daisy. It suits you."

"Thanks, Harold. Do you think I've worn it too long? I mean, is it out of fashion yet or anything?" I read *Vogue* at the library and kept up with current fashions, but I wasn't sure about my comfy blue checks.

Darned if Harold didn't roll his eyes, looking not unlike Sam Rotondo only smaller and rounder. "Don't be ridiculous. That frock will last you for years to come if it doesn't fade."

"That's good to know."

"You look charming, Daisy," said Fred chivalrously. I felt silly. Oh, well.

"So," I said. "What's the not-entirely-good-news you have for me?"

"The patient seems to be doing better," said Fred, carefully avoiding names.

"I'm so glad!"

"She's not out of the woods yet, but she spoke a little to Hazel yesterday evening."

"That's good news."

"Yes, it's promising news. I still wish we could get her to the hospital, but...Well, we can't at the moment."

"Lucky me," said Harold.

"Don't be an old grump," I told him. "You're performing a good deed."

"Lucky me," Harold repeated, even more dourly than before.

"You can't fool me, Harold Kincaid. I know that under that cynical façade lurks the soul of a saintly man."

"Good God," said Harold.

The soda jerk came up to us, smiled, and asked us what we wanted. I looked at the chalked menu behind him and decided to have a tuna-fish sandwich and a chocolate malted milk. I'd only recently discovered malted milkshakes and thought they were delicious.

"Sounds good to me," said Harold.

"And me," said Fred.

The soda jerk appeared pleased with the unanimity of our order and went off to fill it.

"I need your help," said Fred in not quite a whisper.

"Oh? I'll be happy to help you." Then I wished I'd kept my mouth shut. Being happy to help people had landed me in trouble a whole lot in recent years.

Harold, who, as I've already said, knows me well, said, "Don't worry. This isn't an onerous task, but you'll have to work fast. Fred doesn't have all day."

"What do you need me to do?" I asked with some trepidation.

"Take me to a store where I can find ladies' clothing, underwear, nightwear, and things like that. Hazel said our patient is in dire need."

"Oh, my, I hadn't even thought about clothing and so forth. I guess she might well be in dire need if she hasn't changed since she...uh, arrived."

"Precisely," said Harold.

"Hazel is careful to sponge-bathe her every day, and she's made do with the hospital gowns I've brought, but they're not really satisfactory, especially since the patient seems to be on the mend. I hope."

"That's the reason we need you," said Harold. "Hazel can't be spared, and I can't very well accompany Fred on an outing to purchase women's clothing."

"I guess not, huh? Um, did Hazel give you any idea about what sizes you'll need?"

"Yes. I have the sizes written down." Fred removed a note from his coat pocket.

I scanned the list. On it, in neat printing, Hazel—I presume it was

Hazel—had written: *slippers (size 6), two nightgowns and a robe, two day dresses (loose, size 12), cotton stockings, low-heeled shoes (size 6).*

"Hazel says the shoes aren't necessary immediately, but if the patient continues to improve—"

Fred stopped speaking suddenly as the soda jerk appeared before us with three plates, each one containing a tuna-fish sandwich and a dill pickle spear. "Be right back with your malteds," said he, and loped off.

"And you said she's spoken to Hazel?" I asked, marveling at the seeming improvement in Mrs. Bannister's wellbeing.

"A little. But let's eat. We can discuss all this when we drive to... Where should we go? Harold said you know all the stores in Pasadena."

"Yes. I think we can get everything on the list at Nash's Dry Goods and Department Store. They carry pretty much everything."

"Good." Fred picked up half of his sandwich and took a bite. Harold and I did likewise. I followed my bite of sandwich with a bite of pickle. Yum. I wasn't sorry I'd fed Spike most of my omelet. If I kept dining with Harold, I'd be fat as a pig in no time flat.

"And here are your malteds," said the soda jerk, deftly placing a milk-shake and a straw in front of each of us. He left the metal containers in which he'd mixed the malted milkshakes next to our glasses, so we could refill them if we wanted to. Obliging chap.

After I swallowed a couple of bites of my sandwich, I said, "What has she said? Anything coherent?"

Harold snorted inelegantly. "I don't think so, but Fred begs to differ with me. So does Del."

"Ah, so Del knows about all this, does he?"

Harold looked at me as if I were a monkey that had got loose at the Griffith Park Zoo. "For God's sake, Daisy, Del *lives* there. Of course, he knows."

"Of course," said I, feeling silly.

"Hazel thinks she asked for a Bible and her rosary beads," said Fred, then he took a big sip of his malted milkshake.

"Idiotic woman. If it weren't for the Catholic Church, she'd have been rid of that pig years ago."

"People take their religious beliefs seriously, Harold. I know you don't take anything seriously, but religion means a lot to many people. I have to say that in my line of work, I've found people of strong faith able to withstand things that others might not."

"Well said," I told Fred. Then I took a slurp of my own malted milkshake. Oh, my, it was good!

"If you two say so. I still say the church is very much at fault, along with her parents, for the condition Mrs.—uh, the patient is in."

"You may be right," I said, admitting as much because it was the truth. I mainly blamed her parents. They might at least have shielded poor Lily Bannister from her brute of a husband.

"Well, eat up. We have to get going, and I have to get back to the hospital." Fred shook his cuff back and looked at the splendid gold wristwatch he wore. "It's one o'clock now. I need to be back at the hospital for my rounds at three."

"I guess I can take the items to Harold's house after we finish at Nash's," said I, thinking I'd got off easy that day.

TWENTY-TWO

Naturally, I was wrong about that last part.

The shopping went well. As I said, Nash's, which sat on the corner of Fair Oaks Avenue and Colorado Boulevard and was, therefore, not far from the Pasadena Police Department, carried all the items Fred needed to buy for Mrs. Bannister. Vivian Blake, a young woman with whom I'd gone to school and didn't like, operated the elevator to the second floor where the ladies' fashions resided. I decided to heck with Vivian, and smiled and made small talk with Fred. If she thought Fred and I were an item, so be it.

On the second floor, Fred and I both looked at the ready-made dresses. I'd gone to school with the clerk who helped us in the ladies' dress department, which presented a slight problem. But I just smiled at her and said, "Dr. Greenlaw here needs to purchase some items for his aunt."

"Ah," said Mildred Phipps, looking dubious. I didn't dislike Mildred as much as I disliked Vivian, but it was a close race between the two.

"Yes," said Fred. "She broke her leg and can't get around. So she needs loose clothing."

"And a nightgown and a robe. And stockings and slippers, too," said I.

"You'll have to get those items in the hosiery and lingerie departments, but I can certainly help you with dresses." I guess Mildred was too happy to be selling things for her to think much about why I might be accompanying the handsome Dr. Greenlaw on a shopping expedition for his broken-legged aunt. Thank God for small mercies.

I chose two loose-fitting frocks that were subdued in color and would be comfortable on a woman who'd recently undergone a bad beating. Because Fred turned bright red at the thought, I tackled the hosiery and lingerie sections by myself. I got some sturdy cotton stockings, some ladies' drawers, and what looked like it might be a comfortable brassiere, although you never knew about those pinchy things. Fred had stopped blushing when I returned to walk with him into the shoe department. We found what looked like a comfortable pair of canvas shoes that probably wouldn't hurt poor Mrs. Bannister's feet and a pair of fuzzy slippers that looked as though they'd feel like fur on a foot. If you know what I mean. Soft, I mean. Oh, never mind.

We walked through the rest of the store, searching around for anything else we might need and that Hazel might have overlooked. It appeared as though we'd done a good job. I didn't ask the clerk about a Bible and rosary beads, figuring Mrs. Bannister would prefer her own, if anyone could ever get them for her. I'd already given her some money, but she couldn't go anywhere to spend it. Mercy sakes, what some people do to some other people is just...awful.

It was only about two-thirty by the time we'd finished at Nash's. Dr. Greenlaw, gentlemanly fellow that he was, carried the parcels as we tramped to my Chevrolet, which I'd parked in front of his Marmon Wasp on Colorado near Nash's.

Aaaaand, we nearly bumped in to Sam Rotondo as we left the store.

"Sam!" I said, aghast.

Sam looked from Fred to me and back to Fred and said, "Daisy. What have we here?"

Oh, dear. "This is Dr. Greenlaw, Sam," I said, smiling a huge, false smile. "He asked me to help him shop for his aunt, who's broken her leg and can't get around very well."

"I see. And the poor woman has no clothes of her own?"

"She needed larger sizes to accommodate her cast," I said, improvising furiously.

"I see," said Sam again. He looked unconvinced and sounded rather like an iceberg might sound if one could talk. I wished I could fault him, but I really couldn't.

"And now, since Dr. Greenlaw has to get back for his rounds at the hospital, I'm going to take these things to Mrs.—" My imagination failed miserably.

"Mrs. Greenlaw. She's my uncle's wife," said Fred, valiantly trying to save the situation.

"I see."

"Well, we'd better get going. Will you be coming for dinner tonight, Sam?"

Sam took another long look at Dr. Greenlaw. "I don't know. Am I invited?"

"Of course, you are!" I said, trying to sound indignant.

Then I remembered I hadn't introduced the two men and fumbled with an introduction. "Sam, this is Dr. Fred Greenlaw. He's Dr. Greenlaw's son."

"Funny how that works," said Sam dryly.

"And Fred, this is Detective Sam Rotondo. My..." I gulped and then said, "My fiancé."

Sam stared at me, astounded, for a second or two.

"Very pleased to meet you, Detective Rotondo. I'd shake your hand, but mine are full at the moment. I appreciate your fiancée's help in shopping for my aunt."

"I see," said Sam, not sounding quite as frosty as he had before.

"Gotta go, Sam. See you tonight." And I skedaddled to the Chevrolet, wishing Fate were kinder to me. But it never had been yet; why should it start now?

I drove to Harold's, thinking the day couldn't get much worse. Fortunately for me, it didn't. In fact, when Roy opened the gorgeous door to Harold's mansion, he gave me a big smile and reached for the parcels in my arms. "Good day, Mrs. Majesty." He set the parcels on the floor next to the door.

"Good day to you, Roy. Could you help me get some more packages from my car?"

"Happy to do that for you," said he, sounding as if he meant it. So we went back to the Chevrolet, and Roy picked up the remaining packages. He carried them into the house and said, "Are these for the poor lady?"

"Yes. Dr. Greenlaw said she seems a little better today."

"Yes, ma'am. Miss Hazel, she says the lady is getting better."

"I'm so glad to hear it."

"Miss Hazel, she'd like to see you. I'll take these things upstairs, and you can speak to her for a bit."

"Thanks, Roy."

Roy carried the huge bundle of paper-wrapped parcels up the magnificent staircase, and we both walked to Mrs. Bannister's door. I knocked upon it lightly, not wanting to wake her up if she were sleeping.

When she opened the door, Hazel beamed at me. "Oh, thank you, Daisy! Harold said you'd be glad to help with the shopping. Fred is a hopeless shopper, so I'm extremely grateful to you."

"He did pretty well with the sheets he gave me," I said in Fred's defense.

"I'm sure his nurse got those," said Hazel with a grin. "Fred doesn't shop. Thank you so much for helping him today."

"You're more than welcome. It honestly didn't occur to me that the poor woman might need clothes to change into."

"Yes. Well, she didn't at first, but she seems to be feeling a little better. I'm not sure she's out of the woods yet, but she's at least speaking a bit."

"That's good."

"Indeed. Although she mainly seems worried about her Bible and her rosary beads." Hazel sighed, and I didn't ask her if she held the same opinion about churches as did Harold, or if she were more inclined to her brother's point of view. Not that it mattered.

When I tiptoed to Mrs. Bannister's bed, she still looked like the wrath of God to me. "Oh, dear," I said, wishing I could wave a magic wand and make her well again. "She's better, you say?"

"Yes. A little."

"She still looks awful."

"Yes, she does, but she's opened her eyes a few times and spoken a few words."

As if on cue, Lily Bannister opened her eyes, which weren't as swollen as they had been, although they were still a hideous combination of colors. She whispered, "Leo?" in a scared-sounding voice.

"Leo isn't here, Mrs. Bannister," said Hazel in a soothing voice. "Leo can't find you here. Ever."

"Ah," said Mrs. Bannister. She closed her eyes for another moment or two, then opened them again. "My Bible. Someone...my Bible?" Her words were mushy, but that was because her mouth was still swollen and a virulent purple and green. At least her split lip had stopped bleeding.

"I can find you a Bible, Mrs. Bannister," said Hazel. "Would you prefer to have your own?"

"Own," said Mrs. Bannister faintly. "Ros'ry bees."

"Mrs. Majesty has brought a new nightgown and robe for you, dear. And some slippers, for when you can get up and walk."

"Wah?" said the poor women, not opening her eyes.

"Yes, dear. You'll be well again one day, and then you'll be able to walk. In the meantime, I'm going to let you rest. After Dr. Greenlaw sees you, I'll bathe you and put you in a new nightie. That will be nice, won't it?"

"Ros'ry bees," said Mrs. Bannister.

We both understood that. It appeared the woman wanted her Bible and rosary beads more than she wanted new clothes or a bath. And, I'm sure, neither one of us had any idea how to get Mrs. Bannister her own Bible and rosary beads.

"We'll surely try to get them for you," said Hazel. She didn't say how.

"Ah," said Mrs. Bannister, and she seemed to slip off into either sleep or unconsciousness once more.

Hazel motioned me to a couple of chairs across the room from the patient's bed.

"The poor woman hasn't yet been told about her husband's death," said Hazel.

"I didn't think anyone would have told her yet. I wish we could.

Maybe she could say whether or not she shot him. This whole situation is terribly confusing."

"Yes, it is." Hazel frowned at the figure on the bed. "I can't imagine her shooting anyone, even that monster she was married to."

"I can't, either," said I, only without quite as much certainty. After all, I'd never met either of the Bannisters until Flossie showed up at our front door with the black-and-blue Lily. And no gun had been found at the scene. Perhaps Lily had shot Leo and taken the gun with her when she escaped from the house?

That seemed unlikely. When she came to our house on Marengo, she couldn't even walk. It was difficult to imagine she'd had the wherewithal to remove a murder weapon from the scene of the crime. If it was a crime. Nuts. I was driving myself crazy.

On the other hand, I might just be able to go to the Bannisters' home and find Lily's Bible and rosary beads if they meant that much to her. According to Fred, whom I had no reason to doubt, the objects of her religious beliefs might help her heal. Hmm...

"Say, Hazel, do you think there's any way I might get into the Bannisters' house? I'm sure the poor woman didn't have a handbag with her when Flossie found her. Did she? I don't recall seeing one."

"No. I haven't seen a handbag. Maybe the Bannisters leave a spare key under the doormat like everyone else in the world."

"I wonder. I think the police have finished their search of the place. They even searched the dumbwaiter shaft."

Hazel's eyebrows soared. "The *dumbwaiter* shaft?"

"Yes. I asked Sam."

"The detective? You two are close, aren't you?"

Whoo boy. Well, why not? "Yes. We're engaged to be married, although I haven't quite managed to take my late husband's ring off my finger and wear the one Sam gave me." I sighed. "I'm not being fair to Sam."

"Oh, I don't know. Grief is difficult to deal with at the best of times, although I'm not sure what the best time is for a person to die. Your husband must have been awfully young."

"He was. The war killed him, only it took its own sweet time. He was

183

gassed and shot. He'd probably have been all right if it weren't for the gas." I shook my head. "I know it's a sin to say so, but I hate Germans. Which is completely illogical, because it wasn't 'the Germans' who killed my Billy. It was the maniacal Kaiser. I wish somebody would gas him."

Naturally, tears swelled in my eyes. I swear, I don't know about myself sometimes. Maybe most of the time.

Hazel put an arm around my shoulders. "I don't blame you. So many young men were killed and maimed in that awful war. Fred served on the front in a medical capacity, and he said it was the worse ordeal he'd ever been through, and he was a doctor, not a soldier. He'd never seen such ghastly wounds. And the gas was pure evil."

"Yes," I said, pulling a hankie out of my checked jacket pocket and mopping my eyes. "It was pure evil."

"I read an article by an psychologist or an alienist or one of those folks in which he said the Kaiser had an inferiority complex because of his withered arm, and that's why he decided to take over the world. To prove he was better than everyone else."

"Good Lord." I stuffed my hankie back into my pocket and thought wicked thoughts about Kaiser Bill and his minions, for all the good that did anyone. "An inferiority complex, eh? And for that he killed thousands of people? The man's mad."

"Quite possibly."

"But that doesn't get us any closer to Mrs. Bannister's Bible and rosary beads. Fred said that sometimes a person's faith can help him or her through dark times, and this is about the darkest time I've ever seen a person go through. Well, except for my Billy." I took out the handkerchief again. I know, I'm hopeless.

"If she wakes again, perhaps I can ask her if she has a key stashed somewhere, so that you might get into the house. I suppose that's breaking the law, isn't it?"

"I don't know that it matters at this point."

Hazel and I exchanged a significant glance.

"It might be dangerous," said she.

I frowned. "I can't imagine why. The police have already searched the place, and it should be empty now."

"Should be," said Hazel, still sounding significant.

"What do you mean?"

"Well, if Leo Bannister was doing something horrible with children, maybe they're being stored in the house or something. The place must be locked up and empty now, what with both of the Bannisters gone their separate ways. So to speak."

"Merciful heavens! I hadn't considered that. If they are, I'll let them go and call the police instantly."

"But how will you explain your presence at a crime scene to the police?"

Darn. I hadn't thought about that. "Well...I'll wait and call from somewhere else. But I'll still let them out." The notion of children being held captive for the pleasure of depraved Pasadena men made me sick.

"I guess that might work." Hazel sounded doubtful.

"I'm going to try. Providing you can figure out from Mrs. Bannister if there's a spare key and that it's somewhere I can get at it."

"I'll see what I can do."

"Thanks, Hazel. I'd better get home now. I'll be *so* glad when this whole disaster is over."

"You're not alone there," said she.

TWENTY-THREE

I t was a surly Sam Rotondo who knocked upon our door that evening at about ten minutes until six, when Vi always served our evening meal.

With great trepidation, I opened the door, making sure Spike was by my side and barking his joyous welcome-to-a-friend bark. I had no desire to be alone with Sam just then.

"Hey, Sam," I said, trying not to sound as worried as I felt. Even though I'd introduced him to Fred Greenlaw as my fiancé, it couldn't be denied that the good doctor was a *very* handsome man. If I'd seen Sam walking around on the main east-west street in Pasadena with a beautiful woman on his arm, I'd be upset.

"Hey yourself," said he in a perfectly neutral tone of voice. Then he bent over and petted Spike.

"Vi's fixing that salad I told everyone about for supper this evening. She made some of her delicious dinner rolls to go with it, and I think she has a coconut cake for dessert. With ice cream."

Sam straightened until he loomed over me like a volcano about to burst. "Sounds good."

"It is. Vi's meals are always good."

Suddenly, Sam grabbed me by the arm and dragged me outside, leaving Spike indoors and probably gaping with dismay at the front door.

"Sam! What are you doing?"

"What are *you* doing, Daisy Gumm Majesty. Shopping with Dr. Greenlaw because his aunt has a broken leg? Tell me another one, why don't you? Only this time, make it believable. If you can."

"I wasn't lying!" I lied.

"Yeah? Your shopping expedition today wouldn't have anything to do with the woman Flossie Buckingham so conveniently found beaten to a pulp, would it?"

"No! Johnny couldn't help that woman. If Johnny and the Salvation Army can't help anyone, how should I be able to?"

"I'm sure you could find a way. You always do."

"I do not!"

"Nuts. I wish you'd tell me what's going on."

"I wish *you'd* tell me what's going on."

"About what?" His dark eyes gleamed in the late afternoon sunlight.

Oh, dear. Did I dare ask again about the time of Leo Bannister's death? If I did, he'd know I was doing something connected with his case, and he'd hound me. Worse than Spike, was Sam Rotondo when he was on a case.

"About anything!" I said, trying to sound hurt. "You never tell me about any of your cases, and I'm curious about the recent murder. Everyone is."

"Yeah? Define everyone?"

"Why, *everyone*! Even Lucy Zollinger is reading every article she can find about the murder. Murders are rare in Pasadena."

"Not around you, they aren't."

"That's not fair, Sam Rotondo."

"Anyway, that fellow you were with today, Dr. Greenlaw. Do you want to give me back my ring?"

"*What!*" I was shocked. "No, I don't want to give you back your ring! Why would I want to do that?"

"The doctor is a good-looking guy, Daisy. And, as a doctor, I'm sure he makes a lot of money. More than I'll ever have."

"Sam!"

"Well?"

"No, I don't want to give you back your ring. I love you, Sam!"

"You don't act like it."

"Just because I helped Dr. Greenlaw with some shopping for his aunt doesn't mean I like him in that way."

"Helped him shop for his aunt. Right."

"I did!"

Sam heaved a gigantic sigh. "Right. His aunt. Very well, let's go eat this meal your aunt prepared. At least she never lies to me."

"Darn you, Sam Rotondo." I contemplated telling Sam about Fred Greenlaw's sexual preferences but hesitated. Sam had never spilled the beans about Harold, but if he was really mad at me, he might go after Fred. After all, Fred and Harold and Del were technically breaking the law every time they...Well, never mind that. I decided the stakes were high enough for me to chance it. "For your information, Fred Greenlaw is of Harold Kincaid's persuasion."

Sam had his hand on the doorknob, but dropped it and turned to me, looming again, the big galoot.

"He's what?"

"You heard me, Sam Rotondo. And if you *ever* tell *anyone* I told you that, I'll deny it. To my dying day!"

"Huh. Is he really?"

So much for my dramatic declaration. Grumpily, I said, "Yes, he is."

"Oh. Okay. Well, then, that's all right, isn't it?" His big hand went to the doorknob, turned it, and he walked into the house to be greeted by a delirious Spike, who didn't hold grudges.

Shaking my head, I followed him. "You drive me crazy, Sam Rotondo?"

"Likewise."

I'd already set the table for dinner, and the rest of the family greeted Sam as if he were a welcome guest. I suppose he was, even though I wanted to take a baseball bat to his big Italian head at that moment.

Bless Pa's heart, as soon as Sam had hung up his hat and overcoat, he said, "Any news about that Bannister fellow, Sam? The newspapers are having a field day with the murder."

"Yes, I know they are. No news I can share."

Sensing an opportunity, I asked, attempting a tone of innocence, "Are reporters still camped out at the Bannister home? Is anyone looking for his poor wife?"

Although Sam shot me a suspicious frown, he answered my questions. "No. There's no one in the house anymore."

"Nobody's staking out the place in case his wife comes back?" More innocence on my part.

"We don't have the manpower to spare a uniform to watch an empty house."

Oh, good! I didn't say so.

"It's terrible that someone was shot in that ghastly way," said Ma.

"Yes, it is," agreed Sam.

"Well," said I in a wry voice, "from everything I've heard, he was a pretty ghastly man."

"Daisy!" said Ma. As usual.

"Let's all sit down, and I'll bring in our supper salad," said Vi brightly. "Daisy, you'll love this. It's Roy's recipe, only with my own variations."

"Sounds yummy, Vi," said I. I didn't have to feign anything that time.

We always had Pa say grace before our dinner meal, and as soon as he was through, Vi passed the salad bowl. I took a big scoop of her salad and plopped it on my plate. "Looks wonderful, Vi."

"I hope you like it." Vi smiled a secretive smile. Hmm. What did this mean?

My mouth was watering, but I managed to wait until everyone had served him or herself before I dug in. "Oh, my! This is even better than Roy's!" I said, gazing at my aunt with eyes that probably looked like Spike's when he was worshiping at the feet of one of his humans. Only my eyes are blue and Spike's are brown.

"Wonderful, Mrs. Gumm," said Sam, buttering a flaky dinner roll. "I've never eaten anything like it before."

"Me, neither," said Ma, eyeing another bite of her chicken salad with misgiving. She popped it into her mouth, though. I believe I've mentioned, probably several times, that my mother wasn't an adventurous eater.

"Delicious!" said Pa. "I think I'll make myself a little sandwich." And darned if he didn't break open a dinner roll, plop some chicken salad onto it, and take a bite.

"I like it by itself," I said. "What did you do, Vi? I see you used green grapes instead of apples."

"Indeed, I did, and I also used toasted almonds instead of walnuts."

"Ah. And there's another flavor in there that I can't quite place."

"A tiny dash of curry powder is my other secret ingredient." Vi had every right to look as smug as she did.

"Curry powder! Imagine that!" I gobbled more of my salad, trying not to look as though I was gobbling.

"Curry powder can be useful from time to time. I'm glad Mr. Pinkerton introduced me to it."

"And chorizo sausage," I said.

"That was Mr. Larkin, and it was because of the Bannisters and the Gauldings." Vi frowned slightly.

"Hmm. That's right," I said, slipping Sam a sideways glance. "I hope Mr. Gaulding isn't as horrid as Mr. Bannister was."

"Daisy," said Ma. "It's not nice to speak ill of the dead."

"I don't know why not. He was a horrid man when he was alive according to everyone I've talked to about him. I don't suppose he's changed much now that he's gone to hell."

"Daisy!" Ma said again.

Bless Sam, he foiled any scolding she aimed to give me. "Oh?" said he. "Who else have you spoken to about him?"

Drat my too-ready tongue. "Well, Lucy Zollinger and Dr. Greenlaw—the younger one, I mean—both said he was awful. It was Dr. Greenlaw's sister, don't forget, who had the run-in with him."

"Hmm. Yes. An attempted assault, I believe you said."

"Yes. But we'd probably better change the subject or Ma will send us both away from the table," I said, hoping in that way to get out of a ticklish situation.

It almost worked. Ma said, "Daisy!" once more, but Pa and Vi laughed.

Then Vi said, "Evelyn McCracken certainly didn't like the man. Said he was cruel to his wife."

"There. See? I'm not the only one."

But the topic of conversation changed, much to my relief.

"What did you say the anthem was going to be tomorrow?" asked Pa, bless the man.

"It's an oldie but a goodie," I said. "'O Happy Day that Fixed my Choice.' Lucy and I are singing a duet in the fourth verse." I looked across the table at Sam. I always set his place across the table from me, because I didn't want my family getting any wrong ideas. Well, by that time, since we were technically engaged, they'd have got the right idea, but...Bother. "You should come, Sam. Lucy and I sound good during the fourth verse, and the choir is singing it in a round for a couple of verses."

"I don't think I've ever heard that one. You Methodists use different music than we Catholics use."

"Really? I didn't know that. How interesting." I meant it.

"I don't know how interesting it is. Your services are also in English, which is a darned sight more sensible than giving them in Latin, which is what Catholics do."

"Good heavens. How many people do you think know Latin?"

"Except for priests? None," said Sam. "Maybe a doctor or an ancient scholar or two."

"I wonder why they use it then. Don't the priests want folks to know what they're saying?"

With a wry grimace, Sam said, "I expect they don't. The church likes to lead folks around like sheep, and the less they know, the better."

"I've never approved of Catholicism," said Vi. "All those idols and candles and so forth." She shot a startled glance at Sam. "Oh, I'm so sorry, Sam! I didn't mean to disparage your church."

"It's not my church. It's my parents' church. I've never much approved of it, either, if you want to know the truth."

"Sam's late wife used to go to the West Side Congregational Church, which joined up with the Unitarians last year, I think. Didn't they, Sam?"

"I think so." It didn't sound to me as if Sam cared a whole lot. Sometimes—often, in fact—I got the feeling Sam shared Harold's opinion of religion.

"That's interesting," said Ma. "I've always been curious about the Unitarians."

"I think they like to be inclusive," I said. "Kind of like the Salvation Army, but not...Not...I don't know. They don't cater to the dregs of society, I guess is what I mean."

"Dregs? That's not very kind, Daisy," said Ma. She would.

"Well, what I mean is that the Salvation Army doesn't turn people away if they've hit the skids. You know. Poor Johnny had a terrible time when he came back from the war. Lost himself in the bottle and credits the Salvation Army for saving him. And don't forget Flossie Buckingham. She went through a whole lot, too."

"Until you introduced the two," said Sam, looking at me with what I could only describe as a satirical grin.

I sighed. "Yes. I guess I did, but I was only trying to get rid of Flossie at the time."

"Daisy!" Ma cried, truly horrified this time.

"I didn't mean it in that way. It's only that she asked for my help in getting away from that awful man she was with, and I figured if anyone could help her, Johnny could. And he did. And they're now married and have an adorable little son. At any rate, I think the Unitarians take in all kinds of Christians. You can be a Baptist or a Methodist or an Episcopalian and still go to the Unitarian Church."

"Why would you want to go to the Unitarian Church if you were a Methodist?" asked Ma.

"I don't know." I was getting downright frustrated with this conversation. "All I know is that Sam's late wife used to go to the West Side Church. Right Sam? And you went there with her?"

"Yes," said Sam, unwilling to abet me in conversational matters. It figured.

"Anyhow, I've never been there. At least we've been to a service at the Salvation Army. And Johnny conducts a pleasant service."

"Yes, he does," said Aunt Vi. "We should invite the Buckinghams over for dinner one of these days," said Vi musingly.

"Great idea! Say, speaking of Flossie and Johnny, did I tell you that Mrs. Pinkerton gave me five hundred dollars to replace what Stacy and Percival Petrie stole from the children's charity fund?"

"Five hundred *dollars!*" Ma cried. "Was there that much money in the fund to begin with?"

"Not by a long sight. I think they stole something less than fifty bucks. But Mrs. Pinkerton was so crushed and ashamed of her daughter that she gave Johnny and Flossie five hundred dollars. Both Flossie and Johnny were nearly speechless when I handed them the wad of cash."

"I don't blame them," said Sam.

"I don't either," said Vi, lifting her napkin to her eyes to blot tears. "Say what you will about Mrs. Pinkerton, she has a generous soul."

"She does, indeed," I agreed, wishing the woman also had an ounce of common sense. But if she did possess such a commodity I'd probably be out of a job, so I didn't wish it too hard.

It didn't matter. Sam said it for me. "Too bad she doesn't have any sense."

Ma didn't scold him for his harsh words. My mother wasn't any fairer than life itself sometimes, darn it.

TWENTY-FOUR

Sam did condescend to attend church with us the following day. I was engrossed in a front-page article in the *Pasadena Star News* about the Bannister killing when he knocked at the door and Spike went wild with delight.

With a sigh, I set the newspaper aside—it didn't give the time, or even the day, of Leo Bannister's death, drat it—and walked to the door. We'd already had breakfast, thanks to Vi, and I was already dressed in my church clothes. Sam had declined Vi's generous offer to come to breakfast with us, claiming police duties. I'm sure he was telling the truth. Sam never turned down one of Vi's meals if he could help it.

"Morning, Sam," I said when I opened the door to him.

"Good morning to you." He knelt to pet Spike. When he stood again, he said, "You're looking lovely today, Daisy."

"Thank you!" Sam didn't ordinarily compliment me on my excessive wardrobe. Maybe it wasn't truly excessive, but I often felt guilty about making all the clothes I wore, even though I also sewed for the family. Including Spike, who didn't appreciate it.

That day I wore a charming green creation with a low waist, tied with a sash on the side. Of course, Sam's ring would have looked spectacular with the outfit. Again, guilt nearly swamped me. I *had* to get over my aversion to taking Billy's ring off and putting Sam's ring on. I guess I could wear Billy's ring on the gold chain Sam had given me for his ring, but—

Fortunately for my conscience, Pa gave Sam a hearty, "Good morning, Sam!"

Ma and Aunt Vi joined the chorus, and we all went out the front door and climbed into Sam's Hudson. Except Spike. I think dogs should be allowed in churches, but that's probably just me.

As ever, I detoured to the choir room to don my robe. Lucy Zollinger tackled me (not literally) as soon as I entered the room. "Oh, Daisy! They still can't find Mrs. Bannister! Do you think she killed her husband?"

"I don't know, Lucy. I hope not. I've heard nothing good about him, though, so if she did, maybe she did mankind a service."

Lucy giggled. "I've heard he was a real stinker. You may be right."

Mr. Hostetter, our choir director, said rather sharply, "Ladies, please get into your robes and keep your voices down. I don't want the congregation to hear such scandalous talk."

Fiddlesticks. I was pretty sure the congregation couldn't hear anything but Mrs. Fleming playing the prelude on the organ, which would drown out even Lucy's giggles, however shrill they were. The hymn she played this morning was "Crown Him with Many Crowns," which is a lovely tune, and a hymn I particularly like.

After exchanging a couple of eye-rolls, Lucy and I put on our robes like proper Christian choir girls and lined up to process into our choir alcove on the chancel. For the record, we entered the church from the choir door rather than process down the center aisle of the church. The reason for this was because several choir members were elderly and, while they still had intact voices, they weren't able to walk very well. That was all right by me, since singing, walking, and carrying a hymnal could be tricky at times.

Lucy and I always sat next to each other, and this morning we'd use our proximity to advantage when we sang our duet. Neither of us opened a mouth or uttered a syllable until we were seated. We remained silent when our pastor, Reverend Merle Negley Smith welcomed all comers and made a few announcements.

We," were allowed to open our mouths again when the choir sang the introit, which was, that Sunday, "Joyful, Joyful, We Adore Thee," music courtesy of Ludwig van Beethoven, another German, but an old one so I didn't hold the Kaiser's mania against him.

As the lay speaker read the morning's written prayer—you could follow along on the church bulletin if you wanted to—Lucy leaned a little closer to me and whispered, "What do you think you'll bring for next Sunday's covered-dish dinner after church?"

"I don't know. It'll be Vi who brings it. If I tried to cook anything, I'd probably poison the entire congregation."

Lucy smothered her giggle that time, although Mr. Hostetter shot the both of us a frown anyway. We straightened and sat still.

The two of us performed our duet beautifully, and we made it through the rest of the service without causing any further disruptions. Not that we'd disrupted anything in the first place. Sometimes Mr. Hostetter was a trifle fussy.

As we exited the chancel, however, Lucy said, "I'm going to prepare fried chicken for next week. I've been practicing my cooking skills on Albert."

"Good for you! I still can't cook a lick, even though Vi's tried to teach me."

With a little frown marring her brow, Lucy said, "That's probably only because you don't concentrate. My mother gave me a little book in which she wrote down all the family's favorite meals and how to prepare them."

"What a grand idea!" I didn't bother telling Lucy that even when I concentrated, I could spoil milk. I felt like *such* a failure every time I thought about my cooking disasters.

"It is. I can feed Albert the same lovely dishes I enjoyed growing up."

"Ah," said I and whisked my robe off, hoping Lucy would shut up about cooking.

She did, thank the good Lord. I met my family and Sam in Fellowship Hall then, after hanging up my robe with great care because I didn't want it to get wrinkled. Singing in the choir was fun. I'm not sure I'm supposed to have fun in church, even though I did, but the robes wrinkled easily. I'd take a basket full of clothes to iron over a raw chicken any day in the week. I envied Lucy her improving culinary skills.

When I joined the family group, Sam said, "I heard that one hymn in the Catholic Church I went to when I was a kid."

"Which one?"

"I don't know the name of it. It's the one the organist played before the service began."

"Oh. That was 'Crown Him with Many Crowns,' and it's one of my favorites."

"A good Christian girl, are you?" said Sam. I think he was teasing, but I'm not sure.

"I try to be."

"Do good Christian girls lie to their families on a regular basis?"

Trying to remain unobserved as I did so, I whapped Sam on the arm. "Darn you, Sam Rotondo, I don't lie to my family on a regular basis!"

"Oh. Just me, eh?"

"I don't want to talk about this at church," I told him in a furious whisper. "In fact, I don't want to talk about it at all. I'm not a liar!" Very well, so I'd just lied again. I couldn't catch a break in a bucket sometimes. I took Sam's arm anyway, and we headed to the refreshment table, where ladies of the church always provided cookies, cakes and tea and coffee. We Gumms and Majestys—and the Rotondo in our midst—didn't partake of much food during fellowship, since Vi always had something scrumptious waiting for us at home.

"Huh. Well, tomorrow you're going to get a subpoena to appear in court on Tuesday."

"A *subpoena?*" I was scared to death. "What for?" They couldn't come after me for hiding Mrs. Bannister, could they? How could they, when nobody knew I was doing so?

Eyeing me slightly askance, Sam said, "Your old pal, Gerald Kingston, is being tried for murder and attempted murder this week. You get to testify about how he tried to kill you on Tuesday."

I was so relieved, I might have fainted dead away if I weren't holding on to Sam.

That didn't stop me from nit-picking, however, "He didn't try to kill me on a Tuesday. It was on a Sunday."

"Cripes," said Sam. "On *Tuesday*, you'll have to testify about how your old pal, Gerald Kingston, tried to kill you on a Sunday."

"My old pal," I said with scorn. And probably spite, too. "The man tried to kill me."

"Precisely what I said." Sam let go of my arm and handed me a plate. "That's what the judge and jury want to hear about, so try to remember everything so you'll be fit to take the stand on Tuesday."

"As if I could ever forget that incident. Right here in church!" The recollection made me see red. "In *my* church! And the evil man killed his own brother, too!" I picked up a peanut-butter cookie and set it on my plate. It looked lonely there, but I didn't want to spoil my appetite so I allowed it to remain single.

"Just wanted to give you a fair warning so you won't be nervous."

"I won't be nervous."

"I suspect not, given the practice you've had at feeding the world nonsense for so many years." Sam put two peanut butter cookies on his own plate. His appetite was bigger than mine, probably because he was a large man.

"Sam Rotondo, if we weren't in church, I'd break this plate over your thick head!"

He grinned down at me. "I just love winding you up and watching you fume," said he, and he walked over and sat next to Pa at a nearby table.

I followed, fuming, and as I sat, I said, "You're a fiend, Sam Rotondo, you know that?"

"Daisy!" said Ma, as ever.

"Well," I said indignantly, "he just tried to scare the socks off me."

"Not really," said Sam. "I just told her she'll be required to give evidence at Mr. Kingston's trial on Tuesday."

"Oh, my," said Vi. "I'd be frightened to death if I had to give evidence in court."

"Why?" I asked. "I only have to sit there and tell the truth. The man tried to kill me with an injection of insulin."

"You'd better not say anything about insulin," Sam told me.

"Why not? It's the truth!"

"You didn't know what was in the syringe when he came at you. You can only testify to what you saw, not what they determined was in the syringe after you smashed it." He eyed me again. "Good thing there was enough of it left to test."

"Hmph. I didn't want to give him another chance to stick me with it. You can't blame me for stomping on it," I said, and took a big bite of cookie. I don't know who'd made them, but they weren't nearly as good as Vi's.

Sam said precisely what I'd been thinking. "These cookies aren't nearly as good as the ones you make, Mrs. Gumm."

"Thank you, Sam." Vi tittered a bit.

"Want me to go to court with you, sweetheart?" asked Pa. "I'll be happy to accompany you if you'd feel more comfortable to have a family member there."

"Thank you, Pa. That would be nice. I would feel better with you there."

"I'll be there, too," said Sam. "But I'll probably be busy."

I almost said he wasn't a family member because I was still peeved with him, but decided it would be a cruel thing to say. I don't hold my tongue very often but when I do, it's usually a good thing.

"Will that woman who screams all the time have to give evidence?" asked Ma.

She was talking, of course, about Miss Betsy Powell, who had been sweet on Mr. Gerald Kingston, and who did have a bad habit of screeching every time anything upsetting happened to her. She kept it up, too. She didn't stop with simply one scream. She went at it until somebody stopped her. One time I did it by shaking her hard. The last time she did it, Doc Benjamin gave her an injection that knocked her out. His syringe, unlike the evil Gerald Kingston's, was filled with something non-lethal.

In chorus, Sam and I both said, "I hope not." Then we grinned at each other. I guess all was forgiven for the time being. I hoped it would last.

By golly, it did! We all drove home in Sam's Hudson, and Pa and Sam amused Spike while Ma and Vi went to their rooms to change out of their church clothes. I did the same after I set the table. I decided to wear a pink-flowered house dress I'd made recently. It had a green background, and it, too, would have looked lovely with Sam's ring. I *really* needed to do something about this state of affairs.

Vi cooked one of my very favorite meals that day. It was a leg of lamb with roasted potatoes, fresh asparagus, her special garlicky dinner rolls—which one really needed to smother with butter in order to get the full flavorful effect—and leftover coconut cake for dessert. Since there wasn't a whole lot of coconut cake left, Vi had filled in the gap with a single-layer chocolate cake with chocolate icing. If you ever want to die happy, eat some coconut cake on top of a slab of chocolate cake with chocolate icing, and plop some vanilla ice cream on top. Mercy, it was good! Only you'll have to choose your own method of death. Personally, I wanted to live another day to dine on more of Vi's delectable dinners. And cakes.

"I swear, Mrs. Gumm, I've never eaten as well ever as I've eaten since you started inviting me to dinner at your house." Sam spoke almost reverently.

"Thank you, Sam," said Vi, clearly pleased. "But from that Italian sauce recipe you gave me, I can't imagine you not eating well while you were growing up."

"Well, yes, I guess so. But the menu tended to be the same all the time. Pasta with gravy."

"Gravy?" I said, looking at him across the table with a little frown.

"Gravy is what we call the red sauce. We use it on everything. The variety in your kitchen is much more extensive." He grimaced. "Anyway, when I was growing up, I had to contend with my family, and I'd much rather contend with the Gumms than with the Rotondos, believe me. Even with the Majesty still residing here."

"Pooh," said I, but we all laughed.

However, his comment made me wonder about little Sammy Rotondo growing up in the big, bad city of New York. Had his childhood been rough? I know Flossie's had been, although she'd been born in a particularly vile neighborhood in the city. I really wanted to know, but wouldn't ask Sam at the table because that wouldn't be fair to him, and it would probably only rile him again. As we were then at peace with each other, I didn't risk it.

Ma and I cleared off the table when the last bite of cake and ice cream had been consumed. I was pleased to see a good deal of lamb left over from dinner. That would mean lamb sandwiches for Pa and me on the morrow at lunchtime. Yum.

As I washed the dishes and Ma dried, Pa and Sam set up the card table in the living room, and were deep into a spirited game of gin rummy when we joined them.

"Anybody mind if I play the piano for a bit?" I asked. "I haven't played for a while, and I want Sam to hear something."

"Oh?" Sam lifted his eyebrows as if he suspected me of dire intentions.

"I love to hear to you play, dear," said Ma.

"Me, too," said Pa.

Vi said, "I love it, too, Daisy. And your music will go well with the book I'm reading." She sat herself down in an overstuffed easy chair, plopped her undoubtedly tired feet on the ottoman I'd had sent all the way from Turkey, and picked up *The Triumph of the Scarlet Pimpernel*, by Baroness Orczy. As I dug in the piano bench for the music I wanted, I wondered if the woman truly was a baroness. I'd have to ask Miss Petrie when I went to the library on Monday.

Along about six in the evening, Sam said it was time for him to go home because he had paperwork to go through before Mr. Kingston's trial commenced on Monday.

"I thought it was on Tuesday," I said.

"Tomorrow's just the beginning of things. The fun part starts on Tuesday."

"Oh." I didn't ask what the fun part of a death trial was.

Vi fixed Sam two lamb sandwiches for him to eat for dinner, and I handed him a couple of oranges to go along with them. He thanked us both and didn't even tease me about my contribution. After all, oranges didn't need to be cooked. I was glad of both of those things, since we'd been getting along so well.

By the way, the tune I wanted Sam to hear was "Crown Him with Many Crowns," which was right there in the Methodist hymnal I'd brought home from church so that I could practice various hymns. Mr. Hostetter had given his approval, in case you wondered. I might be a liar when I couldn't help it, but I was no thief.

Spike and I accompanied Sam out to his car. "That was pretty, what you played in there, Daisy."

"What was? Oh, you mean the hymn?"

"Yes. It has a catchy tune."

I laughed. "You pick your favorite hymns the same way I do, I think. It's the music that matters most to me. I hardly pay attention to the lyrics half the time. That probably means I'm a terrible Christian."

With a shrug, Sam said, "I doubt it. I think most of us are like that."

He bent to give me a kiss, and I kissed him back. I felt kind of lonely when he drove off down the street. However, Spike cured me of that when he went haring off in full roar after the neighbors' cat, Samson. I swear, if Samson ever stopped to confront Spike whilst being chased, I'm afraid Spike might not come out of the encounter without a few bloody scratches to call his own. Cats' claws are mighty sharp.

I went to bed that night contemplating testifying at Gerald Kingston's trial. I regret to say that most of my thinking time was devoted to what I'd wear to court. Sometimes my mind is so trivial, I can hardly stand it.

TWENTY-FIVE

Darned if Monday didn't turn out to be cold and rainy! This was most unusual weather for May in our fair city. I'd aimed to do a little gardening in the morning, but that was out. It didn't matter much, since Mrs. Pinkerton called the house right after I'd finished washing and putting away the breakfast dishes.

Of course I knew who it was before I picked up the receiver. Nevertheless, I spoke my usual greeting: "Gumm-Majesty residence. Mrs. Majesty speaking." Nobody interrupted me! Maybe it wasn't Mrs. Pinkerton.

It was. "Oh, Daisy, Rolly was so right about telling me to get away for a few days. Algie and I had a wonderful time in Santa Barbara. The coast is so lovely this time of year."

I'm sure. And probably the rest of the year, too. I didn't get to see the coast much, since the entire family, except Pa who couldn't, had to work for a living. "That's nice, Mrs. Pinkerton. I'm so glad." I didn't have time to worry that taking Rolly's advice had cured her of her problems, though.

"But can you please come over to the house, dear? I really would like to consult with Rolly. I know he can't tell me where Stacy is, but...Well, you know. It would be a comfort to me if you'd consult Rolly and the cards for me."

"Of course I can do that, Mrs. Pinkerton." I eyed the kitchen clock. It was only eight, which would give me plenty of time to get dressed and maybe dust the house. Because the rain was coming down in buckets, I couldn't walk Spike, poor thing. "I'll be there at ten."

"That would be so kind of you, dear."

And after I dealt with Mrs. Pinkerton, I could go to the library and chat with Miss Petrie. I didn't think I'd told her that her rotten cousin had stolen money from a church yet. Maybe I shouldn't although I knew I would, gossip, after all, being gossip. Besides, I had a feeling Miss Petrie wouldn't mind hearing more awful things about her cousin.

I'm glad the Petries didn't run around with guns like the Hatfields and McCoys.

Or maybe they did, and Percival Petrie had shot Leo Bannister. Hmm.

But I didn't want to think about that now. I decided to wear my brown, knee-length herringbone tweed suit. It had an unfitted jacket with a high, rounded neck and a double collar. I wore an emerald-green scarf tied into a large bow. As I buttoned up the jacket I once more thought Sam's ring would be a beautiful accompaniment with the outfit. However, I didn't want to think about *that*, either. So I grabbed my brown felt cloche hat, pulled on my stockings and brown, low-heeled shoes, snatched up my handbag and my accouterments, and headed for the door. Naturally, I stooped to give Spike a farewell pat and a word of sympathy about not being able to take him for a walk.

Pa said, "If it stops raining long enough, I'll take Spike around the block. Poor fellow doesn't understand why humans don't like to walk in the rain."

I eyed my hound. "Well...If he could talk to us in a language we understood, he'd probably say he wasn't keen on walking in the rain either. He just hasn't learned that yet."

"Suppose not. It's not as if we get a whole lot of rain in Pasadena."

Grinning at the two favorite men in my life—there would have been three favorites if Sam had been there—I said, "One more thing to love about Pasadena."

Pa laughed. Spike gazed after me with mournful eyes.

I arrived at Mrs. Pinkerton's house at ten on the nose, parking in front of the house and getting as close as I could get to the huge front porch. I dashed out of the Chevrolet, holding my beautifully embroidered Ouija-board cloth over my head. With, of course, the Ouija board in it.

Featherstone greeted me at the door, as usual and, also as usual, said, "Please come this way."

So I went that way and, taking a deep breath for courage and hoping Mrs. Pinkerton hadn't worked herself into a state yet, I entered the drawing room.

Glory be, she hadn't! Rather than weeping copiously or charging at me, she stood upon my entrance and stayed before the sofa, smiling at me. I didn't even have to grab a piece of furniture to keep from falling over, as often happened when she lumbered at me and embraced me.

"Good morning, dear. It's so good to see you."

"It's good to see you, too, Mrs. Pinkerton. I'm pleased Rolly's advice seems to have done you so much good."

"Yes," she said upon a deep and heartfelt sigh. "I still worry about Stacy, but I know there's not a thing I can do to find her or bring her to her senses."

It was my considered opinion that Stacy had no senses to be brought to, although I didn't share that opinion with Mrs. Pinkerton. I only smiled and walked over to one of the gorgeous medallion-backed chairs across from the sofa and the coffee table residing in front of it. "What would you like to ask Rolly today, Mrs. Pinkerton?"

"I've been thinking about that. I thought—and I know Rolly can't tell me where Stacy is—but I thought he might be able to advise me on how to locate her."

Although I wanted to ask why she'd want Rolly to do such a stupid thing, I didn't. I merely smiled one of my more spiritualistic smiles, opened my rather wet embroidered bag, and set the Ouija board on the table before Mrs. P. I'd been doing my job for so long, I could read upside down as easily as I could right-side up, so it didn't bother me that the letters weren't facing me.

"Very well, let's consult Rolly. You may ask the question, if you please."

Fortunately for all of us, Rolly could hold his planchette much better than I could hold my tongue, so he didn't advise Mrs. P to count her blessings and hope the brat never darkened her door again. Rather he spelled out, "Consult a private detective." He'd advised her to do that before, but what the heck. I was proud of thinking about private eyes. I'd read about them in books, but had never met one in person. Sam was a detective, but he was a public one. Hmm. That doesn't sound quite right.

"What a brilliant idea!" cried Mrs. Pinkerton, making me proud of both Rolly and myself, and also wondering why she hadn't said so the first time Rolly mentioned the matter. "Does Rolly know whom to consult about such matters?"

Since I hadn't a clue, neither did Rolly. He didn't say so bluntly, but did suggest she look up private eyes in the telephone directory.

"The telephone directory?" said Mrs. P, as if she'd never heard of such a thing.

Rolly heaved an internal sigh, and suggested she ask Featherstone to consult the telephone directory for her.

"Will Featherstone know what it is?" asked Mrs. P.

Rolly sent the planchette to the "Yes" printed at the top of the board. I didn't even sigh, wince or grimace, proving yet again how good I was at my job.

"Oh, wonderful! That sounds like a splendid idea. Thank you so much, Rolly."

He spelled out, "You're welcome." Mind you, according to the legend I'd concocted about him, Rolly had never been to school and was, therefore, nearly illiterate, but most of my clients had forgotten all about his history by that time, so no one called me on it. Certainly not Mrs. Pinkerton, who couldn't seem to last more than three days without consulting my fictitious Rolly.

After Rolly had finished doing his duty by the Ouija board, I hauled out my tarot cards and laid out a Tree of Life pattern. As soon as I saw the layout, I had to stifle a grin. The top of the tree represented the spiritual side of the person being read for. In this case, the top card turned out to be the hanged man, meaning the subject was spiritually unconscious. Fitted Mrs. P to a T. From there on out, the cards were a mixed bag. There weren't nearly as many swords as I'd dealt the prior two or three times I'd read them for Mrs. Pinkerton, but those lying on the table didn't necessarily predict a smooth trek in her immediate future.

The ace of swords could cut either way, being double-edged as it was. Then there was the two of swords, predicting that poor Mrs. P wouldn't know what to do with herself in all likelihood. That was only normal, as far as I could tell. I didn't like when the tower appeared. According to the tarot arcana, it meant Mrs. P was going to have to change her ways so that she could begin a new path. If she could, and I wasn't sure about that. Of course, if Stacy did anything truly reprehensible, the poor woman would be forced to acknowledge defeat in one way or another. If she was able to, she might be able to build for herself a brighter road in the future.

Truth to tell, I wasn't awfully keen on that tower card, as Mrs. P had up until that point never seemed to change at all. However, the bottom-most card I turned over was the ace of cups, which predicted a more harmonious time in store for Mrs. Pinkerton. We'd just have to see about that.

Not that I believed anything about the tarot, but the various cards were of interest, and I attempted to explain them in the best light I could.

You couldn't tell that from the look on Mrs. Pinkerton's face when I finished the reading.

"Oh, dear," said she. "It looks as if I'm going to have a rough road ahead."

"True, but the ultimate future looks bright." I tried to sound sparkly.

"Hmm. I hope you're right. I just worry so much about Stacy. If she stays with that Petrie creature, who knows what will happen?"

Who, indeed? "Try not to worry too much, Mrs. Pinkerton. You're not responsible for Stacy. And you're definitely not responsible for Percival Petrie. It's not your fault Stacy and he met each other and decided to marry. That had nothing to do with you, and everything to do with the characters they have. Or don't have."

I didn't generally speak so honestly to Mrs. P, but that day I thought she ought to know a little bit of the truth, whether she'd acknowledge it or not.

She didn't. "I'm sure Stacy didn't..." Her words trailed off.

I said, "I think she did, Mrs. Pinkerton. I'm sorry to say so."

The woman sat still as a stone on her sofa for a good thirty seconds. It seemed like eons to me, and I expected her to tell me to leave and never come back. But I'd wronged the poor dear.

"No. You were right to say so, Daisy. Stacy has always been a problem. It's probably all my fault, but—"

As a rule, I don't interrupt my clients but I did so then. "No, it's not all your fault. Stacy is difficult. Her father was a bad man, and you did your best. Sometimes one's best isn't good enough and that's a shame, but it's not a fault. Look at poor Miss Petrie at the library. She's a perfect gem of a woman and honest as the day is long. It's not her fault another branch of her family tree is rotten."

That did it. Mrs. P hauled out a hankie and held it to her now-streaming eyes. "Oh, Daisy," she sobbed. "I don't know what I'd do without you!"

How nice. In truth, I didn't know how I'd do without her, either, but I elected not to say so. She'd been my best client for years, but I was pretty sure I could find others to pick up the slack if she fired me. If telling a spiritualist to go to heck means the same thing as firing.

Anyway, I got out of there as soon as I could after that, and walked down the hall to the kitchen. When I pushed open the swing door, Vi was putting the finishing touches on a platter of sandwiches. They looked like ham and cheese to me, and she'd bedecked the platter with pickle spears, tomato slices, lettuce, and very thin slices of onion. Made me hungry to look at it, and it was only eleven o'clock! I remembered the lamb residing at home in the Frigidaire, however, and didn't pester Aunt Vi for a ham sandwich.

I did say, "Boy, that looks good, Vi."

"It does, if I do say so myself. Mr. Pinkerton will be here for luncheon, so I decided to prepare a manly one. These are hearty sandwiches, and I know Mr. Pinkerton likes onions on almost everything."

"So do I. Say, Vi, would you like me to get you more books from the library? I'm going there right after I leave here."

"Oh, yes, please, dear. You always choose the best books."

"It's Miss Petrie who guides my choices," I said loyally of my favorite librarian.

"She does a good job." Vi eyed me for a moment, then said, "Have you ever heard of a hamburg sandwich, Daisy?"

"A hamburg sandwich? Is that the same as a hamburger?"

"I'm not sure. Maybe. Mr. Pinkerton said he used to love eating hamburg sandwiches on buns with lettuce, onions, tomatoes and pickles. I thought I might try them out on the family one of these days and see if I might be able to duplicate the ones he likes so well."

"Sounds logical to me. But you say they're made with buns instead of plain old bread? What kinds of buns?"

With a shrug, Vi said, "I guess regular bread-roll buns. A little bigger than my normal buns, I suppose."

"I'm game to try any number of hamburg sandwiches," I said, my mouth still watering. "I think I read something about hamburgers, or hamburg sandwiches, in an article in *The Saturday Evening Post*. As far as I'm concerned, you can try them out on us any old time. Several times even, if you think you need to work on the buns some more or anything like that."

"Good. I think I'll do that tomorrow. I'll call Mr. Larkin and tell him to have his boy deliver a couple of pounds of ground round. Tonight we're going to have curried chicken, because I'm fixing it for the Pinkertons."

"Mr. Pinkerton has certainly broadened your culinary horizons, hasn't he, Aunt Vi?"

"Oh, go along with you, Daisy! You've broadened my horizons plenty enough, what with that cooking book from Turkey."

So, with a laugh, I went along with myself to the library. Fortunately for me it had stopped raining, although the sky remained black. I say fortunately, because I left via the back entrance of the huge mansion, and I didn't fancy getting soaked to the skin running to the car.

Miss Petrie sat at her desk, and I strolled up to her after depositing the already-read-by-my-family books on the returns table. She looked up at my approach and smiled. "Good morning, Mrs. Majesty."

"Good morning, Miss Petrie," I said, smiling at her in turn.

"I have some books for you, although I'm afraid nothing awfully new has come in. Have you read *The Breaking Point*, by Mary Roberts Rinehart?"

"*The Breaking Point*? Why no, I don't think so." I'm pretty sure my eyes were shining with delight. "Except for *The Amazing Interlude*, which involved the Great War and which made me cry, I've loved everything I've ever read by Mrs. Rinehart. Thank you!"

"You're more than welcome. I enjoyed it immensely. It's quite a good mystery."

"Oh, I love mysteries."

"I know you do." She smiled. She, too, loved mysteries. "And here's *Fortune's Fool*, by Mr. Rafael Sabatini. I know you loved *Scaramouche* and *Captain Blood*."

"Oh, my, yes." My little heart pitty-patted a little bit. Both of those books were rip-snorting adventures.

"I don't believe you've read *The Man in the Brown Suit*, have you? It's one of Mrs. Christie's books, but it doesn't contain Hercule Poirot."

"I'll be happy to give it a try." I frowned a little. "You know, Miss Petrie, I enjoyed *The Mysterious Affair at Styles*, but I've been musing about *Murder on the Links*. I liked it when I first read it but after thinking about it some, I'm not so sure it was as good as I initially thought."

Miss Petrie twinkled at me. She could be quite an attractive woman if she wore a little makeup, bobbed her hair, and wore more stylish clothes. I don't suppose there was much she could do about her eyeglasses, but if any man disliked a woman because she had to wear eyeglasses, he probably didn't deserve her in the first place.

That, however, isn't the point.

Miss Petrie said, "Yes?"

"Well, you know, there was a gigantic cast of characters in that book. And, according to *The Mysterious Affair at Styles*, Mr. Hastings was around thirty years old. In *Murder on the Links*, he meets and falls in love with a woman who was only about seventeen. *And* she was a twin and just happened to be an acrobat, who saved the day at the end. I...Well, I don't know. The more I thought about it, the less the plot seemed realistic to me."

"I felt precisely the same!" exclaimed Miss Petrie in a whisper. It's amazing how much emotion one can give way in a whisper. Clearly, she more than agreed with me. Small wonder I loved all the books she handed me. "Here's one you might like. It's not a mystery, but it's...good." She didn't quite sound convinced. "It's *The Little French Girl*, by Anne Douglas Sedgwick."

I took the book and glanced at its cover. "I'll give it a try." I didn't expect to like it much, although that might be because I didn't care about Frenchwomen who went to Great Britain and sought out wealthy Englishmen to marry.

"Here's another good book that's not a mystery, and I don't think you've read it. It's *The Shepherd of the Hills*, by Harold Bell Wright. I think Mr. Wright is a minister."

A minister, eh? Well, who knew? I took the book and thanked Miss Petrie, even though I expected the volume to be filled with sermons in disguise. Not that there's anything innately wrong with sermons, but I prefer to listen to them on Sunday morning, not read about them in books.

"And for your father, here are *The Wanderer of the Wasteland* and *The Call of the Canyon*, both by Mr. Zane Grey. He might already have read either or both of them."

"I can't remember, but I'll take them. Pa doesn't mind rereading books he enjoys. Neither do I, for that matter."

"Nor do I," said Miss Petrie, and she gave a soft giggle.

"Oh, but Miss Petrie, you must let me tell you the latest scandal concerning your cousin."

She closed her eyes and a pained expression crossed her face. "Do I really want to know any more evil about Percival?"

"Probably not, but this might reinforce the negative light in which you view him."

She sighed. "Go on, then. I don't think I can stand many more of those horrible Petries coming to town and spoiling the family name."

TWENTY-SIX

"They did *what?*" Miss Petrie forgot to whisper, instantly slapped a hand over her mouth, and leaned forward after looking around to see if she'd disturbed any library patrons. I looked around too, and didn't see anyone who appeared mortally offended by her outburst.

I nodded. "They stole the children's charity fund from the Salvation Army Church where they'd both been members. Stacy Kincaid had been going there for a couple of years, on and off. I don't know how long Mr. Petrie's been attending services there, but they both skedaddled out of there with their ill-gotten gains."

"The awful man! And that girl! I can't believe even Percival would sink that low."

"Hmm. I've known Stacy for more than half my life, and it didn't much surprise me to know she'd stolen from a church. In fact, whatever evil deeds Mr. Petrie is perpetrating these days, I'm sure she's right there in the thick of them."

"Dreadful," said Miss Petrie. "I feel so guilty that a member of my family would steal from anyone, much less a church."

"Don't fret about it. Mrs. Pinkerton, Stacy's mother, replaced the money. In fact, she more than replaced it. The two brats stole less than fifty dollars, and Mrs. Pinkerton gave five hundred dollars to the church!"

"Oh, what a kind woman," said Miss Petrie, reaching in her pocket for a handkerchief. "I believe I ought to donate something, too."

"Don't be ridiculous. Mrs. Pinkerton has more than made up for the church's loss, and you weren't responsible in any way for the evil deed of your cousin."

"I suppose not. I only wish all those lousy Petries had just stayed in Tulsa."

"I'm sure everyone in Pasadena wishes the same thing, or they would if they knew who they were and what they've done."

"God forbid anyone should ever connect me with Percival," whispered Miss Petrie, shuddering and screwing up her hankie with nervous fingers.

"I'll be sure to quash any rumors if I hear any. Don't fret about it. None of this is your fault."

We left things at that, and I checked out my stack of books and high-tailed it back home. I'd been hungry ever since Aunt Vi had showed me her ham-and-cheese sandwiches and talked to me about hamburg sandwiches. I wanted myself a nice, thick piece of roasted lamb on whatever kind of bread Vi had made for us last.

When I reached home, the weather had started drizzling again, but I managed to get into the house via the side entrance with my Ouija-board bag and library books without getting any wetter than I'd been when I entered Mrs. Pinkerton's house. Pa and Spike had just returned from a walk around the neighborhood, so I didn't have to feel guilty about the dog, although Spike was about the only thing I didn't have to feel guilty about.

"Hey, Pa! Want a lamb sandwich? I'm going to fix mine with some of Aunt Vi's mayonnaise, a little mustard, and whatever kind of bread she's left in the bread box."

"Thank you! I'll cut the bread for you."

That was nice of Pa, but I know he mainly offered because I can never cut a clean slice of bread. My slices always turn out to be thicker on one end than the other. Yet another instance of my stupidity when it came to all things culinary. It could get downright depressing sometimes, especially when I considered marrying Sam. Who'd cook for us? If he depended on me, I'd probably poison him within a month of our honeymoon. If, of course, we took a honeymoon. If, of course, we ever got married.

Nuts. Because I was famished by that time, I didn't change clothes, but put on an apron, got out the lamb, put it on the cutting board, and cut two fairly tidy thick slices of lamb. "Oh! There are some grapes in here, too. Want some grapes with your sandwich?" Even I couldn't hurt grapes. "They're the little green ones Vi put into that delicious salad she made for us."

"Sounds good to me."

Spike seemed interested, too, but I decided he probably wouldn't like grapes. So I tossed him a little bit of fat from the lamb roast. Clever dog that he was, he snatched it right out of the air, and it didn't even hit the floor.

"Good dog, Spike!" I told him. He wagged at me, clearly hoping for more.

But I'd been trained well by Mrs. Hanratty and Mrs. Bissel, and didn't dare allow Spike to get fat. Not only would such a condition hurt his back, but neither Mrs. Hanratty nor Mrs. Bissel would ever forgive me. And, since Mrs. Bissel gave me Spike in the first place and was my second-best client, I didn't want her angry with me.

I slathered the four slices of white bread Pa had cut with mayonnaise and mustard, and placed the slices of lamb on the bread. I had to move one over a little, since I'd missed the middle and it flopped over the side of the bread. See? I can't even make a sandwich without failing in one way or another.

"Harold called," said Pa as I set his plate in front of him on the kitchen table. I'd cut his sandwich in two neat triangles, and washed, dried and set a stem of green grapes on the plate beside it.

"Harold? What did he want?" As if I didn't know.

Eyeing me curiously, Pa said, "He didn't say, but I expect it has to do with all the commotion you and he have been dealing with in the past several days."

"Commotion? Whatever do you mean, Pa?"

Shaking his head, Pa said, "Never mind." But he grinned, so I guess he wasn't angry or anything.

"I'll call him after lunch. Say, Pa, Aunt Vi is going to prepare something she calls hamburg sandwiches for us tomorrow. Have you ever heard of a hamburg sandwich or a hamburger? I read about hamburgers in a magazine recently."

"I do believe they're ground beef sandwiches served on a bun, aren't they?" Pa swallowed his first bite of sandwich and popped a grape into his mouth.

"Exactly. We're having chicken curry tonight, according to Vi, but she's fixing us hamburgers tomorrow night."

"Sounds good to me."

"Anything Vi fixes is good with me," I concurred.

I took another bite of scrumptious lamb sandwich—

And the telephone rang.

Sighing, I rose from the table, pushed in my chair in case Spike got any clever ideas about climbing onto my chair and devouring my sandwich, and went to the telephone.

"Gumm-Majesty res—"

"Oh, shut up! I know who you are," came Harold's querulous voice over the wire.

I heaved a sigh. "Do I need to shoo my party-line neighbors off the wire?"

"No. Just get over here as soon as you can. Developments."

And with that, he hung up. Well!

I resumed my place at the kitchen table and popped a grape in my mouth. "Harold," I said.

"So I gathered. What's up?"

"Well, you know I've been trying to assist him with a somewhat knotty problem lately. I really can't talk about it, but I think it's getting him down."

"I gather you and he have been having...dealings, of late."

"Yes. I wish I could tell you about them, but I can't right now."

"I hope it has nothing to do with his health," said Pa, who liked Harold in spite of his (Harold's, I mean) proclivities.

I seized on an opportunity. Or maybe not. These things are difficult to judge when they first pop out of one's mouth. "Not his, but a dear friend's. Harold is tending to..." I swallowed another grape before I could blurt out the word *her*. "To his health. I fear Harold isn't a natural-born caregiver. I know exactly how he feels, because I felt the same way when I was caring for Billy." I had to wipe away a tear. Silly me, but there you go.

Pa reached across the table and patted my hand. "You did a wonderful job caring for Billy, Daisy. Don't ever think otherwise. I know Billy could be snappish."

I sniffed and took another bite of sandwich, irritated with myself for succumbing to grief. For Pete's sake, I was engaged to another man! Moreover, Sam was the man Billy had ordered to take care of me on the event of his demise which, I am certain now, he was planning then. After I'd swallowed and before I could begin wallowing, I said, "That's only because he was in such great pain and felt like such a failure because he couldn't work."

"I know, sweetheart. The war was hard on lots of people."

"Not on the stupid Kaiser. He's still prancing around in the Netherlands, damn his blighted heart."

Pa's eyes opened wide. It wasn't like his daughter to swear in front of the family. "I agree with you," he said mildly, "although I wouldn't necessarily put it that way."

Finally summoning a grin, I said, "That's because you're nicer than I am, Pa."

He chuckled, and we finished our delicious sandwiches and grapes. Truth to tell, I enjoyed the sandwich more than I did the grapes.

Since I hadn't bothered to change clothes before lunch, I didn't have to put on anything fancier than the outfit I was already wearing. I kept my apron on as I washed and dried the lunch dishes, and then, since I didn't need the Ouija board when I visited Harold, I got my trusty old umbrella out of the stand beside the door, gave Pa and Spike a fond farewell, and dashed out to the Chevrolet, conveniently parked at the foot of the side porch stairs. The drizzle had picked up, and was now raining in earnest, although not torrentially. Fortunately for me, the Chevrolet had a windshield wiper, which worked like a charm.

I pulled up in front of Harold's house about a half-hour after leaving my own home, mainly because I drove slowly in the rain. Nothing rash about Daisy Gumm Majesty, except for hiding the occasional woman who might or might not be a murderess. Nuts.

Roy must have been looking for me, because he dashed out to the Chevrolet and opened my door, carrying a huge umbrella with which to protect the both of us as we splashed up Harold's beautiful front walk-way. I wished I'd worn my galoshes, but hadn't. We Pasadenans didn't have to deal with real weather very often.

Harold met me in his hallway, looking rumpled and annoyed. "Took you long enough," he said by way of greeting.

"I'm sorry, Harold, but Pa and I had just sat down to eat lunch when you called."

"Untrue, Daisy. I called while you were out. Didn't your father tell you so?"

"Yes, he did, but I was hungry. Therefore, I fixed Pa and me lamb sandwiches for lunch, and we were eating them when you called again. I came here as soon as I was able."

"Hungry. Huh. I could have fed you."

"Yes, but you couldn't have fed my father." I was feeling a trifle snap-pish myself by that time.

Harold threw up his hands. "All right, all right. Sorry I sounded peeved. I *am* peeved, and it's all your fault! Dammit, the woman is speaking now, and she's driving Hazel batty with her constant demand for those stupid rosary beads and her Bible."

"Oh, dear. Well, maybe I can help." I remembered what lay before me on the morrow. "Only it will have to be on Wednesday, because I have to give testimony at the trial of Gerald Kingston tomorrow."

"Oh, God. I don't think I can stand another full day of this."

"Can't Dr. Greenlaw knock her out or something so she can't pester Hazel? Anyhow, why are *you* so worried? *She's* the one who has to take care of Mrs. Bannister."

"I know. I know. But just knowing she's here and I might be harboring a criminal in my home is enough to give me the heebie-jeebies. Plus, Del isn't pleased. He thinks it's a scandal for a wife to leave her husband."

"Del thinks that? What with him living here with you? Do you think he'd remain here if you beat him? His reasoning doesn't make any sense, Harold."

"I'll tell him you said so. But come upstairs. Maybe you can make sense of what the woman's saying. Hazel isn't quite sure because the woman's speech isn't too clear yet."

"All right." I didn't want to look at Lily Bannister again. Ever. However, Harold was right in so far as I'd thrust her upon him, so I figured I owed him. Hmm. So did Flossie. Well, I'd just talk to her about this, whatever it turned out to be.

Hazel responded to Harold's light knock on the door and smiled at me as she stepped aside for us to enter the room. I sort of tippy-toed up to Lily Bannister's bed. It looked to me as if she were sleeping, thank God.

Then she opened her eyes. They weren't as swollen as they had been, but they remained colorful. Not pretty colors. She peered at me without recognition. Small wonder.

"Good afternoon, Mrs. Bannister," I said, trying to sound pleasant. What I wanted to do was run for the hills.

"Hehhh?" is what it sounded like coming out of her mouth.

Hazel stepped up to the bed. "This is Mrs. Majesty, Mrs. Bannister. She's the one who brought you here so you can heal."

"L-Leo?"

Hazel, Harold and I exchanged glances. Hazel spoke up first.

"You needn't worry about Leo, Mrs. Bannister. He will never find you here."

Or anyplace else, now that he was deceased, although Hazel didn't add that part.

"Sh-shure?"

"Yes, we're sure, dear. Mr. Bannister will never bother you again. Believe me, because it's the truth."

"Sh-shure?" said she again.

"Yes. But Mrs. Majesty might be able to help you with getting the property you're concerned about. What is it you need from your home?"

Mrs. Bannister's gaze slid toward me. If she were able to, I do believe she'd have appeared puzzled, but evidently puzzlement was too much for her, because she only said, "Ros'ry beads. Bi'le."

Hmm. Her pronunciation was getting better. Her mangled mouth still looked as if it hurt a great deal.

"Where are they?" I asked.

"Be'room," she said.

"They're in your bedroom?"

"Yeh."

"Is your bedroom upstairs or downstairs?"

She seemed to contemplate the question for a second or two, then said, "uh-stairs."

"Upstairs?"

"Yeh."

I thought about asking where it was in relation to the other upstairs rooms in the house, but thought I'd better not. The woman clearly wasn't well enough to be interrogated. "Um...Do you have a key to your house?" I knew it was a forlorn hope, but figured I might as well ask.

The poor woman shook her head, winced, closed her eyes, and I saw a couple of tears leak there from. I felt like a brute.

"Is there a key outside where I can find it?" I asked then, hoping not to strain her faculties too much.

Evidently the question didn't fuddle her for too long. After gazing at me for a moment, she said, "Maa."

"Maa? Oh! Do you mean the mat? The front doormat?"

"No. Ba' door."

"Under the back doormat? Is the key there?"

"Yeh."

"Thank you, Mrs. Bannister. I'll do my best to get your rosary beads and your Bible for you." I thought about telling her it wouldn't be until Wednesday, but didn't. The poor thing probably didn't even know what this day was, much less when Wednesday would be.

"Thans."

219

"You're welcome. Happy to help you in your hour of need."

Lie, lie, lie. It seemed to me that all I did that dismal May was lie.

"Thanks, Daisy," said Hazel.

"Yes, thanks, Daisy," said Harold, evidently appeased for the moment. "I don't suppose you can go to the house after your court appearance tomorrow?"

"I don't know. I have no idea how long it'll take. I'll see what I can do."

"Very well."

Harold didn't seem awfully happy when I left him that day. Small wonder.

TWENTY-SEVEN

That night's chicken curry, which Vi served over rice, was very good. Sam joined us and, as usual, said, "Delicious meal, Mrs. Gumm."

"For heaven's sake, Sam Rotondo, will you please call me Vi? We've known each other long enough by this time. I call you Sam. Why don't you call me Vi?"

Believe it or not, Sam blushed. His skin, being olive-toned because he was of Italian extraction, turned kind of puce. It wasn't an altogether becoming color for him.

"If you say so, Vi." Sam gave Vi a tentative smile.

"And call me Peggy," said Ma.

"Thank you. Peggy."

"There," I said. "Now we're all on a first-name basis."

My mother said, "Daisy," although I'm not sure why. I wasn't trying to be disrespectful of anyone.

Good old Sam saved the day. Or the dinner. "Are you ready for your court appearance tomorrow, Daisy?"

"Yes. I even think I know what I'll wear. If it's rainy, I'll wear—"

"Daisy," said Sam, "nobody cares what you'll wear! They'll care what you say."

"Well, *I* care what I'll wear. Anyhow, I already know what I'll say. I'll tell the court and the jury that Gerald Kingston came at me with a syringe after luring me into that Sunday-school room under false pretenses. I won't mention anything about insulin. Can I tell them what he told me in order to get me into that room?"

Sam shrugged. "I don't know. Depends on whether or not the judge is a stickler. Strictly speaking, since Kingston lied to you, I don't suppose it can be considered hearsay."

"Hearsay? What's hearsay?"

"It's when you report what someone said to you."

"But that's not fair! I'd never have gone into that room if he hadn't told me Miss Powell needed me!"

"That's why the judge might allow it. If it comes up, just tell the truth."

Huh. Telling the truth would be a nice change.

"Will do."

"It'll be a nice change for you, won't it?" said Sam, who always seemed to read my thoughts, drat him.

I scowled across the table at him. "Cut it out, Sam. As I told Pa today, I'm trying to help Harold out of a tricky situation. It's his story to tell, not mine." I'm so glad I came up with that fib. It had stood me in good stead twice on the same day.

"If you say so," said Sam. He winked at me.

Good heavens. I don't believe Sam Rotondo had ever winked at me before.

"Thank you," said I, and dug into my chicken and rice. And, as a nice change of subject, I said, "Vi told me she's going to make hamburg sandwiches for us tomorrow night."

"Hamburg sandwiches?" asked Ma, looking worried. She didn't much care for variations in her diet.

"Don't worry, Ma. These will be delicious. Mr. Pinkerton said so to Vi, and Vi never prepares anything that doesn't taste good."

"Well..."

"I used to eat them all the time in New York City," said Sam. "People back there sell 'em out of carts, like they do sausages on a long role. What do they call them? I think they're called hot dogs. They're good. So are hamburgers. That's what we called them. We'd get 'em on Coney Island, where they called the sausages on a roll Coneys."

"I read an article about hot dogs somewhere!" I said, happy to keep the conversation rolling along safe ground. "Evidently, some fellow had the idea of serving sausages on long rolls in the eighteen-seventies. He called them frankfurters, and then some guy decided to sell them, and he wanted to call them hot dachshunds because they were long." I smiled down at Spike, who generally sat beside various family members during meals, hoping someone would drop something. "A reporter wanted to write an article about them, couldn't spell dachshund, so he called them hot dogs."

"You mean frankfurters—I mean hot dogs—got their name because some reporter couldn't spell? That's rich!" said Pa, bursting into a big laugh.

"I thought it was funny," said I.

"Me, too," said Sam, smiling.

It always made me glad to see Sam smile. His smiles didn't come often enough, especially when he was around me.

Naturally, Ma frowned. "I don't believe a spelling error should change the course of culinary history."

"I don't think you can call hot dogs—or frankfurters—exactly culinary delights or any sort of cuisine," said Pa.

"Maybe not, but they're sure good. I like mine with mustard and onions," said Sam. "And hamburgers are good with mustard, tomatoes, pickles and onions. And probably anything else you want to put on them."

"I'm glad to know that, Sam. I'll be sure to slice some onions and pickles."

"And tomatoes, too," said Sam.

"And tomatoes," Vi agreed.

"If I weren't already full, I think I'd be hungry by now, thanks to this conversation," I said.

Everyone laughed again. Thank God!

Sam had to leave shortly after dinner was over because, he said, he needed to go over the paperwork in the Gerald Kingston file to get ready for the trial on the morrow. As it had begun raining again, Spike and I didn't see him to his Hudson but left him at the front door. I was glad of that, because I didn't want to have to fib anymore.

As Sam shrugged into his overcoat and plopped his hat on his head, I said, "I'm glad I don't have to study anything. All I have to do is tell what happened." Remembering that awful day, I shuddered.

"Right," said Sam. "And one of these days, you'll be able to tell me what's going on with you and Harold won't you?"

Trying to sound and look self-righteous, only not overly so, I said, "I hope so, Sam. As I said, it isn't my story to tell."

"Right." He stooped to kiss me on the cheek. Then he hurried out to his Hudson, umbrella-less, although we wouldn't have minded if he'd borrowed one from our umbrella stand. Tough guy, Sam Rotondo.

Tuesday Morning dawned cool and gloomy, so I put the outfit I'd chosen to wear if the weather remained ugly on my bed to change in to after I ate breakfast and tidied up the dishes. It was a gray-blue two-piece suit with a single-breasted hip-line and a notched collar. I wore it with a white shirt and a dark blue tie. Since women's fashions had dictated women as well as men should wear neckties, I'd had to learn to tie the stupid things. By that time, I was as good at tying ties as anyone, I imagine. With my black low-heeled shoes, black handbag, and black turban-like hat, I looked perfect (I hoped) for my appearance in court.

I straggled into the kitchen in my robe and slippers, Spike at my heels. Spike, if anyone cares, had accompanied me to the bathroom for my morning ablutions, etc. I tell you, when you have a dachshund, you're never alone. Maybe that's true of all dog breeds; I only know about dachshunds.

"Morning, sweetheart," said Pa from his place at the dining room table. "Ready to go to court with me today?"

"Sure am. I'm really glad you wanted to go. I think I'd be nervous if I had to go all by myself." I eyed my father, who was clad in his neat blue Sunday suit, definitely not his usual morning attire. "I see you're all set."

"Yup."

"Good." It figured. Pa didn't have to cook breakfast or clean up the dishes, so he didn't have to worry about getting his suit stained or sopping wet. Not that I begrudged him his leisure. He'd worked hard before that heart attack, and I sure didn't want him having another one.

"Vi thought you should fortify yourself well for your ordeal today, so she left one of her breakfast casseroles in the warming oven for you."

"Bless Vi's heart!" I scooted over to the cabinet for a plate, then went to the warming oven and scooped out a big dollop of potato-bacon-and-egg casserole. I don't know where she'd got this particular recipe, but it was one of my breakfast favorites.

"I peeled an orange for you," said Pa.

"Bless your heart, too!"

I loved my family. You can see why. I sat and ate happily with Spike at my feet looking mournful. I tossed him a piece of egg and potato.

"Tut, tut," said Pa, grinning.

"I know. We can't let him get fat. Mrs. Hanratty would beat me with a stick, and Mrs. Bissel would cease hiring me for séances if we let Spike get fat." I eyed my dog carefully. "He doesn't look too pudgy, does he?"

"How can you tell if he's pudgy?"

"I'm not sure. I do know dachshunds are supposed to have waists. He hasn't lost his waist, has he?"

After peering ad Spike judicially, Pa said, "Not at all. He gets lots of exercise anyway, so I don't think a little drop of food from the table every now and then will hurt him too much."

"I hope not."

After I'd finished my breakfast and washed the dishes, I went to my room with Spike, and he helped me dress. I'm joking about that last part. However, I looked neat as a pin and quite the sober-sides when I left the kitchen and joined Pa. He drove to the courthouse. He loved to drive and tinker with automobiles, and he didn't often get the opportunity to drive these days.

Back then the courthouse sat at 117 East Colorado Boulevard, not far from City Hall and police headquarters. Pa parked across the street from the building, and we both noticed Sam, wearing his bulky overcoat and the same black fedora he'd worn the night before. The hat didn't look any the worse after having been rained on. Sam saw us at about the same time we saw him, and he crossed the street, dodging cars, to greet us.

"You're going to get run down if you keep doing that, Sam Rotondo," I told him.

He shrugged. "If you're more comfortable crossing at a corner, let's go to Euclid."

So we did.

"You ready to give your testimony?"

"Yes."

"Don't be nervous when you see Kingston at the table with his attorney. He'll probably be frowning at you and thinking dire threats."

"Phooey. I'll just think dire threats back at him."

Both Pa and Sam smiled.

"The trial's in courthouse number three on the second floor. I'll take you there."

"Thanks, Sam," said Pa.

"Yes, thank you. I didn't know Pasadena had so many courtrooms."

"There are four in all."

"Ah." Golly, I didn't know my fair city needed so many courtrooms. I'd always thought Pasadena to be a fairly safe city filled with law-abiding citizens—with the occasional bad apple of a Bannister or a Petrie gumming up the works. Shows how much I knew about it.

After we got into the elevator, which conveniently transported us to the second floor of the courthouse, Sam said, "You'll have to wait outside the courtroom until the bailiff calls you in."

"Why?"

"So you won't hear testimony from others. They fear other people's stories might affect your own."

"Huh. It wouldn't."

"Maybe. But those are the rules." Sam left us and entered the courtroom. I guess he'd have to give his own testimony, since he'd been the one to arrest Mr. Kingston. After he'd punched him in the jaw, but I doubt that would come up. After all, Mr. Kingston had tried to murder Sam's fiancée, and Sam didn't take kindly to people abusing me, bless him.

Hard benches lined the corridor on either side of courtroom number three. I gazed at the other folks who had gathered for various reasons. There weren't many of them, which made me glad. I guess Pasadena wasn't *too* crime-ridden. Then I spotted someone I was hoping I wouldn't see that day.

"Duck your head, Pa. Here comes Miss Betsy Powell. If she sees us, she might start screaming."

Pa looked directly at Miss Betsy Powell. I guess he didn't believe me until the woman took one gander at the two of us seated on that hard wooden bench, and let out a screech that could probably have been heard by my kin back in Massachusetts. My gaze paid a visit to the ceiling which, I noticed, looked as if it might have leaked during yesterday's hard rain.

"I told you not to look," I muttered as uniformed men appeared from several rooms in the area.

"I thought you were kidding."

"No, I wasn't."

Miss Powell had her hands pressed to her rosy cheeks, and continued shrieking like a banshee until a policeman took her arm and dragged her into a room. Don't know what kind of room it was, but her screams stopped abruptly. It's wicked, I know, but I hoped the copper had knocked her on the head with his nightstick.

"Good Lord, I'd forgotten how loud that woman could be."

"I hadn't," I muttered.

Just then the door to courthouse number three opened, and a uniformed police officer stepped out and called, "Mrs. Majesty."

Pa and I both rose. The policeman eyed us and said to me, "You Mrs. Majesty?"

"Yes."

"I'm her father," said Pa. "May I come in, too?"

After thinking the matter over for a second, the policeman lurched forward an inch or two, glanced over his shoulder, frowned, and said, "Yes, sir. You may accompany your daughter, but don't say a word."

"Promise," said Pa.

I saw what had precipitated the poor man's forward movement as soon as I walked to the door of the courtroom. Sam stood directly behind the uniform, and I figure he'd used a little nudge to reinforce his preference that Pa and I enter the courtroom together. Pa sat in a forward bench in the courtroom, and Sam escorted me through a little swinging wooden gate to the witness box.

The court clerk—I learned that's what he was later when Sam told me—had me hold up my right hand, place my left on a Bible and said, "Do you solemnly swear to tell the truth, the whole truth, and nothing but the truth so help you God?"

A little edgy by that time, I said, "Yes, sir."

"Please be seated."

So I climbed the short two steps into the witness box and sat on the chair provided. I was really glad that chair was there as I peered out at the courtroom and saw Mr. Gerald Kingston at a table with his attorney. As Sam had predicted, Mr. Kingston scowled at me, and I could tell he wished me ill. Well! If Spike had been there, I'd have ordered him piddle on Mr. Kingston's shoes. I wished the wretched Kingston at least as much ill as he did me. He'd not only killed a terrible man, but he'd also murdered his own brother and rigged up a bootleg distillery in the San Gabriel Mountains. *And* he'd kidnapped Mrs. Wright's butler and held him captive for three weeks. Mrs. Wright is an extremely wealthy woman who lived in an estate on Orange Grove Boulevard not far from Mrs. Pinkerton's place.

I was surprised to see quite a few women sitting in the courthouse pews, if that's what they're called. They were mostly middle-aged, hatted, fairly well-dressed, and seemed to gather in groups of two or three. Perhaps they came to court every day in order to get a dose of excitement. I'd have to ask Sam after this ordeal ended. If ordeal it proved to be.

TWENTY-EIGHT

Fortunately for me, the attorney for the state (I think that's what you call the district attorney) questioned me first. He merely asked me what had happened that awful Sunday after church, and I told him.

"And why did you go into the Sunday-school room with Mr. Kingston, Mrs. Majesty?"

"He told me a woman named Miss Betsy Powell needed my assistance."

Kingston's attorney leapt to his feet and said, "Objection, Your Honor! Hearsay."

The DA said, "It's a statement relevant to the subsequent events, Your Honor."

His Honor, a bald man with a white moustache and masterful features, said, "Objection overruled."

Kingston and his lawyer, who sat with a thud, huddled together, both looking grim.

So I told the court why I'd gone into that room, what happened there, explained how I'd thwarted Mr. Kingston's evil intentions by knocking a pile of Bibles from a shelf, thereby tripping him and making him drop the syringe.

"And what did you do after Mr. Kingston dropped the syringe, Mrs. Majesty."

"I stomped on it and ran for the door."

Titters erupted from the audience of hatted women. Pa smiled. Mr. Kingston's scowl deepened.

"And what happened after that?"

"I unlocked the Sunday-school room door and ran out."

"Where was Mr. Kingston during this time?"

"I think he followed me. I didn't look back because I was so scared."

"You ran into the hallway outside the schoolroom?"

Actually, I'd run into Sam, but I figured it would be better not to say that. I only said, "Yes. Fortunately, a number of people from the congregation had come looking for me, so I was safe as soon as I left the room."

"Did you ever learn what the syringe contained before you broke it?"

"Objection, Your Honor," said Mr. Kingston's lawyer, rising once more and looking peeved. "This woman isn't an expert. She has no personal knowledge of whatever was in the syringe, if, indeed, it contained anything at all. If, indeed there was a syringe."

Before the judge could respond to the objection, I said, "There certainly was a syringe! Mr. Kingston said it contained insulin. He said it would be harder to detect than the poison he used to murder Mr. Underhill."

"Objection!" shouted Mr. Kingston's attorney.

The judge sighed and spoke to the court stenographer, a youngish man who was taking everything down in shorthand. I was impressed by how quickly he wrote. "Strike Mrs. Majesty's last statement, please."

Dang. Oh, well. I guess you couldn't win them all. I expected Dr. Benjamin to testify sometime or other. He'd certainly confirm that there had been a syringe and that it had been filled with insulin.

"How did you feel after your encounter with Mr. Kingston, Mrs. Majesty?"

How did I feel? What did that have to do with anything? Nevertheless, I answered the question. "Terrible. I was just getting over a serious bout of influenza, and being frightened nearly to death didn't improve my health any."

"Objection, Your Honor!"

"What precisely is your objection?" asked the judge.

"Er...Mrs. Majesty's state of health at time of the incident doesn't matter, Your Honor."

The DA rose to respond. "I beg to differ with my fellow counsel, Your Honor. If Mrs. Majesty's health was already impaired, she could have been even more seriously hurt by the attempt on her life than she might have been otherwise."

"Alleged attempt on her life," said Mr. Kingston's lawyer.

The DA rolled his eyes and said sarcastically, "*Alleged* attempt on her life."

"Objection overruled," said the judge, sounding bored.

Easy for him to be bored. He wasn't the one who'd been threatened with a syringe filled with insulin. Alleged, my eye.

I decided to proceed with my testimony, since the objection had been overruled. "I had a relapse after the attack," I said, realizing as I did so that I'd just committed perjury. Oh, well. Anyhow, it wasn't a complete untruth. I'd been so worn down by that day's events, I'd collapsed on the sofa after we all got home.

"Thank you, Mrs. Majesty," said the DA. "No further questions, Your Honor." I later learned the DA's name was Mr. Abraham Silverman. I never did learn Kingston's lawyer's name. Didn't want to.

"You may cross-examine the witness," said the judge to Kingston's lawyer.

"Thank you, Your Honor." He strode aggressively to the witness box and frowned at me. I frowned back at him. "Now, Mrs. Majesty, you say you were *lured* into that room by Mr. Kingston?"

"Yes. He lied to me and said that Miss Betsy Powell had become ill with the same influenza that had knocked me out for a couple of weeks."

"Objection, Your Honor," said he. "Mrs. Majesty didn't know at the time that the defendant was lying to her." He seemed to consider what he'd just said and added, "*If* he was lying."

"He told me Betsy Powell was in that room and that she was sick. I knew he'd lied as soon as I stepped foot in the room, didn't see Miss Powell, and heard him lock the door behind me," I retorted.

"Objection, Your Honor!"

"Objection overruled." The judge turned to me. "Please wait until a question is asked before you answer it, Mrs. Majesty."

Hmph. "Yes, Your Honor." Fiddlesticks.

Kingston's lawyer eyes me balefully for a moment or two, then said, "No further questions, Your Honor."

"Any re-direct?" the judge asked Mr. Silverman.

"No, Your Honor." Mr. Silverman grinned and gave me a wink.

"You may step down, Mrs. Majesty."

So I stepped down, not quite sure what I was supposed to do next. I wanted to stay in the courtroom and see the rest of the trial, if I were allowed to do so.

Sam rose from Mr. Silverman's side and walked over to open the swing gate separating the audience side of the courtroom from the business side. I smiled my thanks at him.

"May I stay here with Pa and watch now, Sam?" I whispered.

"I don't know why not. Just don't blurt out anything." He gave me a grin, though, so I don't think he was annoyed with me for my plain-speaking.

"Thanks, Sam."

So I sat next to Pa, and we got to spend the rest of the morning watching Dr. Benjamin, Reverend Merle Negley Smith, and—glory be!—Miss Betsy Powell give evidence. Miss Powell had stopped screeching, but she sobbed through her testimony, and both attorneys and the judge had to tell her to quit blubbering a few times. They didn't use the word "blubbering," but that's what she did.

She was obviously irritated as all heck that the man she'd aimed to marry had turned out to be a villain. Not that she had a whole lot to complain about. After all, she'd tried to kill the man Mr. Kingston eventually *did* kill before the man died. If that sounds confusing, I beg your pardon. It was a complicated series of events.

The judge adjourned the court at about five past twelve, and Sam joined Pa and me. "Want to take lunch at the Chop Suey Parlor?" he asked.

"Sure," said Pa. "This courtroom stuff in interesting."

"It sure is," I said with enthusiasm.

"You don't have to sit through the boring parts," said Sam. "I get to testify this afternoon, lucky me."

"Just don't mention that you socked Mr. Kingston in the jaw, and you'll be fine," I told him.

Sam glanced around to see if anyone was close enough to have heard me. Blast my too-ready tongue. "Daisy!" he whispered angrily.

"I know you didn't sock him in the jaw, Sam! That was supposed to be a joke." Boy, oh, boy, if I lived to see the end of the Bannister affair, I was going to have to have a long chat with God and ask if he'd please forgive me for telling all the whoppers I'd been spouting that month. Sam had socked Mr. Kingston in the jaw. Hard. Thereby making me quite happy and pleased with him for wanting to defend me. But nobody else needed to know that.

Pa chuckled. Pa knew, too, because he was there.

"Right," said Sam punching the elevator button savagely.

The elevator clanked to a stop before us, we stepped in, the elevator girl pulled the lever, and we went from the second floor of the courthouse to the first floor and out onto Colorado Boulevard. From there we walked to Fair Oaks Avenue, turned left, and walked north a bit until we got to the Crown City Chop Suey Parlor, where we entered.

The place was full of uniformed policemen, the restaurant being only a short hop from the police department. Sam nodded to friends as he ushered Pa and me behind the waiter who'd come to the door to greet us. I noticed a few of the hatted courthouse-sitting ladies in there, too.

"Do those women come to court every day, Sam?" I asked after we were seated at a nice table against the back wall.

He sighed as he slapped his menu down onto the table. "Yes. It's their idea of a fun outing."

"I suppose it might be if they don't have to work and they're home alone all day. It might be entertaining for them if their lives are boring." I seldom had the luxury of getting bored.

"Yeah. Entertaining. That's what it is."

I decided not to speak again. The waiter assisted me in this endeavor when he returned to our table with cups of tea and a pot. We gave our orders—I ordered a number one, and Pa and Sam ordered a number four, which contained a few more items than number one—and he returned shortly with our plates and lots of dishes. I loved Chinese spareribs, so I snatched a couple of them and some shrimp. There was also chop suey, some kind of interesting vegetables with crunchy things in them, fried rice and...oh, all sorts of delectables. I love Chinese food. Heck, I love food.

When we'd finished our meals—Sam insisted on paying, which was nice of him, although it was true that he dined at our house most evenings, and I guess he figured he owed us—we walked back to the courthouse. There I detoured to the ladies' room, and then met Pa and Sam at the door to courthouse number three. Sam knocked on the door and a few seconds later, the bailiff appeared. He allowed us entry. This time Pa and I sat closer to the action. I didn't want any lady with a tall feather in her hat to sit in front of me.

The trial continued. Sam was his stolid, stoic self as he gave his testimony. When Mr. Kingston's lawyer asked Sam if he'd punched Mr. Kingston, Sam said, "He resisted arrest." It was the same thing he'd told his copper friends at the church that day last winter. Good old Sam.

The judge adjourned the trial at about four-thirty that afternoon. I was disappointed, as I'd hoped to see Gerald Kingston get sentenced to spend the rest of his unnatural life in prison. Or, better yet, sentenced to the electric chair. I'm not really bloodthirsty, but you have to remember that the man had tried to kill me.

So Pa and I went home. Sam said he'd be over at six to take dinner with us. It was only then I recalled that Harold had asked if I couldn't try to fetch Mrs. Bannister's rosary beads and Bible that day. Oh, well.

Harold called shortly after we got home. Vi was already there, cutting round buns in half, I presume for the chopped hamburg meat to sit on after she'd prepared the beef patties and cooked them in her big cast-iron skillet. I could barely lift the thing; I wasn't sure how Vi managed it. She was used to it, however, so I guess she had muscles where I didn't. I recalled the days when I used to have to wrestle with Billy's wheelchair and got all misty for a moment. I told myself to cut it out, so I did.

I changed into my old blue day dress, and Pa and I took Spike for a walk around the neighborhood. "There," I told my dog. "That should work off the piece of whatever it was I gave you at breakfast this morning."

Spike wagged at me. He was such a good dog.

Pa laughed.

Sam arrived at our house at six p.m. on the dot.

"Hey, Sam. Did anything happen after we left the courtroom?"

"No. I went to the department and finished up some paperwork."

"I thought you wouldn't have any paperwork now that the trial's almost over."

"Kingston isn't the only case I'm working on, don't forget." He eyed me meaningfully, and I wished I'd kept my mouth shut. Not, I assure you, for the first time.

The telephone rang right before Vi called us to dinner. I scurried to the 'phone. "Gumm—"

"Oh, for God's sake, shut up," Harold growled. "So did you get the stuff?"

"I couldn't. I was in court all day. The Gerald Kingston trial."

"Oh, cripes. I'd hoped you'd get out early."

"Sorry, Harold." I felt a little guilty, but not too much.

I felt Sam looming behind me, so I said, "Tomorrow, for sure."

"It had better be for sure. I'm about to go 'round the bend."

"I'm sorry, Harold. I just couldn't do it today."

"Right." He hung up on me.

I turned and smiled at Sam.

He didn't smile back. "Harold needs you some more, does he?"

"Yes, he does."

"For this problem he has that you can't tell me about."

"Yes."

"Right," said Sam, sounding remarkably like Harold, only in a deeper voice.

I decided not to say another thing, but only walked into the dining room and took my place at the table. Some joker—I suspected Ma or Vi—had changed the seating arrangement so that Sam and I sat next to each other that evening.

It didn't matter. The hamburgers, or hamburg sandwiches if you prefer, were absolutely delicious. Vi served fried potatoes with them, and we loaded our buns with mustard, some of Vi's mayonnaise, some of her pickle relish, pickle slices, tomato slices, onion slices, and leaves of green lettuce.

The verdict was unanimous. We all wanted hamburgers more often.

I put on a sweater after dinner, and Spike and I walked Sam to his Hudson, since he said he had paperwork to do back at the office. Poor guy never had much free time.

"Let me know when you've solved Harold's problem," he said. "Then maybe you can clue me in on what's been going on."

"I will, Sam."

Sam said, "Huh," bent to kiss me on the cheek, bent further to scratch Spike behind the ear, got into his car and drove home.

"I'll sure be glad when this mess is over, Spike," I told my loyal hound as we walked back to the house.

Spike, bless his heart, wagged at me.

The telephone had commenced ringing as Spike and I entered the house. With a small groan, I went into the kitchen to answer it.

"Gumm-Majesty home. Mrs. Majesty speaking." Whoever was telephoning allowed me to finish my routine greeting, from which I deduced Harold wasn't on the other end of the wire.

"*Daisy!*" wailed Mrs. Pinkerton.

Shoot. I guess Rolly's cure didn't last as long as I'd hoped it would.

TWENTY-NINE

The weather had turned mild again by the time I woke up on Wednesday morning. I was glad of it. I also almost wished I could go to the courthouse and hang around with all those other bored housewives who used the courtroom as entertainment.

I, however, was a working woman and didn't have time for such nonsense. After I ate breakfast and cleaned up the dishes, Pa and I took Spike for a walk. When we got home, I called Flossie Buckingham at her home behind the Salvation Army Church.

"Good morning, Daisy!" She was happy to hear from me; I could tell.

"Hey there, Flossie. Um...Is it possible for you to get away for a few minutes today? Maybe an hour? I need to pick something up from that woman's house, and I'd feel better if someone came with me."

"Oh, my. How...No. I won't ask over the telephone. What time do you need me?"

"Would ten o'clock be all right? I have to visit Mrs. Pinkerton at eleven because she's having another nervous attack about her stupid daughter. I don't think this will take very long."

"Let me ask Mrs. Bond if she'd be able to watch Billy for an hour or so, and I'll telephone you back. Is that all right?"

"Bless you, Flossie. I'll pick you up."

"Sounds good. Mrs. Bond loves Billy, and she's usually available, but I need to check to be sure."

"Thanks, Flossie. Hope to see you at ten."

"I'll call you right back," she promised, and we both hung up our receivers.

While I waited for Flossie's call, Spike and I retired to my bedroom, where I eyed my overstuffed closet with an eye to the warming spring-time weather. I decided on my trusty white-and-cream spotted voile dress with a wide boat-shaped neck trimmed with some embroidered ribbon. I'd worn this same outfit the day Billy died, but I tried not to think about that.

The telephone rang before I was fully clothed, but I was at least decent when I ran to pick up the receiver. I recited my regular spiel, and Flossie said, "I'll be happy to go with you today, Daisy. Mrs. Bond is delighted to care for Billy for an hour or two."

"Wonderful. I'll pick you up at ten."

"See you then."

After hanging the receiver on the cradle, I hurried to my room and dressed quickly. Then I patted my darling Spike and said farewell to my darling father and I exited the house via the side entrance. After carefully backing out of the driveway—I don't care what anyone says, driving back-ward is harder than driving forward—I drove to the Salvation Army, where Flossie awaited me outside the church. She looked fresh and spring-like in a pink dress, which she wore with bone-colored shoes, hat, handbag, and gloves. She hurried to the Chevrolet and climbed in on the passenger side.

"So what are we going to do today?" she asked.

"We're going to go to the Bannister place to get Mrs. Bannister's rosary beads and Bible."

"Is she any better?"

"Yes. She can talk a little bit, although her words are still pretty mushy. I still think she should be in a hospital."

From the tail of my eye, I saw Flossie shake her pretty head. "That poor woman."

"Indeed. She'd probably have died if it weren't for you, Flossie."

"I don't know about that. It was you who took her to Harold's. Bless Harold's heart."

"Yes. He doesn't like to admit it, but he's got a big heart."

"So how are you going to get into the Bannisters' home?" asked Flossie, her voice trembling with trepidation.

"Mrs. Bannister said there's a house key under the back doormat, and her beads and Bible are in her bedroom, which is on the second floor of the house."

"I guess this can't be called breaking and entering, since the owner of the house sent you on an errand. Can it?"

"I guess not, although I'm not sure."

With a sigh, Flossie said, "It's for a good cause."

"What did you tell Johnny about today's jaunt?"

"I just told him you and I were going out for a while. He's been pretty busy helping some recent attendees who are quite needy."

"You and Johnny are both saints, Flossie."

"Johnny is, at least."

"Nuts. You both are."

"I don't feel awfully saintly, keeping Mrs. Bannister's hiding place from Johnny."

"I don't, either, but we really are performing a good deed. If the police knew where she was, they'd probably smash down Harold's front door, arrest the poor woman, and then arrest you, me, Harold, Fred, Hazel and Roy."

"Hideous thought."

"Yes. So don't think of it as a criminal act. Think of it as an act of mercy."

"Right."

I could tell Flossie was of two minds about that "act of mercy" thing, but she said no more.

The Bannisters had lived in a gorgeous, huge house in the San Rafael hills, not far from a former client of mine. The house didn't have a locked gate, for which I was grateful, and at least the drive was empty. Therefore, the house must be empty too. I hoped. I parked the Chevrolet in back of the house, praying no one would see my car from the street. Not that the streets in this part of town were busy. These were the mansions of people who employed minions to work for them, and most of the minions had to take busses to get to and from work. They didn't have cars of their own to clutter up the streets. I hoped none of the Bannisters' minions had been retained to keep the house dusted. I doubted it, since the mister was dead and the missus was presumed to have killed him and run off.

I turned off the motor, looked at Flossie, who looked back at me, and we both sucked in huge breaths.

"Nothing ventured, nothing gained," said I as I opened my door and got out of the machine.

"Absolutely," said Flossie, doing likewise.

As Mrs. Bannister had said, the key to the house lay under the back doormat. So far, things were going well, although we hadn't entered the house yet. I stuck the key into the back door keyhole and it turned like a charm. Flossie and I exchanged another couple of glances, and I pushed the door open.

We both stepped into what looked like a service porch and stopped still. I don't know about Flossie, but I strained my ears until they nearly popped, trying to hear any noises that might be coming from anywhere in the house. I heard nothing. I glanced at Flossie, who shrugged and shook her head. The place was dark, what with no lamps lit, and I didn't think it would be wise to turn on any switches.

I whispered, "Let's look for the staircase."

Flossie nodded.

We both tiptoed, even though I was sure the house was empty. Still and all, one could never quite tell about these things. The staircase was easy to find, being off the front entryway, which was tiled in what looked like Mexican-patterned tiles. But that was a guess on my part, and based on the fact that I'd seen similar tiles in Mijare's, the Mexican restaurant in town where I liked to dine occasionally. The whole family did. So did Sam, for that matter.

Flossie and I quietly ascended the staircase. Unlike Harold's home, this staircase didn't have any odd bends in it. It led onto the upper story, and Flossie and I commenced opening doors, looking for a bedroom that might belong to Lily Bannister. It didn't take long. Not only did we discover Mrs. Bannister's bedroom, but we also discovered dried blood-stains on the carpeting. Ha. So the evil Mr. Bannister *had* beaten his wife to a pulp. Unless those stains were where Mr. Bannister had fallen after Mrs. Bannister shot him. I wondered why the police hadn't taken up the carpeting, but didn't dwell on the matter.

Bother. I wish I'd asked Sam where in the house Mr. Bannister's body had been found. Too late by that time.

On the table beside the bed—a single bed, leading me to believe Mr. and Mrs. Bannister occupied separate bedrooms—lay a Bible. On top of the Bible sat a string of rosary beads. I didn't know much about rosary beads, but these looked expensive to me. Not bothering to stifle my sigh of satisfaction, I stuffed them into my pocket and handed Flossie the Bible.

"Thank God," whispered Flossie, taking the Bible from me.

"You bet," I whispered back.

We weren't as quiet going down the staircase as we'd been going up. That turned out to be a big mistake on our part.

We'd just left the tiled entryway and walked back to the service porch, when whom did I see but Stacy Kincaid, in all her evil glory.

"*You!*" she bellowed. "Percy! Come here!"

"What?" came a masculine voice.

I searched for where the voice had emanated and saw a door opened to what was probably the basement. Crumb.

"Come here!" Stacy shouted again. "Get in here now! Daisy Majesty has come to spoil the day!"

"What the hell?" the man's voice said.

And darned if I didn't see a man emerge from a set of steps leading to the Bannister's basement. Flossie gasped.

Then Stacy attacked me. She belted me one in the mouth with her closed fist, and I fell down like a wet mop.

Flossie shrieked, "Oh, no you don't!"

I'm not sure what Flossie did, but Stacy joined me on the floor shortly thereafter. The man—Percival Petrie unless I missed my guess—bounded into the service porch from the basement steps. I looked to see what

Flossie had done to fell Stacy and saw her standing there with a kitchen chair in her hands, looking shocked.

I crawled toward the back door, hoping we could escape with little more damage than had already been done. I'd just slithered to the top of the basement steps when darned if Flossie didn't hurl herself and her chair at Percival Petrie. He bumped into me hard, said, "Shit!" stumbled over my inert form, and bounced down the basement steps.

Stacy cried, "Percy! *Percy!* What have you *done,* you bitch?"

"Be quiet this instant, or I'll wallop you again," Flossie said, the threat in her voice clear to hear.

"That's enough, all of you," came a female voice I didn't recognize.

When I turned my head to see who had spoken, I didn't recognize the woman from whom the voice had come, either. I sure recognized the big gun in her hand, though. Not it's model or make, but it was definitely a gun.

Flossie dropped the chair. I got to my feet.

Stacy wailed, "Percy! *Percy!*"

"Shut up!" said the woman, aiming the gun at Stacy, which was a nice change, as it had been aimed at me.

Flossie and I backed toward the basement steps, and we both raised our hands in a gesture of surrender. Don't ask me why, but I wondered what Flossie had done with the Bible.

Before I could ask, a voice I *did* recognize came from the back door. "Put down the gun and turn around slowly."

"Sam!" I cried. "What are *you* doing here?" He held a gun aimed at the woman who'd just aimed her gun at Stacy.

Sam didn't have the chance to tell me why he was there, because the woman whirled around and pulled the trigger on her gun. Sam fell with a huge *thump* onto the service porch floor. His gun went off with a big *boom,* and the strange woman staggered and dropped her own weapon.

I saw red. I really did. Before the woman could catch her balance or threaten anyone again, I grabbed the chair Flossie had dropped and swung it at her. The woman, not Flossie. Caught her on the side of the head, and darned if she didn't drop to the floor with another, smaller *thump.*

Without thinking, I grabbed the unknown woman's gun from where it had slid across the floor toward me and cried, "Flossie, call the police! Call the doctor! Call an ambulance!"

She'd run to Sam, and I handed her the gun.

"If either Stacy or her precious Percy or that woman so much as moves a finger, shoot 'em."

"You bet," said Flossie, holding the gun on Stacy and backing into the kitchen, where we'd both seen a telephone hanging on the wall.

"Sam! Sam! Where did she hit you?" I started crying. "Oh, Sam, why did you come here? How did you know to come here?"

"Shut up," said my beloved. "Get a dishtowel and tie it around my leg above the wound." I saw a pool of blood gathering beneath his left leg and nearly fainted. I guess Sam knew that because he said, his voice fainter, "I'll bleed to death if you don't."

His face was horribly pale. I rushed into the kitchen, kicking Stacy Kincaid in the head as I passed her—didn't want her to get any ideas—snatched several towels from a rack, and raced back to Sam. He'd passed out.

I cried some more as I tied a tourniquet around his upper thigh. I also prayed and prayed and prayed.

THIRTY

As soon as the ambulances left with their occupants—Sam got an ambulance by himself while Stacy, the woman whom I soon learned was Mrs. Gaulding, and Percival Petrie crowded into the other one—I called Pa and asked him to telephone Mrs. Pinkerton and tell her I couldn't attend to her wishes that morning at eleven.

"Sam's been shot," I sobbed into the receiver, not caring if all the party-line neighbors in the entire city of Pasadena heard me.

"He's *what*?"

"Come to the Castleton Hospital, Pa. I'll tell you all about it there."

If I had anything to tell. At that point in time, Sam was still out cold. He'd been taken to the emergency room, and been attended to by a host of doctors. They wouldn't let me in to see him. Flossie sat in a hard chair in the waiting room and held me as I cried.

Damn! I didn't want to lose another man I loved. What's more, I didn't want another man I loved to become a cripple! I hated life during those perilous hours.

Pa soon arrived and came over to sit in another chair on my other side. He held the parts of me Flossie couldn't get to.

Standing, Flossie said, "Now that your father's here, I'm going to telephone Johnny. I guess I'll have to tell him what happened."

Sniffling pathetically, I said, "Did you get the Bible?"

"Yes." Flossie held it out to me.

"Thank you," I whimpered. "I still have the rosary beads."

"Bible? Rosary beads? What are you two talking about?" asked Pa.

"It's to do with Harold's problem," said I, still clinging to our subterfuge with both hands, even though they were now wet with Sam's blood and my own tears.

"Who shot Sam?" Pa asked.

"Some woman named Gaulding, according to the police," Flossie told him. "Sam's bullet winged her in the arm, I think. Then Daisy nearly battered her to death with a kitchen chair."

I looked up through watery eyes to see Flossie smile a loving smile at me. I tried to respond in kind, but couldn't because I was still crying.

"Who's Mrs. Gaulding?" said Pa, understandably confused.

Because I felt like a fool, I tried to swallow the rest of my tears and answer my father. "We-we don't...really know." Sniffle. "Some lady who's..." Sniffle. "...in cahoots with Mr. Leo Bannister, Stacy Kincaid, and Percival Petrie."

Pa shook his head. "I still don't understand any of this."

"Neither..." Sniffle. "...do I."

Flossie had left the waiting room in search of a telephone. Shortly after she vacated the room, a contingent of policemen, some in uniform and some not, entered the room and walked over to Pa and me.

"Mrs. Majesty?" said one of the non-uniformed policemen.

"Y-yes?"

"Did you know there were twelve children chained together in that basement?"

My tears dried instantly. *"What?"*

"There were twelve children chained up in there, ranging in age from eight to approximately fourteen, although it's difficult for us to tell, since none of them speak English very well."

"I had absolutely no idea," I told him. "Not that it surprises me," I added bitterly.

"Good Lord!" said Pa.

"I *told* you Leo Bannister was an evil man," I said.

"Do you know how Mr. Petrie met his death?" the officer asked next.

"He's *dead*?" I shook my head, trying to take in his words.

"Yes, ma'am. He died from a broken neck after he fell down the basement steps."

"Good! He was an evil, no-good son of a gun! And yes, I guess I *do* know how he met his end. After Stacy punched me in the jaw, I fell down. That Petrie creature tripped over me and fell down the stairs. I'm sure I have a hideous bruise to show for it."

And darned if I didn't rise from my chair and attempt to show the officers the bruise on my side over my ribs. I don't know where my modesty had gone, but it wasn't with me at that moment.

"Daisy, it's all right," Pa said, grabbing my hand so I couldn't pull up my skirt. "I believe you. Your face is a swollen mess. And you say Stacy Kincaid did that?"

I felt my cheek and winced. My eye hurt, too, so I felt that, and discovered it was swollen. "Yes. She punched me in the face, damn her to hell and back."

"Daisy!" cried Pa, shocked by my language.

"She's right, Mr. Gumm," came Flossie's voice.

I looked up and saw she'd come back to the waiting room. "Johnny's on his way, Daisy."

"Oh, dear."

"It's all right," she assured me. "He only knows you've been hurt, Sam's been shot, and Stacy battered you. Did I hear someone say that horrible Petrie man is dead? Good!"

"I'm still confused," said Pa.

"I don't blame you," said the officer not in uniform. He stuck out his hand. "Detective Roland Oversloot," he said to Pa.

Pa shook his hand. "Do you know what these two are talking about?" asked Pa, nodding at Flossie and me. Flossie had retaken her seat at my side. I reached for her hand, and we squeezed each other for comfort.

Detective Oversloot said, "We were investigating Mr. Leo Bannister for various crimes against children. He also ran a disorderly house."

"What's a disorderly house?" I asked.

Flossie clued me in. "A brothel."

"Oh, my."

Oversloot said, "Mr. Bannister's death came as a surprise to us."

"And you think his wife killed him," I said in disgust.

"Not any more. We're fairly certain he was shot either by Mr. Petrie or Mrs. Gaulding. But we can't find Mrs. Bannister. For all we know, they killed her and buried her somewhere."

"Huh. I told you she wasn't guilty," I said to my father.

He held his hands up in a gesture of bewilderment. "I don't remember ever accusing her of anything."

I pierced Detective Oversloot with an icy glare. "Precisely when did Mr. Leo Bannister die, Detective? I *really* need to know the day he was killed."

Oversloot squinted at me, but he said, "Wednesday, May thirteenth. Why?"

I swear, I nearly fainted dead away. Flossie and I squeezed each other's hands again, and this time Flossie started crying.

After gulping audibly, I said, "What time on Wednesday?" What if he'd been shot on Tuesday and was only discovered in Wednesday?

"Why do you want to know?" Oversloot asked suspiciously.

"I don't *want* to know. I *need* to know. You'll have to trust me about this."

Oversloot paused for fully long enough for me to get the impression he didn't trust me one tiny bit.

"Trust her, Detective," sobbed Flossie. "It's really important."

"Around four o'clock in the afternoon," said Oversloot. He sounded grouchy.

"How do you know the time?" I asked.

"Cra—Why do you need to know the time of his death?"

Then it was my father stepped nobly into the breach. "I think it's important, Detective Oversloot, or these ladies wouldn't be asking about it. I'm Mrs. Majesty's father, and a long-time friend of Mr. and Mrs. Buckingham and Detective Rotondo. Please tell us how you can know the time Mr. Bannister was shot."

"The butler and the upstairs maid heard the shot," said Oversloot grudgingly.

Flossie and I sagged in our chairs.

"Then Mrs. Bannister didn't shoot her husband," I said.

"Oh, Daisy!" cried Flossie, and we hugged each other once more. By that time I'd resumed crying.

"How do you know that?" demanded Oversloot.

I let go of Flossie, sniffled once more, and mopped my face with my already sodden hankie. "Because Mrs. Buckingham found Mrs. Bannister nearly beaten to death on Tuesday, May twelfth. She brought her to me, I called a friend of mine, he called a friend of his who's a doctor, and the doctor fixed her up as well as he could, although he said and still says she should be in a hospital. His sister is a nurse, and she's been tending to Mrs. Bannister."

"Why didn't you just take her to the hospital?"

"Because she feared her husband would find her. He beat her up all the time. Her parents wouldn't help her. She's a Roman Catholic, and even her *priest* wouldn't help her! But now that there's no way Mr. Bannister can hurt her again, we can bring her to the hospital."

Frowning, Oversloot said, "Perhaps we should send an ambulance to pick her up."

Flossie and exchanged a couple of meaningful glances. I said, and firmly too, considering my state of blubberishness at the time, "That depends on whether or not any of us will be charged with anything. She's no murderess, but I suppose someone could make a case of...I don't know. Obstructing justice or something, although we didn't obstruct anything. The poor woman hasn't even been conscious until a day or so ago, and she still can't talk very well because that brute of a husband bashed her face in. He also kicked her in the ribs and the head. Dr.—Uh, the doctor who tended to her said she might have permanent brain damage."

"Good Lord," whispered Pa. "No wonder you've been nervous as a cat this past week or so."

"Precisely. So, before I tell anyone where she is, I need to know if any of the people hiding her can be charged with anything."

Oversloot and his fellow police officers glanced among themselves.

Finally, Oversloot said, "Did Detective Rotondo know anything about this?"

"*No!*" I hollered. Then, realizing where I was, I said more softly, "No, he didn't know a thing. He's been pestering me for days to tell him the secret I've been holding, but I couldn't do that because then he'd have been obliged to report Mrs. Bannister's whereabouts to the police department. At that time we didn't even know when Mr. Bannister died. Now that we know she couldn't have killed him...Well, we'll just have to find out if anyone can be charged for hiding her."

"Aw, Jes—heck," said Oversloot.

A doctor came into the waiting room. His white smock was dotted with blood. I feared it was Sam's. I leaped to my feet. "Is he all right? Sam? Is he all right? Detective Rotondo, I mean?"

The doctor looked from me to Detective Oversloot and spoke to the man, blast him. "He's lost a lot of blood, but he'll recover, barring massive infection. He'll be laid up for a while and won't be able to walk any time soon."

"Is he awake? May I see him?" I asked, desperate to see my beloved.

"Who are you?" the doctor demanded.

I took a deep breath and blurted out, "I'm Detective Sam Rotondo's fiancée, is who I am!"

Three or four people in the room gasped, but I'm not sure which three or four they were. I suspect Pa and Flossie were two of the gaspees.

The doctor alone seemed unimpressed. "You're his fiancée, are you? How can I know that?"

"Because Sam gave me this engagement ring." I plucked the golden chain from beneath my formerly pristine white-and-cream outfit and flashed the beautiful gold ring with the sparkling emerald at the room in general.

Flossie said, "Oh, Daisy, that's just gorgeous." She hurried to me and picked up the ring. "Perfectly lovely!"

"Thank you. Sam's father designed and made it. He's a jeweler in New York City." I shot a peek at Pa, but he merely sat there with his mouth agape.

"Why don't you wear it on your finger?" asked Oversloot suspiciously.

Out of custom I suppose, I clasped my left hand with my right and started leaking tears again. Boy, was I a mess that day! "B-because I couldn't quite make myself take my late husband's ring off my finger. But I will now." Defiantly, I unclasped the chain and slid Sam's ring from its links. Then I slipped Billy's ring from the ring finger of my left hand and shoved the plain gold band into the pocket still holding Mrs. Bannister's rosary beads, and put Sam's ring on my finger. Then, naturally, I burst into tears once more. Pathetic.

Both Pa and Flossie hugged me.

Officer Oversloot said, "Oh, for God's sake."

The doctor said, "Hmm. In that case, I guess you can see him. But only you. And only for a minute or two."

"I'll have to question him," said Oversloot in an aggressive tone of voice.

"If what this lady says is true," said the doctor. "I think he'd rather see her first. He's been asking for someone named Daisy. You can question him when he's in better shape."

And darned if he didn't lead me into Sam's room.

THIRTY-ONE

Once the doctor sat me down beside his bed and Sam half-opened his eyes, I asked, "How did you know I was at the Bannister house?"

"Followed you," said he in a voice of gravel.

"Why?"

He shut his eyes and grunted. "Knew you were lying."

"I wasn't lying! I just...didn't tell the entire truth."

"Huh."

So I finally told him where Mrs. Bannister was and why Harold, Flossie, Hazel Greenlaw, Fred Greenlaw and I had been hiding her. Then he grumbled and mumbled and carried on so much, you'd have thought *I'd* shot him.

"Oh, be quiet, Sam Rotondo." I clasped his hand, and he turned to glare at me.

Then his gaze slid to my hand holding his, and his eyes opened wide. "'S'at my ring?" His voice was sort of a gasping croak.

"Yes."

"Be damned." And he passed out again.

So here are the results of those awful lie-filled two weeks in May of 1924.

None of the conspirators who'd hidden Mrs. Bannister were arrested for anything. In fact, Dr. Fred Greenlaw was thanked politely by the surgeon at the hospital for taking such good care of Mrs. Bannister. Flossie and I visited her several times when I could get away from Sam's bedside.

When I left Sam's room that first night, I dug into the pocket of my dress and pulled out Billy's ring and Sam's gold chain. I carefully slid Billy's ring onto the chain and clasped it around my neck. Pa patted me on the back and held me while I cried some more. Huh. I was a wreck.

Mrs. Bannister lauded Flossie and me with thanks and, a little later, money. I graciously accepted my portion of her largesse. Flossie tried to refuse hers, but I elbowed her in the side. I whispered to her that she would hurt Mrs. Bannister's feelings if she didn't accept the woman's reward. Flossie whispered she didn't believe me, but I told her I had scads more experience dealing with wealthy women than she did, and besides, the Salvation Army could use the funds. She shut up after that.

Mrs. Bannister was ushered from Harold's house to the Castleton Hospital via ambulance after I was assured (several times) that no charges would be brought against those of us who had helped and hidden her. Her stay at the Castleton lasted for two months, and she still had trouble seeing and walked with a limp when she was released from the hospital. Fortunately, she was a wealthy widow, thanks to her rotten husband's demise, so she could hire people to take care of her. Hazel Greenlaw stayed on as her private nurse for several months.

Harold gave Mrs. Bannister the Bible Flossie still had and the rosary beads I still had, and he scrammed out of her room like a spooked rabbit when she started crying at him. I know about that last part because Harold told me.

The day after Sam was shot, I was sitting at his bedside watching him sleep when I heard a subdued commotion coming from the hallway. The door opened, and I looked up to see Mrs. Jackson, a genuine Voodoo mambo from New Orleans and the mother of Joseph Jackson, Mrs. Pinkerton's gatekeeper, standing in the doorway. Mrs. Jackson always made quite an impression, as she dressed in the most alarming colors, wore fantastic turbans and dripped with beads, some of which sparkled even in the dim lighting of the hospital room.

I blinked hard and whispered, "Mrs. Jackson! How good of you to come." I rose and would have walked over to her, but my legs gave out and I had to grab the foot post of Sam's bed, thereby waking him. He growled.

Waving at me to sit again, Mrs. Jackson lumbered to Sam's bedside and gazed down at him. "He's hurt bad," said she.

"Yes," said I, sniffling slightly.

Sam's eyes slitted open, and he gazed up to see Mrs. Jackson looming over him. She was a very large woman. He said, "Huh?"

"Quiet, young man," she commanded. "You wear this."

And darned if Mrs. Jackson didn't pull out a Sam-like Voodoo juju from her enormous handbag and set it on his chest. As Sam tried to look at his juju, his eyes crossed, then shut, and he slept again.

Naturally, I was sobbing by that time. "Th-thank you, Mrs. Jackson."

"Huh. Just be sure he wears that. It will heal him and help him."

"I'll be sure he does," I told her.

She said, "Hmm," shut her eyes and, I presumed, prayed silently over Sam's inert form for a few moments. Then she patted me on the head, said, "You're a good girl," and left.

That was probably the most exciting thing that happened during Sam's hospital stay.

Percival Petrie had died from tripping over my body and falling down the Bannisters' basement stairs. My ribs hurt for a month, but Dr. Benjamin said they were only bruised and not broken. I silently took issue with the word "only," but didn't let on. They hurt, darn it.

Stacy Kincaid was arrested and charged with abetting at least one murder, and for assisting her evil boyfriend in kidnapping and hiding children for immoral purposes. I'm not sure if she was also charged with assisting in running Percival Petrie's and Leo Bannister's so-called "disorderly house," and I don't care.

Mrs. Gaulding turned out to be Eloise Frances Petrie Gaulding. The next time I went to the library, roughly a month or so after everything happened, I told Miss Petrie about her evil schemes. I also told her I'd been shocked to learn Mrs. Gaulding was another one of the rotten Petries.

"Small wonder," said she, aghast anyway. "She was Percival's older sister and an awful woman in her own right. I know this is sinful of me to say, but I'm glad Percival is dead. Was Eloise's husband in on her crimes?"

"Apparently not. When Detective Oversloot came to our house to talk to Sam, he said Mr. Gaulding had broken down and sobbed his heart out when he heard the news."

"That doesn't surprise me, either. They're all good actors on that side of the Petrie family. I'm sure he had no idea what his wife was up to."

"Oh, and Stacy Kincaid and Percival Petrie never got married. They lived together in sin. Evidently they took up residence in the Bannisters' home once the police had finished searching it."

Miss Petrie humphed. Then she handed me *The Step on the Stair*, by Mrs. Anna Katherine Green; *The Mystery Road*, by Mr. E. Phillips Oppenheim; *Lucinda*, by Mr. Anthony Hope; and *The Cask*, by Mr. Freeman Wills Crofts. Then, because I wanted to, I fetched Mrs. Mary Roberts Rinehart's *The Window at the White Cat*, Mr. Anthony Hope's *The Prisoner of Zenda* and Mr. R. Austin Freeman's *Dr. Thorndyke's Casebook* from the stacks. These were all comforting books in my life. What's more, I aimed to read at least *The Window at the White Cat* to Sam. That would shut him up for a while, and he'd never again be able to doubt the efficacy of dumbwaiters as hiding places.

Johnny and Flossie Buckingham had their hands full when they took in the children who'd been held captive in the Bannisters' basement. I'm sure Mrs. Bannister's monetary gift to Flossie helped them a great deal.

I also know, although he wasn't the one who told me, that Harold Kincaid was instrumental in locating the families of the children who had been kidnapped. He assisted them all to immigrate to the United States. As far as I know, they're all still here, working hard and being useful almost-citizens.

Sam was laid up at the hospital for three weeks, whining and complaining the whole time. He didn't admit to whining, but did say, "You'd complain, too, if you couldn't get around."

"I suppose so," I said, wanting to slug him. Not that I didn't still love him, because I did. However, he was a most exasperating patient.

The notion of Mrs. Pinkerton calling and wailing at me for having her daughter arrested plagued me for the several days I remained with Sam at the hospital. When the doctors finally declared Sam out of the woods at the beginning of his second week at the Castleton, I drove home and dropped dead on my bed. Not really, of course, but boy, was I exhausted. Spike, elated to see me, kept me company.

When I finally crawled out of bed ten or twelve hours after I'd fallen into it, I noticed the telephone receiver dangling from its cord. I blinked my gummy eyes at Pa, who sat at the kitchen table. This was on a Wednesday morning.

Pa winked at me. "Mrs. Pinkerton has been telephoning you daily six or seven times. She claims she's in a crisis."

"Whoo, boy. Did she say she wanted to fire me for getting her daughter into trouble?"

"You didn't get her daughter into trouble! Stacy Kincaid did that all on her own."

Plunking myself onto a kitchen chair and cupping my head on hands supported by my elbows, which were planted on the table, I said, "I know that, and you know that. Flossie, Harold and everyone else involved know that, and the entire Pasadena Police Department knows that, but Mrs. Pinkerton has her own version of reality sometimes. Most of the time, actually." Something occurred to me. "Oh, Lord! She hasn't fired Aunt Vi, has she?"

With a chuckle, Pa said, "No, she didn't say she wanted to fire either of you. Vi's over there now. She wants you to rush to her side and ply the Ouija board and the tarot cards for her."

I groaned.

"But first eat a good..." Pa's words trailed off as he glanced at the kitchen clock. "Well, it's lunchtime, so eat some lunch. Your aunt fixed a great pot roast yesterday, and I'll cut some bread for you."

"Thanks, Pa. Think I'll take a bath first." I felt sticky and sweaty. The month of May was almost at its end, and I kind of hoped June and July would be foggy and cool, because I was hot. June and July were often cool and foggy, even though they were supposed to be summer months. Talk to God about it; I have no idea why it happens.

So Spike and I retired to the bathroom, and I took a bubble bath, washed my hair, brushed my teeth, combed out my hair, and retired once more to my bedroom. There I put on a clean housedress. I felt more human after that, and resumed my seat at the kitchen table. Pa had fixed a sandwich for me!

Naturally, I burst into tears. I swear, I was worth absolutely nothing at all in those terrible days.

Nevertheless, after I'd eaten my sandwich and an orange from our Valencia orange tree, I took my heart (and perhaps my livelihood) in my hands and telephoned Mrs. Pinkerton.

"*Daisy!*" she shrieked after Featherstone had called her to the telephone.

"Mrs. Pinkerton," I said in a subdued tone. "I want you to know how very sorry—"

She interrupted me with another screech. "*Noooo!* Don't be sorry! You finally opened my eyes to what a truly awful person Stacy is. She's her father's daughter, and there's no getting away from it." She sniffled a bit.

It was true Stacy was her father's daughter. That she was also Mrs. Pinkerton's daughter I thought better to keep to myself. She already knew that, and was probably ashamed. I didn't blame her if she was.

"Oh, but Daisy! I want you and Dr. Greenlaw and Miss Greenlaw and those two Salvation Army people and Detective Rotund"—she *never* got Sam's name right, darn her—"to come to a dinner at my home. It will be a thank-you dinner to all of you for saving poor Lily Bannister's life and keeping her safe."

"I didn't think you knew her that well," I said, slightly puzzled.

"I didn't, but I made it my business to get to know her better. She's a lovely woman, and she's been through hell. That horrible husband of hers nearly killed her!"

"I know he did."

"So I want to have a dinner party in honor of all of you. I have no idea what's going to become of Stacy and quite frankly, I'm not sure I care."

She sobbed a little. "That's not true. I *do* care. But, oh, Daisy, she's gone far too far this time."

"I agree."

"So you must come to a dinner party in your honor."

"Um...That's very kind of you, Mrs. Pinkerton, but right now both Mrs. Bannister and Detective Rotondo are hospitalized."

"I know that, dear. But when they're better, I want you to come over. I mean it, Daisy. I can't tell you what good you and Rolly have done for me over the years."

"That's very kind of you," I said, feeling a wee bit stunned.

"Kind, my foot. And could you please come over in a day or two to consult Rolly and the cards for me? I'd appreciate it *so* much!"

Golly, she'd never asked me to come to her house at my convenience before. Maybe the tarot cards and that tower had been correct, and she *was* changing her ways.

"I'll be happy to do that, Mrs. Pinkerton." I swear, that was the first time I'd lied since Sam got shot. "Will tomorrow be all right? I have to visit the hospital, and then I can be at your house at...Say eleven o'clock?"

"Perfect. Thank you so much, dear. Tomorrow at eleven."

Stacy and Mrs. Gaulding were still in jail by the time Sam was released from the hospital and transferred to our house via ambulance.

Ma, Vi, Pa and I made him up a bed in my sewing room. Flossie and Johnny helped by bringing us a bed and mattress that had been donated to the Salvation Army. We assured them we'd return same when Sam recovered.

Flossie and I had decorated the sewing room so that one would hardly know its original purpose in life unless one checked in the closets. We used the White side-treadle sewing machine as a table for storing Sam's medications and so forth.

Sam was a terrible patient when he arrived at our house in an ambulance. I nursed him. As I had become a trifle rusty in the art of nursing men, I might not have done the world's best job, but I did my best.

"I hate being laid up!" he griped.

"I know you do," said I, bathing his heated brow with a damp wash-cloth. "But you have to be still and recover. If you don't rest, you'll never get better."

"Hell."

After about a week of moaning and groaning, he was well enough to limp into Billy's old wheelchair. He was a much larger man than Billy had been, but he complained considerably less when he was slightly more mobile.

Dr. Benjamin came every day to check up on him. Sam never swore or griped at him. He didn't moan and complain to my parents or Aunt Vi, either. I was the only one who received his nasty complaints. He complained *about* me, too.

"Why the hell didn't you tell me what was going on? We could have had that poor woman in the hospital a week before she eventually got there."

"You refused to tell me when Mr. Bannister died. We didn't know if Mrs. Bannister had killed him or not, although if she did kill him—which she didn't—it would have been a clear case of self-defense."

"Huh."

"Don't you 'huh' me, Sam Rotondo. I asked you and asked you, and you still wouldn't tell me. You didn't have to follow me and get yourself shot! You could just have told me when that lousy so-and-so died. But oh, no, you weren't allowed to tell me anything about the Bannister case. Nuts to you!"

"I'm never allowed to tell you about my cases."

"Phooey. If I'd told you where we were hiding her, you'd have had to arrest all of us, wouldn't you?"

"Well..."

"Admit it, Sam."

"Oh, hell. Yes, I'd probably have had to cite you."

"By cite you mean arrest, right?"

"Aw...Yes."

"All of us?"

"Dammit. Yes. All of you."

"Well, then, can you blame us? *We* didn't know when that awful man was murdered! *We* didn't know anything! All we knew was that Lily Bannister had been battered to within an inch of her life and was frightened to death of her husband. For good reason."

"Nuts."

"Phooey."

Fortunately for us, at that moment Aunt Vi entered Sam's room with a bowl of chicken soup and some soda crackers. By that time he could sit up with help. He *hated* being helped. I helped him anyway, the big lout.

What's more, I made him wear Mrs. Jackson's juju, whether he wanted to or not. Naturally, he didn't want to. He did anyway.

You should have heard Sam rant when, about a month and a half later, in mid-August, I told him we had to attend a dinner party at Mrs. Pinkerton's house. He'd graduated from the wheelchair to a cane by that time, but his leg still hurt him a lot and I could tell he loathed the fact that he limped.

"Damned if I will!" he declared.

"You will, too," said I.

"Will not!"

"Will so."

And he did.

He griped and whined as I drove him in our Chevrolet to Mrs. Pinkerton's house, and continued his whining until Featherstone opened the door and said, "Please come this way, Mrs. Majesty and Detective Rotondo." At least he pronounced Sam's last name correctly.

So Sam and I walked to the drawing room where everyone else, including Flossie and Johnny Buckingham, awaited us. Mrs. Bannister still looked pretty bad, but at least her face was no longer swollen and purple. Her eyes were kind of weird, but when I asked Fred about that, he said they might recover as Mrs. Bannister continued to heal.

As soon as Mrs. Pinkerton spotted us, she rushed over. I stood slightly in front of Sam to prevent her knocking him over if she hit too hard. But she surprised me. She stopped short of bumping into either one of us.

"Oh, Daisy, I'm *so* grateful to you for coming tonight. And you, Detective Rotund—"

"Rotondo," Sam growled.

"Of course. I beg your pardon, Detective Rotondo."

"We're happy we could come," I fibbed nobly.

"Yeah," said he, still growling. He perked up some when he noticed Flossie and Johnny standing beside the fireplace. August had been warm so far, so there was no fire lit. He excused himself to Mrs. Pinkerton, limped over to them and began chatting. I spoke a few more words to Mrs. Pinkerton and then made my way to Mrs. Bannister, who cried when she thanked me for what she called her "salvation."

After that, I moseyed over to talk to Harold, Dell, and Fred and Hazel Greenlaw. Fred was as handsome as ever, and I felt sorry for the maidens of Pasadena who'd never have the chance to snabble him.

Harold was still telling me how awful had been his ordeal whilst hiding Lily Bannister when Mrs. Pinkerton lifted her arms in the air and said in a loud voice, "Please, everyone, let's give a round of applause to all of these heroes!"

I guess she meant us. Since there was no one there to applaud except the heroes and heroines of whom she spoke and Mr. Pinkerton, the applause was scanty. Mrs. Pinkerton didn't seem to mind.

She sighed happily. "Oh, I'm so very glad you took care of Lily! She's led such a hard life! Now," she said with a smirk at me, "if only Harold and Daisy would marry, I'd be a truly happy woman!"

I saw about twelve starts of surprise in the room, and I realized I hadn't broken the news of Sam's and my engagement to Harold's mother.

"Um, thank you, Mrs. Pinkerton, but I fear Harold and I can never marry."

Her face fell comically. "Why not?"

I walked over to Sam, lifted my left hand and showed her my ring. "Because Detective Rotondo and I are already engaged to be married."

The applause after that announcement was uproarious. I do believe the only person who didn't clap was Mrs. Pinkerton. She only stared, astonished, at the two of us.

Ah, well. Such is life.

Oh! I forgot to tell you what happened at the end of Mr. Gerald Kingston's trial. The information was related to Sam by several of his cronies in the police department when they visited him at our house. Truth to tell, I'm glad I wasn't there when the verdict came in. The jury found him guilty, and the judge sentenced him to death. Miss Betsy Powell nearly screamed down the courthouse. I understand she had to be carried out of the courtroom kicking and screeching. I don't think she was ever charged with attempted murder (although she did attempt to kill someone). Honestly, I think charges weren't brought against her for fear she'd keep on screaming.

The End

SPIRITS UNITED

DAISY GUMM MAJESTY MYSTERY, BOOK 12

"Miss Petrie!" said I upon arriving at her desk. "Please let me introduce you to my fiancé, Detective Sam Rotondo. He's with the Pasadena Police Department. Oh, I guess you already knew that."

"How wonderful to meet you at last, Detective Rotondo," said Miss Petrie in a thrilled whisper. She held out her hand and Sam shook it.

"Pleased to meet you," said he, not snarling for once. He actually behaved properly and smiled as he shook her hand. Sort of like a tranquilized rhinoceros, if you know what I mean.

"Oh, Daisy," said Miss Petrie after Sam had let her hand go. "I have so many books for you!"

"Thank you!"

"Hmm," said Sam. "You're the one who feeds her detective-novel reading habit, I've heard."

"You betcha," I said.

"Yes indeed," said Miss Petrie, her smile faltering slightly.

"Don't mind him," I told her. "He acts grouchy on purpose."

"Do not," said Sam grouchily.

"He's a man, Daisy. I know what men are like."

She did? Her words surprised me since, as far as I knew, Miss Petrie was an unmarried young lady and, also as far as I knew, had never been engaged or anything. Maybe she grew up with brothers.

Naturally, Sam said, "Huh."

"So what do you have for us today, Miss Petrie?" I nearly rubbed my hands with glee.

"Two new arrivals from Mrs. Agatha Christie!" she exclaimed. Naturally, she whispered her exclamation. It can be done; believe me. "*Poirot Investigates*," which is a collection of short stories, and *The Secret Adversary*. The latter isn't about Hercule Poirot, but introduces two young people at loose ends after the war. They get together in this book. I loved it. It's ever so much better than *Murder on the Links*. The two young people are Tommy and Tuppence Beresford, although they aren't married at the beginning of the book. Rather like you and the detective." Miss Petrie giggled.

"Oooh, thank you!" I hugged the two volumes to my bosom. Not that women were supposed to have bosoms in those days. But I wore my bust-flattener and did my best. Because of my profession as a spiritualist-medium, I always attempted to look fashionable when I went out in public. Nobody wants to hire a sloppy spiritualist, trust me.

"And we just got a couple of books by Mr. E. Phillips Oppenheim, too. I think I've told you that it sometimes takes a while for books to get here from England."

"Oh, I love his books!"

"Good. Here we have *The Wicked Marquis*. It was published in 1919, but it still holds up today."

As 1919 was only six years prior, I imagined it did. "Thank you."

"And this is *Jacob's Ladder*, also by Mr. Oppenheim. I think you'll enjoy the tale of Mr. Jacob Pratt. He does have his ups and downs." Miss Petrie giggled again. I think the presence of the large, looming figure of Sam Rotondo by my side intimidated her. I'd never heard her giggle twice in one visit before. I didn't fault her for feeling daunted. Sam was rather like a granite obelisk when one first met him.

I said, "Thank you," again, feeling positively gleeful.

"But the best is yet to come," said Miss Petrie, her eyes sparkling behind her spectacles. It's long been my belief that she could be quite a pretty woman if she did something with her hair and used a little makeup. Not that it's any of my business. "Here we have *The House Without a Key*, by Mr. Earl Derr Biggers. I think you'll love his detective, Charlie Chan."

"Charlie Chan?" said Sam incredulously.

"Yes. He's a Chinese detective in Hawaii."

"Goodness. Thank you!" I said in hopes of preventing more comments from Sam.

I needn't have bothered. At that very second, an earsplitting shriek pierced the silence of the library. I dropped my pile of books. Fortunately, they landed on Miss Petrie's desk. Another scream followed the first one, and then we heard loud sobbing coming from the biography section of the library stacks.

Miss Petrie leaped to her feet, and she and I ran toward where the commotion had emanated.

Sam said, "Wait!"

Naturally, we didn't. I heard him thumping after us, and I could tell he was angry by the loudness of his cane as it made contact with the floor. His feet weren't terribly quiet, either. Sam was a big man.

"Whatever happened?" Miss Petrie whispered.

"I don't know."

We reached the biography section, and we both stopped still in our tracks. There, before us on the formerly pristine library floor, lay the body of a woman in a pool of blood. Another woman with her hands pressed to her cheeks stood, trembling, beside the body. I presumed she was the shrieker.

"Good heavens, what could have happened?" Miss Petrie said in a hushed voice.

"I don't know," said I. "She couldn't have been croaked with a gat, or we'd have heard the shot."

From behind me I heard a disgusted, "'Croaked with a gat?' Is that what all your reading has taught you?" Sam. Angry, unless I missed my guess.

Then it was I saw an old school fellow of mine, Mr. Robert Browning —not the poet—swing around the end of the biography stack, a bloody knife held in his hand. He stopped dead when he saw the body on the floor, and his mouth fell open.

"Robert!" I cried, appalled. The last person in the entire universe I could imagine killing anyone was Robert Browning. Well, except me and a couple of other folks I knew.

"Wh-what happened?" he asked, sounding and looking dumbfounded. "Good God, is that a dead woman?"

"We don't know yet," growled Sam, pushing Miss Petrie and me aside so he could get to the body. He knelt beside her, even though I knew doing so would hurt his leg. He pressed a finger to where the pulse in her neck would be if she were alive. Then he picked up a hand and felt for a pulse there. Turning to Miss Petrie and me, he snarled, "Call the cops and an ambulance. Now." He got painfully to his feet. "And you," he said to Robert. "What the hell are you doing with that knife?"

"I-I found it on the other side of this row of books. It looked...out of place. I don't know why I picked it up, but when I heard the screams, I ran over here." He looked from Sam to me and back again. "I didn't do anything! I just found the knife."

"And picked it up." Turning to Miss Petrie and me again, Sam said, "Well, get going!"

So we got going.

Available in Paperback and eBook From Your Favorite Online Retailer or Bookstore

ALSO BY ALICE DUNCAN

The Daisy Gumm Majesty Mystery Series

Strong Spirits

Fine Spirits

High Spirits

Hungry Spirits

Genteel Spirits

Ancient Spirits

Spirits Revived

Dark Spirits

Spirits Onstage

Unsettled Spirits

Bruised Spirits

Spirits United

Spirits Unearthed

Shaken Spirits

Scarlet Spirits

The Dream Maker Series

Cowboy for Hire

Beauty and the Brain

The Miner's Daughter

Her Leading Man

ABOUT THE AUTHOR

Award-winning author Alice Duncan lives with a herd of wild dachs-hunds (enriched from time to time with fosterees from New Mexico Dachshund Rescue) in Roswell, New Mexico. She's not a UFO enthusi-ast; she's in Roswell because her mother's family settled there fifty years before the aliens crashed (and living in Roswell, NM, is cheaper than living in Pasadena, CA, unfortunately). Alice would love to hear from you at alice@aliceduncan.net

www.aliceduncan.net

f facebook.com/alice.duncan.925

CPSIA information can be obtained
at www.ICGtesting.com
Printed in the USA
LVHW030150020323
740759LV00006B/106

9 781644 570678